Carnival

of

Cannibals

A Modern Pastoral

JAMES J HOUTS

Copyright © 2011 by James J. Houts
All rights reserved

Cheyenne Publishing Inc.
1740H Del Range Blvd., Suite 130
Cheyenne, Wyoming 82009
USA

Library of Congress Cataloging-in-Publication Data

Houts, James J.
Carnival of Cannibals / James J. Houts

ISBN 13: 978-0615469379
ISBN 10: 0-615-46937-X

Carnival

of

Cannibals

When asked by Zeus why he had stolen fire for man, Prometheus, one of the last Titans, answered, "Because I loved man, whom with the help of the gods I had created, I longed to give him some gift that would raise him high above the brute creation and bring him nearer to the gods. I knew of nought that could do this save fire from heaven, and to ask the boon from you, O Zeus, would have been to ask in vain. So I scaled the walls of your city and lit my reed at the flame, and now all over the earth fires are kindled; and in men's hearts too has arisen the flame of pure and high ambition. Not all of your power, O ruler of heaven and earth, can put out those fires, or bring men back to the easy content which marks the beasts of the field."

—Amy Cruse, *The Book of Myths*

Jeri's vision flared suddenly white; the handgun's unexpected discharge was as bright and blinding in the darkness as a photo flash. They had only been a few feet away from the struggling men when the shot stunned them, its dazzling explosion in the small, dark room lingering on in their eyes, its deafening crack ringing in their ears.

Shapeless phantoms drifted in the void as she blinked, ghostly afterimages that remained long after the instant of brilliance. She was reminded of a sunny day on the mountain, when she had skied toward the sun, huge and strong in the thin, clear air, doubly blinding after reflecting off the snow. She leaned back and felt Ted behind her, holding her firmly, and then she remembered the day they had met, skiing up on that mountain.

Jeri had feared then that he was yet another Texan looking to get laid on his Colorado ski vacation, and had scolded herself for not paying more attention on her way to the lift. They had arrived at the chair at almost the same time, alone together on that part of the mountain. She had thought, at first, that he had adjusted his speed to cause the meeting, and she had dreaded the inevitable come-on. But instead, he had seemed surprised and somehow subdued. He had watched her for a long time, hiding behind his dark glasses, but he hadn't seemed to be leering at her. He had seemed quietly isolated and mysterious. His body language had indicated that he was not going to speak, and she had wondered if he would board the chair up to the summit or take the lower trail back to the chalet. Then he had reached up to his face, his ski pole still held in his hand, and his glasses had dropped to dangle around his neck, exposing his dark eyes. They had been shockingly sad and shy.

"Shall we ride up together?" he had said in a halting, almost stuttering voice, and she had known it would be all right to ride with him. She had even been pleased when he had asked. Then, when she had nodded and moved to the chair, his eyes had changed, filling with pleasure and confidence, and that too had pleased her.

Ted and Jeri had watched the four men as they struggled for the weapon, immobilized by the suddenness of the violence. The shiny barrel had pointed in wildly unpredictable directions as the hand holding the gun was pounded mercilessly into the dirty wooden bar. Now they could see nothing beyond the white shroud of their light-stunned eyes, but the ringing was subsiding.

"Remember the mountain that first day, Ted?" She felt suddenly very tired. "So white? So bright? So cold."

"Yes, Jeri, I remember." He pulled her closer, her softness familiar and comfortable.

Ted had been unprepared for the encounter at the lift, disinclined to approach the young stranger with curly blonde hair billowing from under her cap, reluctant to make the obvious suggestion that they ride up the slope together. He had first studied her from behind the small anonymity of his sunglasses, fearing rejection, searching for hints of hesitation or aversion. But their meeting had seemed a rendezvous of chance, a serendipitous pairing at a surrealistically deserted chairlift station. The methodical machine had seemed to operate without human guidance or intervention, with no lines and no wait, not even the usual bundled-and-gloved chair attendant. They had arrived together after completing their separate runs; converging slowly, they had skied across the hard, flat snow from different directions, the sun's gleaming white light reflecting blindingly from it. Then he had spoken to her, and she had boarded the double lift beside him.

They had spent the day together, skiing and getting to know each other. She had discovered him to be intelligent and interesting; he was vastly experienced when she compared his life to her own, yet reticent and shy about his past. He had seemed worldly and sophisticated when he bought the wine they had shared at the Powder House, but almost boyish in his shyness with her.

A soothing calmness filled him as he recalled their first day together, on a mountain devoid of other skiers, skiing and riding lifts through the silence. They had become comfortable with each other as they had challenged the first run, stopping briefly to discuss and select each new path before proceeding. Initially, their discourse had been impersonal discussions about the mountain and the terrain. But as the day continued, they had shared long, quiet conversations, traveling suspended over the lonely white slopes, revealing increasingly more personal information about themselves. They had lunched on cheese, French bread, and icy, crisp white zinfandel at the Powder House, midway between the summit and the chalet. And after spending the rest of the day together, they had sat close on the old resort bus as it bumped down from the mountain to the Iron Horse Inn. He had become a guest at the resort a few days before, disjointed from his old life, his memories, and his doubts; she had been scheduled to work there, waiting tables in a dining room without diners.

She remembered their second day together: waiting impatiently for his call, and her excitement when it came; their trip in her Toyota up to the Tamarron resort, where they had shared a slow, romantic dinner; and surprisingly, how easy and comfortable it had been to stay with him on that night of their first real date.

He remembered his fears before their first nervous night together. He had been afraid that, in private, he would prove to be another man than the one she had met on the mountain. But his fear had been baseless. He had been relieved to discover that the intimate element of their relationship would be as good as, possibly superior to, the public aspect of their friendship. And as the few full days of their love affair cascaded through his memory, he was overwhelmed with the wonder and impossibility of it. She wasn't just perfect, she was perfect for him.

Jeri had the careless, unself-conscious beauty of one who had always been beautiful and carried it without conceit. She was half a head shorter than a six-foot man, but her light bone structure made her seem tall when standing alone or with other women. Her figure, when seen from behind, was almost boyish, with slender hips and delicately squared shoulders; yet when seen in profile, dabs of woman-softness curved flawlessly, as if placed carefully there by an artist of great subtlety. Her long, narrow neck rose gracefully upward to a round face of perfect features: gently angled chin, gleaming even teeth, small straight nose, naturally colored high cheekbones, and large, disquietingly blue eyes with long lashes. She wore her wavy, almost curly, blonde hair parted simply in the center to fall thickly below her jaw. The white softness of her small hands and long, slender fingers belied the hard work they had always performed. Beautiful, smart, and tough, she asked few favors of men, but when she did ask, it was rare for her to be denied.

My God, he thought, she seems so light in my arms.

Ted and Jeri

But it is more important for analysis to treat humans in most systems as mere parts. We kill about 5,000 people a year outright in U.S. industry. The vast majority of these "accidents," however, are only "incidents" in our scheme, for no subsystem or system damage is entailed. Only a "part" has been destroyed.

—Charles Perrow, *Normal Accidents*

Ted Johnston was content. The San Elejo project was ahead of schedule, and the planning meeting had ended earlier than he had expected. The road wind buffeting the open car pulled at his dark hair as it whipped around his head, muting the drone of the engine behind him. He reached for his ball cap. The logo sewn to its front reminded him of the larger version hanging in his Porsche dealer's showroom. The larger logo was on a sales banner that quoted from a forgotten book, a book written about the old California of vast Spanish haciendas and expansive cattle ranches, a California that had been destroyed forever by the great gold rush a decade later. He smiled as he remembered the quote: "'The Californians can hardly go from one house to another without getting on a horse.' Dana's *Two Years Before the Mast*, 1840." Below that, in slightly smaller but still giant lettering, was: "Some things never change: Porsche for a new millennium." An onshore breeze, normal along this beach in the late afternoon, carried the richly thalassic scent of the breaking waves, and briny-tasting aerosols arrived damp and cool on his face. He turned his eyes to the soothing pastels of the evening sky and he felt happy. It had been a good decision to move back to Southern California.

His consulting business was thriving. A series of successful projects had improved his reputation and expanded the prestige of his company, earning him the respect of other engineering professionals within the small community of nuclear energy. He found the elevated status among his peers personally satisfying, but more importantly, it had brought larger projects with more lucrative consulting contracts for his company. He was established in his profession and comfortable with his lifestyle.

The sun was setting. The orange disk seemed artificially large as it descended toward the dark hump of the ocean. He remembered an old sailor's myth he had heard during his time in the navy: the setting sun was said to flash green light at the moment it disappeared beneath the horizon. He decelerated into a turn-out, braking and downshifting hard before the sports car left the pavement and bumped onto the compacted sand shoulder of the road. He pulled up close to the edge of the sandy bluff, turned off the ignition and got out to watch the fading moments of the day. Leaning back against the car with his legs crossed at the ankles and his arms folded across his chest, the soft wind fluttered his tie and massaged his face. He studied the interface between the sun and the sea carefully, as he had many times before, waiting for that final instant of light, hopeful that at last he would see the mythical green flash. As he waited, he thought about the extinction of his family and regretted that they could not be with him to share this calm moment by the sea. He recrossed his legs to make himself more comfortable, and the synthesized musical ringtone of his cellular phone played from the inside pocket of his jacket. He activated the device by memory and touch, maintaining his focus on the horizon as he answered.

"Hello, this is Ted Johnston."

"Hi, Ted. This is Mary. What are you doing?"

Mary Peralta was an attractive, strong, and successful woman. She had a nice figure, delicate features, and disarmingly large black eyes; she was charismatic, witty, and opinionated, especially regarding women's rights and her Latino heritage; and she was vice president of information technology at a moderate-sized aerospace firm located in western Los Angeles County. Ted was surprised it was Mary and thankful the call did not involve business.

"Hi, Mary. Good to hear your voice. How are you?"

"I'm great. Just leaving the office. Where are you?"

"Well, I'm standing on the beach watching the sunset. It's beautiful tonight. You should see it."

"Lucky you. I'm sitting in traffic going about two miles an hour. I wish I was there. Do you have plans for tonight, Ted?"

"Just laundry. Why? Want to get together for a drink or something?"

Ted recalled the comfortably subtle attempt at matchmaking that had resulted in his introduction to Mary six months earlier—the wives of his business associates seemed confident he needed to marry. Mutual friends had arranged for them to sit next to each other at an intimate dinner party. The match had been a good one, and they had pursued an intermittent relationship for several months before gradually drifting apart. The short love affair had not ended badly. The time demands of challenging careers and the geographies of separate lives had simply made each encounter more difficult, each date less spontaneous than the one before. They had stopped seeing each other without agreeing to do so.

"Better than a drink," she answered. "I have tickets to the Laguna Arts Festival Pageant of the Masters. A software salesman gave them to me a month ago, but I've been so busy that I totally blew off the date. I realized it today and, well, since you live in Laguna, I thought of you. How about it? If you don't want to go, I'll probably just stay home."

Ted liked Mary, although their previous attempt at a relationship had floundered in the nightly flow of congested freeway traffic. He realized there was little chance of them succeeding as a couple, and his happy mood dipped a little when he remembered the death sentence for an LA relationship: GU—Geographically Undesirable. Still, she was a very interesting person, and he did want to see her, and the Pageant of the Masters had a local reputation as a "must-see" event.

Ted's education and experience had been dominated by science and technology, but since his return to LA, he had tried to broaden his exposure to the arts. He had taken several art appreciation classes at night and had purchased season tickets to the LA Philharmonic for use when entertaining clients. One of the night classes had included a day trip to the Laguna Arts Festival. The Pageant of the Masters was the culminating event of the festival, an experience as much social as artistic, a performance art unique to the festival.

"Well, Ted, what do you say? These tickets are hot, you know. They're only sold one day a year—the day after the pageant. I'd hate to miss this, but if you don't want to go, I'll be damned if I'll go alone."

"No, I want to go. I was just thinking." The last yellow edge of the sun dipped below the horizon and was gone. He blinked his eyes, trying to recall the last instant of light, to decide if he had seen the green flash, but the moment was lost. He couldn't be sure if he had seen it or not. "Damn."

"What? You can't go?" She sounded annoyed.

"No, I was thinking about something else. I'd love to go. What time does it start, and how should we meet?"

"Great," she said. Her voice sounded happy and excited now. "I'll just come down to your place—if that's all right. I should get there in forty-five minutes or an hour. That should give us enough time to relax for a while before we leave. Sound good?"

"Sounds perfect. I'll be waiting for you."

"OK. Looks like traffic is starting to move. I'll see you in a little while. Good-bye."

"Good-bye, Mary. Drive safe, and I'll see you soon." He heard her break the connection as he was speaking. He turned off the phone and returned it to his pocket.

The sunset was still beautiful above the ocean; bright yellows and reds were dappled with the blues and grays of scattered clouds. He turned from the watercolor sky, got back into his car and went through his short routine of getting back on the road: seat belt, mirror, ignition. He pulled onto the smooth pavement and accelerated through the gears, bringing the car up to speed, matching the pace of the fast but light traffic.

Earlier, as he had walked across the parking lot from his office to his car, he had found the day transformed into another of the near-perfect evenings of late summer in Southern California. So after twelve hours indoors, planning the work his company would do during the upcoming San Elejo Nuclear Generating Station (SENGS) Unit Number Two refueling, he had put down the convertible top and taken the old road by the beach. The coast road was only rarely visited by the Highway Patrol, and sometimes, if his mood was right, he would disregard the risk of a citation and speed through the tight turns on his way home.

He braked hard as he approached the next curve in the winding two-lane highway; shifting into a lower gear, he allowed the engine to race as he steered the sports car into the apex of the turn. The car gripped the pavement firmly, slowed, and turned. He applied throttle, and the car responded powerfully out of the turn. He enjoyed the car he drove because of its mechanical excellence, and yes, if he was honest about it, somewhat because of the prosperity it symbolized. He realized that ego was a poor reason to own a car, and he didn't believe that he was one of those insecure men who used his car as some substitute for masculine virility. He was a Californian—he loved to drive and he loved his car.

Driving the old coastal road home from his office near the San Elejo Nuclear Generating Station was one of Ted's few concessions to frivolous pleasure. His crowded professional life as a nuclear engineering consultant was otherwise a well-regulated and carefully planned testament to time management. He looked forward to the drive home as a high point in his day, and when he could leave the office before nightfall, he would drive with the top down and the stereo loud. He could take the old road almost all the way from his office near SENGS to his home farther south in Laguna Beach. The challenging drive in the open car could, in a few exhilarating minutes, dissipate stress accumulated over tedious hours behind his desk and prepare him for the few free hours he could spend at home. He needed the freedom of the drive, with the wind tugging at him and his blood pumping fast through his body. It was a drive that fortified his belief in his own success, even after a day of work that might argue of his failings. He enjoyed this car and he enjoyed this road. He reveled in the cool coastal air and the panoramic ocean views from old Highway 1. He found the smooth, even power of the car's engine reassuring and exciting as he accelerated through the narrow turns. He had worked hard and long all his life, and he believed he deserved this one small pleasure. He felt no guilt for owning such an extravagant car.

Although he spent the majority of his waking hours at his engineering office up the coast, Ted lived in a quiet upscale beach community that depended on retirees, tourism, and outside money to survive. It was a great place to live, but it had precious few employment opportunities. He was one of the lucky citizens of the beach town who worked near enough to avoid the excruciatingly long commute into LA. That commute, he knew, would quickly remove any enjoyment he found in driving. When he thought about adding a three-hour commute to his workday, he realized he would rather live in LA than make that exhausting daily drive. And when he thought of living in LA, he remembered his childhood home in Cerritos and his life growing up in the smoggy, congested suburbs of sprawling Los Angeles County.

He had been raised in one of the cloned bedroom towns that had developed south and east of Los Angeles. Nice enough when he had been a child, the neighborhood had gradually succumbed to the cancerous death from within common to large American cities. But throughout his youth, the degenerating suburb had been his universe; in high school, it had never occurred to him that anyone could live in any other way. Then his life had changed forever and had evolved unpredictably: the Naval Academy for college, majoring in nuclear engineering; a short, impatient career in the navy working on reactors, not fighting wars; his first civilian job at General Electric, training young navy people how to operate nuclear reactors; then independent consulting to public utilities. Finally, he had returned to Southern California, where he joined the private engineering firm of one of his old instructors at Annapolis. He had wasted little time on frivolities since his days in high school; he had worked long hours and invested his money. He had succeeded in the ways he had always wanted to succeed: he owned his own company, he was financially secure, and he lived in a great beach house in Laguna, surrounded by other successful professionals.

He was proud and satisfied with his work, and he accepted the demands it made on his time and his energy. It was challenging and unforgiving work, but for Ted, it represented man's mastery over the primal forces of the universe and his dominance over energies that, if unbridled, could destroy the world. He felt great pride in his role as one of the gatekeepers, who by acts of will and intellect kept the beast corralled and controlled, compelling it to toil for the benefit of humanity.

When Ted thought about the brilliant engineer who had brought him back to California, and who had once taught reactor design at Annapolis, he was bewildered. He couldn't comprehend the man's eventual dissatisfaction with the work and his final rejection of it. He was still astonished by his mentor's sudden retirement and subsequent move to Costa Rica. None of it had ever made sense. At one of their last meetings, during the final negotiations of Ted's purchase of the company, he had asked his old friend about the perplexing change in his ambitions. He remembered the puzzling response verbatim: "I'm just not a believer anymore, Ted. It's time for me to move on."

They still exchanged e-mail and the occasional letter, but increasingly less frequently, and with each exchange the replies were shorter and the information less personal. Ted hoped his old friend was happy and healthy, and that the developing world lifestyle he had chosen was all that he had expected and everything he had needed.

Driving the Porsche through the turns, Ted realized he was looking forward to the night with Mary. He hadn't been out on many dates since their relationship had languished. He used work as an excuse when friends asked about his tame social life, but he knew he had just been leery of beginning yet another dead-end romance. He hadn't admitted it to himself before, but now he accepted that he was eager for a good night out with a woman he had missed.

The evening still held the glow of the day when Ted pulled into his driveway. He could hear the loud electric fan of the car working to cool the hot engine as he walked up the slate sidewalk to the entranceway. Inside the door, his mail cluttered the floor below the slot. He shuffled through it as he walked to the beach side of the house. It was the usual, uninteresting mail of someone living well in Southern California: junk mail, store fliers, bills, bank card statements, an offer of free gifts if he would visit time-share condos in Palm Springs. He tossed the pile on the bar and made himself a scotch and soda. From behind the bar, he looked across the room and out through the French doors that made the far side of the enclosed patio more a window than a wall; the last colors of the sunset were fading from the graying blue horizon. He took a long drink from his scotch, sat down on a bar stool and shook his head. He had made it. All his youthful dreams had been fulfilled. His parents would have been proud.

His had been a simple middle-class family that had worked hard and lived frugally. Ted had been the second of three sons in a generation without daughters. He had been the first in the family to have gone to college, and if it hadn't been for the navy, he probably wouldn't have managed to go either. After the navy, he had moved to Idaho to work at the GE Nuclear School. He had bought a cabin to avoid paying rent, but the timing had been fortuitous. When he had left Idaho, he had made a nice profit on the sale of the cabin. Eager to reinvest, he had arrived back in California to find the property market depressed and flat. He had been unsure how to invest sensibly, so he had rented a small apartment.

Then he had been introduced to Tony Parker, an attorney who had given up the law to become a successful real estate investor. Tony seemed to make money in any market and viewed the low property values as an opportunity. Tony had given Ted a tip on his first condominium deal, and as they had become friends, they had partnered on several investments: first condos, then houses and apartment buildings. Ted had even been a minority partner in one of Tony's strip mall deals. Five years after arriving back in LA, he had bought the Laguna Beach house.

Although the property deals had been profitable, Ted enjoyed the solitary challenge of the stock market more. He went about investing in stocks in the same measured way he had led his life—lots of homework and a reluctance to accept the easy path as the right path. He did use one risky investment tool, stock index options, and these had made him, in a small way, wealthy. When he became concerned about the faltering economy, he had bought index put options, and the markets complied with a severe and extended decline. When the Dow had dropped to new lows, he had bought index calls, riding the trend for two years as the Dow repeatedly reached new highs. Then, when the fears of future inflation began to make him nervous, he had engineered a portfolio heavy in commodities and inflation-protected bonds. He had been lucky with his guesses and aggressive with his investment of capital. Now he was content to leave his savings in conservative and diversified mutual funds.

He took another drink of his scotch and considered his good fortune. At times he felt he was an impostor living a counterfeit life. It was like the farm kid from Kansas who joined the navy and was put behind the controls of a sixty-million-dollar fighter plane. In his role as jet pilot, the kid was an expert at operating the ultimate machine of an advanced technological society, yet beneath the flight suit and helmet and the veneer of training, he would always remain the same Kansas farm kid. It seemed that random accidents of fate made dreams become reality.

His thoughts about dreams made him remember something his father had said when he was still in high school: "Old age is a place where memories are more exciting than dreams." Then he remembered his family—his father and mother and two brothers—and he was saddened. They were all gone now, lost to disease and drugs and disastrous fate. Then, in a hot wave of unwanted remembrance that beaded cold sweat on his scalp, the bad memory stole into his consciousness.

He remembered his brothers, one older and one younger; they had been best friends, close in age and interests, the three of them an overwhelming team in young life. He remembered how they had been then: his older brother interested in fast cars and beer, his younger brother into motorcycles and pot, and himself a teenage mediator between the two, a bridge between the cultures. When he remembered them, he longed for them; usually he tried not to think about them, because when he did, he felt the emptiness they had left inside him. But now his thoughts went back to the time he had shared with his two brothers in high school; a time of beer and football, pot and girls, cocaine and death; a time when they had learned so much about life and themselves and the lengths to which the government would go to control the use of drugs.

He had lived a nightmare at the end of that period. No, it had been a real-world tragedy of life-altering force. It seemed that the pain of his loss would continue throughout his life unabated, unaffected by the passing of years. Then, aware of his unwanted drift into the memory, he brushed it to the back of his mind with the easy skill of a well-practiced expert and turned his thoughts to the night before him. He carried his drink to the master bedroom where he would prepare for his date.

A few minutes later, while he was undressing, the doorbell rang through the house. He yanked his pants back up to his waist and pulled a sweatshirt over his head before trotting barefooted to answer the door. Outside, leaning on the bell, was Mary; she was still in her business suit, her purse over one shoulder, an overnight bag over the other. She smiled a girlish smile that didn't quite match the businesslike way she was dressed or the conservative bun that held her hair tightly at the crown of her head.

"Mind if I take a bath? I had to come straight from work to be on time. Do you mind?"

"No, of course not. Come on in." Ted took the plump overnight bag from her; the implications of it stirred a small conflict in him. He knew Mary to be a sexually aggressive woman, and they had not seen each other for months. He had to assume that she had been active during their time apart, and the realization filled him with a sudden weariness. He was still physically attracted to her, and had once nurtured hopes that they could become serious, could somehow be together always. But now, holding the weight of the bag, he feared further involvement with her, feared being hurt by another failed relationship. In an instant he knew there would be no relationship, no emotional involvement, no risk of being hurt.

He remembered something Hemingway had written when he was young. In the story, the boyfriend had grown afraid of his feelings and had sent his girl away; later, he had realized that something had gone from him. Some part of his essence had been lost with the loss of the relationship. Ted believed it was a common feeling; everyone had probably felt it. It was like the memory of a bad burn; not the actual pain, but the sick feeling after it, a kind of emptiness. When he had first noticed this emptiness in himself, he had thought that the essence that was lost each time was reduced, like the power in nuclear fuel, and that if enough was lost he would eventually run out. Each heartbreak would lower his reserves of emotional essence until finally none would remain. He would be empty, devoid of essence to lose or pain to feel. But over the years, after many relationships, he had decided that the essence wasn't a finite resource at all. Somehow, the relationships themselves created it, and it could never be depleted. It reminded him of the mythological character that had been punished for giving man fire. He had been chained on his back to a stone, spread wide and vulnerable, exposed each day for a giant bird to devour his liver; then each night he would be miraculously cured, to await the new day and the undiminished pain of the bird. There was never an end to the pain through the loss of the life-giving part of himself. It was like that with love, Ted thought.

The overnight bag implied sex without commitment, pleasure without the investment of emotion; yet he feared a physical involvement with Mary because she had the capacity to damage him emotionally. She stepped into the entranceway, and he closed the door behind her.

"Would you like a drink before you get cleaned up?"

"I'd love one. The San Diego Freeway was its usual mess coming down here, and my air conditioner is on the blink."

She followed him through the house to the beachside patio. He dropped the overnight bag on the floor beside a bar stool and went behind the bar. She looked windblown and tired. A strand of hair, still wet with perspiration, fell across her eyes, and she brushed it away with an index finger. "The BMW dealership kept my car all day, and the damn thing is worse than when I dropped it off."

"Yeah, car dealerships can be a real pain in the butt. If they can't sell you a new one, they grind you for working on the old one. Have a seat and relax while I play bartender."

"That's OK, I'll stand. I'm still cramped up from the drive." She leaned her back against the bar, turning to face the ocean. "I just love this house, Ted. You are so lucky."

"Well, I don't feel so lucky when I make the mortgage or pay the insurance. What can I get for you, Mary?"

"White wine?"

"One white wine coming right up. So traffic was slow tonight? It's good that you came directly here. I hear parking up at the festival is hell. We'll probably have to walk a mile." He gave her the glass of wine. "I mean, literally, a mile."

"Well, I better get started or we'll never get there." She picked up her bags, pulled the straps over her shoulder, took her glass of wine and turned to walk back into the main house.

"There should be clean towels in the big cupboard behind the door," Ted called to her as she passed out of sight. Then lower, more to himself, "I see you remember the way."

Ted finished the remainder of his drink and made another. He peeled the rind from a slice of lemon and squeezed it into the scotch. Sitting backward on one of the bar stools, he watched the evening sailors tacking home and wondered how often Mary Peralta brought her traveling bag to work, prepared for spontaneous overnight dates. Then he realized he too needed to take a shower. He walked through the house to the bath in the master bedroom. He would shower and shave in the bathroom he considered his own; he rarely used the others. It would be interesting to see how well the hot water lasted with the two of them showering at the same time.

When he rejoined Mary on the beachside patio, he found her behind the bar, pouring herself another glass of wine.

"This seems so pushy, I know, but I suppose you already know I'm a little pushy. You get like that after a while. Woman in a man's world and all that."

"Make yourself at home. I don't mind. The only room that really feels like it's mine is my bedroom." He looked slowly around the darkening patio. "And this room a little bit, I suppose. The maid is in more of the house, more of the time, than I am—and I live here. It's too big for me, but it was a good investment."

"It is just beautiful. Did the fires come close to here? I saw so much damage on the hillsides."

"Well, the houses on the hill took the worst of it. I did worry for a while, though. I swear, I'm going to tear off those wood-shake shingles with my bare hands."

Sitting across from her at the bar, he could see the upper half of her body as she replaced the cork in the bottle. She wore a white blouse made of very thin nylon or silk. The contrast of her olive skin with the whiteness of the material caused both to seem rare and beautiful. He could see that under the filmy blouse she wore some mysterious, lacy one-piece undergarment. At that moment she seemed to him to be at once sophisticated and innocent, worldly yet prim. He found himself wondering what else lay below the layer of affected professionalism, the suits and billowing scarves.

What other secrets did she conceal from her business associates, and from him?

"How about making me another Scotty while you're back there?"

"Be glad to; just tell me what's in it."

"Pretty simple, really, scotch and soda, but you do need to cut me a little piece of lemon peel."

They spoke about work and joked about meaningless things the way people who are strangers will do, and gradually they each became more comfortable with the other's company.

Soon it was time for them to leave for the festival, and they went outside to his car. Ted offered to put the top up, but Mary insisted that she would enjoy the ride more with it down. The drive was short and Ted drove fast. At one point, Mary leaned into her seat belt to increase the stereo volume, and Ted could see the definition of her breast and the tight point of one hardened nipple. She looked up into his face suddenly and he was embarrassed; it was obvious that she knew where he had been staring. She looked down at her breasts and smiled broadly, her straight white teeth shining as she leaned back in her seat.

The entrance to the pageant was on a narrow two-lane road that wound up into the foothills. Ted found a place to park about a half mile up the hill from the entrance. As the electric top slowly came up, Mary unbuckled her seat belt and opened her large designer bag. While he finished latching the top, he noticed her looking at herself in the sun-visor mirror, dabbing carefully at her makeup. She turned to him and smiled, took one last look in the mirror, turned off the vanity light and dropped her makeup into her purse.

"OK, I'm ready now," she said, and she leaned over and kissed him happily. They got out of the car and began the long walk down the hill, arm and arm.

Inside the Irvine Bowl, well-dressed people huddled under a clear, star-filled autumn sky. Mary and Ted sat near a bronze colored sculpture of a riderless stallion, and she hugged his upper arm close to her breasts, resting her chin on his shoulder.

"This feels good," she said, as she pulled his arm closer to her. "I'm getting impatient for it to start. I know you'll love it."

"Is this horse part of the show?"

"Oh yes, wait until you see it."

At that moment, the lighting in the outdoor theater dimmed and the stage lights brightened. An unseen narrator, who sounded a lot like a recording in a Disneyland attraction, began to introduce famous works of art. After each introduction, the curtain would be drawn to expose a group of people in front of a carefully painted backdrop. The people were disguised as the figures in a famous painting and were posed, motionless, so that the entire stage took on the appearance of the introduced work of art. Occasionally, a spotlight would angle into the audience to illuminate an impersonation of some sculpture—the horse near them, at one point, took on a bronzed rider to become a life-sized imitation of a Remington cowboy. Although novel at first, it seemed to Ted that the presentation was a little pretentious, verging on pompous. It was not art, after all, but the imitation of art. By the end of the presentation he had become quite bored. He began to wonder about all the people involved. All these people were pretending to be something they were not—some pretending to be lifeless bronzed figures for sixty seconds, and others pretending they understood the significance of the charade.

Ted found this art of impersonation, of pretending to be something one was not, to be the perfect art form for California's Orange County. In Orange County, almost everyone was pretending to be something. It reminded Ted of his thoughts earlier about the fighter pilot from Kansas. The farm boy pretended to be a technologist so well that the pretend character functioned very well in the real environment of fighter planes and pilots. Then he thought about himself. Was he also only pretending? Was he really an Idaho ski instructor underneath his disguise of technology and business? His thoughts stopped drifting when the amphitheater lights came up, signifying the end of the pageant.

They drove to a trendy restaurant in the touristy part of Laguna Beach for a late dinner. While they waited for their table, they had cocktails in the bar that overlooked Pacific Coast Highway and the beach volleyball courts that lay between the road and the quiet surf. They sat close together, sipping their drinks and watching the whiteness of the low breakers on the black water. The diffuse light of the beachside businesses illuminated the wide beach and the foamy waves. He held her hand in her lap, and she held his in return. When he turned away from the windows to look at her, she was watching him with a sweet white smile and inviting brown eyes. She leaned to him and they kissed, softly and without passion, yet with the excitement and anticipation of intimacies to come. He thanked her for taking him along to the pageant, and told her what he thought she wanted to hear—that it was truly one of the best things to do in Orange County.

They ate seafood dinners in a lonely corner of the restaurant, drinking a dry chardonnay and talking extensively of their separate lives and their unrelated careers. Mary was intelligent and interesting and sexy. Ted felt glad he had broken his routine to go out with her; she was everything he had remembered her to be. They finished the fish and the wine, and then ordered cognac and coffee for their after-dinner drinks. The strong brandy warmed him and made him feel content and confident—ready for the short trip to his house down the coast. They left the restaurant holding hands and waited outside for the valet to bring around the car. They stood together, embracing as they waited, and before the car came the hug evolved comfortably into a long, intimate kiss.

His desire to be close to her and the separateness of the sports car's bucket seats made him feel far away and isolated, and the short drive seemed longer than usual. He reached over to rest his palm on her leg, and she responded by leaning into him, embracing his upper arm with both of her own. At his house he made drinks. They sat close together on a sofa overlooking the bright sea, the reflected moonlight filling the room with soft, cool light. They didn't speak and they didn't drink, and very soon he took her by the hand and led her to his bedroom.

Ted found the process familiar at first: the mutual desire to please a partner, the slight mistakes made and immediately forgiven, the clumsiness of drink and the forced humor used to negate it. Then, as the excitement of the act built, he lost the reality of the moment, and in the darkness he lost the memory of Mary's face. And for a time, his partner became the woman he had known before ever having met this one; the woman for whom he had started to feel love before his fear and distrust drove him to senseless tests of her love, tests that had eventually soured her feelings for him. Then the memory of that woman was gone, and a stream of ghost lovers from the past took her place. He remembered the small things they had asked, and he gave them now. He felt and smelled and tasted each woman as he made love to her in the darkness, before the next ghost took her place. Then in an instant it was over; the ghosts were gone and he was alone once again, in bed with Mary Peralta.

Jeri Singleton awoke suddenly from a deep, comfortably warm sleep. The harsh ringing always seemed to come too early, but it never failed to wake her. Still clumsy with sleep, she struck out at the alarm clock rattling on the nightstand beside her. With the bell silenced, she checked the time. The radioactive coatings on the hands and numbers glowed green against the black face of the clock. It was five a.m. She rolled out of bed and stood for a moment in the darkness, bare feet on the cold hardwood floor, her fingers shivering as she reset the alarm to seven. Steve's shift at the gas station didn't begin until eight, and that gave him two extra hours of sleep. She reached down and touched the sleeping form of her husband; the down comforter was cold to her touch, but she could feel the hard bulk of him underneath. She carried the clock across the dark, frigid bedroom and placed it silently on the dresser. Steve would only wake up if he was forced to get out of bed to turn off the alarm. She walked to the bathroom rigidly, feeling ahead unconsciously with her toes before every step. In the silence of the black morning the creaking of the tired wooden floor seemed much louder than in the day, especially when she was trying to be quiet. After carefully closing the bathroom door, she found the light switch by feel and memory, and with a night amplified click the small bathroom was instantly bathed in glaring white light. She looked at herself in the mirrored door of the medicine cabinet; her face was still red and puffy from the night of tears. Her eyes were a mess: the normally bright irises were deadened and dull; the surrounding sclerae, usually an unblemished white, were fogged red with inflamed blood vessels. Her blonde hair was tangled and dark, and her lips were pulled down in an ugly, sad frown. She smiled forlornly at the image of herself, and she was, in spite of it all, instantly beautiful.

Naked, she reached into the shower stall to turn on the beckoning hot water, noticing her condensing breath without interest as it rattled uncontrollably from her shivering chest. The hot shower flowing and the small, cold room quickly filling with steam, she stepped into the saving heat of the hot cascade. She stood face up to the flow, her eyes closed and her arms held tightly to her body, shaking hands fisted under her chin, the hot water hitting her full in the face, and she gradually grew more awake. She remembered the discussion of the night before with dread and regret.

It was always a discussion—never a fight, nor even an argument—but the pain the discussions brought could not have been worse if they resulted in physical violence. She cried into the hot water silently, her tears joining the cleansing flow as it ran down her face and body. She knew she would be late for work if she lingered, but the hot water seemed to warm the coldness she felt inside. She dozed as she stood motionless in the shower's soothing jets, her mind drifting to her childhood on the farm, to high school and marriage. She followed her adult life path through a journey that had been variously joyful and dispiriting to the present, to this moment of closure that was both promising and hopeless, to a point in her life that was an end while it was a beginning.

Jeri had met Steve when she was still a little girl. He had been the best friend of her older brother, and being two years her senior he had always seemed an alluring and knowledgeable older man. In the beginning, when Steve had come across the fields of eastern Colorado wheat that separated the Singleton farm from the farm of his own family, she had felt like an unwanted nuisance to the two boys as they played their boy games. But in Jeri's heart, Steve had already become the object of faithful and overpowering love. Then as they grew older, and their child bodies changed into the preadolescent promises of adults, the way Steve looked at Jeri had changed, and by the time she entered high school his visits across the separating grain were made in a somewhat dilapidated pickup truck to see Jeri, not her older brother.

They spent two years together as a couple in high school, his last and her first, their small school's perfect pair: Steve, successful in athletics, if not one of the best students; and Jeri, spirited in her cheerleading, yet dedicated to her college prep class schedule. They were in love and innocent, their strict Christian upbringing reining in the powerful physical drives that pulled them together across the ragged bench seat of the pickup truck. But with Steve's graduation and his entrance into the adult world of work and regular paychecks, their young relationship changed into something more serious. A relationship of longer and deeper kisses, of lonely drives and extended stops, of quiet hours when one or the other of their families were away from home, and finally a relationship of discovery and responsibility, of desire and fear, of satisfied lust and birth control pills.

During her last two years of high school, Jeri played the not uncommon double role of student/lover; an ambiguous life of womanhood and childhood. In her life at school she was the star student and the darling cheerleader, vice president of her senior class and leading lady in the school play, president of the physics club and homecoming queen. In her life away from school, her life with Steve, she was a thoughtful counselor and a sensual woman, a sympathetic listener and an ardent lover, a supplier of solace and of sex.

Jeri's approaching graduation brought Steve's inevitable proposal of marriage. At eighteen the dichotomy in Jeri's life was overwhelming. One part of her yearned to agree, to become one with him, but another part of her rebelled at the obvious loss of self that marriage would require. Her life with Steve was everything she had always thought she wanted in a relationship, but as the year brought acceptance letters and scholarships and offers of financial aid from colleges across the country, she began to fear a missed opportunity, a passing by of life, a mistake that once made would limit her life forever. She decided to fight a delaying action with Steve. She would avoid giving him an answer in words while her eyes and lips and body told him not to worry, everything would be fine, she just needed more time. But as her senior year passed swiftly, Steve's proposals came more frequently, and with each asking he became more insistent and she became less able to delay. Her fear of losing either side of her life, and Steve's overpowering needs, led to a compromise: they would marry, but would move to where Jeri could go to college.

They were married the last week in June and moved to Durango, Colorado, in mid-July. They crossed the Continental Divide in the old pickup truck, the bed piled high with used furniture donated by their families and new kitchen aids, towels, and sheets received as wedding gifts. They started a new life together in a small rented mobile home a few miles outside town. Jeri enrolled at Fort Lewis College and started working as a waitress in the restaurant of a tourist hotel. Steve found a job in another gas station, and Jeri knew he wondered why they had needed to move. She knew that in his mind the move was an unnecessary waste of time. He had argued that they should stay where they belonged; that his father's farm would someday be theirs; that their future was the farm and a family. He had complained that Jeri's stubbornness about going to college would only delay their start and postpone their family. Only his confidence that Jeri would want to return home in a short time had allowed her to convince him to make the move.

Steve had been painfully wrong. One year in Durango had passed, then two, then three, with Jeri's education and experience expanding and her ambitions growing. Through the years, Steve had lived a temporary life, clinging obstinately to his dream of returning home to his father's farm. But it was a dream of a home that no longer belonged to Jeri, nor she to it. Now, at the beginning of Jeri's senior year, they were living partially estranged in the same house; rarely touching sexually, they slept desperately close in the same bed.

The end had come the night before, during yet another discussion about returning home. It had come as a powerful anticlimax to months of quietly grinding conflict. Steve had once again declared that the trouble they were having in their relationship was rooted in Durango and caused by the abandonment of their home. He had insisted that if only they were to move back home, where they belonged, everything would be as it should be. Then he had described the complicated plans he had made for their move; a move to be completed as soon as possible after Jeri's graduation. As he had recited his plans, Jeri had known she could no longer postpone sharing the ambition she had been working toward for the last two years.

Her appetite for life didn't include a return to Steve's father's farm. Jeri aspired to be a medical doctor; her hopes and dreams were to use her intellect and drive to learn the mysteries of science, and to leave her dull rural existence behind and live in a thriving modern city. She had submitted applications to six medical schools around the country and felt her chances of being accepted were better than average. And if her applications to the medical schools were all rejected, she would pursue the subtle invitation she had received to do graduate work in biochemistry at UCLA in California.

The water jetting in her face began to grow cool as she remembered her quiet announcement of the night before. "Steve, I'm not going back. I've applied to several medical schools, and if I don't get accepted I'm moving to California to go to graduate school." She remembered the pain and astonishment on Steve's face after she had explained her plans. She hated to hurt this man she had loved most of her life, but she had to go on. She had to keep growing. She couldn't stop being herself any more than he could change himself.

"California?" he had responded. "Oh, Jeri. Not more of your college. I don't think I can stand anymore of that. It's tearing us apart, can't you see that? All those phony Joe College guys always trying to take you out, and you always at class or in the library. Even when you're at home you're always studying. We just can't go on like this anymore. Don't you see that?"

"I see it, Steve. We can't go on anymore—we've changed. I've changed. We're not good for each other anymore. I'm not sure we ever were." Jeri had tried to hold back the tears, but her emotions had been overpowering. She had wiped the moisture from her eyes roughly with the heels of her hands, wanting to maintain her composure during the critical discussion.

"What? What are you saying?"

"I need to go on with my education, Steve, and I need to do it alone for a while. I think you should go back home until we sort this thing out. You want to go back more than anything else, and I think you should do what you need to do."

"But we're married. Man and wife. We have to stay together. We can make it work if we only stay together."

"Yes, we're married, but what kind of a marriage do we have, really? Steve, we haven't made love in months."

"I knew it. I knew you were thinking about that. Come on, honey, we still love each other. We just got off track, that's all. We're too tired to solve this now. Let's go to bed, and we'll talk about this in the morning."

His desperation and pain had disarmed her. "All right, Steve," she had said as he took her into his arms. "Let's go to bed." The discussion had ended, still unresolved, and they had walked, holding hands, to the bedroom.

Jeri was forced to finish her shower with cool water, as she had let most of the hot water run down the drain while she had been musing. As she dried herself, she remembered the failed attempt at lovemaking with which the night before had culminated, and she shivered. It was useless to go on, it was over. They were two totally different people now, and it was probably her fault. She wondered how it would have been if they had stayed home and begun a family rather than following her desire for learning. No, that would never have happened. If Steve had insisted, she would have gone on alone. Maybe that would have been better; certainly the pain would have been less.

She dressed and quietly left the house. It was a nice little house she had been elated to find after their leaky mobile home. She remembered how happy she had been the first Christmas they spent in this house, and once again fought back tears of regret.

There had been several inches of snowfall during the night, and it made the yard look clean and familiar. She unplugged the heater from her old Toyota station wagon, brushed the loose snow from the windshield with the sleeve of her down jacket, and scraped the remaining ice free with the plastic tool she had brought from the house. At first she couldn't get her key to work in the door lock, so she heated the key with a match and tried again. The tumblers turned reluctantly and the door finally unlocked. But before the door would open, she was forced to yank on the handle with all her might to break the icy seal the mountain night had made of the rubber weather stripping. Thanks to the electric engine heater the old car started with relative ease on the second try. She sat with her hands in her coat pockets as she let the car warm up and remembered with another twinge of regret how impossible it had been to start the car before Steve had replaced the battery. She again felt waves of sorrow and pain wash over her. She turned around in her seat to look into the back of the car. Steve had anchored a three-foot section of log in the back to give her little car more weight over the rear wheels. It had helped the car's traction in the snow immediately. She realized that she had always depended on him for the mechanical things, and wondered if she was making a mistake. In that moment she doubted she could make it on her own. She forced the thought out of her mind as she put the car in gear and bounced bumpily out of the driveway.

The last and biggest bounce reminded her of the sunny fall Saturday they had spent together, shoveling the first snow from the long driveway. They had worked in shorts; Steve had gone shirtless and she had worn only her bathing suit top, happily letting their skin burn in the clear mountain sunlight. They had worked through the early afternoon, drinking iced tea and occasionally tossing a little snow on each other. They had stopped just short of the paved roadway, planning to finish the job the next day, but during the night winter had come again and covered their world with another two feet of snow. The unfinished end of the driveway had become a hard terrace, a teeth-rattling shelf that banged violently each trip out to the road. For a long time that last big bump had reminded her of a happier and more hopeful time with Steve, but on this morning it seemed to her that this newest snowfall had somehow flattened the step and softened the bump. She hardly felt it at all.

She had to hurry, as she was opening the restaurant at six and it was already five thirty. The new snow would make for good skiing, and that would make for a busy breakfast crowd. She thought about the side work she needed to finish before she could begin to serve breakfast, the coffee to be brewed and the bread to be toasted. She drove carefully south to the hotel, where hungover skiers would be getting up and looking for orange juice and coffee.

The highway hadn't been cleared, but the thin layer of snow was passable with the added weight carried in the rear of her car. The turnoff to the hotel, however, was a steep downhill incline that made a hairpin turn of almost 180 degrees. As she turned in to the entrance she noticed, too late, that the storm had picked this spot to redistribute the snow into a small drift. She realized that a touch on her brakes would begin a slow slide, but the only alternative was to be buried in the drift. Having no choice, she gingerly toed the brake pedal. The first tiny pressure on the brakes caused the car to go slowly sideways. Her speed, when she entered the driveway, had been barely faster than a walk, but the steep hill of the drive allowed gravity to supply the energy for the slide. She moaned quietly to herself as the car inched its way into the drift. Then, with a muffled bang the car stopped, driver's side blocking the narrow driveway and passenger's side buried in the drift. She got out of the car to survey the problem. She could see the dimly lighted restaurant just a few hundred feet away, but knew it was too early to expect help from there. She opened the hatchback of the car and removed the tattered cardboard box that held her tire chains. Then, digging with her gloved hands, she uncovered the half-buried right rear wheel, jacked up the back of the compact car and put on the chains. After tossing the jack in next to the log and closing the hatchback, she restarted the car, backed out of the drift, and drove the last frustrating three hundred feet to the parking lot.

It was six fifteen before she entered the restaurant to find a small group of resort guests being served coffee by one of their ski-panted own. Jeri rushed through the dining room, walking below the disembodied heads of elk, deer, sheep, and buffalo that were mounted on the walls, remnants of the beautiful animals that had been taken as trophies by nameless hunters in some long-forgotten past. She pulled off her gloves and down jacket, throwing them over the back of the first chair she passed.

"Sorry I'm late, but I had a small car accident. I see you've already found the coffee. Let's see if I can't get you some food before the bus leaves for the mountain." She smiled at each person as she rushed past the group of skiers, and their faces gradually lost their angry expressions. She called out to them from the waitress station, where she was trying to do a half hour of side work in thirty seconds, "Anybody want some orange juice?"

The Ram Restaurant, as Jeri had expected, filled quickly with expectant skiers as six thirty approached. She knew if she could just hold her own for fifteen or twenty minutes help would arrive in the form of two additional waitresses and a busboy. She sped into the kitchen to find the cooks standing, as always, behind the steam counter and the deep metal pans filled with neat rows of precooked breakfast meats. They looked at her cheerfully over their carefully prepared food.

"Hey, guys, I'm in trouble out here. Think I could get one of you to help make coffee and toast?"

Jeri knew that, as far as the cooks were concerned, the only question was which one of them would be the lucky one. They loved to get out of the kitchen, to have an excuse to linger in the dining room and watch the vacationing guests. They were also her friends; most of the cooks had been her co-workers for the four years she had lived and worked in Durango. On her birthday, only a few months before, she had worked a double shift so another server could study for an important exam. A few days after the test, the cooks had discovered that not only had Jeri taken the same test, but had earned the highest grade in the class. In this part of the country, in the mountains, favors like that were remembered and, if possible, repaid. And, simply put, she knew they liked the way she looked—the guys, anyway. The male cooks were always flirting with her and constantly coming up with reasons to spend extra time with her. It was general knowledge among the hotel workers that one of the youngest cooks, Patrick, had an uncontrollable but innocent crush on her.

It was Patrick who came out of the kitchen to help her. Jeri quickly took orders and delivered breakfasts to the first early arriving throng of skiers. Then, just when she began to think she would fall dangerously behind, the busboy arrived, and with his and Patrick's help she was able to keep up with the mounting work until the other two waitresses arrived and began to take tables. At eight o'clock it was over. The large room full of excitedly talking skiers emptied out into the snow, and as they boarded the resort bus the room became quiet. Jeri helped the busboy clear the tables and gave him a larger-than-normal percentage of the tips she had earned. She then went into the kitchen to find Patrick, the wholesome-looking young cook who had saved the morning. She found him already preparing a large prime rib roast he would cook in anticipation of the hungry skiers' return that evening.

"Here, Patrick, I want you to have this for helping me out this morning." She held the bills out to the young cook.

"Oh, Jeri, all I did was make some coffee. I wasn't doing anything anyway. You go ahead and keep it. You work for tips and I don't."

"Well, you did today, my love." She took his hand in one of hers and pushed the bills into it with the other. She noticed the remaining doubt in his face and continued, "Don't worry, Patrick, I'm working a double and will be back for dinner tonight. You can make me something special to eat before you go home." She saw the doubt in his eyes change to concentration as he thought about what he could make for her, and she knew he would take the money. "Well, I have a biochemistry lecture at nine and I don't want to miss it. Got to go. See ya." She turned and left the kitchen before he could reply.

When Jeri got outside to her car, she noticed the parking lot and driveway had been bladed clear and the morning sun had turned the small amount of snow that remained into glistening water. She once again went around to the back of her car and opened the hatchback to get the jack. It seemed so futile to have had to put the chains on for the last few hundred feet of her drive, just to have to take them off a little over two hours later. *But that's the southwest Rockies*, she thought.

She had back-to-back lectures until noon. She attended them all, but could do little more than take notes for later understanding. She was still distraught from the heavy discussion with Steve the night before and couldn't concentrate. She did care very much for him; it was just that they wanted such different things. All he wanted in the world was to go back to the farm and hide out for the rest of his life. She wanted to feel the modern world around her, to live in a city and enjoy the fruits of culture and technology. She wanted to go to the theater, the ballet, and the symphony. She wanted to learn the intricacies of medicine and to become a respected member of the profession known for knowledge and wisdom. She wanted a new car that was stylish instead of practical. She wanted to take vacations to exotic places, to fly across the world in high-speed jets whenever she felt the desire and to feel jet lag and traveler's sickness. She wanted to be a part of the complex matrix of science and technology that held the great cities of the world together with metallic strands of commerce and communications, strands which in her mind looked like the red lines on a map of commercial airline routes.

She pulled up to the front of the house at about one o'clock, and as she got out of her car she sensed that something was wrong. Steve's truck wasn't parked in its usual spot in the driveway, but that wasn't it. She hadn't expected it to be there; his shift wasn't over until five. It was something else, something she felt inside. She rushed to the front door, walking quickly up the drive and the stone walk.

When she opened the door and stepped inside, the near emptiness of the living room shocked her. She moved into the bedroom and it was totally bare. She found herself in the living room again and dropped into the single old chair that remained. It was the used recliner her family had given them when they first moved from the eastern, more rural part of the state. She looked around her at the empty room; everything Steve's family had given them, and everything Steve had bought since their life in Durango began, was gone. And so was Steve.

T ed awakened as he did almost every morning: long, quiet minutes before his clock radio interrupted the predawn silence. He remained motionless, waiting in the darkness for the radio to switch itself on, concentrating to maintain his stillness, ignoring the morning aches and itches that demanded he move. Then, after an electronic crackle, the room filled with the garish traffic report of an AM radio station. He leaned over, hit the snooze button, and returned to lying on his back and staring into the darkness.

The warm form next to him rolled quietly under the bed-clothes, apparently without waking. He waited with his eyes open to the darkness, listening to the soft sound of the air conditioner, wondering about the sleeping woman in bed beside him. Their first date in months had gone well. Mary was an impressive woman; she was smart, beautiful, and interesting. But he felt uneasy about her life away from him and was reticent to resume a relationship. There was something about her that made him feel the need for caution. Although she had seemed eager to have sex with him, she had suggested they use protection. They had never taken this precaution while dating before and her new wariness disturbed him. Either she had been worried about some sexual activity he may have had after their drift apart, or she had been protecting him from some high-risk behavior of her own. He knew he should question her regarding her life during the time they had been separated, but if they were not going to continue seeing each other, the discomfort caused by the effort would be pointless. Then, as he sighed, resigned to forgo the questioning, the insistent tone of a text message pierced the dark silence. He felt for his phone on the nightstand, pushed the acknowledge button and held it so he could read the message. The lighted window of the device was bright in the blackness of the morning. The text was from Diane Thomas; she needed him to call.

Diane was a good engineer and his best project manager. She was managing their part of the SENGS refueling project, and was scheduled to meet with the contractor's manager at the site later in the morning. It was unlike her to contact him so early, so the message could only indicate she had met with some unexpected problem. He switched the clock radio alarm to the off position and rose to sit on the edge of the bed, lingering there for a moment to muster his will to get up. He walked to the bathroom, confident of his way in the darkness, trusting the mental compass gained from familiarity with his home and uncounted repetitions of his morning routine. After closing the door, he turned on the overhead light and dropped heavily to the bath settee. Blinking from the light in his eyes, he dialed Diane's cell phone number. Ted wondered what the day's emergency would be. Diane was a very independent manager, and he knew she would never have contacted him if it wasn't something critically important. She picked up his call on the first ring, answering by saying his name.

"Ted, I'm sorry to bother you so early, but we have a little disaster brewing with the maintenance contractor."

"No, it's all right. I was getting up anyway. What's the problem?"

"The contractor's manager just called me. He disagrees with our critical path. He wants to start the work inside the containment first. Says he has jumpers on the payroll, and he wants them to go to work right away."

Ted disliked the use of jumpers, but it wasn't his call. His company just provided the engineering for the outage activities; the maintenance contractor provided the labor and did the work. Jumpers were temporary, unskilled laborers hired for short trips into the hot areas of the containment. The maintenance companies were notorious for going into the most depressed areas, usually minority neighborhoods, to open their temporary employment offices. It was impossible for the poor, unemployed people living there to resist the offer of top-dollar jobs, even if the jobs were dangerous and lasted only a few weeks. However, in Ted's opinion, workers hired in this way were terribly unreliable. There were stories of jumpers who had deliberately caused themselves to be contaminated in some misguided effort to outwit their employer. Exposing themselves during their first excursions into hot areas, they had quickly reached the legal maximum for radiation exposure. Once they had accumulated the permissible dosage, they were no longer permitted into radioactive areas and their usefulness to the maintenance company was over. They were paid for the full duration of their contract and sent home early. There were other, equally frightening rumors, not the least of which had been the story of jumpers smoking pot inside the containment.

Ted wondered what changes the contractor wanted to make. His team had worked long and hard to perfect the critical path of the activities involved, optimizing the sequence of work and minimizing the dangers.

"Diane, try to set up a meeting. I'll go directly to the plant this morning. It's a little late to be changing things now."

"Don't I know it. I'll call him back and set it up. I'll call you on your cell once I get it confirmed."

"OK, Diane. I'll get there about six or so. Call me when you get the details. Bye."

Diane said good-bye and he hung up the phone. Ted tried to avoid interfering with the responsibilities of his subordinates; it irritated his engineering managers and signified a failure of the management system he had put in place. But it was his company, and his was the last name on the buck list. Although he preferred to allow his field managers to handle the day-to-day plant activities, he was always prepared to go to the site to help. Maintenance activities at SENGS started at seven o'clock, an hour after the operations shift changed. This gave the operations people time to get settled in to their duties before the added responsibility of monitoring contractors began. Ted tried to be at his desk in his office when his people began their field work, so he would be easily available to them if needed. But he started most of his days much earlier, sitting at the bar on his patio, usually wearing only a robe or a pair of sweatpants. He would drink coffee and read the morning newspaper long before the rising sun transformed the night outside the windows to the silver and gray of dawn.

This morning he showered and dressed quickly before moving through the dark house to the patio, where he put on the coffee. Preparing the coffeemaker seemed uncharacteristically long and slow; he normally had at least one cup of coffee before his shower, and the change to his routine made the exercise seem tardy and sluggish. He walked to the front of the bar, sat on a stool, and listened impatiently to the gasping sounds of the brewer, loud in the silence of the morning. He remembered Mary, wondering if he would need to wake her, but it was only moments before she walked briskly into the room. She was again in the business suit from the previous day and wore full makeup. She dropped her overnight bag at her feet, rummaged through her purse, and finally pulled her key chain out with a jingle.

"I have a pot of coffee here. Want a cup?" He filled his own cup as a few late-brewing drops fell onto the hot plate with steamy sizzles.

"No thanks, Ted. I need to go home and change my clothes before I go in to work. I have to go." She bent down for her bag.

"I'll walk you out." Ted stood up and put his cup on the bar. They walked outside together silently. Ted wanted to say something to make the moment seem less awkward, but he couldn't think of anything that wouldn't sound forced or phony. As she warmed her car, he leaned inside and they kissed each other lightly. Her lips felt sticky and tasted faintly sweet. They said good-bye, and then she turned her head away from him to back out of the driveway.

He knew it was thoughtless, but he was glad she was gone. It would be a busy day since he was going to the site. Entering the nuclear plant was a much more time-consuming process than simply parking his car at his office. As he thought about the complex security procedures at the plant, his cell phone began to ring. He answered as he entered the house.

"Ted Johnston."

"Ted, this is Diane. The meeting is set for nine at the turbine lab conference room. Can you make it?"

"No problem, Diane. That gives me plenty of time. But I thought they wanted to meet right away. What's the deal?"

"Oh, their project manager wants to get his boss in on the meeting. He has to wait for him to come down from Irvine. Do you want me to call him back and try to get them to meet earlier?"

"No, nine is fine. I have some things I need to do around here. I'll see you at the turbine lab at eight thirty or so. We can talk before the meeting. OK?"

"That would be good. I'll see you then." Diane sounded relieved that the meeting was finalized. They finished the call and Ted went back to his first cup of coffee of the day.

The meeting time of nine o'clock had given him some unexpected time for himself; a luxurious hour and a half he could devote to private tasks around his house. He had been working sixty- and seventy-hour weeks for so long that he had learned to do most of his personal duties early in the morning. The cleaning woman he paid to come in twice a week had taken a week of vacation, and the house showed it. He didn't care for housework and was not very good at it. He decided to leave most of it for the cleaning woman's return, but he was running low on clean socks and underwear, so he put a load of whites into the machine. While his laundry washed, he ate a small breakfast of dry toast and black coffee. He watched the business channel on TV, ignoring the irritating monologue of the announcer as he concentrated on reading the electronic ticker tape at the bottom of the screen. He put his plate and cup in the dishwasher and moved the laundry from the washer to the dryer. The brief time he had had to himself was over and it was time to head out to the site. He collected his laptop and SENGS paperwork, locked the house and went out to his car, all the while thinking about the morning's meeting and ways the critical path could be safely altered to accommodate the contractor's changing needs.

His business placed huge time demands on him, and he wondered if that had been one of the reasons his old boss had quit and sold out. Ted liked the money and security that came with a successful business, but with the exception of all-too-infrequent vacations, he never seemed able to fully enjoy that success. Maybe his boss had just decided it wasn't worth it. Ted realized that he too was prepared financially; he didn't need any more money. If he chose a less expensive lifestyle, he could live comfortably on what he had already earned and saved. It was much more expensive for a working professional to relax than the retired, or even the unemployed. He remembered the camping trips he had taken with his brothers during high school; the total expense of all those happy adventures was certainly a fraction of the amount he had spent the previous winter on a bungled ski trip to Switzerland. Then he thought about the Colorado ski trip he had purchased for the coming winter, a single-occupancy trip to Durango. The tickets and reservations were still sealed in the travel agent's envelope, until that moment forgotten in his desk drawer at the office. He tried very hard to buy a fulfilling use of his limited recreational time, but most often, it seemed, he went unsatisfied. The vacations ended without providing the happiness he sought, and he was content to return to LA where he would again immerse himself in work.

The drive to the plant was slowed by intermittent fog, and Ted began to worry that he would be late. Each time he entered a clear section of road, he would accelerate the sports car quickly, but when he approached a foggy patch he would slow and many drivers would pass him. He would have liked to be as oblivious to the unseen dangers lurking in the fog as the other drivers, but this youthful carelessness had left him long ago, unnoticed at the time, along with the many other curious symptoms of adolescence. Now it seemed that he always measured the dangers inherent to an act before he performed it. Today he would just have to arrive at the plant a little later than he had planned. He would still be early, but the security systems at a nuclear complex were unpredictable; it was possible they would delay him long enough to make him late for the meeting.

He parked his car in the contractors' parking lot, far from the main gate of the plant, and caught a ride on the parking lot tram. The tram was almost empty, most of the contractors having arrived much earlier in the morning. He hoped the few workers riding with him were an indication that there would be no line for the security checks.

After the tram stopped at the main gate, the riders milled into a short, ragged line to present their identification badges. The badges were hard-won; contractors received them only after background searches and a required program of intense safety training. They were color coded to designate the level of freedom the holder would have inside the plant. Ted's badge allowed him general access to the balance of plant systems, but he would need a health physics chaperone if he had to enter higher-security areas of the nuclear facility. When his turn at the head of the line came, he gave his laptop and the metal contents of his pockets to the security guards for inspection, then slid the magnetic strip of the badge through the electronic card reader. After the digital codes on the badge were identified and approved by the plant's security computer, the steel gate to the threat detection system opened and he walked through the rectangular body of the metal detector. On the other side of the electronic portal he was stopped and taken aside. By waving a portable unit around his body, a suspicious guard verified the slight positive result his walk through the metal detector had produced. A few buzzing cheeps exposed his zipper and belt buckle as the source of the positive indication, and he was cleared to wait for his things. Other guards booted up his laptop to confirm its operation, then swabbed the edges of the plastic case with absorbent sample cloths. They checked the samples with an explosive detection instrument before passing the computer through and returning it to him.

Once he had completed the security checks, he signed in on the plant log and made the long walk to the turbine lab. He hurried because Diane was probably waiting for him. She would want to talk to him before their meeting.

The turbine lab, by design, was not a radioactive area. The giant steam turbine that the turbine lab technicians monitored was part of the secondary cycle. The steam that drove the turbine never entered the reactor core itself. The primary system carried the heat from the reactor to the secondary cycle by way of a massive heat exchanger. The heat exchanger generated the steam for the turbine. Theoretically, the systems were separate, and the secondary system was nonradioactive. But Ted knew through long experience that nothing man built ever functioned exactly as the theory predicted—there was always deviation. Leaks from the primary system into the secondary system or the surrounding environment were not supposed to happen, but Toyaimra and Three Mile Island and Chernobyl had proved that nothing was impossible when dealing with nuclear energy.

Ted accepted that he would be exposed to insignificant amounts of radiation in the course of his working day; however, the amounts were closely measured and monitored by the health physics department. He had never received a dosage that exceeded a small fraction of the amount typical of a common tooth X-ray at the dentist's office. He felt secure in the collected technological expertise that made the plant function safely and efficiently. He knew his job, the health physics people knew theirs, and the control operators running the place certainly knew theirs. Together, they operated this pinnacle of technological complexity, and operated it well. When Ted walked through the plant, he felt pride in the intellectual accomplishment of the dangers understood and controlled. The problem, he knew, was not the power-producing part of the plant, but the complexity of the systems designed to make the dangers safe. The more complex a system became, the more prone it was to failure.

He found Diane in the turbine lab, sitting at a technician's desk. She was talking to a group of chemical radiation technicians composed of both those going home and those coming on shift. Ted walked over to the group to eavesdrop on the conversation. It was shift turnover time; the procedure was for the newcomer to be briefed by the technician going off duty. The briefing was an informal affair with a casual oral format. The departing technicians explained the notable events of their shifts to the relief crew, summarizing the log books and itemizing tasks they had not completed, that would need to be finished on the next shift. Although the plant was very busy with coming off-line for the outage, all the parameters monitored from the turbine lab were normal. All the physical and chemical limits were being maintained, all the instruments were functioning and calibrated, and no radiation out of the normal range had been detected. All in all, it was a good day for a chem rad tech to come on shift.

Diane picked up her things and motioned him to a quiet part of the lab. When they were far enough away from the technicians not to be overheard, she put her laptop and briefcase on the lab bench. He swung his own laptop off his shoulder and put it down beside her things.

"So what's the deal, Diane, are we screwed or what?" He knew Diane to be both intelligent and direct, so he thought it would be best to get to the point.

"I don't really know, Ted. Maybe, maybe not. We planned on him working on the stuff outside the containment for three days before he went inside. But I just heard the SENGS people have decided to clear the containment as soon as possible. If he has the labor to do both simultaneously, we may not be delayed. But then again, if he puts off turbine work to get inside, we lose at least three days. Maybe more, if things are as slow as they normally are in there." She seemed to be asking him for advice, so he felt better about telling her what he had decided on the drive to the plant.

"What do the SENGS people want? Do they want to get into the containment first?" He watched her face as he spoke, and a small expression of defeat passed over it.

"I think so. They sure seem to be in a rush to shut the reactor down and get ready."

"Well, the customer is always right, Diane, and it is their plant. We just have to go along with the flow and try to get him to work on both paths at the same time. Let's play it by ear. I know you don't want a delay, but it's really out of our control. They can't penalize us for a delay of their own making."

"OK, then it's settled. Let's go on in, they should be getting here by now." With the quickness of the professional he knew her to be, she seemed to understand and accept his decision not to fight the contractor. They shouldered their computers and moved out of the lab to the conference room.

The meeting was much longer than Ted felt was necessary, but then they always were. The SENGS people would be ready to proceed inside the containment in thirty-six hours, and the contractor had only the manpower to proceed with the jobs inside. The outage would be delayed or not, depending on the efficiency of the maintenance performed inside the containment. The SENGS people allowed that Ted's company would assume no financial responsibility of a delay if it occurred. If the contractor could get in and out quickly, the outage might even be shortened, and that was what they all wanted. At one point in the meeting Ted could see that Diane wanted to explain why she thought the change to the sequence of work was a bad idea, but she had remained silent. She looked over to him and he raised his eyebrows and shrugged. It was out of their hands now.

After the meeting Ted explained to Diane that they had done what they had been hired to do. They would be paid regardless of the changes. Changes like this sometimes happened, and sometimes they even worked for the best. There was nothing wrong with the new plan; the SENGS people were just betting the contractor could save them some time. Diane didn't have the same confidence in the contractor as the plant people, and for this reason believed that time would ultimately be lost. Diane knew that lost production time at a big nuke meant big dollars in the freewheeling, deregulated electricity market. She had agreed to the changes, but was still very sure she had been right.

"Ted, this is going to cost them a lot of money. The contractor is going to find some unexpected problem inside the containment, and he will prove it is all SENGS's fault, and all his people will be sitting around drinking sodas while nothing is getting done. I can't believe they are buying his shit."

"Well, like I said, it's their money. We can always say we told them so later." He tried to disarm her with a smile, and she responded with a halfhearted grin.

"Yeah," she said, "and don't think I won't."

"Hey, Diane, I haven't gone down to take a look at the condenser or condensate pumps yet. Why don't you try to patch it up with the contractor's guy while I go walk it down? OK?"

"All right, Ted. Have fun down there, but it's all in the drawings." She smiled a real smile and left to find the contractor.

Ted walked across the wide concrete floor of the turbine deck to a steel grate stairway. The stairway led down to the surface condenser below one of the sixty-ton steam turbines. As he descended, he could see through the steel grating of the stairs and it gave him a feeling of walking on air. When he had first begun working in plants, the feeling had given him a mild case of acrophobia, but repeated exposure to the open heights of power plants had deadened the feeling. When he got down to the solid concrete of the ground floor, he walked to the condenser area and studied the layout of the condensate system. He took out his pocket notebook and began sketching the system. He knew that Diane had prepared detailed computer drawings of the system and each step of the work that was to be performed, but he had always made sketches to understand systems and old habits were hard to give up. Sketching the piping and the control valves, he forgot about the politics of the meeting and began to enjoy the work. It was the uncompromising and steady work of an engineer, not the perceptional, expedient work of the business manager. He was walking to the other side of the condenser when he thought he heard the distant sound of a siren. Suddenly alert, he put the notebook back into his pocket and listened to the muted call of the alarm over the loud noise of the condensate pumps. He wondered from which part of the plant the sound was originating. On every occasion in Ted's experience, the sound of an alarm in a nuclear facility had resulted from an alarm malfunction. Every time an alarm sounded it was by mistake or because of a planned test. But, Ted realized, he would have been informed during the briefing if a test of the alarm system had been planned. He was sure it was a mistake, an error of the monitoring system, but the skin on his arms pulled tight and the tiny hairs there stood on end. He tried to convince himself it was a good thing that the monitors and alarms were so sensitive. He wanted to believe that their tendency for false positives protected him from the real dangers of the plant, but as he listened to find the source of the threatening sound through the loud noise of the pumps, he began to feel a hardness forming in his stomach. He was in the open area beneath the turbine deck where many large pumps and compressors were located. He could see for at least fifty yards down a concrete runway used to drive heavy vehicles into the area to work on the equipment. He remembered from his safety training that there would be alarms—sirens and red lights—placed strategically along the length of the indoor street. He looked down the long roadway to find the red light at its far end blinking emphatically from within a growing cloud of foggy steam. Accompanying the light was the muted call of a siren, engulfed by machine noise it was almost too far away to hear. He had just started back to the lab, to wait out what he hoped to be another false emergency, when he heard a second siren—much louder than the first. He looked down the street to see that another red light, one nearer to him, had begun to blink, and as he stood immobilized by the unbelievable events, a white wall of steam-generated fog rolled toward him down the narrow road. Then, as he watched the cloud fill the corridor, he became aware of the lights and sirens the length of the street, warning him to be somewhere else. But it was already too late. As the warm, wet steam engulfed him, his heart pounding in his chest, Ted knew this was no malfunction of the detection equipment. He ran away—away from where he had seen the first blinking red light— away from the place where the menacing cloud of steam had begun its advance toward him. He ran from the terror, without thinking of a destination, until he saw a grotesque shape at the bottom of a steel staircase. The figure, a man protected by a full-coverage radiation suit, was motioning for him to proceed up the stairs. The sight of the health physics technician in the radiation suit made Ted feel exposed and naked; he held his breath unconsciously as he climbed the stairs. When he reached the top of the stairway, another technician in a white full-coverage suit led him to the decontamination area.

The leak from the primary system had been small. It had been detected quickly and the system had compensated immediately. Ted had been the only person near the secondary system pump when it had failed. The ruptured and rapidly depressurizing secondary system, normally operated at a higher pressure than the primary system to prevent just such an event, had sucked lethal primary coolant solution through tiny, hitherto unknown, cracks in steam generator tubing. The lacerated secondary system had flashed contaminated steam in the area where Ted had been standing. A frightening vaporous cocktail of primary system radio nucleotides had quickly flooded the air around him; radiocesium, iodine-131, strontium 90, and uranium atoms of several masses and lethality had diffused around him and penetrated his body. There had been no criticality, no characteristic flash of blue light, and the total amount of radiation to which Ted had been exposed had not been exceptionally high. But he had breathed the nucleotides into his lungs and they had been in intimate contact with very sensitive tissues.

After he was scrubbed clean in the decontamination room, the site doctor and the health physics people had said that his full body external exposure, his dosage in gray units, had been low. It was the effective dosage—the dosage that depended on organ sensitivities—that concerned them. Adults near Chernobyl had received seventy millisieverts and had survived, while a worker at Tokaimura had taken seventeen full sieverts, each a thousand times as great as a millisievert, and he had died quickly. They guessed that Ted had received between twenty-five and one hundred millisieverts, radiation that had reacted with his tissues and had remained in his lungs. Ted felt as if he was in a dream—a very bad dream. He had not made a single mistake; no one had made a mistake. A piece of metal had cracked and the system had compensated for it, but a little radiation had been released, and Ted had been in the wrong place at the wrong time.

"Crapped up" was the slang term commonly used by the people who worked at the plant. Ted had been crapped up in one of the worst possible ways—in the lungs. He had breathed a very tiny amount of radioactive material, and most of the radio nucleotides he had ingested had very short half-lives—they were already dissipating from existence—but the damage was done. No one could be sure of the effects of the damage; only time would show that.

After they had washed him down and dressed him in new paper coveralls, and after they had given him pills of nonradioactive potassium iodide—pills that might protect him from the radically increased risk of thyroid cancer the exposure had caused—and after having him fill out piles of paperwork, Ted was finally sent home. In a single morning, he had accumulated all the radiation he was permitted by law to receive in a quarter of a year. If he had been working for a utility, he could have been reassigned to a job that was not within the plant itself, a job with no further risk of exposure. As an independent contractor, he would simply be banned from the site for the remainder of the quarter. There would be no more visits inside SENGS or any other nuclear facility until time refilled his health physics checking account.

He was almost dizzy from the speed of it all. In four short hours his life had changed, yet his body felt absolutely the same. He was nervous and a little afraid, and was exhausted from the extended period of adrenal stimulation, but basically he was the same person. He hadn't been in any pain, and there was no overt damage, yet he knew the damage the radiation had caused at a subcellular level within his lungs was real, even if he could not feel it. No one could say how much radiation would be too much for his particular biochemistry. He could only wait the twenty or thirty years it would take for the answers to become obvious.

When he left the plant, he was wearing white paper coveralls and overshoes. They had scrubbed him down until no more radiation could be detected—on the outside of his body, anyway. They had taken his contaminated clothes and sent them to the radioactive waste area. Driving home, he realized he needed a drink, and it would be nice to have someone talk to while he drank it. It would be easy to stop in at one of the bars along the way, but he was afraid his outfit would cause terror in the local populace. They didn't care very much for the workers at the plant under normal circumstances; a guy in paper pajamas who was still giving off alpha radiation would probably cause a riot. He drove home instead, careful not to drive faster than the posted speed limit.

S teve was gone. Jeri sat in the old comfortable chair that had once been her father's favorite, alone in the middle of the now largely empty living room. She watched as a rectangle of weak sunlight, beaming through the picture window, moved gradually across the shiny hardwood floor. She had wanted Steve to go home, even needed it at times, but the reality of his leaving her like this was a loss both saddening and terrifying. He hadn't even said good-bye; he had just packed up and run away.

She remembered disconnected images of their long relationship, beginning as a girl, with her first realization of him, and ending with their fruitless discussion of the night before. Memories of wonderful moments they had spent together contrasted with disappointing moments spent alone at school functions; thoughtful things he had done for her opposed rejected things she had felt were important. She remembered their first ambiguous sexual encounter on the sofa in the den of her parents' house and the anxious days until her next period; the fear and embarrassment of her first physical examination for birth control pills and the feeling of freedom they created; and, near the end, her attempts to initiate lovemaking and his rejection of her caresses. She remembered many things, both pleasant and distasteful, but again and again her mind recalled the night before—the words she had spoken and his astonishment at them—his desire to please her physically and her inability to respond.

She shivered. A gradual perception of her own coldness drew her back from the replay of memories, and she realized that the room had become quite dark. When she had arrived home to the empty house, she had not thought to turn on the lights or raise the thermostat setting. She stood quickly, noticing she still wore her down jacket and gloves, and then walked to the door.

Soon she was back in her car and on the way to the Ram to work the dinner shift. This time the roads were clear and dry. She made excellent time south, arriving half an hour early. As she entered through the pair of glass outer doors, Patrick was coming through the doors on the inner side of the tiny foyer.

"Hi, Jeri. There is something special for you in the kitchen, but I still don't want this money." He thrust the folded bills out to her and she took them without thinking.

"Oh, Patrick, you're a sweetheart, but you really should take this." Before she could insist further he was gone through the slowly closing outer doors. She took two quick steps across the foyer, leaned her head and shoulders outside, and called to him just as he was getting to his car. "I'll get you for this, Patrick. You just wait. Now I'm going to do something really nice for you." Before getting into his car he signaled the "get out of here" sign, a beaming smile filling his face. She smiled and waved, turned, and entered the restaurant.

"Hello, Jeri. Patrick sure put together some meal for you tonight." Donna's voice teased in the good-natured way of old friends. "Did he get you to take back the tip you gave him? He's been moaning about it all afternoon. I've never seen him feel so bad about anything. I think he's in love with you, you know." Donna walked beside Jeri as they moved across the dining room to the kitchen.

"Darn, I didn't mean to make him feel bad. He saved my life at breakfast this morning. This place is empty tonight, isn't it?" Jeri had been hoping for a fast dinner pace to keep her mind off her crumbling world.

"It's been slow all day. They only did nine lunches today. And this afternoon I've only had the handymen come in a few times for coffee."

"Well, the bus should be back from the mountain in a little while. Those Texans will need some grub and whiskey." They laughed at her mildly anti-Texan joke. Jeri's laugh was more at herself for sounding so local. She remembered her initial puzzlement at the locals' resentment of the affluent young skiers who flooded into Durango from Texas and California each winter; now she sounded just like them.

In the kitchen, the night shift cooks greeted her happily, teasing her relentlessly about Patrick's love for her. She went out to the station, taking off her outer clothes as she walked. She put her gloves into the pockets of her jacket and piled it on top of the coats and hats of her co-workers. She had just started back to the kitchen when the three cooks filed out through the swinging doors and physically turned her around.

"Oh no, you don't," the chef said. "I have strict orders from Patrick on this. You just go and sit down to dinner." He carried two large steaming plates in front of his heavy torso. Jeri thought he looked cute carrying the plates; his long white apron covered worn-out Levi's and a red plaid shirt with rolled-up sleeves. The kitchen crew herded her around the waitress station barrier to the table closest to the kitchen, the one the hotel workers called the employees' table.

Jeri was stunned. The table was set formally for one, the china and flatware shimmering on a lacy white tablecloth. Donna was lighting the second of two tall white candles.

"Et tu, Donna? I thought you were my friend."

"What do you mean? I had to drive all the way home to get this tablecloth. That's friendship, girl."

The cooks guided her to the seat of honor and began serving the meal: two plump and golden brown Cornish game hens with Patrick's own special stuffing, mashed potatoes with gravy, steamed snow peas, and freshly baked rolls.

"Do you expect me to eat all this food alone?"

"Well, that is what Patrick said. Isn't that right, everybody?" the chef asked the smiling group. There was a general nodding of heads and a chorus of affirmative-sounding grunts in reply. "And he did go out special to shop for the hens…"

"And spend most of the afternoon babysitting them."

"So the very least you could do would be to eat every last morsel," Donna said, following up on the series of statements from the cooks.

"Oh, nooo," Jeri groaned. She had raised her eyes to look across the length of the dining room, past the stuffed bear and stuffed mountain lion that bracketed the entrance to the bar. There, passing between the silent beasts, strode a tall, broad man with graying hair and a white beard. He walked toward her stiffly, a small serving tray held chest high. Draped over his forearm was a neatly folded white towel and on the tray was a single glass of white wine. He walked up to her left shoulder and served the wine.

"Your wine, madam. Will there be anything else at this time?" He was affecting a French accent that Jeri considered quite good.

"Big John, I should have known you had a hand in this."

"I'm hurt," he replied, the French accent gone. "I'm only doing what I was told to do." There was a wide toothy smile between his mustache and beard.

"I don't think I'm going to believe that. You probably put poor Patrick up to this entire thing, didn't you?"

"Well, I might have mentioned something…"

At six feet four inches tall and 240 pounds, the man known as Big John to the employees of the Ram Restaurant seemed even more massive to Jeri because of her seated position and the closeness of his stance. His huge size made him different from the others standing around the table, but size was not the only thing that made him different. All the others were young, generally less than twenty-five years old; Big John was well over forty, how much over was difficult for Jeri to guess. His thick, wiry salt-and-pepper hair gradually paled in tone as it moved down to his face, where it became a full grayish white beard, clipped short. Rosy cheeks with minuscule red blood vessels lay prominently below his ash gray eyes. The deep laugh lines that converged at the ends of his bushy gray eyebrows were accentuated by the broad smile he seemed to wear whenever Jeri was near. His appearance was a curious contrast to the aspect of the others: the young, mostly thin, mostly clean-shaven restaurant workers.

But he was also different in other, more subtle ways than age or size—veiled, elusive ways that were no less incongruous. Most of the others had been born nearby, with the mountains an ever-present tutor as they grew. Their life experiences were generally limited to and guided by the cold snowy winters and the lush green summers of the southwestern slopes of the Rocky Mountains. The young restaurant workers who stood around Jeri's table were a candid, openhearted, unselfish group, many of whom held deep-seated born-again Christian beliefs. To them, Big John, the graying middle-aged bartender, was an enigma. The stories of his life that he sometimes told them across the bar after a long, slow night of steady drinking were both romantic and foreign to them. He was a drifter who used his knowledge of the restaurant and bar business to find employment as he needed it. He seemed to have been everywhere: from Seattle to Fort Lauderdale, and Bar Harbor to San Diego. He had arrived into their lives in the fall, a month before the first snows, driving his big four-wheel-drive camper van. He had been hired as a hotel maintenance man, but when the snows brought the crowds of skiers and the bar was opened on a nightly basis, he had become the little resort's regular bartender. Although garrulous and likable, he was reticent, almost secretive, about his personal beliefs and goals. This reluctance to expose his inner nature was effectively masked by a boisterous, bawdy, jocular, teddy-bearish personality. Above all else he was a practical joker. The others had learned that none of them were exempt from the almost continuous flow of creative practical jokes. Most of them found the pranks innocuous, and there was no denying that they were amusing, but sometimes he went too far.

"John, you're always playing a joke on someone. I think it's time you took a little of your own medicine. I feel a payback coming along." Jeri was smiling and happy, but she really felt that it would be good to pull one over on the big prankster.

"It's been tried by experts, my dear, and I've got to admit, I've been had a few times, but not very often. No, not often at all."

"Well, I can never eat all this food," Jeri said, glancing around her to smile at each of her friends. "You all better get some plates and help me." She motioned to the big plates of food and the other workers complied by picking at the meal without sitting down.

Jeri worked the dinner shift with Donna. It was steady and they both made good tips. During the work Jeri's mind was kept off the recent upheaval in her personal life, but after closing, as the two young women set the tables for the next day's breakfast, she felt a rush of nauseating self-recrimination and dropped heavily into one of the wooden dining room chairs.

"Jeri? What's wrong? Are you all right?" Donna was by her side in a moment, one arm around her shoulders. "What's bothering you, Jeri?"

"Yes, I suppose I'm OK. Steve moved out today."

"Oh, shit. Do you want to talk about it?"

"I don't know that it would do much good, really. I asked him to go back home last night, and today, when I got back to the house after class, he was gone. No good-bye, no note, nothing."

"Hell, Jeri, you sit here while I get those last couple of tables, then we're going to get a drink and talk."

"No, I'm all right. I'll help finish tomorrow's setup, but you know, I would like to talk to someone."

When the two young women walked into the empty bar, the big bartender's face lit up with a brilliant, welcoming smile. He put down the glass he had been polishing and began to walk down the length of the bar toward them. "Well, hello, ladies. I must say this is a pleasant surprise." He spoke as he walked from behind the bar, turning into the room as he reached its end. "I have a very nice table right over here by the fire." He led them across the room to where a river-rock fireplace dominated the far wall of the bar. A large fire burned quietly in it. The area was quiet and dark, lighted only by the flickering light of the fire and the crimson glow of the table lamps. The room was empty, and the two young women were seated where a casual glance inside could easily overlook them.

"Now, just what is it that I can do for you two lovely ladies?"

"I don't know, how about something icy and creamy?" Donna said to the bartender, and then turned to Jeri. "What about you, Jeri?"

"I'll have the same." Jeri was not a frequent drinker, she rarely had the time. Her favorite drink was usually what everyone else was drinking.

"I have just the thing for you two mountain flowers. Be back in a minute." He turned away and again walked the length of the bar.

At the far end he raised a section of the bar top and passed through the gap to get behind the counter. At the table there was a moment of strained silence that ended with the loud sound of a blender crushing ice.

"Tell me what happened, Jeri. It seems so sudden and all. You two have been married so long."

"Almost four years, but we were together nearly eight. Not counting childhood."

"Well, that's what I mean. What happened?"

"I don't know. I guess we just grew up. Grew up and grew apart. I still love him, but we just don't seem to have anything in common anymore."

Jeri stopped talking when the bartender brought the drinks. He carried a small tray holding two large decoratively curved glasses containing what looked to Jeri like chocolate frozen yogurt, and a third, less ornate glass of dark amber liquid.

"Do you ladies care if I join you?" He served them their drinks and began to sit down.

"Well, to tell you the truth, John," Donna answered, before he could transfer his weight into a chair, "this is kind of...well, girl talk."

"That's OK, Donna," Jeri said, as she took one hand away from the stem of the tall cold glass and moved it to touch Donna's bare forearm. "I don't mind, really." She took her hand away and motioned toward the chair. "Sit down, John. We were just discussing my life, or what's left of it."

"Are you sure? I'm not one of those phony drinkers who won't drink alone, you know. I don't mind a bit." His mass was moving back upward.

"Don't be silly, John. Sit down." Jeri reached up and tugged gently on his big arm, and the upward momentum was instantly neutralized. He settled in the chair to the accompanying squeaks and creaks of straining wood.

"You know, kids, I really don't want to interrupt anything private." He seemed serious, an uncommon thing for him.

"Steve's moved out, probably halfway over the mountains by now." Jeri stated it as if it were news of a bad storm or an avalanche; something that was bad, but could not be avoided.

The bartender was visibly surprised. "You know, I don't like to make a fool of myself by saying something negative about someone at a time like this. As soon as I do people make up, and I can't take back the words. But I will say this," he said, looking directly into Jeri's eyes, "any man who would knowingly leave a woman like you is either insane or very stupid." It seemed obvious to Jeri that the man was not shamming the hurt that filled his gray eyes. "I know, Jeri, because I did it once...a very long time ago."

"I asked him to go." Jeri said quietly, almost to herself.

There was an immediate change in the character of the man's eyes. The pain there changed to a merry, cynical gaze that seemed to Jeri somehow more natural for this strange older man.

"Well then, that's different. That is probably the best move you've ever made. Let's celebrate." He brought his glass to his mouth and drank with long, deep gulps.

"John, don't make a joke of this." Donna's voice was harsh and scolding. "Can't you see that Jeri is hurting? Sometimes you are such a jerk."

"It's all right, Donna. Please don't get upset." Jeri stirred her thick malt-like drink with the two oversized plastic straws that had been standing vertically in its center. Unconsciously, she had assumed the role of peacemaker.

The man smiled at both of the young women in turn; his eyes soft, but with a hint of condescension. "Why, of course she is hurting. The thing she has to get straight in her mind is: why?" He directed his remarks to Jeri. "I don't think you're hurt because you want him back. I think you feel bad because you think you've betrayed him or some such nonsense. That, and because you've been with him for so long there is a big hole where he used to be. Well, let me tell you something about betrayal. You're not betraying anyone now. The two of you betrayed each other, and yourselves, when you went off and got married before you had a chance to learn anything about who you were or what you wanted from a partner. You have to put that part of it, the betrayal part, out of your mind. That's the logical part. You can do it if you just try. The emptiness, though, that's different. No amount of logic will make that go away. That space is there and it will always be there. All you can do is refill it...with another man."

"Shit," Donna said, looking at the bartender. "And I suppose you know just the guy to fill her back up, don't you, *Big John?*" She said his nickname with a vicious sneer. "You can never get your mind off it, can you?"

When Donna spoke, Jeri thought she detected something beyond sisterly concern in the sharp edge of her voice. There was something there, but Jeri was having trouble believing it could be the way it sounded. She looked from one face to the other; there was quick, hot anger in Donna's eyes and flirtatious amusement in John's. Maybe there was something going on between them. It just seemed so surprising and incredible.

"Now, Donna, don't get your pretty hackles up. I'm not currently available for the heart-healing position. I never liked that job anyway—too easy to get burned." He smiled, even as he was drinking.

"Don't give me that, you old coot. You're always available." Her words were hard, but her eyes had softened.

"Well, I need another drink. Anybody else ready?" He stood as he spoke.

Jeri noticed that all that remained of his drink were a few small pieces of ice and that Donna's drink was now only a milky film on the inside of her glass.

"Sure, this is really good." Donna bent the tops of her straws down the outside of her glass and tipped the drink up to her mouth to finish the last drops. Jeri sipped through her straws for the first time; it tasted much like coffee ice cream, but she could also detect the unmistakable tang of alcohol. She took another, larger sip from the drink and only the coffee ice cream taste remained.

"Wow, this is good. What is it?" Jeri called to him as he rounded the far end of the bar.

"It has a lot of names, but it's really just a frozen white Russian with a little extra Kahlua." He spoke as he poured from several bottles at the same time.

Jeri sucked another long pull through her straws. The icy drink seemed to freeze the tissues of her throat, and she felt a tingling coldness travel downward in her chest.

"It's so cold I can feel it all the way down." She laughed happily and Donna joined her. It was the first time in months that she felt truly relaxed. She felt as if the smoldering stress of the failing relationship, searing her mind and soul for so long, had somehow been quenched by the icy drink.

The three of them stayed in the lonely bar until midnight, drinking and talking and laughing. They discussed work and the funny things that had happened to them or to their customers. They talked about skiing and the quality of the snow currently available up at the Purgatory ski area. The bartender told amusing stories about other bars in other towns and cities, and Jeri answered with anecdotes, usually at her own expense, of funny things that had happened in vertebrate anatomy lab or organic chemistry lab. When twelve o'clock neared, Donna got up, cleared the dirty glassware and walked behind the bar. The bartender stood quietly, his bulk graceful as it rose slowly out of his chair. Jeri watched his eyes as they followed Donna on her walk to the bar. She wondered about the other side of life, a side of which she had been little aware, a world where people stayed up late at night drinking and laughing. Donna stood behind the bar, bent over at the waist, water running loudly in the metal sink, and washed their dirty glasses. A steamy mist rose from the hot water, encircling her down-turned face, dampening her thick dark hair. She looked up from the sink toward the table, her right arm pumping as she moved the glass rhythmically on the rotating sink brush.

"Let's go over to my place. I'm too awake to sleep," Donna said over the noise at the sink.

"That, my friend, is an excellent idea." John shook the ice in his glass as punctuation before bringing it to his mouth and draining the remainder of his drink.

Jeri and Donna left through the lobby door as the bartender locked the liquor cabinets behind the bar. They each held Styrofoam cups full of the icy coffee drink, surreptitiously balanced under the folds of their coats. Jeri rode with Donna on the short drive south into Durango. Donna lived only a block off the main street of the old mining town turned tourist destination. The street was actually Highway 550; outside town it connected Colorado to New Mexico, Silverton to Farmington, but in town it sliced the little mountain community in two.

Donna's apartment was a small two-bedroom with one large bath, and Jeri was surprised to see how well furnished it was. But the first thing she noticed when they entered was that it was wonderfully warm inside.

"It's nice in here. Our place is always cold. Steve says it's a waste of money to heat it when we're not there. Well, I mean…" Jeri realized with a moment of pain that she shouldn't be speaking of him in the present tense, and quickly continued to cover her exposed feelings. "It seemed like it would just start to warm up, and we would be ready for bed. He would always turn the heat back down when we went to bed because he said we were warm enough there. Getting up at five is like walking into a refrigerator. Worse, like a freezer."

"Yeah, I tried that, but I like coming home to a warm place. Maybe it's because I live alone. That is, except for Boris, the meanest, biggest castrated tomcat in the world. Have a seat, I'll be right back." She walked to the back of the apartment as she stripped off her coat. "Boris, baby, where are you? You better not have shit in the house. Oh, there you are. Such a good boy."

Jeri could hear the loud crying of the cat as her friend spoke to it. Donna came back into the room with the big cat draped from neck to waist.

"Good little cat. You want to go outside, don't you?" The gray cat wiggled out of her arms, jumped to the floor and ran to the door, crying loudly as he looked back to her. Donna pulled the door open and the cat was gone before the gap was more than three inches wide. "I hope he doesn't get into any trouble. He's too damn mean for his own good." She retraced her steps to the back of the apartment, shaking her head. She called back from some unknown location, her voice muted by the distance, "I thought getting his balls cut off would calm him down, but I don't think it made any damn difference. Except maybe he got fatter, that's all."

Jeri put her drink on the low coffee table and hung her coat over the back of the sofa. She sat so that the coat was behind her and looked around the living room. She noticed again how nice the furnishings were, quite a contrast to the hand-me-down things she and Steve had used to fill their modest house. It all seemed to her to be so well matched, so modern, and so new. That was the real difference, the newness. It was all new and it looked expensive.

Her thoughts about the furniture and the money it would take to buy it were interrupted by the sound of ringing phones. There was a phone with a long cord on the coffee table, which stopped ringing after only two rings. Jeri could hear Donna in the back of the apartment talking in muffled tones for a few minutes, and then she reappeared, smiling. She carried an intricately carved wooden box in one hand and her Styrofoam cup in the other. She placed the wooden box on the coffee table as she sat down next to Jeri.

"Your apartment is just great, Donna. Everything is decorated so nicely. I'm impressed."

Donna smiled broadly. Jeri could see that her comment had been received as she had meant it, a compliment to Donna's taste.

"Oh, it's OK. I call it home." She bent over and pulled the box to her, but hesitated before she opened the lid. She leaned back and turned her head to look directly into Jeri's eyes. "It's still not exactly how I want it, but it's hard to pull the money together, to get the things I want."

"Well, it's just lovely. I don't know how you do it on the tips we make at the Ram."

"Oh, I have some money saved up. I part with a little of it when I see something I like."

"I love it. I'd give anything to get my place looking half as together." Jeri giggled; it sounded silly to her and she realized she was a little tipsy. "You should see it now. Steve just about cleaned the place out. Just as well, I suppose. It's too big and too cold and way too expensive for me now." Jeri looked around the room longingly and sighed. "My time will come. Someday, I'm going to have everything I want."

Jeri noticed a strange look in Donna's eyes, an oddly interrogating look, as if she was trying to make an important decision and was unsure of her facts. The look made Jeri suddenly uneasy; she got the feeling that Donna was unsure of their friendship, that she was somehow frightened by her. It made her want to reassure her friend, but she didn't know how.

"What is it, Donna? Are you all right?"

Donna stared into her eyes for a long, silent moment, then finally shrugged her shoulders, bent back to the coffee table, opened the wooden box and removed a white hand-rolled cigarette. She lit it adeptly with a disposable lighter she had also taken from the box. She leaned back into the sofa and carefully inhaled the joint. Her eyes closed, and Jeri could see that she was holding the long breath of smoke deep in her lungs. In a few moments her eyes opened and she exhaled the smoke. She looked into Jeri's eyes with a glassy, out-of-focus gaze.

"Do you smoke, Jeri?"

"I've tried it a few times. You know, at parties. Steve found out and almost died. He really hated it."

"Want some now?"

Jeri had tried smoking pot, but not a few times. It had been only once. She had on that occasion, like this one, been drinking. It had been at a party where a large bamboo water pipe was being offered to each person around a kitchen table. The pipe could be lighted only once before needing to be refilled. She remembered with disgust that the water in the pipe was putrid-smelling and black in color. Of the intoxication, she remembered only that she had been first dizzy and then nauseous. She remembered being sick to her stomach, kneeling in the snow just outside the door of someone else's house, Steve holding her head and scolding her gently. She had not enjoyed the experience.

Donna took another expert drag on the joint before setting it on the edge of the ashtray.

"I wonder what Super Cat has gotten himself into." She stood quickly, seemingly unaffected by the drug. She opened the front door, placed each of her pinkie fingers into her mouth and sounded a single ear-piercing whistle. In moments the cat came bounding through the door, snow in his coat and a hamburger wrapper in his mouth. Donna closed and locked the door carefully as she called to the animal, already vanishing into the rear of the apartment.

"Oh, you are such a trash picker. Just can't wait for your dinner, can you?" She was smiling at Jeri as she stomped into the small kitchen. She used an electric can opener on a can of cat food and the big cat was back, leaping onto the breakfast bar that separated the living room from the kitchen, the wrapper still in his mouth. He gave it up without a fight when Donna pulled on it with one hand as she held out his bowl of food in the other. He stood on his back legs and stretched his neck toward the bowl, trying to see or smell the contents.

"Well, it's showtime, Jeri. Do you want to see Boris do his tricks?" She moved to the center of the room and the cat jumped heavily to the floor to follow the food. Jeri got out of her comfortable seat and also went into the kitchen.

"Your cat does tricks?"

"He'll do anything for food." She made the cat sit, sit up and beg, and speak—meow—on command, before she placed the bowl on the floor. He ate slowly, making loud purring sounds throughout his meal.

Jeri laughed and praised both cat and trainer before the two women returned to the living room, sitting in the same places they had occupied before the cat's feeding. Donna reached down casually and recovered the cold marijuana cigarette from the ashtray while she picked up the lighter with her other hand. Holding the lighter and the joint up in front of her face, she carefully applied fire to the blackened end of the cigarette. When it began to glow red, she held the shortened joint to her mouth and inhaled. The burning end flared several times as she drew on it.

Jeri knew she would again be offered the pot. She felt comfortable and safe with Donna, in the warm living room with the big cat purring in the next room. The concept of gaining enjoyment from the drug was alien to her, but Donna was her friend, and she wanted to complete the bond forming between them. She had, in the past, done many things to please others without gaining pleasure for herself; at work and school, in her marriage and with her family. She was good at making other people happy, and she knew that Donna would be pleased if she smoked with her. It was as if Donna knew what she was thinking; silently, she held the joint out across the coffee table. Jeri took the small smoldering cigarette, squeezing it clumsily between her thumb and index finger. She could feel the heat of the thing, telling her to let go, to drop it. She tried to imagine herself, looking at herself through Donna's eyes; as she held the hot, dirty, brown, wet, smelly thing called a roach to her mouth. *What,* she asked herself before she breathed in the smoke, *would Steve think?*

She tried to look experienced as she drew a small puff of smoke into her lungs. She tried to hold it in, like she had been taught, but the smoke burned her lungs and she was forced to exhale in a small, painfully suppressed cough. She passed the joint back to Donna, still choking. Donna repeated her experienced inhalation and handed it back with a smile. Jeri took an even smaller puff on her second attempt and didn't have as much trouble holding it in her lungs. She felt her mind drifting away until the phone rang again. The ringing startled her back to the warm, well-lit living room. The telephone rumbled on the glass top of the coffee table until Donna picked up the receiver.

"Hello? No, not tonight, I'm going to bed now. Yes, it did. Eighty. Yeah, call me back tomorrow, after noon. OK, bye now." She smiled at Jeri, affecting irritation with her eyebrows. "I'm turning this damn thing off." She placed the receiver on the cradle with one hand and switched off the ringer with the other.

"But what if it is something important?" Jeri was surprised by the slowness of her own speech, and the feeling of thickness in her lips and tongue.

"Well, it really isn't off. Just the bell is disconnected. My answering machine will still pick up. Not pick up, but it will answer. Hell, you know what I mean. I'm a little high."

"I guess you get a lot of telephone calls." Jeri spoke without thinking about what she was saying. She was very high and felt like she was babbling. Donna turned to her with suspicion in her eyes, and Jeri worried that she would think her untrustworthy. But Jeri was already so intoxicated that she was incapable of guile or of making statements containing double meanings.

"No, not many. A friend was just asking me if I knew where he could find some smoke, that's all."

The doorbell rang, and Donna looked first at the silent phone before realizing someone was at the door. She quickly replaced the contents of the box, closed it, and carried it back to the bedroom. The doorbell rang a second time and Jeri rose to open the door; she felt light-headed and awkward. As she neared the door she heard Donna call to her from the back of the apartment. "Don't get that, Jeri. I'll be right back." Jeri shuffled back to the sofa and sat down.

Donna reappeared and walked briskly across the room. Jeri was surprised to see she was apparently sober, unaffected by the drinks or the pot. She walked to the door and leaned forward to peer out through the peephole. "It's just John," she said, as she worked to unlock the door. She turned the dead bolt first, then twisted the doorknob lock, and finally removed the security chain. The big bartender moved through the door sideways, as though he didn't want to force Donna to open it more than necessary, and came into the room carrying his Styrofoam cup. Donna secured the three locks in reverse order and followed him as he walked toward Jeri.

"Well, hello again, Jeri." He smiled at her knowingly. "Looks like you ladies have been having a little party of your own. Sorry I missed it." He directed his last comment to Donna as he sat down without invitation. Jeri noticed he seemed comfortable in Donna's apartment, familiar with his surroundings and confident of his welcome.

"Don't worry, you're included, John." Donna answered him as she walked into the darkness at the rear of the apartment.

"Wake up, Jeri," the big man said. "You look like you're going to fall asleep any second." He spoke over the top of his cup.

Jeri was having trouble focusing her vision, but it seemed to her that his eyes were not smiling in their normal way.

"I am tired. This is way later than I usually stay up. And I'm not used to drinking this much," she answered, her head leaning back onto her coat, her eyes almost closed.

"Not to mention the pot, Jeri."

"Yes, I'm not used to that either." Her eyes closed completely, and she fell into a deep pot- and alcohol-induced sleep.

Ted was very drunk as the sun began to set on the long and horrifying day. He had been crapped up, contaminated by radioactive isotopes, and his only sensation was one of common drunkenness. He was sitting at the patio bar, wearing a pair of loose-fitting slacks, drinking scotch on the rocks and making long-distance phone calls. The paper coveralls he had worn on the drive home from the SENGS site were now cold ashes in the living room fireplace.

He had been placing calls to neglected friends and past girlfriends for several hours without much success. He had not contacted many of the people for years, and the old phone numbers were mostly out-of-date. When he did get through, it was usually an answering machine that received his call. There had been a few good conversations, but he had been unable to talk about the accident and they had not satisfied his need. He had started at the beginning of his address book and was into the P's when he came across Mary's number. He realized he hadn't thought about her since he kissed her good-bye through the window of her BMW that morning. It had been only that morning, yet it seemed an impossibly long time ago. He was stunned when, after counting them, he accepted that it had been a mere fourteen hours earlier.

He dialed her home number, and when there was no answer he tried her at work. A computerized receptionist answered, and he fumbled as he entered her name using the phone's number buttons. After a short pause she picked up the phone.

"Hello, this is Mary."

"Hello, this is Ted. You're working late tonight."

"Not really. I usually work late, but I'm about ready to call it a day. I was up late last night." She said the last part with a mischievously light tone of voice. The playful tone surprised him and a long silence followed. "What is it I can do for you, Ted?" She sounded businesslike, impatient.

"Oh, I don't know, I just wanted someone to talk to, I suppose." He tried not to sound depressed, but he could hear the darkness in his own voice.

"Where are you, Ted? Are you OK?"

"Yeah, I'm all right. I just tangled with the wrong technology today and came out on the short end of the stick."

"What happened, Ted? Were you injured? Are you sure you're all right?"

"I'm just fine, just drunk, a little. The effects won't be known for years."

"Listen, Ted, you don't sound fine at all. I need to get home right after work and take care of a few things, but if you like, I could come down later this evening and we could talk. Would you like that?"

"Sure, come on down. Bring your overnight case, and we'll talk." He realized that in his drunkenness he had probably insulted her, and he waited for her to respond angrily, to tell him that he was a jerk, to rebuff his rude invitation. He was surprised at her calm response.

"Ted, just stay home, OK? I don't want to miss you. Don't go driving off if you've been drinking."

"Never happen, my dear. I'm having much too much fun staying home and getting drunk. I'll see you when you get here." They exchanged good-byes, but he was still talking when he heard Mary break the connection.

He put down the phone and became aware of the nostalgic rock music playing softly on the sound system. The old songs reminded him of the past, and he let himself be drawn into thoughts of his vanished family. He listened to the music for a long time, remembering the night his brothers had died and the way his mother had wasted away afterward, devoured by grief and cancer. But when his memories advanced to the night he had found his father, he rejected them.

He finished his drink without tasting it, stood up, and tried to walk behind the bar to make another. But standing made him suddenly dizzy; he lost his balance, stumbled forward and sprawled across a stool. He laughed at himself, surprised at how drunk he had become, but still he wanted to drink more. He pushed himself up and made himself another scotch on the rocks. As he tried to cut the peel from a lemon, he found himself unable to focus his vision on the work. He blinked his eyes and concentrated on his effort, but the shiny blade of the sharp knife would not stay steady on the yellow surface; his body was weaving far too much. Then the damp lemon slipped from his hand, his left arm followed it across the cutting board, and with one quick flash of the blade he opened a long, shallow cut in the skin of his left forearm.

For a moment the tissue of his arm lay open, pink and dry, without bleeding; then, blood oozed out from the wound and dripped onto the cutting board and the undamaged rind of the lemon. There was very little pain, and for a moment he stared at the wound and the blood without understanding. Then, when he finally comprehended the accident, he opened the linen drawer and took out a clean white bar towel. Winding it tightly around his forearm several times and tucking the triangular tips under the edges of the wrapping, he cobbled a crude bandage. The blood continued to seep from the cut, darkening the towel in a long, thin line, but he recovered the knife and finished cutting his twist. When the simple garnish was completed, he twisted the tiny rectangle of peel over the drink, squeezing the flavorful oil from it, and dropped it in the scotch.

The doorbell rang as he was moving to the front side of the bar. He weaved through the house to the front door and pulled it open. Outside, standing in the chill of the early night, he found Mary. Her overnight bag was hanging from her shoulder.

"Hi, Mary. How the hell are you? Glad you could make it."

"I'm fine, but how are you? You look a mess. What happened to your arm?"

"Oh, nothing. It's just a cut." He looked over her shoulder to the driveway. His car was still open and the damp night had taken it. A thick layer of dew was twinkling on its surface, inside and out. "I guess I should have put the top up on the car. Oh, well, it'll dry out tomorrow. Come on in. Come in out of the night. You need a drink." He reached for her with his rudely bandaged arm, but she turned slightly to one side, avoiding his grasp, and moved past him into the house.

"Jesus. What's happened to you? Are you all right?"

"Just fine. Just had enough to drink, I think. You know what Fitzgerald said: you never know how much is enough until you've had too much. I'm working on the too much part now."

He led Mary through the house to the beachside patio, trying very hard not to stagger. He went behind the bar, convinced that he had concealed his drunkenness.

"What can I get you? Sit down, relax, and have a drink." She didn't answer, so he reached into the speed rail and pulled out the first bottle he touched. He presented it to her, imitating the formality of a waiter, and discovered it was a bottle of Rémy Martin. "Hey, cognac. Excellent choice, my dear. Here, I'll even get you a glass." He placed the bottle on the bar and bent down to the glassware cabinet to find snifters for the brandy.

He pushed inappropriate glassware out of his way until the sounds of breaking glass came from the blackness deep within the cupboard. Transfixed by the sounds, he paused in his search, listening to the rumbling thumps, metallic rattles, and glassy bangs of something tumbling down behind the shelves. When the noises ended, he found a pair of large crystal brandy snifters. They tapped together, ringing musically, when he put them on the bar. As he poured the drinks, his bloody bandage hovered near the rims of the glasses, and when he offered one of the snifters to Mary, she wouldn't accept it. She left the drink—and his bloody arm—waving in the space between them.

He raised his eyes to look at her for the first time since he had begun the long process of making her drink. She sat at the bar stiffly, hands clasped in front of her, her lips thin and her eyes

70

narrow, with tiny vertical lines in her forehead indicating her exasperation.

"Look, Ted, I like to party, but I don't like sloppy drunks. I had to fight the Orange County commute—on the San Diego Freeway—and I find you shit-faced and disgusting?" He realized that she was angry and revolted by his appearance. "Look, I don't know you that well, but this behavior—well, it just doesn't seem to fit with what I've learned about you so far. Just look at yourself." She pointed to his reflection in the mirrored wall behind the bar.

He turned and stared at his reflection. His skin was gray and puffy around eyes that were red and swollen. He hadn't shaved since early morning, and his evening beard made the lower half of his face look dark and dirty. The bar towel around his left arm was crusted with blood, and there were brown patches of dried blood on his bare chest.

"How long have you been drinking? And what have you done to your arm?" Her voice was still curt, but growing less angry.

"Since about three or so. I nicked myself cutting fruit, but it's not bad, really, just showy." He tried to smile.

"Let me see. She reached across the bar to take his left arm, and he allowed her to have it. She gingerly unwrapped the upper end of the bar towel with the tips of her thumbs and index fingers, exposing the long, shallow slice in the flesh of his lower forearm. The blood had clotted messily around the wound, but he didn't think it looked too serious.

"It probably isn't deep enough to have cut anything too important. A little deeper in that part of the arm and you would have been in where there are important tendons and blood vessels." She spoke as she inspected the injury, holding his arm gently in her hands.

He waved his fingers and twisted his wrist. "See. No loss of movement and the bleeding has almost stopped. I'll be OK. I just need a clean towel, is all." He put the arm in the sink and turned the water on slowly. "And I know you are a safe sex kind of girl now, so you'll be happy to hear I gave blood about two weeks ago. I'm clean as a mountain stream." He used the old towel to clean up the arm around the cut, then threw it in the sink. He took a clean towel out of the linen drawer and once again wrapped the arm.

"Now I'm ready to party." He moved around the bar and sat on the stool next to her. He felt himself swaying slightly as he tried to focus his eyes.

"Look at you, you're a mess. Let's go in the bathroom and get you cleaned up."

"Yes, I am all crapped up. Let's go and get cleaned up." He laughed as they walked together to the bathroom.

She swabbed him down as he stood leaning against the wall. First, she scrubbed the clotted blood from the wiry hair on his chest; then, she gently daubed his cheeks and eyes, like a mother washing her little boy's dirty face. He stood quietly with his eyes closed, letting her wash him and dry him. When she was finished, he opened his eyes and watched her hang the washcloth and bath towel neatly over the edge of the sink. She looked at him with resignation and shrugged.

"All done. You're all cleaned up."

"No, not all cleaned up. You forgot my lungs."

"What? What are you talking about? I think maybe you ought to go to bed and get some sleep. Don't you think so, Ted?"

"No, Mary, let's stay up all night and drink and talk. I need to talk." His speech was slow, but not slurred; he felt more tired now than drunk.

"OK, Ted. Let's go back out to where we can sit down." They left the bathroom and walked down the hall toward the patio. "Let's go sit down and get comfortable, OK? You can tell me what happened that sent you off the deep end."

They sat side by side on a patio sofa, a glass-topped coffee table in front of them. Ted stared across the room and out the windows; he could see the sliver of the new moon floating in the blackness. He was very tired, but was starting to sober up, and a headache was beginning to throb in his temples.

"Ted, do you feel like telling me what happened?" She was offering to listen, but not demanding an explanation. He felt she would not press for the story if he chose not to speak, but he needed to tell someone about the accident, and it might help her understand why he had gotten so drunk.

"OK, Mary. I was working at the SENGS plant today. Just a meeting, really, but I wanted to take a look at the equipment. I was out in the plant when a pump casing failed. I breathed some air that contained radioactive material, enough to keep me out of any potentially radioactive area for three or four months. It made me a little crazy, I guess."

"Oh, Ted," she said, shaking her head slightly, her voice a sad whisper. At first, the expression in her eyes was so foreign to him that he didn't recognize it. Then in an instant he identified it as pity, and he was terrified by it. He fumbled with his words as he tried to explain his radioactive contamination in a more favorable light.

"The duration really wasn't that long, and the levels weren't that high. It is all just governmental red tape, really. I've been needing a vacation for a while anyway." But she didn't seem to be listening to the brighter side; she just stared at him, her eyes wide and empathetic.

"That's terrible, Ted. I can understand why you wanted to get drunk. But alcohol is a depressant. It will just make you feel worse." The look on her face changed a little; the pity disappeared and something else replaced it. She still stared at him, but her expression was steady and serious, as if she wanted to ask him something very important.

"What is it, Mary? What are you thinking? I'm not dangerous or anything—to you, I mean. It was just an unlucky accident. I'm the same guy, you know." He wanted desperately for her to accept him, to want him in the same way she had wanted him before.

"No, I understand that. It's just that I think I can help you feel better." She waited for a moment before she continued. "Ted, you don't know everything about me—any more than I know everything about you. And it's just that—well, I have something that will make you feel better, and I'm afraid to tell you about it."

"What is it, Mary? Don't be afraid of me. I won't hurt you, please understand that."

"OK, Ted. I hope this is OK." She stood and walked across the room to the bar, picked up her purse, and returned to sit down next to him. She reached into the purse and removed a small colorfully beaded bag. She held it on her lap for a moment before leaning to the coffee table and inverting its contents onto the glass surface. He recognized the paraphernalia at once.

"Is that cocaine, Mary?" he asked, as he studied the group of objects on the table: a small brown vial with white powder inside, a short stainless-steel tube, a box of razor blades, and a tiny metal spoon.

"Maybe I shouldn't have told you. You seem so conservative about everything. I wanted to get to know you better before I asked if you got high. Well, now I'm asking. Do you get high?"

"No, not really. I tried it once in high school. My brother was into everything. He wanted me to try it." He remembered his younger brother and the night after a football game, when he had shown Ted the mechanics of snorting cocaine. He remembered he had sneezed. His brother had punched him in the upper arm and accused him of wasting it.

Then, before he could suppress it, he remembered another football game on another night: a game in which his younger brother had thrown him a long touchdown pass in the final seconds to win the contest, a night that led inexorably to the deaths of his only two siblings. He pushed the memories of his brothers from his mind before his thoughts could move on to the rest of that terrible night and the events that followed.

"Well, you don't need to have any, but it would do you some good. It will pick you up. And boy, do you need something to perk you up. Anyway, if it's OK with you, I'm going to have a line." She raised her eyebrows, seeking permission to take the drug in his presence.

He was reminded of his younger brother and the coaxing he had given him—urging him to "lighten up," to "get a life," to "stop worrying so much," and in general, to stop acting so conservative. He remembered him and his arguments, and his resistance to Mary softened. If she wanted to take some cocaine that was her business. She had come down at a moment's notice to take care of him. Who was he to tell her she couldn't do as she pleased?

"You go ahead, Mary. Maybe I'll try some later."

He was surprised by her. He knew that many people still took drugs, but he had been so far from that culture for so long that it seemed impossible that a woman like Mary, an intelligent and successful business executive, would be involved in it. His perception of the drug culture had evolved over the years; television news shows about crack cocaine and inner-city violence had led him to believe the problem was limited to the poor, to minority men living in slums and carrying assault weapons. He was astonished to learn that another culture still existed in the world of business, BMWs, and wealth. He wondered if this culture had gone further underground in the conservative environment of mandatory drug testing and political correctness, or if he had simply been insulated from it, and denied the truth because he had been considered an outsider, a person too conservative and boring to be included. He sat back into the soft cushions, feeling tired and drained, as Mary leaned over the table to prepare the cocaine.

It didn't seem so dangerous to him now, when compared to everything else that had happened. His life, his understanding of his life, had been somehow changed by the events of the day. A subtle rearrangement of the order of his universe had occurred; a change that was immense in effect, yet imperceptible from his close vantage point. Cocaine, in his exhaustion and drunkenness, now seemed to him innocuous, benign when compared to nuclear contamination. It might perk him up. Then he realized he was afraid to sleep. Although he was overwhelmingly tired, he was afraid he might have the dream.

He watched her repetitive motions as she worked on the drug; they seemed mechanical and somehow powerfully hypnotic. She upended the brown vial onto the middle of his coffee table, tapping it against the glass to empty it. Then, she removed the brown paper from a new single-edged razor blade—it had appeared suddenly in her hands. He heard the scrape of the blade against the glass, and he opened his eyes to see her chopping at the small pile of white powder. He listened to the clicking of the blade, and when it stopped his eyes opened again. The cocaine was separated into four long, thin rows. When she appeared satisfied that all contained about the same amount of the drug, she turned to face him and smiled.

He was suddenly, overwhelmingly sleepy. He watched her disappear between his heavy eyelids, his efforts to keep his eyes open insignificant opposition to the exhaustion of stress and drunkenness. He fought the overwhelming weight of them for a moment, and then just closed his eyes and fell into the deep, dreamless sleep of the alcohol poisoned.

He was awakened by the sound of Mary's voice. He realized it was morning and opened his eyes; the light in the room made his head ache. He was lying on the sofa, a blanket tucked around him. His head was splitting and he felt nauseous. He wanted to get up, but he felt weak and sick. Mary was talking on the phone at the bar, sounding strong and businesslike. He pulled the blanket over his head, wondering how it had come to be across his body, and drew his knees to his chest. He lay motionless, his head pounding, too feeble to move, but then the stirring in his stomach forced him up and he stumbled to the bedroom bath to vomit.

When he was finished being sick, he washed his mouth and face with cool water, dried his face on a hand towel, and turned back to the sink and brushed his teeth. He dried his face again, then took off his clothes and stepped into the shower. The water came out cold at first because he hadn't let the hot water run through the cold pipes to warm them. He hid from the freezing water by shrinking into the far corner of the stall. When the water grew hot, he stood under it with his face fully in the steamy stream, balancing himself in the flow by holding the shower nozzle above him with both hands. The water felt soothing on his aching head, and he dozed off for an instant, losing his balance and waking suddenly. He turned off the water, stepped out into the humid bathroom and leaned against the wall. He rested his forehead on a bath towel that hung beside the stall, burying his face in its fluffy softness. When he felt himself dozing again, he pulled the towel from the rack and draped it around his neck. Still wet, he put on his heavy terry cloth bathrobe and walked slowly to the front of the house and the kitchen. He was incredibly thirsty and wanted a glass of cold water or some juice.

He found Mary in the kitchen; the sky in the window behind her was the bright clear blue of a perfect morning. She had found the coffee and the big coffeemaker he kept on the counter but rarely used. She stood behind the breakfast counter drinking a mug of the coffee, and when he entered the room she nodded to another mug. Then she reached down, picked it up and held it out to him. He took the mug and walked past her to the cabinet where he kept vitamins and aspirin. He really didn't want the coffee, and set the mug down on the countertop before he reached for the jars of vitamin C and aspirin.

"That's not a very good combination for an upset stomach, Ted. They are both very acidic. You'll be sick again."

"I know, but it's all that works. If I can keep them down, that is. You could hear me all the way out here?"

"No, but I didn't think you were running to the bathroom to call your stockbroker."

"No, I suppose not." Normally, he thought, he would have found the situation funny, but he felt too sick and his head was pounding. He tossed the aspirin and vitamin C pills to the back of his mouth and leaned over the kitchen sink to drink from the faucet. Standing up, he tilted his head back to wash the pills down his throat.

"You look like you're in pretty bad shape. How about some milk or something to go with those aspirin?"

"I'm out of practice, I'm afraid. I've got milk?" he asked in astonishment, knowing he never did, but thinking it was possible the maid had brought some in to have with her lunches.

Mary opened the refrigerator and surveyed its contents. "Nope. Beer and wine and water and juice, but no milk."

"Too bad, that sounded good. I'll have some juice."

She took out a cardboard carton of orange juice and began opening cabinet doors in search of a glass. "Are you accustomed to having women take care of you or do you just learn fast? Where are the glasses, buddy?" Ted pointed to a cabinet and she opened it to reveal the glassware. "More acid for an irritated stomach coming right up. You really are out of practice." She filled a water tumbler with orange juice and handed it to him. He took a long drink while he looked at her over the glass.

"I'm a little shaky this morning. Please excuse me." He put down the glass, pulled up the sleeve of his robe and inspected the new cut on his forearm. Its origin was a mystery to him; he had first become aware of it when he undressed for his shower. It was a neat, straight, shallow cut; the edges had already closed and it was not too painful. "Seems I cut myself last night. I must have been very drunk. I'm sorry you had to see me."

77

"You were a mess, a drunken, lonely slob. To tell you the truth, I don't know how any of you men survive."

"We have women, of course. Mary, I remember calling you yesterday, but I'm afraid I don't remember your coming."

"You didn't last long after I got here."

"Sorry. No excuse but drink, I'm afraid." Ted remembered that on the morning after their date Mary had been long gone by the time the sky turned blue. "Don't you have to work today?"

"I called. I've been needing a three-day weekend for a while anyway. But I don't have to stay if you would rather be alone."

"You called in on a Friday? Don't you know it's not nice to call in sick on Fridays or Mondays? The personnel people keep a wary eye on that sort of thing, you know." He spoke between sips of the orange juice.

"I'm not in a position where I need to call in sick. I just call and tell my secretary I won't be in. They have learned they need me since I saved their ass on Web security. Funny, none of the big boys wanted that project, they all thought it was below them, but when the shit hit the fan I was there to be the hero. Now the ones who are still around report to me."

"Well, right now I don't feel like going in at all for a while. Not after yesterday. It won't matter much if I hang around the office or not, I have good people there to run things. I just don't want to think about nuclear plants for a while. I told you what happened?"

Mary raised her eyebrows slightly and nodded confirmation that he had explained the accident at the SENGS site. He looked at her more closely; her hair was combed neatly and her makeup was freshly done. She was wearing jeans and a baggy Stanford sweatshirt. She seemed at once casually and deliberately dressed.

"Where did you sleep, Mary?"

"On the other patio couch. Not very comfortable—for someone sober, I mean. Did you sleep well?"

"Me? I was passed out. Lots of sleep, but not much benefit. I suppose it was you who covered me with the blanket. Thanks for taking care of me. I'm still tired. I think I need a nap." He lifted the bath towel over his head to rub his damp hair, letting it linger over his eyes to block out the light.

"Oh? That would be nice. I could use a nap too." She giggled suggestively, holding her coffee cup in front of her face with both hands, her beautiful dark eyes smiling over it.

Ted felt surprise in his desire for her, but it seemed normal, a connection with his life of two days ago, before a failed pump had changed him. He was aroused by her straightforward yet girlish suggestiveness. She was a very attractive woman, and he realized he felt better; his headache was improved and his stomach had settled. He moved across the kitchen to her and put his arms around her shoulders. She responded by putting her coffee down on the counter and circling her arms around his waist. She looked up to him and he leaned down and kissed her, the mild coffee flavor of her mouth tasting clean and pleasant.

They walked together, holding hands, through the patio. The room was bright with morning light and Ted could see just how drunk he had been the night before; the room was a shambles. The blanket and a bedspread were stacked, neatly folded, on the arm of one of the sofas, and he thought about stopping for them. But the day looked like it would be warm and sunny; they probably wouldn't need them. He looked down at the coffee table as they walked past it. There, on the glass surface, were the four rows of cocaine lying among the paraphernalia used to prepare and ingest it. He remembered it had been Mary who had put it there. He remembered the way she had revealed her secret lifestyle to him, and he remembered her using a razor blade to make the drug ready. He stopped and stared down at the collection of forbidden things on his coffee table, unable to remember more. He felt Mary's hand move in his own and he turned to face her.

"Ted, do you want to do a line first? I think I'm going to have some." She released his hand and sat down opposite the drug on the table. He was confused by the new direction of the morning and his incomplete memory of the night before. She seemed comfortable asking him the surprising question, and he had the feeling of having missed something important.

"I don't think so, Mary. The accident I had yesterday is rare and usually turns into a big deal. I don't know if they are going to make me take more tests, but I need to be careful. They took samples of just about every bodily fluid I have yesterday, but it wouldn't do for me to test positive for drugs now."

"Well, I think you need something to pick you up, and if you think they will be testing you for drugs, it's a little late to worry about it now. It's already in your system. You had some lines last night...You insisted." She spoke without looking up to him, as she wiped the edge of the razor blade with a tissue she had taken from the little beaded bag.

"I don't remember." Could what she was telling him be true? Had he taken cocaine? It didn't seem possible. It didn't seem like him. And how had he misjudged Mary so completely? He was stunned into silence by his own bewilderment.

"I should have made you wait until you were sober," she went on, as she buffed the edge of the blade. "It's all my fault. I'm so sorry, Ted." She looked up to him and he recognized the terrifying pity in her eyes he had seen the night before.

"No, Mary. I can take responsibility for my actions. It's probably not going to make any difference now anyway."

He sat down beside her and watched as she prepared the drug. She pushed the four stiff rows from the night before back together into a chunky pile; the night air had obviously dampened the stuff and fused it together. Then she chopped it back into a very fine talc-like powder before dividing it into four new rows. She extended the tube to him with a smile on her face and encouragement in her dusky eyes; the pity he had seen there moments before was gone.

Ted was finding it hard to believe he had made the important decision to take drugs while in his drunken stupor of the night before, especially considering the way he felt about it now. But that was probably why they made recovering drug addicts give up booze; one thing made it easier to do the other. He still couldn't remember doing it, and he was angry at himself for allowing it to happen.

"No thanks, Mary. You go ahead. I don't mind if you do it, but I think I'll pass. What happened last night is done, I can't change it, but I'm sober now and I'd rather not."

"OK, Ted. I understand. I guess I just made a mistake telling you I do it sometimes. You will probably never want to see me again."

"It's not that, Mary. I don't think less of you, really. I'm surprised and I'm concerned for you, but I don't think less of you. It has to do with my brothers. I lost them both to drugs and I still have very strong feelings about their deaths."

"I'm sorry, Ted, I didn't know. This is bringing back bad memories for you, isn't it? You must have been devastated when it happened."

"Yes, but not as much as my parents. I was pretty bad at first. They called it post-traumatic stress, but it was over before I got out of high school. That was a long time ago. Now I just miss them and wish it could have been different. That's why I'm worried about you."

"You're so sweet, Ted, but it's OK. I don't do this all the time. I've done it a little, off and on, since college. And I've never felt a need to do more. You can't get in trouble if you only do it occasionally. Your brothers couldn't possibly have overdosed on coke."

"No, they died in an automobile accident. The drugs sort of caused it." He tried not to visualize the accident as he spoke about it, forcing himself to be abstract and verbal. "You go ahead, I'm going to go and get dressed."

He stood up, leaned down to kiss her on the forehead and began to walk out of the room. At the entrance to the hall he turned back to watch her. She was bent over, face close to the table, holding the steel tube to her nose. She moved her body sideways as she vacuumed the cocaine into each of her nostrils. When she was finished, she sat up, leaned her head back and sniffled hard.

He felt sorry for her, pity like that she had felt for him when she learned he had been crapped up. They were the same, really; the coke and the isotopes, both were products of the modern world. There had always been coca trees and naturally occurring nuclear reactions, but it had been man's collection and refinement of the innocuous things that had created the danger. Mary was getting crapped up by the same forces of technology that had caused his own contamination. It was too late for him, but not for her; she didn't have to do it, and maybe he could draw her away from it. Maybe he could make her understand the danger, protect her, as he had been unable to protect his brothers—or himself.

Jeri awoke sluggishly; she felt pain in one ear and moved. Her head was resting on a hard pillow formed by her hands, joined prayer-like, palm to palm. Discomfort in her neck, face, and head caused her body to shift position autonomously, and she became vaguely aware of indistinct activity at the boundary of her consciousness. She moved again, extending her knees from where they had been tucked against her breasts, and her cloudy mind came slowly back to full wakefulness. She rubbed her sore ear and opened her eyes. Donna was standing over her, a bulky pink bathrobe wrapped tightly around her torso, her dripping hair dangling in wet ropes around her smiling face. Jeri realized she had been sleeping on the sofa in Donna's living room. She could hear the unmistakable sound of shower water spraying in the bathroom.

"Good morning. How did you sleep?"

"What time is it?" Jeri jerked her head around, turning to look for her bedside alarm clock, confused momentarily by her surroundings. The sudden motion caused a dull pain deep behind her eyes. "I've got to go home. I have to get up for work tomorrow."

"Forget it, Jeri. We overslept. You better call in. It's already ten o'clock."

"Oh God." Jeri's head was pounding painfully. She allowed herself to drop back, flat on the sofa, her arms folded across her eyes. "How could I have done this to myself?"

"Use the phone on the coffee table, Jeri. You can call the restaurant from here. Don't worry, they'll understand. I do it all the time."

Jeri dropped her arms heavily to her sides and nodded. She slid her legs off the edge of the sofa and pulled herself into a slumped sitting position, her face propped in the palms of her hands, her elbows piercing sharply into her knees. She paused there for a while, gathering her thoughts and her strength, then pulled the phone toward her across the table. She was dialing the Ram Restaurant when she heard the squeaking turns of bathroom water valves accompanied by the cessation of the shower water sounds. She looked up to Donna, who was still standing with her in the living room, and the other girl smiled at her mischievously.

Jeri felt dizzy and her head was throbbing. She realized suddenly she was going to be sick; she knew it, but she couldn't let it happen. She couldn't let herself be sick in Donna's house, with the insensitive bartender there to witness it. She hung up the phone and tried to stand, felt her stomach turn over, and was forced to sit back down. Then her mind manufactured a humiliating mental image of herself kneeling before the commode, puking uncontrollably; Donna was standing in the bathroom doorway, and John, clothed only in a wet bath towel, was holding her head and smiling that amused but not amusing smile. She stood again and fought back the nausea, tasting the bitter hint of it at the back of her throat. She stood unsteadily for a moment, a swaying instant just long enough for Donna to notice her loss of poise.

"Jesus, Jeri. You look like shit. Are you all right?" Donna started to move closer to her as a bass voice began to sing in the bathroom. The voice catalyzed the moment; Jeri started as if pricked by a needle. She turned back to the sofa, rolling her head, birdlike, on her limp neck and shoulders, spotted her belongings, measured the distance visually, and bent over to pick up her coat and purse. Hoping Donna couldn't see her distress, she stopped, immobilized by rising nausea, concentrating hard to keep her stomach under control.

"I'm hung over as hell. I've got to get out of here." She moved for the door without slowing to put on her coat or gloves.

"Jeri, wait a minute. Where are you going? If you wait a minute I'll give you a ride."

But Jeri was already fumbling through the multiple locks on the apartment door. "No, it's OK. I want to walk. The air will do me more good than anything right now."

The locks seemed embedded in some thick, sticky fluid, and her fingers seemed dull and unresponsive. Security chain, dead bolt, and finally the lock on the doorknob, slowly she opened each one. She turned the knob, and as the door opened to the small portico a splash of icy air hit her in the face. She forced herself out onto the icy stoop and down the slippery steps, contemplating each dangerous footfall as she negotiated the slick concrete. The path to the street had been cleared during the night by some unknown and unseen Samaritan, while she had slept—while she and Donna and John had slept.

The day was clear and sunny; the sun shone bright and sharp and the sky was the post-storm powder blue of the mountains. The cold, dry air caused her skin to pull tight, and the little blonde hairs of her forearms stood on end, each one atop a tiny pinnacle of flesh. But she did not feel cold; the welcome sun warmed her more quickly than the cold air could wash way her warmth. She put on her coat more to avoid carrying it than to keep warm and did not zip it closed. As she breathed the clean, icy air of the brilliant day, the nausea fell back into the pit of herself, like some frightened nocturnal creature dreading the light of day.

The long walk to the Iron Horse Inn cleared her mind and settled her stomach. She went directly to the Ram Restaurant to explain her irresponsible absence, but to her surprise, no one seemed very interested or the least upset. It shocked her that getting drunk, passing out in someone's living room, and missing work without calling in would have few, if any, repercussions. The lunch crew just laughed, and joked that it served the other morning waitresses right to get along without her for once. They seemed to be saying that she had actually done something that was inherently correct instead of something terribly wrong. Even the food and beverage manager laughed and told her not to worry, explaining that everyone overslept once in a while. She rejected Jeri's solemn apology as something comical, meaningless, and unnecessary.

She drove her Toyota home, wondering if she would ever understand the surprising values of her co-workers at the Ram Restaurant. Inside the cold, empty house she took off her down jacket, but not the heavy sweater she wore underneath. She looked around the kitchen and found that Steve had not bothered with taking any of the food or even the cooking utensils. She made herself a cup of tea and a dish of pasta flavored only with olive oil and seasonings, then carried her lonely meal back to the quiet, empty living room to eat. Sitting in the old recliner with her plate on her lap, she picked at her food silently, thinking about Steve's drive over the mountains, wondering if he was now sitting with his family in the warm living room of his father's farmhouse. An involuntary shudder shook the fork above the plate of food and she felt suddenly cold. She put the plate on the wood floor, walked to the thermostat and pushed the needle up to eighty degrees. She didn't need to explain her desire for warmth any longer. Back in the chair, she recovered her cooling meal, and eating in silence, anesthetized by doubt, she watched through the windows as the occasional car drove by on the street.

The television was gone, but she had plenty of homework to keep her busy until bedtime. She studied her physical chemistry text through the late afternoon and early evening. When she began to feel tired, she realized she had nowhere to sleep. The bed had gone with the television and the rest of the furniture. She remembered a magazine article she had read about the Japanese style of sleeping on the floor; they used thick pads they rolled out at the end of each day. *They call them futons,* she thought, *and they are very popular, even stylish in California and New York.* She would simply become more adventurous and sleep on the floor. She would pretend she was living in New York, in a high-rise apartment, with the lights of the city outside her windows and interesting people, artists and writers and struggling young actors, living in the apartments around her, all of them sleeping on the floor.

She built her futon from her sleeping bag, three blankets, and two sheets, putting it under the windows in the living room to make the house seem more like an apartment and to avoid the bedroom she had always shared with Steve. She put on her nightgown and some heavy white sweat socks before crawling between the cold sheets of her new bed. The floor was much harder than she had imagined it would be; she tossed and turned on the hard surface for a long time without being able to fall asleep. Eventually she realized she had grown hot under the layers of bedding and pulled the blankets down from her body. She lay quietly, with only the top sheet upon her, trying to get drowsy, but still she did not sleep. She got up and turned the thermostat down to a cooler sixty degrees. When she got back into the nest of blankets, she was less uncomfortable and better able to relax. She fell asleep in the twilight of the day, forgetting to turn off the kitchen lights. She awoke after it had grown darker and colder, the kitchen lights shining in her eyes and her arms and legs feeling chilled. She rose once again to turn out the lights, but she did not change the thermostat setting. She got back under her blankets, pulling them up around her neck, and soon fell into a deep night-after-the-party sleep.

The next morning when she awoke, she felt as cold and empty as the little house that had once made her so happy. She washed and dressed, and cleaned every room before making herself something to eat. She tried to sit in the old chair in the living room to eat her breakfast, but the empty room filled her with sadness and regret; she finished her breakfast standing at the kitchen counter. While she stood over the sink looking out the small kitchen window, she decided to find another, smaller place to live. A place that was more her own, she thought, maybe a place like Donna's. No, that would be impossible; it would take much more money than she made just to pay the rent, and she would still need furniture. She would just get a small place that didn't need much. Maybe she would just rent a furnished room near school.

She drove her station wagon to her landlord's house at the southern outskirts of town. Her rental managers were really just another young couple. They made their living by managing several properties for some people who lived in Denver. They were a very spiritual couple, devoted to Jesus and to each other. When not working their property management job, repairing some broken thing in one of the rentals or doing the books, they cross-country skied or, in the summers, worked in their garden.

Actually, there were two gardens: one planted by the moon and another planted randomly. They had planted them during the early days of the summer on either side of the driveway that led up to their double-wide mobile home. Jeri smiled forlornly as she drove, remembering the harvest party the couple had thrown after the first signs of fall, a party she and Steve had attended together. One side of the driveway had grown into a respectable garden; the other side had become an overgrown jungle. Almost everyone at the party had agreed, as they stood on the gravel driveway between the two halves of the garden drinking beer from plastic cups, that the old ways of planting by the moon had produced the obvious difference. Jeri had been the only one to disagree with their evidence; she had argued, unsuccessfully, that something else had been at work. She had explained that the subconscious bias of the gardeners could have tainted the experiment, and that they may have unknowingly treated the two gardens differently. But the others at the party had come to the aid of the two gardeners with friendly vehemence, stating categorically that this test was just a rehash of many others performed over the years. They had all known beforehand what the result of the experiment would be; it was just a waste of garden space to plant without taking the phases of the moon into consideration. In the end, Jeri had given in to the weight of numbers and had surrendered her argument, but she had secretly retained the goal of somehow reproducing the experiment, under rigorous experimental conditions, in some future garden of her own.

When she pulled up to the mobile home, she could see the remnants of the taller plants sticking up brown and brittle through the snow. She parked at the end of the driveway, in a spot that had been roughly cleared of snow, the frozen mud dark beneath a crust of ice. She pulled up the hand brake a moment too early and the car slid a few inches on the slippery surface. She got out of her car and walked carefully up the narrow path to the wooden porch. The subsurface of the path had been compressed by the many footfalls that had passed along it, and she could feel the thin layer of ice between the packed snow and the frozen earth breaking like peanut brittle under her weight. She stomped up the steps, noisily pounding the loose snow and mud from her boots, and before she could ring the bell Annette answered the door.

"Hi, Jeri, how are you? It's nice to see you. Come in, come in."

She was almost as young as Jeri, but seemed older. Jeri knew her to be comfortable with the rural life of flannel shirts and loose denim pants. She had long, straight black hair that she wore parted in the middle, the sides hanging heavily to her shoulders before falling down her back where she usually gathered it in a thick ponytail. She had large brown eyes and the smooth, healthy brown skin of her Navajo mother. She pulled the door open wide and Jeri walked into the warm living room of the home.

"Hello, Annette. How have you been?" Jeri pulled off her boots and stood them by the door. "It's nice and warm in here. And what is that I smell? Corn bread baking? You're such a homemaker, you're always baking something."

"Come in and sit down, I'll get you some coffee."

She followed Annette into the kitchen and sat at the small dinette table. Its Formica top was covered with receipts, checks, bills, and cash register slips, all organized into piles of significance known only to Annette. A big ledger was open where Annette had been working on the books of the rental management job; a mug of coffee was steaming at one side of the book and a four-inch square of corn bread was at the other, resting on a folded paper towel, with a large lump of butter melting on top.

Her landlord and friend walked past the table to the kitchen counter, where she poured a cup of coffee and cut another slab of corn bread. When she returned to the table with the bread, it was on a white china plate, a pat of butter and a tiny butter knife at its side.

The two women sipped coffee and ate corn bread while they gossiped about the local events around the small tourist town. When there was a break in the casual conversation, Jeri brought up the reason for her visit.

"Annette, Steve and I have split up. He has gone back home. I can't afford to live in the house anymore. You know that I have kept the place up, and I was wondering if you could apply the cleaning deposit to one more month's rent."

"My God, Jeri. I'm so sorry. Steve came by yesterday and told me you two were moving out. I knew the place was clean so I gave him the deposit."

"That bastard." The words burst from her before she could control her anger. When she heard them, she was immediately embarrassed. The voice had not even sounded like hers. "I'm sorry, I didn't mean to be rude."

"Hell, he is a bastard. You don't need to apologize to me. I'm the one who believed the selfish ass."

The two women sat facing each other, looking across the three feet of paperwork, both of their expressions taut with anger, eyes squinting, jaws set. They looked into each other's eyes and Jeri felt a new level of friendship, a common bond of womanhood. Their eyes, two brown and two blue, opened a conduit through which their anger and their knowledge could pass. They stared, immobilized for long, intimate moments, then slowly the eyes softened, and the lips loosened, and the hard wrinkles at the corners of their eyes turned up and began to become the wrinkles of amusement. The more Jeri tried to remain hard and angry, the more difficult it became, and when she saw a tiny smile pulling at Annette's lips, she realized they were both trying not to laugh.

"Those bastards." Annette emphasized the second word with a fist pounding on the table. They watched as coffee lapped at the rims of their cups and they laughed without restraint.

"They really are, aren't they?" Jeri could barely push the words from her throat for her laughter, squeezing them between gasps for breath.

"Only good for one thing."

"Bimbos."

"Whores."

Annette spilled her coffee on the tabletop, and the two friends scrambled to save the papers from the growing flood of brown liquid, cleaning the mess away in a few minutes of sponges and paper towels. When they were finished, Annette refilled their cups and they sat together quietly sipping coffee for a few minutes, each involved with her own thoughts. Then Annette got up and walked to a cabinet over the kitchen counter, opened the door and reached inside with both hands.

Sounds of rattling china came from inside the cupboard, followed by the rasping noise of a lid closing on a ceramic pot, and Jeri wondered what her friend was doing. Annette came back to the table with a small glass ashtray and a single marijuana cigarette. She sat down and put the clean white cigarette in her mouth with one hand while lighting a plastic disposable lighter with the other. She lit the joint like another person might light a tobacco cigarette on a street corner.

Annette smoked the joint without any of the theatrics Jeri had seen performed by the other people she had watched smoke pot. She smoked it without consciousness, the way a person would place a stick of gum in her mouth and begin to chew it, seemingly unaware she was doing something outside the norm of a casual cup of coffee. Jeri thought, as she watched, that this domesticity with the ingestion of the drug was most likely caused by reiteration; Annette probably smoked it every day, maybe all day every day. Then, as she set the burning joint in the ashtray, she suddenly looked up to Jeri's face, apparently guessing her thoughts.

"Shit, Jeri. I'm sorry. I didn't even think about your feelings before I lit this up." She quickly moved to put the cigarette out. "Sometimes I can be a real jerk myself."

"No, that's OK. I don't mind. Really." Annette looked up from the ashtray with the joint still smoking between her fingers. Jeri could see that she would much rather finish smoking it than put it out. "I smoke sometimes, too. Occasionally, I mean."

"Really? You know, I would never have guessed it." She was smiling once again as she passed the joint to Jeri.

"Well, I wouldn't have guessed you smoked it either. You always seemed so—well, spiritual."

"I'm Christian, if that's what you mean. But I really don't buy into pot being a sin."

Jeri looked at the marijuana cigarette that was being offered to her; it was clean and white and neatly wrapped. It seemed safe here in Annette's warm kitchen. Bright streamers of light were shooting between gaps in the curtains over the sink, reminding Jeri of happy summer days. A thin wisp of smoke rose from the burning joint, wafting straight up to a cylinder of light where it rolled in upon itself before disintegrating into a hazy cloud. Jeri felt secure, and the marijuana seemed remarkably wholesome and natural. She took the joint carefully so as not to appear clumsy and inexperienced, and the heat from the smoking end, an inch or so away from her fingertips, felt only warm. She held the joint to her lips, and the smoke coursed into her eyes and burned, causing her to close them. Tears flowed freely down her cheeks and she wiped at them with her free hand. Self-conscious, she forced herself to inhale the puff of smoke before pulling the source of her tears away from her face. When she was able to open her eyes and blink the vision-clouding moisture from them, she saw Annette smiling at her.

"Got in your eyes, huh? I hate that."

"I suppose it is pretty obvious that I am not very experienced with smoking pot—or anything else, for that matter."

"Jeri, it gets into everyone's eyes. You just sort of get used to it, I suppose." She held the joint up to her own lips and expertly inhaled from it. "Here, try this." She went to the kitchen cabinet and retrieved a short length of copper tubing. She stuffed the unlit end of the joint into the tube and passed it back to Jeri. When Jeri took another puff, she was surprised to find that not only was the smoke not getting in her eyes, but it was much cooler and milder to her throat and lungs. She took a deep breath of the smoke, but didn't try to hold it in; instead, she let it surge out quickly, without panic or discomfort. She was instantly dizzy and momentarily completely incapacitated; she had never really been intoxicated by pot until that instant. She had felt the drug's effects before, but only mixed with the overwhelming consequences of alcohol. This was different; she felt her self-awareness and control come back slowly, and she was left feeling happy and silly and good. When she was able to focus her eyes on Annette again, she was aware that the joint had somehow been passed back without her cognizance. Annette finished taking a puff from the copper tube and placed the joint, tube and all, in the ashtray. She picked up the ashtray as she stood up from the table and returned it to the kitchen cabinet.

"Come on, let's go outside and get some fresh air."

"OK." Jeri was in no condition to argue. They went outside only after Jeri had some difficulty getting her boots on. She had hopped up and down, one foot at a time, trying to force the tight boots on her feet without much success, her awkward effort bringing them both to teary-eyed, stoned hilarity. Once they had donned their boots and coats, they walked from the mobile home past Jeri's car to the highway. They walked single file along the shoulder of the quiet road, in a narrow path in the snow cut by the passing of other walkers before them.

It was another brisk, clear day, and the mountain air was cold and clean. Jeri was amazed at the taste of the air and the feel of it against her face. She listened to the crunching below her and watched a few grayish clouds race through the blue sky. She stopped and turned her face to the bright sun, letting it heat her cold skin. She was happy for the first time in so long that she could not remember the last time. She was stoned and she knew it, but she liked it—she liked it very much.

"Annette, where do you get your pot?" She immediately felt she was prying, asking a very personal question, and Annette would think her rude. She felt embarrassed and ashamed of herself and began to apologize. Annette stopped her with a laugh and didn't seem at all upset.

"We grew it ourselves, in the garden this summer. That was why we had the big party. No one wanted to tell you because you seemed so straight." She laughed again. "I guess it would have been all right to tell you. You just got high on the best herb in our garden."

"I don't know, Annette. I think I've come a long way since last fall. It feels like it was a hundred years ago."

"Oh, that's just the pot. Let's go back, I have work to do. If you want, you can have a couple of joints to take with you. I can't do anything about your deposit, but I can sure make losing it a lot easier to take."

They turned around and walked back the way they had come. Annette's comment about the deposit had ended her pot-induced contentment; she still had the problem of where to live after the first of the month.

"Oh, I had forgotten about that. I just don't know what I'm going to do."

"See what I mean? Best homegrown we've ever harvested. Makes you forget your troubles. But seriously, Jeri, I know of several small apartments. The biggest part of your problem will be finding a truck and some big dumb men to move your stuff."

"I won't need a truck. He just about cleaned the place out."

"So what you need is a furnished one-bedroom. No problem. Just leave it up to me."

"You are such a good friend, Annette. I don't know how to thank you."

"Don't mention it. We women need to stick together. We can't have those drunken men screwing us over all the time." When Annette finished speaking, Jeri wondered why she sounded so bitter toward men. She wanted to ask how her marriage was going and hoped that her intuition was wrong, but she had a bad feeling that Annette was not as happy as she seemed. Stomping loudly up the wooden steps of the mobile home, Annette recited a tongue-in-cheek, overused witticism. "You know what they say. Can't live with them and can't live without them."

"Oh yeah? Who says that? I'm sure going to give it a try."

Inside, Jeri waited at the door without taking off her boots while Annette went into the kitchen. She soon brought back two perfectly rolled marijuana cigarettes. Jeri inspected them carefully, interested in how different they looked from others she had seen at parties and at Donna's apartment.

"Annette, how do you make them so perfect? The others I've seen are so irregular and twisted."

"Oh, we have a little machine. Neither one of us can hand roll so we just bought a machine to do it. It uses too much pot, but since we grow our own it doesn't matter. If you have to buy it, it's better to hand roll it." She looked to the kitchen and the paperwork on the table. "Well, I'm back to my books. It was great having you come by. Please come by again whenever you want. We'll have you in a nice one-bedroom in no time, and then I can come visit you all the time."

Jeri hugged the other girl tightly and began to cry softly. "I can't thank you enough. You've been so good to me. I love you so much." She felt Annette patting her back, and she felt good about having someone so nice for a friend.

"Just don't worry. Everything is going to turn out just fine. You may even like being the beautiful young bachelorette."

They separated slowly, kissing each other lightly on the cheek before Annette opened the front door. Jeri heard the door closing behind her as she stepped carefully down the icy wooden stairs. Once she was in her car, she put the two joints in an old envelope she found in the glove box, then placed the envelope delicately in her coat pocket. As Jeri drove down the frozen driveway, she was happy she had found such a supportive friend to lean on.

Ted was nervous. He could avoid work no longer; his excuses, those given to his employees and the ones he used on himself, were depleted. He had to go to the office. The environment there would prevent any further evasion of his business, preclude his denial of the accident, and unavoidably end the seductive retreat he had taken during the three weeks following the SENGS excursion. He had to go in today; Diane's calls had gradually increased in frequency and desperation after his first week out, and she seemed to be reaching the limits of her patience. But more importantly, the SENGS people wanted to meet with him about his exposure during the radiation excursion.

Work at the office had progressed routinely without him at first, as work on existing projects was plentiful, but in the last week the calls and e-mail messages had grown increasingly frantic. He needed to make some decisions regarding new bid specifications and the assignment of new projects. He had once believed that he had created a system that would function without him, but there were important decisions that only the boss could make, decisions that would define the health of his company in the future. He had tried, in the beginning, to delegate to Diane and when necessary, make final decisions over the phone, but he had been away too long and was losing touch with the new projects. He realized that he could no longer make informed choices on some of the stickier details. He had to go in and get caught up on the data if he hoped ever again to make a good decision. There was also the SENGS meeting. They had been calling Diane every day, trying to set up a meeting, pressing for her to produce him. She had finally called Ted, angry and exasperated, when they told her that he should obtain legal representation.

In business, the unexpected involvement of lawyers almost never signified anything good; Ted considered them deal breakers. Over the years he had reached handshake agreements with customers many times, only to have the lawyers, the customer's or his own, come in and squeeze the meaning of the deal until no one wanted to sign the convoluted contracts they produced. He had to meet the SENGS people and find out what they wanted. Diane had scheduled a meeting for eleven this morning at his office.

Ted had gotten up early, as he had always done before the accident, but it had been difficult. His biological clock had become inverted by the late nights he had been keeping and by sleeping in each day. In fact, not since high school had he slept as much has he had during the previous three weeks. He seemed always to get at least twelve hours a night, although now, partly in the mornings before noon. Lately, he even found himself taking naps, adding to the daily sleep totals. When the radio had clicked on at five, it had been a struggle to wake up and roll out of bed. Only a first cup of coffee and a shower had brought him to full alertness, but his eyes still felt raw and dry.

He was dressed in a dark business suit, and although he had not used it for weeks, his laptop case was at his feet. He looked out the patio windows at the dawning sky and gray water, and realized he felt nervous—more about going into his office to resume his routine than about the meeting with the SENGS lawyers. He had done nothing wrong; he was the victim, after all. He reached across the bar and poured himself another cup of coffee before checking his watch: it was already six thirty, and the shifts at SENGS would be changing.

He brought this last cup of coffee with him when he left the house and walked to the car, his laptop case hanging from his shoulder. The car was filthy. The elegant red paint was coated with a veneer of grime, water spots, and bird excrement; splashes of mud caked its sides where it had sprayed up from the wheels; and there was paper debris scattered inside: an unread newspaper, several empty cardboard coffee cups, used tissues, a fast-food bag with the discards of a hurried meal. He had not had the car detailed since before the accident and it was suffering from the neglect. But it wasn't just dirty; it seemed tarnished in a more fundamental way. He was no longer excited by the sports car the way he had once been. The car seemed to him only a means of travel, a necessary tool. He had lost interest in the Porsche soon after the accident; its high-tech mechanical engineering now represented the life he was trying very hard to forget. It was going to be another pleasant morning, but he didn't consider putting the top down to enjoy it; he wanted only to make his commute. He pulled out of the driveway and made his way to work without interest, driving slowly, the elaborate sound system silent.

He thought about Mary, his image of her transformed by her use of drugs. She had reentered his life at a critical time, her influence catalyzing self-evaluation and emotional mutation. On dates of her planning and some of his own, sometimes at his place and sometimes at hers, they had been dating several times a week since she had disclosed her secret lifestyle. He had tried to keep the dates simple, dinners and shows and trips to museums in Los Angeles, but she had wanted excitement—parties, clubs, and crowds of loud people. She seemed to be trying to convert him to her secondary lifestyle, the parties and clubs and the young people who frequented them, while he was attempting to hold her back from the edge, discouraging her use of drugs. It was a hopeless effort, for both of them.

He wondered why he was still seeing her, and also why she wanted to spend time with him. They were similar in some ways, in the world of professionalism and business, but they were so different from each other in other important yet subtle ways. She had agreed not to take drugs when with him, and she had retreated from the openness of her night of disclosure, but still he often suspected her of being under the influence of cocaine. He liked her and wanted to help her, but their relationship seemed overwrought. He was drawn to her in some inexplicable way, and she continued to pursue him, but their time together had a strange quality of exertion and strain. He would have liked to see her every night, the satisfying time in bed with her reducing the lonely time he spent at his bar drinking and listening to old music. But she seemed always to have something more exhilarating to do, limiting their nights together to two or three a week. She often invited him to go with her to the parties and the clubs, but he felt she was happy he usually refused. He suspected she was seeing someone else, but he feared asking her about it. They were not promised to each other in any way, and he was afraid she would interpret any questioning as jealousy. He had the nagging feeling she would bolt at the first signs of jealousy or even need.

He arrived at the office and parked in his usual place, sitting in the quiet car for a long time before gathering his strength and going inside. He was careful to approach each of the administrative staff, exploring cheerful reunions as if he were returning from a long business trip, asking them about their spouses and children, the office and their work. Each of the engineers working in the office, not out in the field, greeted him casually, without mention of his unlucky day at the SENGS plant. Diane had remained in her office, but seemed to be waiting for him when he went in to say hello.

"Good morning, Diane. How are you doing?" He tried to sound normal, as if he had not been away, as if he had not thrown the management of his business onto her shoulders without asking.

"I'm good, Ted. It's good to have you back. Do you have a few minutes? I'd like to talk to you." She stood from her desk and closed the door, barring his escape by standing with her back against it. "Ted, things are starting to unravel around here. We have half a dozen bids in the works and no one knows what you want them to do." She stepped around him to her desk and with both hands picked up a six-inch pile of bulging manila file folders. "Look at this, Ted. You have to make some decisions or we won't have any work in a couple of months." She spoke softly, imploring him with her expression and her eyes.

"I know, Diane. I haven't been fair with you lately. And I want to thank you for all the work you have been doing to keep things together while I have been out."

"Ted, it's worse. Some of the guys are thinking about leaving the company. They're worried about their careers, their futures, their families."

He realized by her tone that she was probably one of the guys thinking about changing jobs before it was too late, and with that realization the solution to the problem became obvious to him.

"Diane, have you ever heard how I came to own this company?"

"Look, I know it's your company, but there are other people around here who have a vested interest that you don't run it into the ground." Her voice and face were angry now.

"No, listen, Diane. I wasn't telling you that. I wasn't saying it is my right to neglect the company because I own it. This is important. Do you know how I got the company? Come on, let's sit down."

She seemed to calm herself as they moved to the chairs opposite her desk. "Well, I understand you bought it from the previous owner. When he retired."

"Yes, that's sort of the way it happened. You know, he built this company from nothing. I was just a senior engineer when he decided to quit. He sold me the company, but what you probably don't know is he also loaned me the money. Every month his payment is one of our biggest outlays, after compensation and insurance. It started out as the largest debit I had. It was difficult at first, but we have grown a lot since then, and his loan is relatively small compared to our gross now. Can you see where I am going with this?"

"Not really. It is all quite interesting, but if we don't win some contracts soon, in six months we won't even be able to pay the rent on this place."

"Do you think you can win those contracts, Diane?"

"Sure, we just need to decide on the details of the bids. You need to approve the quotes and assign the engineers who will be working the projects."

"No, I think it's time you did that. If you want it, the company is yours." She stared at him, the pile of folders in her lap and surprise on her face. "Do you feel up to it?"

She didn't speak for what seemed to be a long time, and Ted was beginning to think she lacked the confidence to take on the responsibility.

"Yes, of course I can run this company." Her voice held the strength and determination he had learned to recognize over the years she had worked for him. It indicated she had taken a stand and was ready to fight for something. "I just don't understand how we go about it."

He understood that her initial silence had been due to questions regarding the transfer of ownership, and not because of any doubts about her ability to be a successful manager.

"It's very easy. You buy me out, and I hold the note. We just have to agree on the details. The price and the interest rate. That sort of thing. I'll make it as easy as possible for you to succeed. It won't do me any good if you can't make money. Well, do you want to own your own company?"

"Shit, do I. I can't believe this. You are just going to walk away? Turn it all over to me like this?"

"Yep. That's how it happened to me. How about I get the lawyers to draw up an agreement for us? They'll try to screw it up, but we can rein them in."

They spent the rest of the morning in Diane's office, the door still closed, discussing the value of the company and the details of the sale, with Diane making copious notes in a lined yellow notepad. Ted felt as if a great threat had been averted, as if he were coming back from a very dangerous place. He warned Diane that he wasn't sure he was doing her a favor, but she swept the concept aside as ridiculous, a nonsensical joke. He was wondering about her inability to perceive the risks he knew so well when the intercom interrupted them. The office manager excused himself for the interruption before informing them that the SENGS representatives had arrived. Ted instructed that they be taken to the conference room and requested that Alice, his personal secretary of many years, be asked to join them there. He left Diane working on the figures of their deal and went to the outer office. He joined his visitors in the conference room as they were being offered coffee and sodas.

The meeting was extraordinarily short. The SENGS lawyers had come to settle the question of liability arising from the accident at their plant. They presented an agreement that exchanged Ted's right to sue for a one-time monetary payment. They would admit no responsibility for the accident, and Ted would agree to forfeit any future claims against them. The possibility of litigation came as a surprise to him; he had not considered it. He had always accepted that working with nuclear reactors presented risks, and he had long ago accepted these risks as a personal choice, his to make and if necessary to reevaluate. The option of suing someone else for his decision to accept these risks had never before occurred to him. It was a surreal concept, and the compensation they offered seemed grotesquely large.

Ted tried to agree to the offer immediately, thumbing through the pages for the signature line as he took out his pen to sign. The SENGS lawyers would not permit it, explaining that he must receive the legal advice of his own attorneys before any agreement could be binding. They left the paperwork with him and were gone before lunch. His first day back in the office had become more eventful than he could have ever expected. His life was changing at a dizzying rate, seemingly without his guidance, yet he felt a strange calmness about the metamorphosis.

Later, while sitting at his desk in his own office for the first time in weeks, Mary called. He was studying the agreement the SENGS lawyers had drafted and preparing pre-call notes prior to phoning the law firm that represented his company in business contracts.

"Sir, Mary Peralta is on line two." The sudden sound of his secretary's voice blurted from the intercom, saving him from the confusing legal jargon of the document.

"Thank you, Alice." He picked up the receiver and punched the blinking button. "This is Ted."

"Hi, Ted. This is Mary. You sound formal today. How's the first day back in the salt mine going?"

The happy, teasing tone of her voice made him feel good; the serious issues of the day retreated to some remote part of his consciousness.

"The mine? I think it's just about played out. One more set of charges to place and it will be history. How are you today, Mary? Got big plans for the night?"

"I sure do, and you are included if you want to be. How about a date, big guy? Want to go out and raise hell with me tonight?" She sounded happy and excited, teasing him in a soft, friendly way.

101

"You know, I think I could use a little excitement. Things have been pretty boring here today. What do you have going tonight?" He felt elated, buoyed by the unexpected events of the day and her upbeat bantering.

"Oh? You want to go?" She was obviously surprised by his readiness to go out and party. "Well, some friends of mine are playing at a club in LA—in a band, I mean. It's the last night of the booking and they're going to have a party after they finish." She was no longer as cheerful as she had been moments before, and Ted got the feeling she regretted her invitation.

"Mary, if you would rather I not go, I don't mind."

"No. No, it isn't that. But it will probably be a late night. The party won't even start until after midnight. I just didn't think you would be interested, that's all. They're rock-and-roll people, kind of wild, you know. But you might have fun. I'm going to the club to listen to them play, and then everyone is coming back down here to the band's studio to party. It will probably last all night. Sure you want to come?"

"I'll drive my own car. If I get tired, I can always go home early. I feel like having some fun tonight, Mary. And I'd like to spend some time with you."

"OK, just remember I warned you this was going to be a wild one." She sounded happy again.

Mary gave him the directions to a nightclub located on Sunset Boulevard in Hollywood. The band she knew would be playing from nine to midnight, and the band's retinue was going in force to show the club owner that the band could draw a crowd. Ted promised to meet her there at nine.

He left the office at about three in the afternoon, hungry and wanting a drink. He had put the SENGS agreement and the notes Diane had prepared in a manila envelope, and as he left he dropped it on his secretary's desk. He asked her to put the documents in a FedEx pack and send it to the company lawyers. On the way home he stopped at a Mexican place to get some lunch and a margarita. The large dining room of the restaurant was quiet and empty, making him feel alone and uncomfortable, so he ate sitting at the bar in the dimly lighted lounge.

The bartender was a pretty blonde girl with the ability, common in good bartenders, to hold a conversation on many subjects. He spent the rest of the afternoon drinking margaritas and talking about meaningless and interesting things with the friendly bar maid. At six o'clock the night shift bartender, a stoic middle-aged Latino with a big belly hanging below a tight red vest, relieved the garrulous blonde and Ted paid his bill. As he left the restaurant the low sun stung his eyes, and he regretted leaving his sunglasses in the car earlier in the afternoon. He walked across the parking lot, the happy feeling of the margaritas filling him with contentment, his hand cupped to his forehead, shading his eyes.

When he got home he sat down on the patio to watch the sunset and fell asleep almost immediately, unaware he still wore his coat and tie. It was eight o'clock and dark when he awoke, remembering his date with Mary. He quickly showered and dressed in casual clothes, knowing he would be late meeting her at the nightclub far across the sprawling expanse of the back-to-back cities that were greater Los Angeles. Although the two-hour nap and the shower had refreshed him, he could still feel the dull influence of the tequila from the margaritas of the afternoon. He put the convertible top down and gathered the trash from the floor and seat of the car, tossing it in a pile on the side of the driveway before starting his drive north.

He drove fast, north on the San Diego Freeway, the deceptively forgiving road-handling characteristics of the German sports car passively persuading him that his driving was both controlled and careful. The cool air of the clear night blew through the convertible, muting the retro rock music playing on the radio, and he felt happy, relieved by the events of the day, free of responsibility and eager for the capricious night with Mary. The Santa Ana Freeway came up fast, and he led the car from the left lane across six almost empty lanes onto the transition road north. As he accelerated through the sweeping turn of the ramp, he realized he was speeding, taking advantage of the light traffic to enjoy the car as he had not done since before the accident, and he was surprised.

During the past weeks, the car and his unused laptop had grown to represent his life leading up to the accident; they had become artifacts of a lifestyle based upon the unthinking pursuit of technology.

But tonight, with the wind in his face and the throaty drone of the engine in his ears, he hoped there could be some intermediate way to accept scientific and technological progress.

His first impulses after the accident had been to reject everything technological, but surely that was impossible. Since the early days of the industrial revolution people had yearned for a more pastoral existence, but humanity could never go back, not all the way back to a time before technology, because man's very essence was in the use of tools. Even the Amish, driving around rural Pennsylvania in horse-drawn carriages, utilized the wheel. Ted realized that before the accident he had been an unknowing participant in this twenty-first-century, first-world culture; working to propagate and extend technology, but occasionally retreating from it to the purity and solitude of the mountains or the desert or an isolated beach. Man was a species with an instinctual yearning for the garden from which it evolved. But with the first spear, the first bow and arrow, the first planned agriculture, the success of the species had depended upon the ability to develop ever more complex technologies. It was a dilemma that had become more difficult to resolve as man's dependence on technology had deepened. But the accident had changed him, had awakened him to his ambiguity and forced him to face the duality of his life. Tonight, driving a refined road machine on wide smooth highways, he felt exhilarated by the products of technology, yet feared his addiction to them. For him, the dilemma had become personal, and he knew he did not know its solution.

When he made the transition to the Hollywood Freeway the traffic became much heavier, but it seemed the rushing commuters cooperated to keep traffic moving at a steady sixty-five miles an hour. The Sunset Boulevard off-ramp was not the ramp he had planned on using, but the famous name beckoned to him and the relatively slow traffic confined him, so he made the turn without thinking, jerking the wheel to the right and braking heavily as he cut across the gore point, the sports car decelerating as wonderfully as it accelerated.

He drove up Sunset slowly, with the car in a low gear, savoring the sensations the smooth vibrations of the engine produced after they made their way through the seat and into his body. The people walking in this part of the city seemed lost and disenfranchised, yet they seemed somehow to belong on the sidewalks of Hollywood. He drove past a timeworn hamburger stand, dirty white paint and garish white lights glaring across the small parking lot and into the street. Standing in front of the dingy fast-food stand were outrageously dressed women: hot pants and spandex, miniskirts and rabbit fur jackets. They looked incredibly vulgar, but he realized the fashions they wore must be the look men liked. That, or it was a means of identification, a fashion-based advertisement. One of the young prostitutes was busily devouring a hamburger, yellow paper framing her jaw as she stared into the street. They seemed comically energetic in their overt attempts to attract him as he drove past, using gross body language and hard eye contact. The one with the hamburger looked sad and desperate in her full-mouthed efforts to appear seductive.

He gently put the car into the next gear and continued up Sunset to find the nightclub. He had never been to the club, but thought a bar with the media history of the Viper Room would be hard to miss. Its mundane façade and inexpensively painted signs surprised him. It was an undistinguished place made temporarily famous by the drug overdose death of River Phoenix on the dirty concrete just outside the door. When Mary had told him the name of the club and given him directions, he had recalled the incident and asked if the bar would be full of movie stars taking heroin. She had laughed and said she wouldn't be surprised if it was.

Parking was down a side street from the club, bumper to bumper and door handle to door handle, in a tiny lot in an alley behind the tremendously successful House of Blues. A parking attendant wearing a rock band T-shirt and Levi's pointed to where he could squeeze the sports car in next to a large green Dumpster. As he parked beside it, he thought that at least one side of his car would be safe from car doors thrown carelessly open by drunken rock and rollers. He raised the convertible top and locked the car before walking up the steep hill to the bar. It was a diminutive entrance located at the side of the building, just off Sunset Boulevard.

Inside, the club was a single room with a stage in one corner and a bar running the length of the opposite wall. The interior seemed to be painted black and there was very little light. Near the stage, a simply constructed wooden structure that barely held the band, a few tables and chairs were pressed against the wall. The room was crowded with people standing three and four deep at the bar and milling around the margins of the small dance floor. The wood of the floor and the stage had the faded look of over-used furniture, as if it had been left out too long in the rain. Ted wondered if this leached look came from the thousands of drinks that must have found their way onto the stage and tables and floor over hard years of rock and roll.

He had pushed up to the bar and was buying a drink, when Mary came up behind him. She put her arms around his torso, pulled herself to his back and hugged him. He turned inside her arms, and she smiled up at him with red lips and dark eyes. They kissed lightly.

"I was beginning to think you had changed your mind. I expected you an hour ago." She didn't seem angry and was still smiling.

"I fell asleep after work. Sorry I'm late. I guess I should have tried to call."

"Don't worry about it, Ted. This isn't a business appointment. Come on, I saved you a seat with us up front." She laughed as she turned from the bar, and Ted felt she thought him ridiculous. Her laughter making him feel a little inadequate, he picked up his change and left too large a tip for the bartender.

The music was loud so close to the stage, and Mary had to scream her introductions to the group sitting around the table. Most of them were in their twenties and early thirties, and wore the timeless denim and cotton of rock-and-roll fans. The men seemed generally older than their dates, and though some of the men were at least his age Ted had a feeling of being from another generation. Mary seemed older than the other women sitting around the table, but she carried herself with the same girlishness as the others, and Ted felt he was the only one to notice. She introduced one talkative guy as the band's business manager; he was his early twenties and wore his long, blond, straight, shiny hair with pride, flipping it from his shoulders often. He interacted with the group at the table with an air of exaggerated secrecy, as though they shared some status-augmenting conspiracy they didn't want to remain hidden. As the night passed, with the group's favorite band playing their favorite music, and the fans at the table covertly snorting cocaine and drinking heavily to maintain the desired balance between the coke and the booze, little business deals were made with affected stealth, making them all the more obvious. It became clear to Ted that the manager made his living selling drugs; his promotion of the band was only a minor distraction that provided him convenient proximity to his customers. Ted felt outside the collusion, isolated in his own heavy drinking and Mary's acceptance by the group. She sat across from him at the table and sometimes tried to bring him into the rock-and-roll-shaded conversation, but he knew he was on the outside of the party looking in, a somewhat unwelcome crasher, and he recognized the discomfort his presence caused her.

During the first break between the band's sets, Mary introduced him to Andy, the leader of the band and her best friend in the group. He was a clean-cut, handsome man in his mid- to late twenties. He had thick blond hair, trimmed short in a modern but conservative style, and blue eyes that gazed happily from his young, smooth-skinned face. While the band performed, Andy stood center stage, played an electronic keyboard and sang the lead vocals. He worked for Mary during the day as a senior programmer, and he had been crucial to Mary's efficient defusing of their company's denial of service logic bomb. During the band's breaks, he and Mary slipped away with some of the others to take coke and smoke cigarettes.

At midnight the band finished their final set, and the live music was replaced by a reverberating sound system. The members of the band, along with a few of the guys from the party table, dismantled the equipment and began the work of moving it off the stage. While they were occupied, Mary moved around the table and sat down next to Ted for the first time since he had arrived. She seemed friendly, but not romantic. Ted wasn't surprised; she had been carefully distant during the night, and he had realized early on that she was attempting to juggle two dates—one with him and the other with Andy.

"Ted, let's go ask Andy how long it will take for them to get back to his studio in Orange County. He may want me to go early and open the door for everyone." She pulled at his arm and stood up. *Of course,* he thought, *she would be the one with the key to the studio.*

"Mary, I'm getting a little tired," he said. "I don't know if I'm going to make it to the party tonight." He resisted her attempts to pull him to his feet, and she sat back down.

"Ted, I know you've been feeling awkward here. So have I, a little. But the party will be better. It won't be so loud, and we'll be able to talk. Besides, I was counting on you for a ride. I came up with one of the other girls and she left a little while ago." She leaned over and kissed him lightly on the lips.

"OK, Mary. I can give you a ride. But I probably won't stay long. I'm not having much luck with getting to know these kids."

"It'll get better, Ted. You'll see. Let me just go and talk to Andy for a minute, and we can go." She stood up, walked to the stage, and climbed the narrow wooden steps with confidence and grace, in spite of the long night of drinking and drugs. He watched her hug Andy and they kissed in the same friendly way she had kissed him. They spoke for a few minutes before Andy reached into the pocket of his jeans and produced a key ring. He manipulated the ring, removed a single key and handed it to Mary. She put the key in her front pocket and came back to the table.

"Are you ready to go? I have the key to Andy's studio. We need to let everybody inside. The band probably won't get there for a couple of hours."

They walked outside and down the hill to the alley parking lot. Most of the cars that had crowded the lot earlier were gone; one car's exit was blocked by Ted's Porsche, and a young couple was waiting inside for it to be moved. Mary recognized the waiting pair and ran up to the passenger window to talk to the girl sitting on that side. Ted had already started his car and was letting it warm up when she came back from her conversation.

"Most of them have already left. They'll be waiting outside when we get there." She looked above her head and reached up to the roof latch with both hands. "Ted, let's put the top down, OK? Let's see if we can be the last to leave and the first to arrive." She was very exuberant, and Ted wondered if the conversation at the other car had included more cocaine.

"I had it down on the way up here. I just didn't know if you would be cold or not." He reached up to help unlatch the top as he spoke. "Buckle your seat belt, Mary, and I'll get you there as soon as

I can." She squirmed in her seat happily as she reached behind her shoulder for the belt.

The drive south was clear; traffic was moving at a steady sixty-five with an occasional car moving at seventy or seventy-five. The night air was cold and loud as it blew into the car, but Mary seemed animated by the speed and the wind. She bounced in her seat, moving energetically to the rock music as it battled the noise of the open car. Ted felt drunk, so he concentrated on his driving. He was worried he would be stopped and arrested for drunk driving, or worse, that Mary would have drugs and he would be incarcerated for their possession. He matched his speed to the flow of traffic in the fast lane and kept the car centered in his own, slower lane. The trip passed quickly and uneventfully, with Mary continually making adjustments to the music, changing stations on the satellite radio and scanning through his iPod. When they grew close to their destination, Mary guided him, turn by turn, through the featureless streets that crosshatched the area of light industry.

In a small parking lot behind a rear building of the single-level industrial park, there were already a dozen cars parked outside the metal roll-up door of the studio. Ted stopped near the other cars and before he could turn off the ignition Mary had jumped out of the car. He put the Porsche's top up as people got out of their cars and followed Mary to the metal door. She unlocked a conventional door next to the roll-up and the mob of partygoers pressed to move through it.

Ted walked across the narrow street behind the building without excitement; he didn't know the people inside, Mary had indicated she was not going to devote her time to him, and he was drunk and getting tired. As he went inside the converted warehouse garage, he could hear more cars arriving in the parking lot, their tires screeching in the night.

The party began quickly; several men were tapping a keg of beer, and the acrid, sweet smoke of marijuana already hung in the chilled air of the tall room. He was surprised to see that much of the garage-like space was occupied by four grand pianos in various stages of repair. The partiers milled between the pianos and some sat on the benches. Beyond the pianos, at the rear of the large garage, was plywood box of a room that spanned the width of the larger room, but reached up to less than half its height. Cardboard boxes, a set of drums, and several large speakers were stored on top. An unpainted wooden door stood open to the interior of the boxlike room. Ted looked around him to find Mary, but she was not among the young people beginning their after-hours party. He assumed she had entered the smaller wooden part of the garage and began to move through the party to check on her. As he walked between the pianos, more people were coming into the room; some of them had been at the club, but others were new, coming just for the late-starting party.

Two teenage girls were working over a small mirror with a pile of white powder on its surface. Ted watched the innocent-looking girls snort the drug and wondered how long it would take for them to become hardened and cynical. How much of their youth would be lost getting drunk and high and wanting to party? Would they join the ranks of the lucky ones, the ones who for some mysterious reason survived those first wild years to become mature and wise enough to control their need to party; or would they become part of the wretched group who were overpowered by the drug culture and destroyed by it?

Mary entered the main room from the doorway of the boxy room and walked to the keg of beer. Ted moved across the crowded room to be with her.

"Where have you been?" he asked, as he pulled a plastic cup from the stack next to the keg.

"Up front, in the studio." She pointed to the plywood addition. "I had to turn off the alarm. I hope I did it right."

"I hope so too. It would not be good if the police came to check for a burglar with all this going on." He motioned to the keg and the girls snorting drugs.

"Well, I guess we'll find out soon enough," she said as she shrugged her shoulders. "Come on, I'll buy you a beer." They handed their cups to a long-haired drunk who had taken the responsibility of pouring the beer.

More people arrived in a continuous stream through the small doorway from the parking lot, rock music vibrating the garage as it quickly filled. The after-hours party was, evidently, more popular than the band's performance at the nightclub. Soon the band arrived in their big step van and the large door was rolled up to receive them. Many drunken volunteers helped haul instruments and electronic equipment into the spaces around the pianos before the metal door was again rolled closed.

When Andy entered the garage his friends and fans rushed him with happy congratulatory greetings. And from across the room full of amplifiers, pianos, speakers, and stoned rock and rollers, as if crossing a stage, Mary moved to him. Ted watched as she zigzagged through the equipment slowly, her body language sexual and inviting. When she got to Andy she kissed him on the cheek and returned the key to the studio door. The kiss had not been overtly sexual, but Mary's body language had been unmistakable and the key presentation overt. Ted felt alone and out of place. He was oddly awake, but it was three thirty in the morning and he wasn't having a very good time. It was obvious that Mary was going to be spending at least part of her time with Andy, and Ted didn't think there was anyone else in the room with whom he could carry on a conversation.

He looked around the room for an inviting glance or gesture. The guests were gathered in small groups talking, drinking, smoking cigarettes and pot—and snorting cocaine. The room was awash with cocaine. In almost every cell of partygoers he could see the activities associated with taking the drug; the mirrors, razor blades, straws, spoons, and pipes passed from guest to guest and group to group as they were needed. There was a wildly intoxicated woman selling cocaine to the party guests; stumbling drunk and wide-awake from her own intake of the drug, she held a plastic cup of beer in one hand and a sandwich bag full of coke in the other. Each time she stumbled, beer would splash in one direction and cocaine would float in the other. Ted wondered if once she had been like the two girls he had noticed earlier, young but pretentiously adult, trying so hard to be something that was such a terrible waste to be.

Mary was still standing with Andy, but they had walked farther into the room, nearer the wooden studio. Ted could see that in this group of young people Andy was a minor celebrity; wherever he moved, people gathered around to be near him. Mary noticed Ted watching them from across the room and waved to him, beckoning for him to join them. As he passed through the crowded room he noticed that some of the pianos were undergoing meticulous restoration. Woodworking repairs of all sizes were in various stages of completion; some were drying under clamps, while others were ready for sanding and finishing. One piano was being refitted with all the metal hardware and wires as well as the wooden hammers and laminated keys. He was impressed by the precision measurement tools that lay within convenient reach of the work. He wondered if the band shared this space with some daytime piano restoration company, possibly owned by the father of one of the band members. When he drew close to them, Mary skipped over and made a show of pulling him into the ring of people talking and listening to Andy.

"Hi, Ted. I hear you two had quite a flight down here after the show." Andy had made of point of directing the conversation to him, bringing him immediately into the group. He was a difficult person not to like.

"We made OK time. It was all I could do not to look drunk. I was too scared to look in my mirrors."

"Our old step van is a slow one, but it can sure haul a lot of gear. I'm happy just to sit in the back after a gig, that way I don't need to worry about drinking too much."

"Andy, I've noticed all the pianos and repair work being done. It's very impressive. Who does it?"

"I do." Ted could see by the expression on the singer's face that he was at once proud of the work and shy about it. "Another one of my hobbies," Andy continued. "Mary is always telling me I have too many. Says it dilutes my efforts. I guess I just have a short attention span." He walked to the nearest piano, leaned over it and spread his palms on the roughly sanded wood, rubbing his hands in gentle circular patterns as if he was imagining he had sandpaper under them. "It's something I really like to do. It's the mechanic in me, I guess."

"Mary told me you were multifaceted, Andy. I'm embarrassed to say that I'm surprised to find out she's right. But you know, I think she's right on the mark. This is art in the true, Old World sense of the word."

"Hell, you know Mary. If you're a milkman she has you owning Wisconsin when she talks about you. She's a great promotion.
According to her, you own the nuclear plant down at San Elejo."

They both laughed, and Ted realized that Andy was very good
at dealing with people. He decided that he liked him in spite of
anything that was going to happen regarding Mary. After all, he
and Mary had no rules to their relationship. It was strange, but even
though he wanted her to want only him, he did not feel jealousy
toward this new man. They walked back to the group where Mary
was standing and watching them, her lips curled in a cynical smile.

"I can just hear you guys comparing notes. I don't think I'm
going to allow you two to be alone together again. A woman must
keep some secrets."

"Come on, Ted, I was just telling Mary that I have a pipe in the
studio office we should go warm up." Andy tossed his head toward
the front of the building and began to walk in the same direction.
"Come on, we'll smoke a little." He held up a vial filled with large
off-white crystals.

"No, I don't think so, Andy." Ted couldn't believe the candid-
ness of his new acquaintance. Surely Mary had not led him to
believe that he would smoke cocaine with them.

"Oh, I'm sorry, Ted. I forgot to warn Andy." She was saying it
didn't matter that he didn't take drugs, but she was smiling at Andy
in a strange, condescending way. Ted felt sudden anger welling
from his center, warming his skin and pounding in his temples.

"I'm going to go get a beer. I'll see you later, Mary. You two have
a good time." As he turned to walk away from them, they both burst
out in laughter. Ted was suddenly not in the mood for more of the
party. He was finished with it and began the walk to the door without turning to say good-bye. On his way across the room he noticed
that the drummer of the band had one of the younger teenage girls
next to him on a piano bench. They were kissing continuously and
the drummer's hand was far up her short skirt.

He reached the door and looked back across the room one
more time. Mary and Andy had disappeared into the privacy of the
wooden studio, but the rest of the party continued unabated. It
occurred to him that they were all also victims; they too were being

poisoned by the technological society in which they lived. Electric music and cocaine, alcohol and marijuana, it was life in the fast lane, just like the old rock song. Enough was never enough, and fast was never fast enough. They lived to party and take drugs and to be with others doing the same thing. It didn't matter to them where they partied, or if there was any particular reason. This garage was as good as the Bon Adventure downtown; maybe better, since they didn't have to worry about strangers interfering with their ability to take drugs.

Ted felt stiff and slow as he walked through the small door beside the roll-up. He knew he was in no shape to drive, but it was just one of those times when he would go slow and try to stay out of trouble. When he got home, he stayed up drinking scotch until the night began to fade into morning.

Jeri had gradually become inured to the distressing monotony of her new life. In the weeks since she had told Annette of her need to move, the friendly landlord had found several small apartments that might be right for her. She had been working double shifts at the Ram Restaurant whenever she could, trying to make and save some extra money, desperately hoarding her tips for a security deposit on the new apartment. Each night, before crawling inside the pile of bedding she thought of as her futon, she had counted her tiny savings, extrapolating to the end of the month. She had also been spending many hours at the library at Fort Lewis, studying hard for her midterm exams. She had lost herself in the extra work, both at the restaurant and at school, and the toil had occupied her mind, crowding out thoughts of her broken marriage and her mounting monetary difficulties. She had worked with Donna several times after the night she had fallen asleep on her sofa, and Donna had usually invited her to come over after their shift. But Jeri had been so busy that she had always declined the invitation, and they had not again spent time together socially.

They were working the dinner shift together, and it had been another slow evening with very few tips. The scarcity of customers produced little work, certainly not enough for both of them, but the resort's general manager wanted two servers on the clock during the dinner shift. She had told all the night servers that she believed it benefited the hotel's prestige to have good service in the restaurant, explaining that room rental was the real profit center of the small resort.

They had finished all the side work they could while still leaving the dining room open for new customers; in fact, they had closed three-quarters of the room and had already set that section for the next day's breakfast. They waited impatiently for closing time, the dining room silent except for the quiet droning of recorded ballads on the ceiling music system. They sat together at the employees' table, Jeri studying a physical chemistry textbook and Donna thumbing through the pages of a *Cosmopolitan* magazine. Occasionally, the muted laughter of one of the cooks or the metallic sound of a pan banging would float from the kitchen into the large room, but mostly it was mockingly silent, the stillness interrupted only by the boring music and the intermittent sound of paper as one or the other of them turned a page.

Jeri was concentrating so hard that she had lost awareness of her surroundings, the mathematical realities of the p-chem filling her preoccupied mind. Then the sudden, explosive slap of Donna's violently discarded magazine startled her from her memorization. She lurched back from the bang instinctively as a miniature blast of air gusted up from the blow, brushing her face and fanning her hair. A heady rush of adrenaline coursed through her body, causing mindless, convulsive rigidity. The yellow highlighter she had been using to mark the textbook flew in a small arc above the table and landed on the cover of the discarded magazine with a quiet plastic clatter. She raised her eyes from the marker to find Donna watching her, a mischievous smile on her lips. She felt her taut body release stale air from her lungs.

"Damn, I'm bored," Donna said. "I wish we could just close this place and go home." She stretched her arms behind her head and yawned.

Jeri realized that the magazine toss had been intended to bring her back into the role of conversationalist. She really didn't mind the interruption. She had been going over the same section of her textbook for twenty minutes, but the music and the sounds from the kitchen and the constant need to glance up to the door, ever prepared to greet and serve a late-arriving customer, had proved too distracting for her to grasp the outlandish concepts of quantum mechanics. She would have to wait until she could get to her favorite cubbyhole at the Fort Lewis library to continue this part of her studies. She closed the textbook and smiled at her friend and co-worker.

"I'm sorry I've been rude, Donna. It's just that I need to ace this test if I want to do well in the class. I didn't do all that well on the quizzes." Jeri didn't want to admit that she was really striving for the highest point total in the class—her A was already a foregone conclusion. "I'll just wait until tomorrow. I'm too tired to study now anyway."

"You know, Jeri, you are the smartest person I know. What are you going to do with yourself when you finish going to school? I mean, it has to end sometime, doesn't it?"

"Maybe. I don't know. Some people never stop going to school, never stop learning. Doctors and scientists, for instance." She laughed as she gathered her books and papers together.

"Is that what you want to be, Jeri, a doctor?"

"I guess I really don't know what I'm going to do. I've applied to some medical schools, and what I do with my life depends on the answers I get back from them. Who knows? I might end up waiting tables my entire life."

"Bullshit, Jeri. I may not have a lot of education, but I'm not dumb. I know you. You're going to be one of those modern, career-driven women who will be wondering about finding a man and starting a family when you're a thirty-five-year-old millionaire." They laughed together at Donna's prediction.

"I don't know, Donna. I was talking to my landlady, Annette, the other day, and we just about decided that men were a bad way to start a family." Jeri was still joking, but she could see that the comment about Annette had affected Donna in a way she had not expected.

"How was she? The last time I saw her she had a broken nose and two terrible shiners. If I were her, I'd kill that drunken son of a bitch in his sleep. He gets all beered up and wants to beat up on someone. She just usually happens to be the closest one."

"Are you are kidding me? That can't be possible. They are a good Christian couple. He can't be like that."

Jeri thought them a normal, loving, almost too dedicated pair. She remembered the way they did little favors for each other and the way they held hands in public. But even as she objected to Donna's comment, Jeri's mind was moving back in time to an evening she and Steve had spent with the other couple, a night they had visited their mobile home for *Monday Night Football* and grilled hamburgers and hot dogs. Both of the men had been drinking beer heavily while they worked and joked outside, first starting the fire and then cooking the meat. Suddenly, Steve had come inside, very angry. At the time, he had only said that he thought the other man an ass, and that he could finish the cooking by himself. Later, after the end of what turned out to be an early night, Steve had explained that Annette's husband had been sloppy drunk and tried to take a swing at him. Steve had said that it had taken all his self-control to avoid getting into a fistfight with his drunken friend.

"Jeez, Donna. I never realized it before now, but you know, now that you've mentioned it, I think he might have a drinking problem."

"Might have a drinking problem? That guy needs to take the cure. And Annette just keeps taking it. She thinks because it's beer it's not being an alcoholic. Don't get me wrong, I don't care how much the guy drinks. I just think a man who beats his wife or kids is some sort of animal—drunk or sober."

Donna had become very excited during her verbal attack on violent men; her opinions suddenly vehement, her emotions impulsive and unbridled. Jeri felt a strong intuition that Donna herself must have been, at one time or the other, the recipient of this kind of violence. Jeri realized that she had been very lucky; she had never experienced the violence that seemed now, surprisingly, all too common.

Her family had been loving and gentle when she was a child, and her husband was never physically threatening. Her husband? She had sent her husband home and now she was alone. She was alone, and the prospect of meeting a man with hidden dangers was terrifying.

"Donna, why does she stay with him? Why doesn't she leave him? She is a beautiful, intelligent woman. She can get any man she wants. If she even needs to have a man, I mean."

"It is not about being able to leave. She loves the guy, even if he's a mean drunk. She can't help herself. She thinks there's something she can do to make him better. And for that, she is as dumb as they come. There is nothing she can do to make him the way she wants him to be. He will keep getting drunk, and he will keep beating her up, and she will keep forgiving him for it when he's sorry and tries to stop. That is the way it is. I know all about it, my dad was the same damn way. Only he beat us kids too, the asshole." Donna was speaking very quietly, her face tight. One tear slid slowly down the side of her nose and she caught it deftly with her tongue as it passed the corner of her mouth.

"I'm so sorry, Donna. I didn't mean to pry." Jeri leaned close to the other women and hugged her around the shoulders. Donna hugged her in return before pulling away and answering.

"You didn't pry." Her voice was strong again. "I brought it up myself. Haven't done that in a long time." She smiled and rubbed her eyes with the corner of a white table napkin, glancing shyly across the long dining room toward the bar. Jeri followed her eyes, traversing the room, seeing but not noticing the mounted trophy heads that lined the dining room walls. At the other end of the room Big John was standing in the doorway to the bar; his hands were at his sides, a limp bar towel hanging from one fist.

He was watching the women closely, but he had not made a move toward them. When Donna saw him she groaned softly. "He will think I'm upset. He is such a big moosh," she said. "He is so big and strong and leathery, but you know, sometimes I think he's more sensitive than I am. He can really get under your skin, that one."

As if on cue, he began to walk through the room toward them, his rolling gait bouncing his gray hair just below the stuffed heads of deer and elk and buffalo. He twirled the bar towel between his hands, a miniature jump rope, as he moved closer, his relaxed walk slow but agile. He approached with a wide grin, but his eyes seemed worried as they remained locked on the damp napkin Donna held in her lap with both hands.

"Now what do we have here. You ladies look like you are up to no good. And if I didn't know better, Jeri, I would say you were the ringleader of this operation." He moved close to Donna, so close that his hip touched her shoulder. He stopped there, maintaining contact with his hip. He leaned over and took the dinner napkin and replaced it with the bar towel. "There, that is much more absorbent. When you ladies are finished closing up, why don't you come in for a drink? I'm buying." He smiled at each of them. "I have drink recipes that will cure anything and everything—a little trouble with headaches so far, but I'm working on it. I do have a patent on one for curing the blues." He touched Donna lightly on the shoulder, turned and strode back through the room, below the mounted heads, to his lair in the bar.

"Didn't I tell you? He can be so empathetic. I don't know if he cares whether I feel bad or good, but he certainly knows which it is. It is the way I always wanted a man to respond to me, but it can be eerie." She glanced at her watch and stood. "Ten more minutes. What do you say we reset the rest of the tables and close this place? If anyone asks we can always say our watches were fast."

She moved to the closest table still set for dinner and began resetting it for breakfast, pulling the white tablecloth from beneath the flatware with a loud metallic jingle. Jeri went to the server station and collected a pile of red paper place mats and followed Donna around the room, resetting the flatware on the mats. When she had finished the last, most distant table, she turned back to the station to see Donna carrying the dark brown coffee mugs four to a hand, her fingers hooked through the handles, one finger to each mug. Jeri joined her, and within minutes they had reset the room for the breakfast servers. They were working on the last of their side work in the server station when Donna asked if she would go with her to the bar for a drink.

"I don't know, Donna. Last time I did that I missed work the next day." Jeri smiled at her friend, but she was serious.

"I don't feel much like getting drunk either. Too bad I don't have a joint. We could go outside and sit in my car and get high first."

"I have a joint," Jeri said without emphasis, not looking up from her work.

"Well, Jeri, aren't you just full of surprises. Come on, let's go do it." She pulled Jeri by the arm, dragging her to the pile of coats and jackets where she grabbed her coat and ran for the exit. Jeri ran too, trying to keep up with her, pulling her own coat from the mound as she went by. They were giggling loudly as they rushed through the double glass doors of the restaurant, and as the room flashed by in her peripheral vision, Jeri caught a glance of the confused bartender standing at the entrance of his bar. They ran to Donna's car still pulling their coats onto their chilling bodies. Once they got in the car, Donna started the engine and turned on the heater; it blew cold air onto their feet and Jeri let out a yelp. Donna laughed at her sensitivity, but turned the fan off while they waited for the engine to warm up.

"Well, girl, light up that number, time's a-wasting." Donna sounded happy now, the tears shed earlier evidently forgotten. Jeri searched deep in the pocket of her coat and pulled out the envelope containing the two machine-rolled marijuana cigarettes. When Donna saw them she laughed. "Now it is starting to come together for me. Looks like you and Annette did more than talk. She is the only person I know who rolls those giant bombers. There has to be three regular joints in one of those things."

Jeri paused, not knowing if she should continue with lighting the seemingly deformed cigarette. She held it between the first finger and thumb of her right hand and stared at it.

"Should I wait? Maybe we should take it apart and make it smaller."

"No way, sister. Flare that baby up." Donna pushed in the dash-mounted cigarette lighter. "No use wasting time reinventing the wheel. Those things are big, but they smoke great."

When the lighter popped out from the dash, Donna helped her light the joint, and shortly they were both high. Donna showed her how to extinguish the glowing end without damaging the remaining unburned portion of the joint, and Jeri returned it to the envelope before putting the envelope back into her pocket. The car's heater was just beginning to produce warm air when Donna turned the engine off and opened the car door. Jeri opened her own door in mindless mimicry. They walked across the parking lot together, but with Donna slightly in the lead.

"You know, Jeri, that's one of the reasons I like pot," Donna said. Jeri at first wondered if she was too high to follow the conversation, but as she studied the comment she realized that her friend had begun the conversation somewhat in the middle of her own thoughts. "I like to get drunk," Donna continued. "It's nice not thinking about things, you know? But alcohol is so hard on you. I can't stand to have a hangover. That's what I like about pot. You don't have to drink so much to get there, know what I mean?"

Jeri was trying hard to follow the flow of the conversation, but she could not. There was no common ground; she had never needed to use anything to deaden her pain because she had rarely felt it. They were back at the double glass doors when she gave up trying to formulate a meaningful answer.

"Yeah, I know what you mean," she finally replied, to be polite, if not truthful.

When they walked into the bar, Jeri was very self-conscious. She had never been stoned in public before and it made her feel as if she had a sign hanging around her neck: "This person is high on drugs." They walked across the darkened dining room to the lounge, entered, and selected two stools at the bar far from the door. They sat silently, neither of them removing her coat, waiting for the bartender to return to his normal place behind the bar. Jeri watched him in the back bar mirror as he delivered drinks to a four-top table of hotel guests; they were still dressed in their ski suits after returning from the mountain. When he was finished, he went behind the bar, moved to a spot opposite them, looked from one to the other and rolled his eyes dramatically.

"Hello, ladies. What can I get for you?"

"White wine."

Donna seemed to have been prepared for the question, but Jeri didn't have any idea what she should order. The big bartender turned to her and raised his eyebrows, his expression restating his question without words.

"Ah, me too." Jeri knew she sounded ridiculous.

"OK, ladies, one white wine and one 'me too' coming right up. I see you two made a pit stop before blessing me with your company." He was speaking softly, as if he didn't want the other customers to hear as he teased them. "Why don't you take off your coats? You look like you are going to run out of here any second."

Jeri watched him remove a bottle of wine from a cooler in the back bar and reach up casually to retrieve wineglasses from where they dangled upside down, their bases in an overhead rack. It seemed to Jeri that he was moving in slow motion, deliberately trying to make her feel uncomfortable. He placed the glasses and the bottle of wine in front of them, leaned forward to rest his hands on the bar and stared. His gaze made Jeri feel exposed in some way, as if he were evaluating her clothing or her makeup. She realized Donna was taking off her coat, and she did too, draping it across her legs, holding it there with her hands. He looked at them for a long time without moving, Jeri's discomfort increasing with each time dilated moment, and then he lifted the bottle and poured the wine with great concentration and elaborate formality.

"Be careful of that, please. I just cleaned the bar." He turned away and went back to the other end of the bar where two cowboys were drinking beer.

"That smart-ass, he likes to try to freak you out when you're high. Don't pay any attention to him." Donna raised her wineglass to drink. She took a shallow sip and the small frown muscles in her face pulled tight. "I don't even want this wine." She turned to Jeri with her eyes wide. "Damn, Jeri, I am toasted. Either that was very strong stuff or that big cigar burned too fast."

"Yeah, I know what you mean." Jeri was having trouble keeping her eyes focused, and her mind was drifting in and out of various dreamlike thoughts. She was startled back to reality by a sudden wave of Donna's arm as she motioned to the other end of the bar. John came back and took up a position across the counter from them, a knowing smirk on his face.

"Yes, Donna? Is there a problem with your wine?"

"Cut it out, John. Could I please have a glass of water? And take it easy on us, OK?" Jeri watched her reach for his hand in a silent request for temporary immunity from his teasing.

"Why, sure, little girl, you can have anything you want." He turned to face Jeri. "How about you, Jeri? I see you haven't even touched your wine."

"Me too…that is…may I have a glass of wine—water—also?"

Jeri was becoming increasingly more embarrassed. She felt that every person in the lounge knew they were stoned on pot. Her embarrassment was growing at such a rapid rate that she was beginning to breathe more frequently, and each breath was much shallower than the last. As she sat at the bar, waiting for the bartender to return with the water, her embarrassment slid into the realm of baseless fear, and the fear grew into paranoia. Her breathing became a staccato tapping, and when John returned she was on the verge of hyperventilation. She saw his bulk in front of her, and she could hear the sound of his voice, but it took a few moments for the sounds to settle into understandable words and sentences.

"Slow down, Jeri, everything is cool. Just take it easy." He was speaking slowly and calmly, holding one of her hands in one of his. "You're OK, little one. Just slow down a little. We're alone here at the dark end of the bar, just you and Donna and me. Isn't that right, Donna? Nobody else in this room but us." His voice was mild, almost monotonous. She felt her breathing slow almost immediately.

"Hey, Jeri, where you going on me?"

Donna was now holding the glass of water up in front of Jeri's face. Jeri reflexively took the glass and began to drink from it. The water was icy cold; its wetness overcame the dryness at the back of her mouth and the top of her throat. When she swallowed the first trickle, she felt momentary pain, as part of her throat was still sticky dry as it worked to pass the fluid. The pain-causing act itself relieving the pain, she continued to drink, and with each swallow she became more composed. She finished the tall glass and pushed it across the bar for a refill without comment.

"There, that's better, isn't it? You were looking like you had swallowed a bone or something. I was about ready to start pounding you on the back or something." Donna was standing close to her stool, one arm around her shoulders.

"Yes, I'm all right now. I just started to feel really obvious, you know. Like everyone was looking at me, and everyone could tell that I was high. It's stupid, isn't it?" John brought her another glass of water and she took another long drink.

"Stupid, maybe, but it happens all the time." Donna was leaning close and whispering in her ear. "Where do you think the saying about being 'paranoid' came from? The smoke makes you feel that way. You get used to it after a while, and it doesn't have the same effect once you learn to recognize it. This is just the kind of place where it happens—public, I mean. There are worse places for me. I hate the really crowded places. I start to feel totally helpless. It was probably a dumb idea to come back inside, but I didn't know how high we were going to get."

"I'm glad we came back inside. I don't know how I would have handled it if I had been driving my car." Jeri's water glass was again empty, and unconsciously she lifted her wineglass and took a drink. She was at first stunned by the change in taste, but then she was surprised because she had actually enjoyed it. She took another, smaller drink and rolled the wine on her tongue. "This wine is good." She turned to Donna as she suddenly changed the subject.

"Damn, girl. You are all right now, aren't you? How about a couple of shots of tequila?" Donna teased playfully. "You are a born partier if I've ever seen one." She was smiling at Jeri as she too lifted her wine to drink.

"Did you call me, Donna?" The bartender was returning from the other end of the bar, where he had gone to get the cowboys two more beers. "I heard you ask for a born partier, and I knew you were looking for me. You have made a very good choice too, if I do say so myself."

"Mr. Modesty. John, you love yourself too damn much."

"Not as much as I love you, my dear." He bent over the bar and placed a quick peck of a kiss on Donna's forehead.

Jeri was almost as surprised by the public display of affection as she was by hearing the big man use the word *love* to Donna. She had known for some time that the two had something going, but she had never considered love. Love meant commitment and rings and marriage and even possibly, under the right circumstances, babies; these things seemed antithetical to the relationship she had witnessed between Donna and John. They seemed too dissimilar to really ever experience the "in love" kind of love; theirs seemed to be more a relationship of convenience and sex. An affair of the body, not of the heart.

"John, may I have another glass of water? I've never tasted it so good before." Jeri was still sipping on her wine, but she wanted to drink water between drinks of the dry white wine.

"Why, sure. Anything you want. You're the customer, you know."
He took the glass and walked away.

"Donna, are you hungry? I only had a dinner salad before work
and I'm starving now. I was just thinking a hamburger would be
wonderful."

"Yeah, or a pizza."

"A pizza, you're right. That would be the perfect thing right
now. You know, A'Roma's is open until midnight. Only thing is they
don't deliver. We'd have to go over there and get it."

"Tell you what. You go call them and order the pizza. I'll run
over to the ski shop and pick up my new skis." She glanced at her
watch as she spoke. "I hope they haven't closed already. Let's go.
We'll pick it up and take it over to my house to eat."

"OK, that sounds like a deal." Jeri stood up from her bar stool
and pulled her clothes straight, surprised that she was not as intoxicated as she had felt only a half hour earlier. "What kind do you
want?"

"I don't really care. I don't like it covered with too much stuff,
you know? But John likes a lot of meat: pepperoni, sausage, hamburger, Canadian bacon, you name it. If it ever walked, flew, or
swam, he'll eat it. He even likes anchovies."

Jeri was mildly surprised, but not disturbed by Donna's pre-
sumption that the bartender would be part of the late pizza dinner.
"OK. I'll order a cheese and mushroom for us and a meat eater's
delight for our resident cannibal. Half an hour enough time for
you?"

"You bet. They're finished with them. I just need to pay. Fifteen
minutes tops, and it only takes ten to get into town. If they had a lot
of rentals out today, they should still be open."

They went their separate ways to pursue their common goal.
Jeri went to the front desk to use the telephone and the phone
book, while Donna ran to the ski shop to get her skis before the
workers there locked up.

Jeri placed the telephone order to the pizza shop and passed
the phone book back to the night clerk with a smile of thanks. She
zipped up her coat and pulled on her gloves before saying good-
bye to the clerk and pushing through the glass doors. Outside, she
spotted Donna walking across the parking lot to her car. She waved

to her, feeling happy and hungry, as she stepped out of the bright light of the hotel entrance and into the cooler, more diffused lighting of the narrow lot.

"I'll follow you," Donna called across the tops of the parked cars before she disappeared below them.

Jeri started her Toyota and put the gearbox in reverse, without properly warming the engine as Steve had so often instructed her to do. She backed from her space and drove carefully out of the frozen parking lot, preparing herself mentally for the icy, curving exit. She stopped just before the steep driveway to gather her composure and concentration, unconsciously looking back into the lot for Donna's car. But instead of finding the other car behind her own, she discovered her friend standing outside her car, waving emphatically for her to return. She backed the little station wagon down from the driveway in a wide Y-turn, taking her time to do it right.

When she got back to Donna, she was standing at the front of her car, leaning her behind on the fender, her purse on the hood, her hands in her coat pockets. Jeri pulled her car close alongside before she stopped, leaned across the passenger's seat and lifted the door lock. Donna opened the door and followed a wave of cold air into the car. She dropped in the seat and fumbled with the seat belt, pulling it far out to give herself enough slack to clear her bulky coat.

"That car. Someday I'm going to get a new one." She was sitting in the passenger's seat, arranged and settled, looking expectantly at Jeri. "Well, let's get out of Dodge. The guys have already closed up for the day. I'll come back for my skis and the junker tomorrow."

Jeri put the car in gear and again started out of the parking lot. "What's wrong with it?"

"It's very temperamental. Won't start if it gets a little cold. It's OK at home, when I have it plugged in, but if it sits in the cold too long it just won't start."

"Sounds like the battery," Jeri said seriously, as she concentrated on driving up the slick driveway and negotiating the hairpin turn at the midway point. She hadn't turned to Donna, and she hadn't thought to temper her opinion.

"What the hell do you know about cars, Jeri? You sound like a mechanic or something." Donna was teasing again, finishing her friendly attack just as Jeri turned onto Highway 550 and started back to Durango.

"Oh? Does that mean you don't think eight years with a mechanic doesn't rub off? Just let me tell you. Besides, I had the same thing. Steve put in a new battery and no more problem."

"Really? How much does a battery cost?"

"How the hell should I know? It cost me eight damn years of my life."

Jeri was joking, but the truth had slipped up from the deeper reaches of her subconscious. She heard her own statement as if spoken by someone else, and at first she thought the comment was thoughtless; then she recognized the statement as truth and was not upset. In the past she would have become depressed at the thought of demeaning either Steve or her relationship with him. She found that now that she was on her own, she could evaluate the past relationship with a more unbiased eye. She felt strengthened by her comment and laughed shyly at it.

"Damn, you are turning into one tough bitch. I love it." Donna laughed loudly, not at all shy in her laughter as Jeri had been, and it was contagious.

The two women drove the short distance into town laughing and talking. Jeri felt as contented and fulfilled as she had ever felt before. She felt alive and happy, but above all she felt free—free to pursue her own life and to explore her own potential. She had loved Steve, and had despaired in the thought of hurting him, but she had feared for long, silent years that he was deliberately holding her back; that he wanted her to fail in her pursuit of knowledge, to fall short of her goals in science and technology. She realized that she had been feeling guilty about asking him for the separation, and this moment with Donna had somehow caused her to suddenly lose the guilt. She no longer felt responsible for Steve's happiness, and the lifting of the emotional burden was more intoxicating that alcohol or pot.

In town, the lights of the many tourist-filled hotels, restaurants, and bars seemed to come into her car with purpose, as if a spotlight was directed at her in acknowledgment of the new, free person she had become. The brightness made Main Street look like a postcard image or a Norman Rockwell print.

"You know, Donna, this is the happiest I've ever been. I mean, I don't have any money, I don't have any furniture, I won't, after the first of the month, even have a place to live, but for the first time in my adult life I'm happy. I must be crazy, but I don't care. I'll take happiness over sanity any day of the week."

"Oh, sanity is highly overrated. Insanity is much preferred." Donna was quietly contemplative for long moments before speaking again. "Why else do you think I'm going out with John? It's certainly not because it is the sane thing to do. I mean, he is fun and all, but he is an old guy. It is strictly insanity to go out with him."

"Is that it, just to do something crazy?" Jeri asked.

"Yes, kind of. But I suppose the biggest reason is he's exciting. Kind of dangerous, you know? Not violent or anything like that, just sort of edgy." Donna sounded suddenly subdued and Jeri thought that she could detect a faraway feature to her words; it was as if she were trying to solve, out loud in their conversation, some personal puzzle with which she had been struggling for some time. When she spoke again she was reanimated, all trace of introspection gone. "I've got it. I have absolutely got it." She was becoming excited, bouncing in her seat.

"What? What have you got?"

"You are going to move in with me. You get the second bedroom, and we split everything down the middle." Before Jeri could react she began eliminating the objections. "No, really. It would be great. We both work in the same place and we could ride together. We are both sexy, single, worldly women, and we need the security offered by numbers." She affected the drawn, hollow-cheeked pose of fashion models when she stated that they were sexy. "You're broke, and I'm always trying to pay this bill or the other. I'm telling you this is perfect. You stay until you have to leave for medical school or wherever. You only pay half the rent and utilities, and there's no deposit or anything. It's perfect."

"Whoa, slow down. I'm convinced, I'm convinced. You are going a hundred miles an hour. It sounds good, I'm convinced." Jeri was laughing again. She could hardly believe how intense Donna had become. It was the perfect solution to Jeri's dilemma, although she couldn't see how Donna would benefit. But if Donna was that intense about her desire for a roommate, Jeri felt she could easily be the very best of roommates.

"I'm telling you, Jeri. This town is going to see some shit now. We are going to turn this mountain upside down. Watch out, you men, two soulless heartbreakers on the way."

"You know, Donna, I'm really not the kind of person that likes to party all the time. You've just caught me when I've happened to have the opportunity. I work very hard at school."

"I know that. Don't you think I know you that well? You just keep on doing your thing. Only now you will have a good friend to have fun with when the feeling strikes."

Jeri drove the car into the small parking lot of A'Roma's Pizza and Italian Restaurant and made two circuits before squeezing into a spot under a large tree. The snow on the ground seemed to make the somewhat destructive exploration for new parking spaces an innocent pastime. As the two young women were unfastening their seat belts and readying themselves to exit the car Jeri turned to face Donna.

"Donna, why do you go out with Big John?"

"Well, sometimes I wonder about that myself. He does turn me on, but sometimes I just can't explain how. He is fun and he has a million stories about places he's been. But it is something else, something that is hard to put into words." Donna closed her eyes for a moment and pressed her lips together tightly. "You know, if I'm really honest with myself, I suppose the main reason I spend so much time with him is he is the biggest connection on this side of the mountains." She raised her eyebrows and squinted her eyes in an unspoken question.

Jeri didn't understand this statement at all. But she nodded, and together they went into the restaurant to pick up their pizza.

Ted was drunk and depressed when he at last arrived home from the band party held in the converted garage. The drive had been a mindless exercise, a nearly autonomic achievement of a brain short-circuited by alcohol. He had driven home without noticing the deserted freeways he traveled, unaware he guided the car, his few thoughts random memories of the failing relationship with Mary, the bad luck at SENGS, his lost family. He passed the remainder of the night alone on his patio, drinking more scotch, listening to sad music and remembering the people and events that had defined his life, an amalgam of romantic betrayals, unhappy circumstances, and personal disasters.

The soft ballads of the cable music channel were still playing, but the gray light of dawn had entered the room when he realized he was dozing at the bar. He woke with his head on his forearms, an untouched drink in front of him, his stomach uneasy and his head spinning. He stumbled through the house only partially conscious, body and shoulders bumping into walls as he wandered through the dark tunnel-vision tube to his bedroom. He left his clothing where it dropped in a heap at his feet, fell naked onto the bed, incapable of another moment of wakefulness, and closed his eyes.

The room began to spin in the darkness, the stomach-turning spirals causing familiar spasms in his abdomen and a painful tightness in his throat. He opened his sticky eyes and pulled his limp body up to sit on the edge of the bed, concentrating to focus his sight, trying to avoid becoming sick. But it was no use; unable to control the reflex any longer, he rushed to the bathroom to allow his body to purge the remnants of the night's heavy drinking. Eventually, there was nothing left in his stomach to expel, and he was tortured by a series of dry, body-wrenching spasms that did nothing to reduce the alcohol poisoning that sickened him.

He never finished being sick; he awoke on his knees, humiliated, his face draped across the edge of the commode. He pushed himself to his feet, shuffled to the sink and cleaned himself up by splashing water on his face and rinsing out his mouth. When he returned to bed, he pulled the comforter up to his neck and drew into a fetal position, holding his eyes painfully open to control the spinning sensation. He used the bedside remote to turn on the television, and sometime during a college football game he fell mercifully into a light sleep. But all too soon he reawakened to the rising progression of nausea; weakly, he stumbled back to the bathroom where the dry convulsions returned. Only this time it was worse. Kneeling in front of the commode, waiting for the next spasm, another need overcame him. He jumped off his knees and pulled down the toilet seat, sitting only just in time for a painful episode of diarrhea.

He was drained, both figuratively and physically. He realized in a painfully lucid instant that, after the accident at the plant, he had regressed into an unnoticed but dangerously self-destructive depression. He had been trying to block out his fears and to medicate the depression in the classic ways of the drug or alcohol dependent. He knew in that instant of understanding that his reunion with Mary had come at absolutely the most inopportune time. He cared for her, but recognized that he could not let that good and pure emotion cause his own destruction. He had wanted to guide her away from taking drugs, but he had instead lost control of himself. After cleaning himself once again he returned to bed and fell back to sleep. He slept until the late afternoon.

When he awoke, his mouth was dry and his head ached dully. The television droned peacefully; a deep, gentle voice was describing the life cycles of African wildlife as staged shots of the animals blinked on the screen. He got up and drank a small glass of water, but it landed in his stomach uncomfortably and he struggled to keep it down. He went back to bed thirsty, for fear of drinking himself sick with a half cup of cool water, and fell quickly back to sleep.

Later, he awakened to an assertive sticky-mouthed thirst and bland movie theme music, the end credits of an unknown film rolling on the television screen. He forced himself to the bathroom and drank two tall glasses of cold water, and swallowed aspirin with part of a third. When he crawled back into bed, the cold liquid sloshed inside him before settling icily in the pit of his stomach. He turned off the television and the room became dark.

The dream didn't wake him; it was almost morning and he had been sleeping intermittently for nearly twenty-four hours. He had simply become awake. He lay motionless on his back, his arms and legs slack and heavy, his eyes unfocused in the darkness. The remnants of the nightmare, lucid in the first moments of consciousness, grew increasingly more illogical with wakeful reflection, the imaginary cinema of the accident gradually fading without his interference. He had slept each night for many months without experiencing the familiar nightmare, but he had experienced long periods without it before, and he accepted that it would probably never leave him completely. Something invariably triggered his memories and catalyzed the dream.

The script was always essentially the same. It would begin with a movie camera vantage point somewhere above the windshield of his older brother's classic 1968 Camaro, his two brothers riding inside the speeding car. He would watch their faces, dream faces without detail, knowing that they were terrified—afraid of being arrested, afraid of what they had done, and afraid of the speed at which they were driving. Then the dream would center around the figure of his older brother as he steered the car through the tight turns, driving madly away from the scene of their guilt. Finally, his mind would produce a wider view of the action as the car flew off the road and tumbled, end over end, down into a lonely desert wash.

Ted had been having the nightmare most of his life, since soon after the accident that killed his brothers, and although it hadn't varied much over the years, its power to frighten him had progressively abated. No longer did he wake in a trembling cold sweat, sometimes screaming for them to be careful, always devastated and drained, filled with feelings of guilt and remorse. Now when he had the dream he would recognize it for what it was while he still slept, and he would watch it run its length with dispassionate interest. It had been that way on this occasion; the dream had screened itself in his mind without causing damage or fear, although it had reminded him of the past he tried to forget.

Ted had not really seen the crash and had no way to evaluate the veracity of the dream, but he had grown accustomed to remembering it in the way his mind had written it. In truth, his information regarding the deaths of his brothers had come in bits and pieces: first from the police reports of the wreck, and then, over the years, from the other teenagers, grown older, who knew what had preceded and precipitated the mysterious high-speed trip to the Mojave Desert.

There had been a party after their high school's most important football game of the year. Ted and his younger had been stars in the game, with their parents and older brother, a year out of school, cheering them on from the grandstands. After the game, Ted's older brother had driven their parents home; he had been scheduled to work early the next day and had planned on a good night's rest. Ted had gone on a big date in the family station wagon, and his younger brother had gone to the party.

Years had passed after the accident with Ted torturing himself with the belief he could have prevented the tragedy, that had he been at the party things would have turned out differently. Though his opinions had not changed and his feelings of guilt had not diminished, the passing years had deadened his ardor for self- flagellation, and the guilt mostly surfaced in the dreams.

It had been a small gathering, a dozen or so teenage boys partying with beer and pot. Maybe there had also been some cocaine or barbiturates, that part of it had never become clear. The stories that had circulated secondhand and thirdhand from the original party attendees had never been consistent. Ted had waited almost a decade to finally listen to one frightened, whispered account from an eyewitness to the events of the night. Ravaged by drugs and alcohol during the intervening years, a few drinks and a few dollars had made the witness an effective if somewhat disconcerted storyteller.

The teenagers had been partying for several hours when some new guests had arrived. One of the partying boys had recognized one of the newcomers as a young-looking undercover narcotics officer, remembering him well from a prior arrest. When the terrified informer had been confronted and encircled by the angry boys, he had panicked, attempting an escape from the ring of drunken, drug-influenced teenagers by fighting his way to the door. The response had been spontaneous and violent. The undercover cop had been mercilessly attacked—beaten and kicked to death in a few minutes of unfettered rage, a short frenzy of madness and fear and drugs.

When the result of their actions became obvious to the young partiers, they had decided that the evidence of their crime must be hidden, taken out to the distant Mojave Desert and buried. The Johnston brothers had been left with the burden, as they had always been left with the burdens of leadership in class, in sports, and in student politics. Ted's older brother had been summoned by phone, and he had allowed the corpse to be loaded into the trunk of his Camaro. The brothers had evidently driven the three hours to the Mojave Desert, as the young conspirators had planned, and buried the body; evidently, since the murdered informer was no longer in the car when the two boys were found dead in the burned wreckage of the Camaro the following day.

Ted put the memory of the fading dream out of his mind and got out of bed to take a shower, a subtle pain still lingering in his temple. The warm water of the shower enlivened him and he realized that he was very hungry. He had to eat. He knew it would help his stubborn hangover if he had something right away, but he couldn't manage the idea of preparing anything for himself. Instead, he decided he would go to a restaurant.

He drove into Laguna and stopped at a small coffee shop, feeling as though it was dinnertime, but it was still too early for lunch. He ordered an omelet and coffee. The food was commonplace and tasteless so he spiced it up with Tabasco and ketchup before he ate. He kept the waitress busy refilling his water tumbler throughout the meal.

After he had finished and was sipping more coffee, he thought again about Mary. He wondered if she had experienced as terrible a Saturday as the one through which he had suffered. He was tantalized by the thought of each of them agonizing in the isolation of their respective homes, oblivious to the distress of the other. He selected her home number from the list on his cell phone and tried to call, but there was no answer, only the familiar sound of her recorded voice. He left a short message and got up to pay his check.

It was a beautiful day, and he felt much better with something in his stomach, so he decided to put the top down and try to enjoy the fresh air. As the engine warmed, he leaned over and scrolled through his iPod until he found the music he wanted to hear. It was a collection of Debussy classics: *La mer, Nocturnes,* and some others that seemed to fit his melancholy mood. He drove the coast road slowly and pulled off to the side in several places to watch the waves rolling in.

He realized that the previous wasted day contained several of the symptoms common to radiation sickness: the nausea, the diarrhea, the fatigue. Yet he knew that these symptoms were not caused by his overexposure to radiation, but by his overexposure to alcohol. Then, with that realization, the poisons he had experienced during his last month, the radiation and the alcohol and Mary's drugs, seemed to merge into a new mental category. They seemed to be artifacts of man's technology that had extended beyond the regulatory influences of his morals or his wisdom. Man had created the technologies, in some mad way had possessed the ability to set them in motion, but could not control their direction. Joseph Conrad said that man had created a great needlepoint machine; only when he started it, the machine began to knit. And no matter how much man wished it would embroider, it continued to knit. It reminded Ted of the cliché about having a tiger by the tail. Once humanity had become dependent on technology, it could no longer do without it; having grasped the tiger's tail, civilization could not let it go without being devoured by the beast. Whether the addiction was nuclear energy, fossil fuels, alcohol, or drugs, the machine that caused it had been set in motion with the first stone tool used by primordial man.

When he arrived back home, he carefully replaced the top of the car and stood back for a moment to question its sleek beauty. He wondered why he had stayed so near home, mindlessly partying in Los Angeles, when he could go wherever in the world he chose. He was bored with the car, and he didn't use most of the house. They were symbols of his past successes, but he felt revulsion toward the technology that had spawned them and had paid for them. His material wealth seemed to him, at that moment, covered with a thin tarnish that could never be cleaned away, crapped up.

Inside, he made himself some instant iced tea and sat down in the living room to watch the NFL on television. The teams were not his favorites, but the game was close and well played. At half-time he called Mary's house again—there was still no answer. He decided that she had probably spent the weekend with Andy, going to more parties and taking more drugs. He would wait until the business week began and give her a call at work. He did not leave another message. Instead, he hung up and dialed Tony Parker's home number. He needed to meet with him to negotiate his way free of the investment partnerships they shared.

Tony had been his real estate partner since his return to Southern California, and they were still partners on several deals, the trickiest a fourplex in downtown Long Beach. It was a teardown they had originally believed would benefit from its location in the Downtown Redevelopment District. The income from the property was barely paying their mortgage, but the drop in Southern California real estate values had forced them to hold on to their position. Dropping out of the deal now would mean a huge loss. Since Ted was determined to liquidate, it would be best for them both if Tony cooperated and bought him out. The phone seemed to ring too many times and Ted was about to hang up when the answering machine came on. He left a message asking for the meeting, explaining his intent to sell everything and leave LA. He felt an emancipating relief as he ended the call.

When the football game was over, he made himself a sandwich and recovered a popular novel he had started months before but had long forgotten. He read until nine and took the book to his bedroom. Once in bed he read only a few pages before falling into a restful sleep, finally deep and natural.

The next day, Monday, Ted awoke early, feeling good. He showered and made himself some toast and coffee. Sitting at the bar he looked out over the ocean as he ate his toast. The morning was still very gray, although the water was shining with reflected light, appearing silver and dense, heavy and languid. As a few power-boats cut foamy white lines across the water's surface, he wondered once again about Mary. She was always so confident about her life and her career. She had every reason to be confident; she was an accepted expert in the field of computer systems design, she had a BS degree in information systems from Stanford, ten years of operational experience, and a brand-new MBA from Pepperdine University. She had broad interests in the arts and literature and could carry on casual yet expert conversation about either. Mary was wonder woman; she had everything it took to get along in the modern world of high-tech executives, and she was burning herself up with drugs. Checking his watch, he decided to wait until nine to try calling her office. It would be a two-hour wait, time enough to start an inventory.

He took a yellow legal pad to the kitchen and began a list of the kitchenware. He already had a fair list of the major furniture, compiled for insurance reasons, but the list was old and he needed an updated inventory of everything he owned. He moved through the house itemizing everything in each of the rooms.

Once the business day had started, Ted tried to locate Mary by calling every one of her numbers: home, work, and cell. She apparently was not at home or work, and her cell phone was unreachable. He called each of the numbers repeatedly, and finally, in mid-afternoon, judged that she had indeed spent a long week-end with her new friend Andy. He decided to wait another day and try her at work again in the morning.

Tony called him back late in the day, and they agreed to meet at a restaurant about halfway between Laguna and Tony's office in West LA. During the call, Ted explained that he wanted out; he wanted out and he wanted someone else to do the business. He asked his friend to buy his shares of the partnerships and sell his house, art, car, furniture, and anything else that wasn't liquid. Ted had decided to put a few personal belongings into storage—clothes, books, photos, files—but he would dispose of the rest.

Tony sounded terrified. "Hey, buddy, what's going on here? I don't know what's brought on the avalanche, but I've seen it before. Let me help."

"I don't know what you mean. I've just gotten fed up, that's all." Ted didn't want to have his friend and partner pity him for his accident at the plant or his period of uncontrolled drinking.

"Whatever you say, Ted. But this call reminds me of a call I got from an orthopedic surgeon I know, someone who had just tested positive for the HIV virus. It always starts this way, you know, with a sudden explosion of business activity. Sometimes it's hysterical and other times almost serene. My surgeon friend was calm and patient, but the force of her personality was like the tide, quietly overwhelming. You know, I've known her since she was a resident, and she has always been preoccupied with medicine. In most of our deals, she'd simply come to the table with her checkbook. She trusted me to find the right opportunity, the correct timing, the good deal. She was a passive investor, a good customer. But once the avalanche struck, she was a new person. She got involved in every facet of the business, she studied the contracts and went to the meetings. Then, once she was liquid, she packed up her family, moved to the South of France and began to paint with oils on canvas. You got a hankering to paint, Ted?"

"Are you kidding? All I want is to lie on some Mexican beach and drink margaritas for a while. And let all you other guys have all the fun in LA."

"All right, have it your way, Ted. Only this kind of thing is tailor-made for abuse. There is fast money in liquidations, and you have to be careful that you don't get swallowed by some shark. This thing has to be done cleanly, and it must look clean too. You're not only my customer, you're my partner. You need some outside, impartial party for this thing. Let me make a few calls. I know a firm up in Santa Monica that specializes in this type of deal. Usually their clients are dead, but occasionally they do divorce estate liquidations."

"What about the properties, Tony? They should be straightforward. Are you in a position to buy my equity? It's a buyer's market."

"Yeah, we can probably do that. Otherwise we both take a hit. How about we get together for dinner and talk it over?"

"Sounds perfect. How about tonight?"

They met for *Monday Night Football* and ribs at a sports bar in the Belmont Shore section of Long Beach. Although the drive had been slow, Ted had left Laguna Beach early enough in the day to make the drive north comfortably, park, and claim a good table before the start of the pregame show. Tony found their table before the opening kickoff. They discussed Ted's decision to sell his interests in their partnerships as they shared a pitcher of beer, listing the properties and sale prices they agreed upon on the back of a paper place mat.

The negotiations were short and pleasant; Ted didn't press for the best prices and Tony realized he was getting good deals. The two old friends agreed to the transfers of property and money without fanfare or discussion. It would be a simple matter for people who liked and trusted each other; quitclaim deeds and personal checks, the escrow would hardly be worth the fees.

The game turned out to be a hotly contested affair featuring two of the best teams in the league. The bar was packed with sports fans, and a group of Bud Girls were making a personal appearance, giving away door prizes at halftime and selling autographed posters of themselves. The Raiders lost the game when the Broncos kicked a field goal with only seconds remaining, and the bar crowd began to dissipate immediately. Within thirty minutes the shoulder-to-shoulder throng was gone, replaced by a few dedicated drunks and several newly formed couples discussing where they would continue their evening. Once the football fans had left, the bar grew quiet and Tony became serious. He looked straight into Ted's eyes, once again the concerned professional.

"Are you going to tell me what the hell is going on, or is this just the end of it?"

"Hell, Tony, it really isn't so surprising. I've just had enough for a while. I want to get away, that's all."

"Really," he said with obvious sarcasm, "and where are you going?"

"That isn't important. I don't care. I have a trip planned for Colorado, to go skiing—but that trip is a ways off. Hell, maybe I'll go to Cabo and go fishing or something, I don't care. I just don't want to stay here anymore."

"Listen, buddy, we've done some good business together. We know each other, and yet we don't. I know the kind of deals you like, and I know you are good for your commitments, but I've never been to your home for dinner, and you've never met my wife. I can't say I know what makes you tick, but I can damn well see when you're suddenly not making the same choices I know you to make."

"Pretty mysterious, isn't it?" Ted smiled before taking another drink of beer.

"Bullshit, Johnston. You are so full of it." But he also smiled. "Here." He tossed a thick white envelope across the wet table. "I knew you wouldn't know where the hell you were going to go." The envelope had the words Silver Star Travel embossed in the upper left-hand corner. "Hawaii, seven days and six nights. Maybe a little clean air will clear the dust out of that brain of yours."

"Why, Tony, this is damn thoughtful."

"Before you get all choked up, my wife suggested it."

"Oh? Maybe I should have come over to meet your wife. She sounds like a very nice lady. But shouldn't you be going with her instead of me?"

"Asshole. Let's have another pitcher of beer." He poured the dregs of the beer into Ted's glass. "You know, she really put me through hell for this one. She's had this trip scheduled for months, but I have a business conflict I can't avoid. We'll go in the summer, but she's still pissed."

"All you married guys try so hard to make it look like your lives are so bad. Hey, Tony, it's OK to be happy."

They stayed at the empty sports bar until after midnight when it closed. In the parking lot they said their good-byes and drove their separate cars in opposite directions home.

On Tuesday, Ted's search for Mary grew more surreal; her secretary wouldn't even talk to him. His mysterious responses reminded Ted of an old spy movie. It was as if Mary had been recruited by some secret agency of the government: the FBI or the CIA. It was probable that Mary's secretary was trying to protect her with his silence. But why should he? With each enigmatic phone conversation Ted's concern for Mary increased. He had no way of knowing if she was all right, and he was afraid he was raising unwanted curiosity regarding her absence with his calls. All her secretary would divulge was that Mary was out on vacation.

Finally, late on Wednesday afternoon, he got through to her at her home. She was subdued and reticent. After a long telephone conversation filled more with silence than words, Ted offered to visit her, but when she refused, growing more excited with each excuse, he convinced her to meet him for dinner. When she agreed to meet, he felt she had only done so after overcoming some powerful need to be alone.

They met in a small seafood restaurant in Surfside that was close enough to Mary's condo for them to have become recognized as regulars during the time they had spent so many nights out together. They sat in the booth they had once favored, tucked into a dimly lighted corner, but this night was different. Ted was sure that her need to meet at the restaurant for dinner, instead of allowing him to visit her at home, was a bad sign for a struggling relationship. The neutral ground and the separate transportation made nasty endings too easy. He felt reasonably sure that Mary was going to tell him she wanted to spend all her time with Andy, and that their relationship was over. He would miss her, but it might be better for him. He knew that if he were to stay involved with Mary, he would have to insist that she give up drugs. He knew that would mean a battle of wills, a battle he wasn't sure he could win. He looked into her face and could see the hard foundations of a wall she had built over the last few days.

"Are you ready to order?" It was the waiter, his second trip to the table.

Ted indicated that he was ready by closing his menu. "Well, what looks good to you?"

"I don't know," she said as she slowly closed her own menu. "I'm not very hungry, Ted. I think I'll just have coffee, but you go on and have something."

"No, I'm not hungry either." He turned to the waiter. "Is it all right if we just have coffee tonight?"

"Sure. Go right ahead. Just let me know if you need anything." He walked back to the more fully lighted part of the restaurant.

"I had one hell of a hangover after Andy's party," Ted began. "I wasted the rest of the weekend nursing it."

As he spoke, he noticed Mary's eyes growing enormous with surprise, and then the corners wrinkled as her face broke into an incredulous smile. Then she was stifling a laugh, the fingers of one hand over her mouth. Soon she was laughing uncontrollably, crying and laughing hysterically, holding her napkin to her mouth. She laughed into the napkin, but she was loud enough to cause the waiter to peek around the corner at them. She laughed too hard and too long and Ted began to worry. It was not normal laughter, especially for the always controlled Mary. She was gasping for breath between the laughter and tears were rolling down her cheeks. Ted moved to her side of the booth and slid close to her. He held her shoulder tight to his own and pulled her face to his neck. The laughter jerked her body into convulsions that quickly became body-wrenching sobs. Then she wept at his throat, and he could feel the tears running down his chest, cold rivulets beneath his shirt. Finally she quieted and rested against him, the occasional, abrupt sniffle causing her to twitch spasmodically.

The waiter walked slowly to the table, sheepishly afraid to interrupt, coffee cups held in front of him. "Is everything all right? Is there anything I can do?" He put the coffee cups on the table in front of them.

"No, everything is going to be fine. Thank you." As Ted spoke he felt the strength coming back into Mary's limp shoulders. "It's OK now, Mary, we're alone. Let me dry your face."

She raised her face from his neck, and he dabbed her with his own unused napkin. He kissed her forehead and she smiled self-consciously.

"Let me up. I want to go to the bathroom."

"Are you all right now? Should I walk with you?"

"No, I'm good now. I just needed to cry. I'm sorry it had to happen in public. Very sorry."

He got up and helped her out of the booth. "Don't be silly, Mary, you have nothing to be sorry about."

She walked proudly, her head held high, to the ladies' room. When she was inside, the waiter reappeared from behind the barrier that shielded his station. Ted motioned him over.

"Bring us two glasses of ice water, please, and more coffee."

The order seemed to calm the waiter's concern. "Yes, sir. I'm glad everything is all right."

He had returned with the water and was gone before Mary came back to the table. When she did return, she was fully made up and her hair was neatly in place.

"How's that for a recovery? Thank God for Visine and makeup." She sat once again across from Ted, but this time her wall was down, destroyed in the onslaught of uncontrolled emotion. She sipped her water and then began to open up.

"It just seemed so funny at first—your bad weekend. But it isn't funny really, is it?" Ted remained silent. "It's just that—well, I had a rather bad weekend myself. I spent three days in the hospital. I tried something new with Andy and it was more than I could handle. I would never have tried it if I was sober, but I was too drunk and too high to know better. I'm normally terrified of needles, but I was so wasted it didn't seem threatening at all."

Now Ted understood. "You don't have to talk about it, Mary. Just relax and know it's over."

"Do you know what a speedball is, Ted?"

"Cocaine and heroin? With a needle?"

"I did that, Friday night. Saturday morning, that is, after you left. I really felt like partying so I did it."

"That is not a very good combination, Mary, especially when you're already full of drugs." Ted caught his rising tone of reprimand before Mary noticed it and changed his direction. "I just wish I had been there to help you."

"You're so sweet. But you're right about doing so much of everything all at once. Andy said that is why it hit me so hard. I shouldn't have done it."

"Don't worry, Mary, it's over now."

"Heroin," she dropped her voice to a whisper and glanced to the waiters' station, "I can't believe I tried heroin. It's so amazingly stupid. And I had to go to the damn hospital and have all those tests and records. I'm trying to keep it from the people at work, but I'm sure they know something happened. I didn't take sick time, but it was so sudden. I had my mother call."

"Slow down, Mary. They won't find out. Please calm down."

Ted was afraid she was about to break down again. Her face was twisted with regret, and her eyes were refilling with tears. Then, in an instant, her face hardened, and she gulped down her water.

"Order me a brandy, please, Ted, it helps my nerves. God, if I can't keep this a secret my career is shot. The pressure is killing me."

Ted leaned out of the booth and motioned to the waiter to come back to the table. He ordered two Rémy Martins and tried to smile so the waiter would relax. But his smile was false; he realized that the emotional scene earlier was not due to remorse for almost killing herself with drugs, but simply fear of being discovered, fear of losing everything she had tried so hard to become. He could see as he watched her sitting there, so proud and so frightened, that she feared the loss of the money, the prestige, and the freedom associated with being a successful young executive. She dreaded the loss of her condo and her Bimmer and her power suits, but most of all, he thought, she dreaded becoming another young Chicana with nowhere left to go except marriage and the mutual dependency of motherhood.

"I can handle just about anything, but heroin is too much. I'm never going near that stuff again—or a needle, for that matter."

Ted could hardly believe what he was hearing. Could it be that Mary thought the overdose was just a once-in-a-billion thing that was solely due to a single new drug? Was it possible that she had no intention of avoiding all the other drugs?

"Or cocaine, Mary. You should stay away from that too. And we should both cut down on our drinking."

"Shit, Ted." Her voice was hard and angry. "You sound just like my mother or those assholes at the hospital. Do you know that they wanted me to go for some kind of a cure? Cut it out, OK? I'm getting enough of that shit already." She was becoming quite loud, and he worried she would again become hysterical.

"Sure, I'm sorry. I got carried away. I'm just glad you are all right, and I want you to stay that way."

"You are sweet." Her voice was again lower and calmer. "I'll be OK if I can just make sure those medical records are closed and locked away. My doctor is an old friend, and I didn't get turned in to the cops, thank God. I was technically in the hospital for exhaustion, but there are some test results that I'm frantic to lose. If I just stay on top of this it's going to be OK."

Ted realized that Mary's life had not been changed in any way by her deadly brush with the darker side of her lifestyle. All she needed to do was bury the evidence and keep going. The career, the life, and the drugs would all keep right on going. He realized that when he had been crapped up at the plant, there had been a matrix of rules and regulations to protect him, but in Mary's world there was no net strong enough to keep her from her own poison. His mind drifted to the list of possessions he had made, and he knew it was time to make a move. He couldn't avoid this woman as long as she was close, and he was afraid to be with her anymore. If he remained in his relationship with Mary the best he could expect would be the lifestyle of an enabler, spending his time involved with Mary's involvement with drugs, waiting for her to kill herself. The worst case would be that he too would become as deeply involved in this second world, a world of hidden culture, a culture below the rules.

The music filled Jeri's head with vibrations. It was so clear and loud that the sound seemed to originate inside her skull, without passing through her ears from the headphones she wore. Jeri's interest in music had been insignificant prior to becoming Donna's roommate, but she had never before had the unrestricted use of such high-quality equipment. When she had first moved into Donna's apartment, she had been reluctant to use her friend's electronics, afraid she might somehow damage the expensive-looking components. But after Donna's teasing and a few minutes of casually incomplete instruction, Jeri had tentatively changed a compact disc.

She had quickly become infatuated with the system and had appointed herself its caretaker within a few days. Distressed by the careless treatment they received, she had carefully cleaned the CDs and organized them alphabetically. No longer did the fragile plastic disks suffer at the foot of the system, on the floor with their protective cases tossed aside in a confusing pile. Donna had praised her efforts, and Jeri believed the small task of housekeeping legitimized her use of the expensive stereo equipment.

She had deliberately listened to Donna's complete collection of CDs, starting at one end of the top shelf and working her way to the end of the bottom shelf. She had learned to appreciate the various types of music and had chosen her own favorites. The little money she had to spend on frivolities was spent on buying new music, but mostly she just listened to Donna's collection. She loved to lie on the floor, flat on her back, listening to the music through the headphones. When she listened, usually resting her head on a pillow, with a glass of wine at one hand and an ashtray at the other, she would smoke a little pot and drink a little wine. She was in this prone position, already slightly high, listening to an older rock recording that had recently been remixed on CD, when Donna came home from work.

With her eyes closed and the music exploding in her ears, Jeri didn't notice Donna's entry into the apartment. She was startled when something touched her shoulder. Jolting to a sitting position, yanking the earphones from her head, she knocked over her glass, spilling the small amount of wine that remained inside. Suddenly alert with adrenaline, she turned reflexively to look behind her and realized for the first time that Donna was in the room and had nudged her from behind with the tip of a shoe.

"Oh shit," Donna said as she bent down, placing her hands on her shoulders, a big smile on her lips and a worried look in her eyes. "I'm sorry. I didn't mean to sneak up on you like that."

"You scared me to death." Jeri's body was throbbing with the power of the adrenaline, her heart pounding and the surface of her skin cold and moist. She sat on the floor for a moment to recover, legs stretched out in front of her and hands braced behind her for support. "You really know how to ruin a good high. The adrenaline rush sobered me right up. I could fly a jet right now—only it would feel too slow for me." She smiled broadly at her obviously amused roommate.

"Well then, you'll just have to get high again, with me." Donna let her purse fall and dropped to the floor beside her, reaching into the ashtray for the partially burned joint Jeri had left there earlier.

"Wait. Let me clean up this spill first."

Jeri lifted the wineglass from the carpet and stood up. She went to the kitchen, put the glass in the sink and ran a dish towel under cold water. She took the wet towel back to the living room, got down on her hands and knees, and wiped away the small damp spot made by the spilled white wine. When she felt the spill had been properly removed, she looked up and saw that Donna had already lit the joint and had finished taking a hit. She was sitting beside her, holding her breath and offering the smoking joint to her.

"Don't mind if I do." Jeri turned on her knees to the stereo and pushed a button to switch the output from the headphones to the speakers. "I've been studying all morning and I needed a break. I guess I sort of dozed off or something." She accepted the joint from Donna and took a long hit from it before standing, the dish towel still balled in her other hand.

"So are you through for the day? Do you have to go to the library or something this afternoon?" Donna asked.

"Yep, done. No point in trying to study until later tonight. I can't understand a thing when I'm high. Maybe that's why I like it. Sort of takes the obligation off. Know what I mean?"

"Yeah. What do you say about driving up to the mountain for a half day of skiing?" Donna was still sitting on the floor, looking up to her. "Sound good to you?"

"Sounds great to me." Jeri loved to ski but rarely had the money for alpine skiing at the big ski area. "But I'm broke. I've been studying more and working less the past couple of weeks, and I just don't have the money saved up." Jeri was disappointed; she had never skied with Donna and the talk around the Ram Restaurant was that Donna was an expert. It would be fun and the day was perfect for it.

"Hey, my treat today. I have a lot more spending money now that we're sharing the apartment. Besides, we've been smoking your pot for a week. Let's just go have fun and worry about money some other time." Donna turned and walked away as if the decision had been made and no discussion was permitted.

"You've got yourself a deal, girl. I'll even drive if you want." Jeri stood energetically, a feeling of adventure filling her with resolve.

In thirty minutes the two women had changed into their ski outfits; had loaded the Toyota with dry clothing, heavy coats, and a bag of cold drinks, fruit, cheese, and crackers; and were finishing anchoring their skis to the rooftop ski rack. When they were ready to go, Jeri started the engine and let it idle to warm. She leaned into the back of the car to see if they had forgotten anything, and Donna got in the car beside her. They were both inside, seat belts buckled, when Jeri turned to Donna and asked, "Do you think we should bring some pot? I have a couple rolled."

"Damn right!" Donna screamed. "I thought that would be the first thing you would take." She took off her seat belt and was out the door before Jeri could answer. She ran up the walk to the apartment, her open coat flapping behind her, bounded up the steps and quickly disappeared inside. Jeri spent the time selecting a CD for the ride. Before she had it in the CD player, Donna had returned. "On the road again," Donna said as she got back in the car. "Let's go, Jeri, I don't want to miss a run."

The drive to the Purgatory Ski Area was over twenty miles, but the roads were wide and well maintained. The old compact station wagon struggled on some of the long hills, and Jeri was forced to put the transmission into a lower gear and race the engine. In the past, she had felt guilty about the loud whine the engine made when laboring in the lower gears. She had been coached so many times by Steve to "keep the rpms down" that she had dreaded the high-pitched engine sound—more because of what Steve would think or say than any desire to "be good to the engine" or to "go easy on the transmission." Now, going up the long grade at forty-five miles per hour, the engine racing and the transmission humming, she felt free; it was her car and she would drive it the way she liked. If it broke, it broke. But she would no longer feel guilty—or worse, stupid—about the way she drove. She wanted to share the feeling with her friend, and she looked across to her, but Donna was busy selecting CDs and adjusting knobs on the stereo, oblivious to the feeling of freedom Jeri gained from the screaming sound of the car as it sought the top of the mountain.

They pulled up to the parking lot of the ski area, one car among a group of cars and sport utility vehicles that had formed a line on the highway, waiting to make the left-hand turn across the downhill traffic. The lot was full, and they had to circle several times before finding a spot to park. Eventually they sat together on the open tailgate of the little station wagon, putting on their ski boots, watching the other afternoon skiers prepare their equipment, measuring the number of skiers already on the mountain by counting the tiny black dots that inched their way down the broad bunny slope. They collected their gear and trudged to the lodge, stepping clumsily, big boots clomping flat-footed, with their skis and poles over their shoulders. Jeri enjoyed the attention they received while they walked across the snow to the ticket booth; they were two beautiful single women, and many eyes followed them on their trek.

Jeri was alive with a sense of her own beauty, and she was able to enjoy the sensation for the first time in her life. Gone were the old feelings of commonness and self-consciousness and imposed guilt that had always accompanied this powerful sensation. Gone was the ill-defined feeling of betrayal; a feeling that had always come with the good sensations, in counterpoint to them, when thoughts of Steve had forced their way into her mind.

Donna bought two half-day tickets, and they followed the growing crowd of afternoon skiers as it moved, animal-like, toward the gate. They were forced to wait for the predetermined starting time, two among the many, using the time to tighten down their boots and bind them to their skis.

When they fell back into the seat of the double chairlift, Jeri wondered how her practiced, graceful style would compare to Donna's more aggressive form. She had heard much about Donna's expertise from the other food service workers at the Ram Restaurant. Even John had spoken with awe about her strength and speed. Jeri's family had been coming to the mountains to ski several times each winter since she was a little girl, and she knew herself to be a clean, well-balanced skier, if not overly athletic. But in contrast to Jeri's Great Plains childhood, Donna had been born in the mountainous country near Boulder. The rumors at the restaurant were that she had been a girl prodigy, spending all winter, every winter, on the snow, becoming expert at both alpine and cross-country skiing. Yet, as so often happens with youthful athletes, the constant, almost daily exposure to her sport and the unrelenting pressure from "stage-mother" parents had caused Donna's strong juvenile interest to gradually fade. Donna almost never talked about skiing, and Jeri couldn't remember the last time Donna had gone up the mountain to do it. She was happy to be with her, feeling there was something special about the day.

They rode the lift up the mountain, talking about work and the Christmas holidays. Donna swung her ski-encumbered feet back and forth in a scissoring motion, rocking the chair forward and back and bouncing it up and down. Jeri was an experienced rider of lift chairs, and she was able to ignore the motion the kicking caused until she tried to take a joint out of her jacket pocket. First with gloved hands, then with one glove off, she struggled to open the zipper on the pocket. Finally, she pulled the binding open, and the sudden release of the zipper caused her to momentarily lose control of her glove. She batted it across her lap several times before Donna caught it in one deft motion.

"Take it easy, Jeri. Lose this glove and you won't have much fun this afternoon. What are you digging for anyway?"

"Just this." Jeri displayed the joint face high between them, holding it vertically by the bottom end with the thumb and index finger of her ungloved hand. She smiled and Donna stopped rocking the chair.

"What a lovely idea. May I help?"

"Well, you already have, now that you stopped rocking the boat. Are you trying to make me seasick or teach me how to fly? Just remember, I've got the pot. Lose me and you lead a boring life for the rest of the day."

"I would never think of it, my dear. Now flare that thing up, we're halfway there." She took off her gloves and dug her lighter from the pocket of her coat. She clicked the lighter, holding her other hand up as a wind screen. Jeri leaned toward the flame, trying not to burn her nose or lips. "Remember that night we smoked one of Annette's bombers at the restaurant and got so damn high? I thought you were going to need medical attention." They both laughed at the memory of the experience, the distance between the joint and the flame jumping erratically. "You should have seen yourself. You had John thinking he was going to get to give you mouth-to-mouth resuscitation." Jeri laughed harder at the embarrassing image of herself, and the flame of the lighter went out, then the marijuana cigarette fell from her cold, numb fingers. She watched it float slowly through the air, twirling and tumbling, a white needle heading toward a mammoth snowy white haystack.

"Jesus." Donna was also watching the joint flutter slowly to the slope. "Look, there is a big tree, right there. Quick, look around for landmarks and get your bearings." They both rotated in the chair and swiveled their necks trying to locate and memorize some distinctive landmark.

"Oh, come on, Donna. Who are we trying to kid? We will never find that number. It has passed into pot-smoking folklore." Jeri began to laugh again.

"You of little faith. Never know until you try. Just remember where we dropped it. Besides, it gives us something to ski for." She smiled at Jeri as she put the lighter back into her pocket and zipped the pocket closed. She was still smiling as she put her gloves back on, but Jeri saw something new in her eyes. It was the look of determination. She had never seen this emotion in Donna's personality and was surprised by it. She watched Donna pull her gloves on tight, clasping her hands together to make sure her fingers were all the way inside them, then reach down to check the buckles of her boots. She kicked the top of each boot with the bottom of the edge of her other ski. "Shit, my bindings are too loose. Will have to do, though, almost there now." She nodded her head forward, and Jeri's attention was diverted from the little show Donna was performing in the small confines of the chair. Ahead was a little hill of snow that was the end of their ride. Donna pulled the straps of her ski poles over her wrists, pulled her goggles up over her eyes and edged forward on the seat. "All we have to do is get to it before some damn Texan finds it."

Jeri followed her lead, and the two women pushed off the chair simultaneously. They turned in opposite directions and headed the tips of their skis down the mountain.

Jeri realized that she was going to have a difficult time keeping up with Donna as soon as they jumped from the lift. A novice skier had fallen and was sprawled at the base of the lift ramp on Donna's side. She avoided him expertly, pivoting slowly in midair around one ski pole, her skis held tightly together as she rotated them around the pole. In a few moments, they were away from the congested area just below the lift and were flying down the mountain like downhill racers, not turning, fully tucked. Quickly, Jeri lost track of the terrain of the run as she concentrated on Donna's line. She tried to imitate each of her techniques as she followed her down the slope. At first she thought about calling out to her, to ask Donna to slow down, but soon she realized that she was still skiing with control, even at the breakneck pace. Oddly, the further they skied, the more comfortable she became, and eventually she felt she was in synchronization with Donna and with the mountain. She had never pressed herself this hard before, and it had, in the beginning, frightened her, but as the snow whisked by under her skis, she gradually felt herself drawn into the exhilaration of the run. She literally did not have time to be frightened; she was skiing much too fast. She only occasionally had the time to look forward, beyond Donna, and in one of these rare instances she recognized something. Yes, she recognized the part of the run where they had dropped the joint. She felt a huge rush of joy and accomplishment. They had made it. She saw Donna pull up in a racing stop, snow flying in a frozen waterfall, the heels of her skis rattling hard into the snow. Jeri stopped too, but she needed to pass Donna and traverse one more time to the other side of the run. When she was sideways to the fall line, the edges of her skis biting hard, she looked back up the slope to Donna. She was standing with her skis together, poles dangling from her wrists as she lifted her goggles from her eyes and placed them crookedly on top of her knit hat. She was looking past her down the hill, and Jeri was surprised at the anger she saw in her friend's eyes.

"Hey, leave that alone. That doesn't belong to you," Donna called down the mountain, as she pointed her skis down the run and pushed off with both ski poles. Jeri turned to look down the run in the direction Donna had called, behind and below her. Two men had stopped skiing near the edge of the run. Their sunglasses were pushed up on their heads and they were examining something one of them held between them. Then they seemed to realize that Donna's call had been meant for them, and both of their heads turned up the slope, surprised expressions on their faces.

As Donna slid past her, still without speed, she said softly, "Damn, Jeri, you are one hell of a skier. Let's go harass these Texans."

Jeri pointed her ski tips toward the bottom of the mountain and also began to gain speed. She was still twenty yards above the men when Donna pulled up to them and leaned suggestively against the one holding the joint. She was almost down to them when Donna reached over, grabbed the joint and leaped into the air, spinning her skis parallel to the line before landing in a perfect tuck.

Jeri didn't need to be coached to know she needed to head downhill. She pushed hard with her poles to gain more speed as she slid by the group. When they passed from the corner of her vision, the men were still standing motionless and erect, stunned by Donna's theft, but Donna was skating hard and pushing on her poles with all her weight to get away from them.

Jeri heard the familiar and happy screech of Donna's voice as she pulled by her, laughing and calling to her, "Let's go, girl, I got it." Then she heard the excited and happy voices of the men as they encouraged each other and raced to catch them. She was at the next turn when the two men came by her, overtaking her slowly, one at a time. She was concentrating hard when she heard the second to pass call to her.

"We're all going to die. Come on."

She pulled herself tight and concentrated on being very slick and very fast. She watched the slower of the men in front of her; he was trying to ski fast, but was obviously inexperienced and it was only a matter of time before he fell. She pulled up next to him and turned to face him.

"You'd better be careful. This is not a very nice mountain."

"You're telling me? Let's let them go fast. I'm slowing down!" he yelled, as she began to gain speed and pull away.

"Not me. See you later." She pulled by and was below him, going much faster and with more control.

"Save me some." She heard his call to her only faintly. Then it was the downhill race again. Only this time she did not have the luxury of imitating Donna's line or technique. She was alone, but she skied as hard as she could. She knew that Donna was much faster than she was, and if the second man was good they would be pulling each other forward. Each level of speed obtained by one would demand still more speed from the other as they competed down the mountain.

Jeri followed the run through a broad turn and passed around a small group of trees. As she rounded the trees, she saw Donna and the quicker of the two men as they turned in to the final section of the run. It was a wide, steep area that had become a field of high moguls. She watched as Donna entered the mogul field first and began negotiating between the little mountains of frozen, compacted snow. She was making dozens of quick turns, staying in the troughs of the stationary waves, skiing very fast but maintaining tight control. The man hit the moguls a moment later than Donna, but he did not follow her into the safer and slower path at the feet of the moguls. Instead, he attacked the mogul field as if he were using each hill as a jump, turning as necessary, but usually at the highest point, at the crests of the waves of snow. Jeri watched him for as long as she could during the more level approach to the moguls; he was quickly overtaking Donna. Then Jeri too entered the bumpy, difficult terrain. Because she was unable to see more than one or two hills ahead, it was difficult to plan her line through them. She tried hard to go fast, but she was quickly forced to slow to a more controlled pace.

The run ended abruptly, the grade dropping to a relaxed, knees-locked flatness. Jeri reached up and pulled her fogged sunglasses from her face, letting them hang from the tether around her neck. She searched the busy area at the base of the mountain for Donna, trying to spot her blue down jacket. But there were numerous blue tops among the skiers dispersed below the redwood deck jutting from the restaurant.

She heard Donna's voice calling her name and turned to face the sound. The other two were standing together at the base of the stone steps to the restaurant. She glided closer and realized that she was hot and breathing hard from the exertion of the fast run. It felt good to have been tested and to have successfully passed the test. Donna and the stranger had arrived at the base of the mountain first, but they were just beginning to unzip their jackets and take off their gloves. As Jeri slid slowly to them, the man pointed to the run and began to laugh. Donna first smiled and then also started to laugh.

Jeri skidded to a stop next to Donna, her ski tips pointing back up the slope, her momentum causing her to slip slowly backward. She saw the second man coming through the mogul run; he was wild and badly out of control. The big bumps were pounding him hard as he fought to stay on his skis. Finally, he went down and began to tumble head over heels down the steep hill. One of his skis came free and sped dangerously down the slope, bouncing from the tops of the moguls and flying spear-like through the air.

It was still traveling very fast when it reached the more level section in front of the lodge. It raced through the parting crowd, miraculously missing everyone, and stopped instantly when it penetrated the mound of snow that bordered the deck. The faster man put his hand on Donna's forearm for a moment and then left her side. He pushed himself forward with his poles and made his way to the embedded ski. He pulled it from the pile of snow and turned to come back to them. Carrying the runaway ski in one hand and both of his ski poles in the other, he moved back toward them using his skis in wide, skating motions.

"That guy can ski. Did you see him take on that mogul field?" Donna was still breathing hard as she spoke. "He was just bashing the tops. Very showy for skis." She was smiling between pants for air, her skin red, her eyes and nose running. She rubbed the sleeve of her jacket across her face to wipe her nose and used the back of her hand on each eye. "Let's go up to the restaurant. I want to go wash my face and comb my hair before talking to this guy."

She reached down to her boots, bending from the waist, to unfasten her bindings. Jeri watched with amusement as her friend, her runny nose dripping on her boots, glanced surreptitiously up to the good skier. Donna stepped out of her skis and lifted them to rest vertically against her shoulder. Jeri was not as practiced, and it took her longer to finish taking off her skis.

"Did you see him crashing through those moguls? Shit, I wonder who he is." When Jeri had her skis up on her shoulder, she noticed that Donna was still staring at him as he waited for his less athletic friend. The novice skier was carefully making his way down the bunny slope on one ski.

Then Donna turned back to her and said, "Come on, we don't have much time to get beautiful before we rudely ignore these guys." She stomped up the stairs to the restaurant and Jeri followed, still breathing hard from the run.

They were sitting comfortably at a window table, drinking hot chocolate, when the two men entered the restaurant. Donna pointed them out as they came in the glass doors and followed their progress carefully as they walked through the cafeteria-style food service line. Jeri was embarrassed by the blatant, physical evaluations her friend made as they watched the two men move through the room, seemingly unaware they were under such critical scrutiny.

Like them, the two men seemed to be in their early twenties. The more proficient skier was taller than the other man by an inch or two and much lighter in build. They shuffled through the food line casually; apparently close friends, they joked with each other with an unmistakable familiarity. When they exited the food service line, they stood for a moment, heads swiveling, looking for a place to sit. They were handsome men; young, tall, and self-confident. The better skier was blond, wearing his hair longer on top and closer to the skin on the sides. The longer hair fell across his eyes as he surveyed the room. His friend, the poor skier, was categorized by Donna as somewhat more of a *Gentlemen's Quarterly* type. His black straight hair was cut immaculately and was stiff with styling gel; his part was sharp and every hair was perfectly in place. Jeri wondered if he had taken the time to add more gel after the run, or if it had simply stayed in place during the head-over-heels tumble they had witnessed. The blond one scanned the room deliberately, obviously searching for them. He turned his head slightly, spoke to his friend, and began to lead the way. They walked straight to them, without detours, in what Jeri's father would have called a bird's flight.

"Hello there, may we sit down?" The blond spoke to Donna, his blue eyes confident.

"Sure. Think you have enough food there?" Donna nodded at the two trays the men held in front of them. Both men looked down at the trays reflexively, and Jeri knew that Donna had made them feel self-conscious.

"I was hoping we could share." The blond was quick. He raised his eyebrows to indicate he did not only mean he wanted to share the cafeteria food. "You know, you are one of the best skiers I've ever met. You must blow the local boys into the weeds. If I had known what I was in for, I wouldn't have been so inattentive when you grabbed that number."

He held his tray in one hand and pulled out a chair with the other. The dark-haired man followed his lead and the seating was immediately boy, girl, boy, girl; Donna had planned the meeting well. She leaned over the blond's tray, making a show of performing a detailed inventory of its contents.

"Growing boy stuff, lots of meat." She turned to the tray in front of the man with black hair and performed a second inventory. "Now this is more like it. Let's see, salad, cheese, crackers. Jell-O?" She looked up into the darker man's eyes and nodded in artificial approval. "And this is nice, a half liter of white wine, and"—she picked up a column of plastic cups, pulled them apart, and continued—"four cups." She turned back to the blond. "You are confident, aren't you?"

"Not really. We hoped to meet you, and Dan wanted to be prepared to be polite, it's a fault of his. This," he said, as he held his palm up toward his friend, "is Dan." The dark-haired one nodded to each of them, and Jeri thought he was a little shy. "And I'm Philip." He smiled broadly at all three of the other people sitting at the rough-hewn wooden table.

"I'm Donna, and this is Jeri," Donna said to the blond.

"Very glad to meet you." He lifted the wine from Dan's tray and poured small amounts into each of the four plastic cups. "We are wandering expatriates from California, here to enjoy the clean air, the rustic beauty, and the downhill challenge of the Rocky Mountains." Finished pouring, he lifted his plastic cup in the gesture of a toast and the others followed his motion. "To meeting new and exciting people." They all tipped their plastic cups to their lips. The one with dark hair, Dan, finished his wine in a single gulp.

"I, for one, am glad to be done with the downhill challenge. You three ski way over my head. I didn't think I was half bad until we came to Colorado. Now I know better." With a broad, white, even-toothed smile enlivening his tanned face, he turned to his friend as he refilled his cup. "Some teacher you are, abandoning your devoted student at the first sign of trouble. Or should I say at the first sign of a better skier."

"At the first sign of a more civilized intoxicant, you drunken lout. My instruction would have been more effective had you not dulled your reactions with wine at the Powder House. Please excuse my spoiled friend, ladies. He is not accustomed to doing anything for himself or by himself. A product of old money inbreeding, I'm afraid. He requires the aid of someone more down-to-earth, such as myself, in order to function."

Philip had not taken his eyes from Donna's face since the first toast. As he spoke, his voice tailed off at the end of each phrase, as if he didn't care at all about what he was saying. When he had finished, the moment was silent and still, with Jeri and Dan watching the other two stare at each other. The silence, which Donna and Philip seemed not to experience, became awkward and long. Finally, Jeri broke it by speaking to the man who had been introduced as Dan.

"Hi, I'm Jeri." She extended her hand to him. "This downhill racer is my roommate. We live here."

"Dan," he said as they shook hands. "No wonder you ski so well. Philip tried out for the Olympic team a few years ago. He is very good."

"I could see that. You say he is giving you lessons?"

"Yes, in a way. We're also roommates, at school. He helps me with surfing and skiing, and I help him with English grammar and bounced checks. We're each codependent, in our own ways." He tipped his cup of wine to his mouth and his head back, pouring the wine into slightly puffed cheeks before swallowing hard. "He falls in love quite a bit. It's hell to pay when he finds his heart broken. Your friend has overwhelmed him, first with her skiing and now her beauty. You are both great skiers."

Jeri noticed that he had not made a blanket statement about their beauty, and she was pleased. She didn't understand either of these unusual young men, but they were attractive and interesting, and Dan was an agreeable person. She looked closer, seeking some answer of physiognomy from his face and upper body. He was a handsome man, possibly the more handsome of the two. He was attractive in the perfect way models were. His friend, Philip, was good-looking, but in the more rugged, outdoors way of the farmers she had experienced in her family and in her hometown. She found she liked the way both men looked, and she liked the way each of them acted, and the way they complimented each other when they were together. She watched Dan as he used the palm of his hand to check if his thick black hair was in its perfect predetermined position, and she didn't mind. She didn't mind because that position was a very good-looking one, and she found it enjoyable to see his hair in place. She watched his black eyes to verify her feeling that he was not watching her as she was watching him, and he was not. He was immersed in some deep, distant saga within the plastic cup.

"So, Philip says you're rich." Jeri spoke only to bring him into conversation, only wanting to fill the silence.

"No, not me. My family. Or I should say what passes for a family: foundations and partnerships and trusts and armies of lawyers and psychiatrists. My sister and I hardly know what to think of it. We're orphans. My mom and dad were killed when my dad crashed his plane. My sister identified them. Not good for her. Now we go to school and get checks to do it."

"God, I'm sorry I pried."

"Don't get me wrong, it's a great life. Can't be beat." He refilled all four of the cups, emptying the thick glass carafe. "I'm going for another half liter. Want to come?" He stood, still holding the empty decanter.

"Sure. Why don't I get this one? It's our turn." Jeri didn't know if she should offer to buy the wine or not. She had little experience with this sort of meeting and hoped she did not sound naive.

"Not at all. How else do you think we are going to make you feel guilty enough to share your pot with us? We didn't out-ski you for it, so now we need to bribe you with wine." Jeri was pleased by how easily he made her feel comfortable. "Come on, these two haven't taken a breath in so long they are starting to turn blue. We may need to call the Ski Patrol." His reference to the other couple brought Donna back into the conversation, from some other, better place.

"Where are you going? Jeri? You're not leaving, are you?"

"No, Donna. We're just going for more wine."

"I'm sorry Jeri. We were just…"

"Yes? You were just, what? This I've got to hear."

"Well, we were just…oh, never mind. Here," she said, as she unzipped one of her jacket pockets and began to dig inside, "take some money, I'm buying this one."

Jeri turned to Dan in silent understanding and they both burst out laughing.

"Oh, that's OK, Donna. We'll take care of it." Jeri was enjoying Donna's confusion. "We've decided that it is only fair for them to buy the wine. That is, since you out-skied the Olympic star, there."

At this statement, Philip also came back from the other, private world. "Wait, why are we staying here? It's cold, the wine is bad, and it is very public." Philip directed his comment to his friend with raised eyebrows; he was apparently trying to communicate some hidden meaning. Jeri was immediately concerned that the two men had some evil sexual motive for leaving the public cafeteria. She tried to make eye contact with Donna, but it was no use. Philip turned to her to plead his case, as if he already knew that Donna would go anywhere he suggested. "Look, we have a condo five minutes' walk down the road. Let's go down there and get warm and drink some good wine." He turned back to Donna. "Smoke a joint?" Donna nodded her agreement. He turned to Dan. "Maybe do a line?" Dan shrugged noncommittally. "We can be comfortable there, relax and get to know one another."

Jeri found his mild arguments unthreatening and very convincing. She found herself wondering if he would someday have a career in law, or maybe in politics. The three of them looked to her for a decision. It was obvious that Donna wanted to go, and she felt as if she were keeping her from having a better time.

"Why not?" Jeri said. "What can it hurt?"

But as they walked out of the cafeteria, she wasn't sure what she had gotten into. She hadn't had much experience with the drug culture, but she thought that "a line" meant cocaine. She had heard a lot about people who smoked crack, and she didn't want anything to do with this drug. She hoped that Donna was not so impressed with her new friend that it caused them to be involved in some terrible crack-house predicament. Then she glanced back to where Dan was walking behind her, head down and disinterested, the least interested in the move, and she felt she had an ally. Someone who would back her if she needed to push for an exit. She slowed down just enough to match his pace. She looked into his face, hoping she would be able to see the truth in his eyes.

"Dan, I'm a little concerned. Is this OK? I mean, I don't want to give you the wrong idea."

"Ha," Dan said, suddenly energized, "don't worry, Jeri, you are in the best of hands, the very safest of hands." He was smiling that same handsome, big-toothed smile she had seen before, and she was attracted to him. There was something compelling in his knowing silence, something that called out and said: "I know what the play of life is all about, I know the ending, but I'm not telling anyone."

Jeri found herself wondering if this might be the night. She and Donna had discussed "the night" and "the man" several times, and each time they had talked she had become so nervous, and so uncomfortable, that she had made Donna drop the subject. But both of the women knew that eventually Jeri would meet a man that did something for her. There would be a man that aroused the sleeping part of her existence, a man that made her feel physical need. Jeri had always thought about the subject in the abstract, but as the two couples walked across the cafeteria, with the late afternoon sun shining horizontally across the chilly room, she felt physical attraction for the handsome, quiet man beside her. In a moment of brave spontaneity, she reached over and entwined her arm around his, pulling his forearm close to her breast. She felt his strong arm against her, and she felt warm and happy inside. She was surprised and gladdened by her own forwardness. *This*, she thought, *could be the night*.

She pulled his arm closer to her and heard him chuckle. "The best of safest hands, Jeri, yes, indeed," he said, as they passed through the glass doors of the cafeteria. He pointed to the frozen pavement with his free hand as he pulled her close, supporting her by the arm he held. "Watch out for that ice, Jeri." She was in his hands now, saved from danger by him, willingly clinging to his body.

They secured the women's skis to the top of Jeri's car and Philip shouldered both sets of the men's skis. Jeri drove slowly down the hill with Dan sitting beside her. He fidgeted with the radio as she followed the other couple the thousand or so yards to the condo complex. The slow part of the trip had been the car. It would have been much faster simply to walk the short distance to the condo, but the car had to be moved from the public parking lot before night fell.

Once at the complex, Dan directed her to the visitors' parking and suggested they remove the skis and store them inside while the two women were there. Jeri thought the suggestion ridiculous, but she had never experienced the rapidity of big-city theft.

"Dan, if you really think we should take the skis, we will, but I can lock them in the rack, you know."

"I'm much too cynical. I'm afraid you just caught me at it. Sure, lock 'em up. Let's go inside. I'm cold and tired and thirsty and hungry. What did I miss?"

"Only horny." Jeri was surprised, but oddly proud, that she had been brave enough to say what she was thinking. She felt sex had been under the surface of the conversation since the cafeteria.

"Oh, Jeri, men are always horny. You mustn't mistake that for anything. We are what we are, unfortunately." He took her by the arm and pulled her close. Then he led her to the condo, passing a steaming Jacuzzi on the way.

When they entered the condo, Philip and Donna were smoking a joint and lighting the fireplace. They seemed very happy together, connected in some intense way. Philip brought the joint to them as Dan closed and locked the door. He held it to Dan's mouth as he inhaled the smoke, then he held it to Jeri's mouth and she did the same. She could taste the pot; it was her own, probably the same joint that had experienced such a full and exciting day. Philip began to pull the joint away from her, and she reached up and grasped his forearm to bring it back to her mouth.

She was tired of alcohol; she really didn't like the feeling it gave her, she hated the hangover, and she had already had more to drink than she wanted. She wanted to get high and they were smoking her pot. She felt she had the right to take the second turn at the joint. She filled her lungs to bursting and did not feel uncomfortable with the smoke in her lungs.

She released Philip's hand and turned back to Dan, who she still held entwined, arm in arm. Then in the mist of her pot-fogged thinking, she thought she detected a little jealousy in his eyes. It made her feel good, desired. She pulled Dan's arm closer to her chest to reassure him and enjoyed the very different feeling the pot had produced. She wondered why she ever drank alcohol. She really hated it, she only liked being high on pot. She felt Dan unraveling his arm from hers, and she followed him to a wood-framed sofa. They sat side by side and Jeri could feel his warm leg against her own. He smiled at her and winked just before he leaned over and reached underneath his seat.

"This is what Philip wants next. Just watch him." He pulled out a round metal canister that looked very much like the kind used to hold holiday fruitcakes. As soon as he brought it up from the hiding place, he nodded, a cynical grin on his face, indicating his friend across the room. Jeri followed his nod to the other couple; Donna was draped around Philip, with her hands interlocked behind his neck and her face buried in his chest, rubbing her body against his. But Philip was seemingly unaware of her; his eyes were locked on the fruitcake canister that had appeared from beneath the sofa.

"See what I mean? Poor Donna." Dan spoke without turning to face her. "Yo, Donna, give it a rest. Come over here and do a little line."

Jeri was astounded by the speed with which Donna lost interest in her erotic activity. Jeri had found the sexual play of her friend surprising enough to understand; the sudden abandonment of the performance was incomprehensible. The other couple moved toward them, still clinging to each other, but both appeared more interested in the stage business being performed upon the table. They dropped to the floor on the other side of the cocktail table as Dan produced the cocaine from the metal can.

Jeri studied them as they watched; both sets of eyes followed every movement of Dan's hands, fixed to each piece of paraphernalia as it exited the can. They seemed entranced by his maneuverings as he carefully organized a mirror, a razor blade, and a small glass vial into the inverted lid of the can. She had heard about cocaine and had even participated noncommittally in cocaine conversation; now it was here, in front of her, ready for her ingestion. She felt strong doubt and discomfort at the sight of this drug because of the many horror stories she had heard of fortunes lost and lives ruined by its increasingly irresistible allure.

But as Dan used the razor blade on the powder he was happy and relaxed. He talked in amusing banalities about the day's skiing, taking special aim at his own unpracticed style. He teased Philip and Donna unmercifully about their clinging togetherness, and Jeri had to laugh in spite of Donna's obvious annoyance with the personal nature of his comments. Then finally, he finished his preparations and pushed the mirror, with the elongated white piles on its surface, carefully across the table to them.

Philip removed a small length of plastic drinking straw from the metal can and handed it to Donna. She smiled at him and took the straw in her fingers, holding it like a dart. She used her other hand to pull her hair back from her face and place it behind her ear, out of the way as she bent over the mirror. With concern and curiosity, Jeri observed her friend as she took the drug. She pressed one nostril closed with the index finger of her free hand and vacuumed the white dust up into the other. She made a rude sucking sound as she moved her head up and down the mirrored glass. Had it not been so serious, Jeri would have been driven to laughter by the ridiculous and unseemly ritual.

Philip was quicker, and it appeared to Jeri more practiced, in the art of snorting cocaine. He sucked the stuff into his sinuses in long, loud, hissing swipes across the glass. Evidently, he did not need to close the other nostril to create the vacuum needed for the operation. When he finished, he placed the straw on the small mirror, tipped his head back, and released a series of absurd piglike snorts. Jeri looked quickly to Donna in time to see astonishment pull her eyes into wide white fields. When their eyes met, they both laughed out loud, forced composure bursting through tight lips as they tried to repress the laughs.

"Don't worry, my friends, he's all right. It is just his way of enjoying himself." Dan spoke through a white-toothed grin as the comical snorts continued. Philip's lips curled into a meek, embarrassed smile as he made the loud noises. "He says it goes farther up. Don't ask me where it goes. By the sounds he makes, it probably comes out his ears." The snorting stopped and became loud sniffles.

"Oh, like you never make any strange noises." Philip was embarrassed, but he seemed to understand the humor in his technique and his smile grew wider. "Sorry. I know how it sounds, but it just works better for me." He winked at Donna before attempting to kick Dan under the low table. The table shuddered slightly, and Dan made an exaggerated move to stabilize it.

"Whoa, boy. Don't spill the goods. Jeri and I haven't even had a line yet." He picked up the straw and handed it to Jeri.

She took it the way she had seen Donna hold it and looked down at the mirror. She still had not made up her mind about the drug, and she paused for a moment.

"Jeri?" Donna's voice was quiet and sweet. "You don't have to do any, you know. No one cares if you don't."

"I never have before. I'm not sure."

"I know. It doesn't matter. But it really isn't as bad as you think. Pot or beer has more kick than this. My first time, I couldn't even feel it. It seems like you learn to recognize what it does, then you really like it." She was beginning to talk rapidly as she leaned over the table, closer to Jeri. "I mean, it's very subtle, sort of just makes you awake and happy."

Jeri looked up from the mirror to Dan's face. She thought she saw something in his eyes; something concerned and thoughtful, tender and sweet. It was strange, she thought, that this handsome, muscular man could emit such strong signals of empathy and sensitivity. She immediately felt safe and protected. He reached out to her hand and grasped it, his big palm engulfing her fist and the straw.

"Jeri, your friend is right. It isn't important to us. You don't have to do a line to please us." His huge black eyes were soft and concerned, communicating a sheltering guardianship. The sudden intimacy between them produced within her a powerful wave of physical attraction and Jeri felt an overwhelming need to please him. She broke the strong hold of his eyes and tried to lighten the moment with a joke.

"I know, you are all just trying to corrupt this little girl with drugs and sell me into slavery." She tried to break the heavy mood that had settled on the group with a laugh and a smile, but still the suspense lingered. Their silence underscored the importance of the moment, a crossroads of conduct and conviction. She thought about the various responses she might have to the experience. Some people tried the drug and immediately rejected it as ineffectual, others encountered its biochemistry a single time and devoted their lives to its procurement, and some seemed to be able to enjoy the occasional use of cocaine and never lose their control over it.

She still held the straw, Dan still held her hand holding the straw, and the only sound in the room was the fire as it crackled in the fireplace. She realized suddenly that she was going to try it. Just a little, just to try it once. Just to be able to say she had tried it and to make the moment end.

"Really, it is all right, Dan." She pulled her hand gently out of his. "Just make sure I do it right. I know this stuff is expensive." She pulled her hair behind her ears the way she had seen Donna do it and leaned over the mirror carefully.

"If you are sure." Dan's voice was smooth and quiet.

"I'm sure."

"Just take a little up at first. It will make your sinuses go a little numb. After that you can do the rest of the line without it burning."

She leaned closer to the mirror and put the straw up to her nose. Again mimicking Donna's actions, she closed off the opposite nostril with her other hand. She paused before inhaling the powder, wanting to do it right so Dan wouldn't think she was a naive schoolgirl. She wanted him to appreciate the strong woman she had lately found herself to be. She wanted the look in his eyes to be male to female attraction and not the look of fatherly concern she had seen there moments before. She guided the straw to one end of the prism of white powder and breathed through it. She saw the end of the pile disappear and felt the sting of the drug as it deposited on the tender membranes of her sinuses.

"That's enough for a minute. Let that work for a minute before you do the rest." His voice was happier now. Gone was the maudlin concern for her lifestyle, and in its place was a teacher's concern that she learned the method correctly.

She could feel the drug in her head; the initial burning, irritating sensation quickly changed to a feeling of numbness. The numb feeling was accompanied by a slightly runny nose. She listened to herself sniffle the moisture back up into her sinuses, and she recognized the sound both Donna and Philip had been making. She tasted the drug, bitter and medicine-like, at the back of her throat, then bent back down and finished the portion she had begun. Dan had been right; the burning felt less uncomfortable as she drew the larger portion of the drug into her nose. She straightened her back, raising her head from the table, and handed the straw to Dan. Donna was watching her, and when their eyes met, she raised her eyebrows and smiled. Her silent message seemed say: "We have fallen into a good thing."

Jeri waited for the impact of the drug, but she couldn't feel anything. After a few minutes, she decided that it didn't have any effect on her. Maybe she was immune or maybe she had a very high tolerance; either way, she could detect nothing.

Philip and Donna got up and went into the kitchen to open a bottle of wine, and Dan moved to a cabinet that contained the television and a small stereo. He put on an old cowboy movie with the sound muted and searched the radio for a station, making small talk and telling silly jokes as he worked with the controls of the electronics. He would make an adjustment and then turn to speak, looking into her eyes as he spoke to her. Jeri was happy and felt very good about being with Dan and this small group of friends. She felt strongly attracted to Dan and hoped he felt the same way about her.

When the other couple came back from the kitchen, they brought a bottle of chardonnay, four wineglasses, and four tall tumblers of water and ice. When Jeri saw the water, she suddenly felt very thirsty. She stood to help Donna distribute the water and glasses before taking her own tumbler of water. She sat down and tipped back her glass, letting the cold liquid flow across her dry tongue and down her smoke-dirtied throat. She didn't stop drinking until the ice cubes hit her teeth and the tumbler held only ice.

"Wow, that was good. I didn't realize I was so thirsty. I've never tasted water that was so good." Jeri checked the glasses of the others, but they had not yet had an opportunity to drink. "I need a refill," she said. "Can I get anyone anything from the kitchen?" She stood quickly, the shaking heads of the others freeing her to leave for more water. In the kitchen, she drank another full glass over the sink to satisfy her thirst, and then refilled her tumbler a second time to bring back with her to the living room.

She stood beside the cocktail table looking down at the others, feeling wonderful. The cold water had given her new life; she felt happy and energetic. She realized that she must have been dehydrated from the long day and the hard physical activity on the mountain, but after the water she felt elated and refreshed. She looked down at the three people seated around the table and felt like they were her closest friends. She wanted very much for them to feel as good as she did. "Are you sure I can't get anyone some more water?"

"No, Jeri, we are all fine. Come sit down, you're making me nervous." Donna was smiling up at her from her position at Philip's side. "You are starting to look like you're going to start cleaning or something."

Jeri noticed that the two men were also smiling at her, so she sat down next to Dan without argument. She was surprised to notice that she was grinding her teeth and consciously ordered herself to stop. Once she was seated she noticed the glass of wine in front of her. She put down her water and lifted her wineglass. The wine was wonderful; dry, but fruity and flavorful. She took another sip before putting it down beside her water.

"The wine is delightful. Does anyone want to smoke another number?"

"What? You mean you two skied that hard and it wasn't your last doobie?" Philip pulled away from Donna's grasp as he spoke. "I can't believe it. All that work, and you had more all the time?"

"How else to meet you?" Donna said, leaning sideways to give Philip a light punch on the shoulder.

"Sure, Jeri. Light it up. I'll line out some more coke." Dan spoke as he reached for the little glass bottle that held his cocaine.

"OK, we can smoke this joint, but I don't think the coke does anything for me."

Jeri's statement caused a moment of silence before the others began to laugh at her.

"Jeri, you have been going a mile a minute ever since you did a line," Donna said, speaking as an older sister might to a wayward sibling. "Don't try to say it doesn't do anything to you. Better watch out. If you don't settle down, Dan may not let you have another line."

"Not to worry, Jeri," Dan said, as he began work on another pile of powder on the mirror. "Just have another glass of wine. It will slow you down."

The two couples smoked pot, drank wine, and snorted cocaine into the late evening hours. They listened to music and watched television while they became increasingly intoxicated. The sun was down when Philip took Donna by the hand and led her up the darkened stairway to the loft bedroom. When Jeri turned back to Dan, he was looking down at his mirror, working on another set of white lines. The clicking of the blade on the glass seemed to have taken on new force. She could only see the side of his face, but she thought she saw signs of distress. There were deeper lines around his eyes and a tighter set to his lips.

"Dan, are you OK?" Jeri asked as she inched herself closer to him. "You haven't been saying much lately. Have I said something that bothered you?"

"No, Jeri, you are perfect. Just perfect. It has nothing to do with you."

"What is it, then? You seem so serious." As Jeri spoke, distant whimpering noises came from the loft overhead. Dan banged his drink down on the table and chopped viciously at the powder.

"Nothing," he said.

But she could see he was becoming increasingly more emotional. He got up and raised the volume of the music, then paced in front of the TV before returning to his seat. He leaned quickly over the table and ingested two heavy lines of cocaine without speaking. When he looked up, she saw that his eyes were moist and his expression pained. She didn't know what to say or do. She couldn't understand why he was so disturbed.

"It's just that he is such an ass. He does this all the fucking time and it really tears me up. He's such a damn whore. I don't know why I put up with this shit."

"It's OK, Dan. I mean, Donna's OK. She isn't sick or anything. She doesn't usually do anything like this." Jeri put her arm around Dan's shoulder and leaned over to kiss his cheek. "I don't normally get involved this way either."

She reached up to his face and pulled it to her own. She kissed him on the mouth, long and soft. She waited for him to respond, but he did not; he was rigid and uncooperative. He neither embraced her nor opened his mouth to her kiss. Finally, in defeat, she pulled her face away from his and released him from her embrace.

"I'm sorry, Dan. I shouldn't have done that. I just thought you might think I was attractive."

"Poor, sweet Jeri. I don't just think you're attractive, I know you're stunningly beautiful. But I'm already in love. I am head over heels, mind out the window, pride down the toilet in love. You don't understand any of this, do you?"

"Understand what?" Jeri was beginning to put the pieces of the puzzle together, but she still could not bring herself to accept the truth.

"It's Philip. Philip and me. I'm in love with Philip, Jeri. We're not just roommates, we're lovers."

Jeri could not immediately comprehend the statement; it was too foreign to her, a different language or thought process. Then, from the loft above, she heard Donna's voice in loud moans of sexual climax—and she suddenly understood everything.

Ted applied the brakes hard, the heavy traffic on both sides of the sports car preventing him from swerving out of the way. A dented step van had crossed abruptly into his lane, cutting off his path. And when he slammed on the brakes to avoid rear-ending the van, his wide-bottomed commuter cup slid off the console and onto the plush carpet with a splash of cold coffee. The dark stain spread into the floor mat relentlessly, but there was nothing he could do to check its flow while still in the frustrating traffic.

Ted was making the long drive north through the multitude of small cities that constituted greater Los Angeles. He had an appointment in Santa Monica with an attorney he hoped would liquidate the remainder of his Southern California assets. Tony Parker, Ted's friend and longtime real estate investment partner, had reluctantly arranged the appointment with the Santa Monica firm, only agreeing to set up the meeting after a series of telephone conversations in which he tried to dissuade Ted from any precipitous activities. But Ted had remained resolute in his desire to leave his life in LA behind him. Although Ted was pleased by the unexpected loyalty Tony had shown, he yearned to abandon the Los Angeles area and escape the constant remembrances living in the familiar city produced. He needed desperately to deflect the painful memories of incidents and relationships that haunted his life in LA.

His route north took him through the congested west side of town, and he had underestimated the extra time he should allow for the heavy rush-hour traffic. It was the morning rush; a misnomer by any measure, as the speed vehicles rushed during peak periods in LA averaged less than twenty miles per hour. But even twenty would have been an exhilaration compared to the stuttering west side traffic that lurched in emotionally exhausting starts and stops.

He had been again accelerating into one of the deceptive gaps in the traffic when he was forced to brake unexpectedly. The step van was an elderly potato chip delivery truck; the old corporate logos showed clearly through a thin layer of white spray paint. It had apparently been salvaged and converted for some handyman's use. Several ladders filled a roof rack and mysterious tools swayed where they hung behind the rear door windows. It produced an almost invisible cloud of toxic fumes that rolled over and into Ted's open car, adding to the sticky soot of the freeway that had already dampened his skin with an unctuous, clammy deposit. Earlier in the morning, in the near dark of the breaking day, he had thought it would be nice to drive along the coast road with the top down, listening to the radio and drinking hot black coffee. But now, in the freeway congestion, riding in the open car only increased his discomfort and depleted his patience.

When he was less than a mile from the Harbor Freeway interchange, traffic stopped completely, trapping him in one of the center lanes, with the dented step van blocking his view forward. Eventually, the brake lights of the van blinked out, and as the noxious fog slowly dissipated, the handyman appeared in the driver's side doorway. He was a leathery middle-aged man with thick brown hair overgrowing a short haircut. He wore faded Levi's, a checked flannel shirt, and dirty white running shoes. He jumped out of the van, a huge bundle of keys jingling like loose change as they bounced at his hip, then walked vigorously to the back of the van, pulling the massive key ring from a chrome machine he had clipped to his belt. He unlocked a padlock, opened the double rear doors, and began rearranging a confusing tangle of baling wire, sheet metal, bricks, plywood, and other, less identifiable, debris.

Ted was enthralled by the determination and purpose in the man's actions. He seemed to find some natural order in the pile of mysterious junk; evidently recently disturbed, he needed only to pull on a wire or push in a board to restore this order, bringing each component in the pile again into perfect concert with the rest of the universe. He seemed to be so sure of himself, so completely confident in every action. He seemed to know his world was only a few yanks away from order and peace. Ted envied his certitude.

He turned off the engine and tried to clean up the spilled coffee with a tissue. The thin paper was quickly saturated and disintegrated, leaving tiny white shreds in the soaked mat of the carpet. As time passed, more commuters exited their vehicles, and people who had been inanimate components of the cars just a few minutes earlier, riding behind walls of glass and steel, began to mill together aimlessly between the helpless machines. Rumors circulated through the useless piles of metal and plastic and glass; a jumper was on an overpass at the interchange, and the Highway Patrol had stopped the flow of traffic until the jumper came down.

Ted was amazed by the festive atmosphere that gradually developed between the emptying cars. Stranded commuters were meeting other castaways and conversations were being initiated, temporary friendships forged. A young uniformed utility meter reader, a gold chain glittering from the open collar of his shirt, approached a Volkswagen with two teenage girls still in the front seats. When he reached them, he leaned through the driver's side window and was soon talking and laughing with the girls. A few minutes later he was in the backseat of their car, leaning forward between them, and Ted could see they were sharing a joint, passing it back and forth as they smoked it.

Ted watched the activities taking place around him, longing to be on his way, but resigned to the delay. He called the Santa Monica law office and explained that he would be late, having no idea how long the traffic jam would take to clear. Farther ahead of the Volkswagen, a dirty and hard-looking biker had left his chopper and was standing with a businessman in a three-piece suit. While they talked, the businessman reached into his BMW, and the two were soon drinking beer from green bottles. Ted marveled at how much it was like an old B movie, a movie with the overused plot of stranded strangers being thrown together to form relationships that would normally be impossible. Only in the old movies the strangers would normally share some common danger: a sinking cruise ship, a ditched passenger plane, or a burning building. The social gathering that Ted was witnessing on the San Diego Freeway, in the middle of stalled rush-hour traffic, was due entirely to the peril of one individual, the one person who could neither be met nor even seen by most of them—the jumper.

The stranded commuters were indifferent to the danger engulfing the lone jumper, concerned only with their own inconvenience. The biker tipped back the final drops of his beer and carelessly threw the bottle over the parked cars and into the deep ice plants of the manicured shoulder. The business-suited BMW driver appeared to object to the littering, but he had been too slow in his offer to take the empty bottle. The biker laughed and shrugged to the businessman before remounting his long, extensively chromed motorcycle. He weaved the machine, clumsy at the low speed, gingerly between the lines of motionless cars, the irregular thumping of the engine a dirgelike drumbeat as it faded from earshot. The driver of the step van glanced back to Ted and shook his head before he spoke to him.

"Looks like a motorcycle is the only way out of here until that idiot jumps. The Highway Patrol should let the guy jump so we can get the hell out of here."

Ted didn't know how to answer this strange man's insensitive comment, so he too shook his head and tried to smile.

As they waited, a small group of strangers gathered near Ted's open car; attracted by the traffic channel playing on his radio, they discussed their collective bad luck and cursed the thoughtlessness of the jumper. Sometime later, rumors came down the line that the jumper was actually a woman, and this sliver of personification somehow made her human. Some of the same people who had earlier agreed vociferously with the driver of the step van, advocating the quick death of the jumper, softened their opinions and tempered their statements. Discussions of why she would want to jump began, and twenty minutes slowly grew beyond two hours.

Then finally, with Ted hours late for his appointment, people began to walk back to their own cars. Somehow the knowledge of the eminent return to normal traffic flow had drifted through the jam-up. They started back to the safety of the cars slowly, but as some reached their objectives and started their engines, others seemed to become uncomfortable as pedestrians and quickened their gaits. The speeds with which they moved back to their cars continued to increase until Ted was reminded of another old movie, a film of a European road race with a Le Mans start. Drivers ran frantically between cars, fearful that they might not be safely in their seats when the traffic flow restarted. Yet after the height of the panic, another half hour passed before anything began to move.

At the Harbor Freeway interchange, the quickening flow north slowed into a huge gawkers' block as the drivers tried to get a glimpse of the tragic collection of ambulances and patrol cars that marked the end of a life. Ted saw that if he rode the shoulder he could bypass the backup and get away from the maddening traffic jam. He sped illegally past the slow-moving cars, riding the narrow shoulder until he could make the transition to the Harbor Freeway north, heading toward downtown LA.

After he had successfully negotiated the congestion, the road opened up and he found himself racing toward downtown Los Angeles, accelerating to put the traffic jam behind him. At first the traffic was light, but soon the increasing number of cars in the metropolitan area forced him to acknowledge his excessive speed. He came up on a group of cars rapidly, avoided them with a series of quick lane changes, and immediately began to slow. He glanced down to the speedometer to find he had been traveling at ninety-five miles per hour—on the Harbor Freeway, in downtown LA. He realized that he had been driving like a zombie, a sleepwalker behind the wheel of a powerful weapon. He continued to slow until he reached sixty and then activated the cruise control.

At the Santa Monica Freeway interchange he directed the car onto the westbound ramp, toward Santa Monica and the northern beaches. His planned day was lost. It was pointless to go to the law office four hours late, but he needed to occupy his mind with something, anything to keep him from thinking about the jumper's fate unfolding as stalled commuters smoked pot and drank beer. He decided he would head north up the coast on Highway 1, drive beside the ocean on the two-lane road and put distance between himself and the dirty, crowded freeways of the city.

The Santa Monica Freeway ended by funneling through a tunnel and onto the Pacific Coast Highway. The midday traffic was light, but beach-goers and signal lights kept his pace slow. After five or ten minutes, he realized that he was very close to the entrance of the Getty Villa, and when the narrow driveway approached, he turned impulsively toward it. Braking as he made the tight right turn onto the bumpy cobblestones, he wondered if he would be able to park without a parking reservation. The car rattled up to the parking structure and he found a spot with uncharacteristic ease.

He parked and locked the car, then walked up to the front of the Roman villa built by an oil industrialist of the modern age. The museum was a re-creation of an ancient complex found buried beneath the ashes of the Vesuvius eruption near Pompeii. It sat on the bluffs of Malibu and overlooked the shining Pacific Ocean, much as the original had overlooked the Mediterranean Sea. He walked past the long reflecting pool to the main building and entered, wondering what portion of the vast Getty collection would be inside, isolated from the new museum in West LA.

As he walked through the galleries he thought of Mary. She was, in some ways, very functional in a complex modern society, yet she was unable to avoid being destroyed by it. The drugs and the need to stay inebriated had her crapped up in the same way he had been crapped up by radioactive isotopes. He felt guilty for not having been there when she had almost died of the overdose, and for having been absent during the first critical moments, hours, and even days after the event. His guilt was intensified by the fact that he had not been there to help her because he had been selfishly nursing his own alcohol-induced sickness. Even while he had been withdrawing his commitment to her because he disapproved of her vices, his own vices had caused him to abrogate his responsibility to her. The thoughts pained him, and he wished he could force them from his mind. He wished he didn't understand the tragedy so clearly, that he could live ignorant and unfeeling as though he was some tiger stalking in the jungle or a shark lurking in the sea.

He stood in front of a Gainsborough portrait of an aristocratic boy. He found the famous portrait beautifully pastoral, but he was taken by the pretense of the boy; he was so childlike, yet he was trying so hard to look like a man. Then he moved on through the collections of Greek and Roman antiquities. Room after room was filled with the artifacts of the Roman civilization that had thrived at

Pompeii until the explosion of a volcano had seared its culture, art, and technology into history. What did it matter that they had strived to build a beautiful city and to fill it with masterpieces of art? In a moment, it had all been destroyed, along with their lives. He came across a painting by Christen Kobke: *The Forum, Pompeii* (1841). The painting depicted the Forum at Pompeii, crumbling from the weather and the sun, with grass growing up through the paving stones of the streets and trees growing wildly through the walls of the buildings. A small typed note at the bottom read: "Theme: Civilization Versus Destructive Nature." Ted immediately knew this to be wrong. Nature wasn't destructive at all, it was restorative. The painting didn't show nature destroying something of inherent value; on the contrary, it showed nature reclaiming itself from the technologies of man. But the technological machine man had created seemed now to be out of control, self-sustaining, no longer vulnerable to the restorative efforts of nature. The technological machine had created plastics that pollute forever and radioactive isotopes so dangerous that the machine itself could not devise methods to dispose of them. The very bay the Getty Villa overlooked was highlighted on the federal government's list of Superfund pollution sites. It was one of the most contaminated spots in the country, with thousands of leaky insecticide drums causing the fish caught there to be covered with festering tumors. Ted felt guilt and despair, and he whispered to himself, "If only nature could wipe away a nuclear reactor without a trace. If only it could instantly clean away the poison in my lungs."

He left the museum feeling a heightened resolve to leave his past behind. He felt hatred for the expensive sports car he drove home, and disgust and fear for the world it represented. He would sign the legal papers to liquidate and go somewhere the machine wasn't so strong. Somewhere in the mountains—he had the trip to the Rockies—or a Mexican beach town where heavy industry meant catching a two-hundred-pound fish with a hook and line. He would find a small town without industry or nuclear power, somewhere pristine and innocent. There must be a place where the machine of modern technology had yet to prevail. Then he remembered the envelope Tony had tossed across the beer-soaked table to him only a few nights before. Maybe Hawaii.

Jeri walked quickly across the slushy parking lot to her car. The noontime sun was rapidly making a dirty wet mess of the night's new snow, and she struggled to maintain her balance without slowing her pace. Five hours earlier, when she had parked outside the Life Sciences building, the snow had still been falling through the darkness. Her advanced biochemistry final exam had finished only minutes before. She had been one of the last to turn in her test and leave the testing room, but she had spent most of her time checking and rechecking her work.

She knew she had aced the test, but there was one equation she had been unable to remember. She was frustrated because she had memorized the recalcitrant chemical formula weeks before and had studied it again several times in the days leading up to the exam. She knew it. But during the test, when she really needed to remember, the structures had refused to be organized into the correct equation. Now she was rushing to her car because the answer waited inside her heavy biochemistry textbook. She could picture the book where she had left it, tucked safely inside her nylon backpack resting on the passenger's seat.

She was impatient to get in the car, and her cold hands felt stiff and clumsy as she fumbled with her keys. With her hands stuffed deep in her pockets and her legs pressed tightly together, she waited for the car to warm up. She tried again to remember the equation that had eluded her, but it was no use. She couldn't remember it. When the car was warmer, she pulled the oversized textbook out of her backpack and turned directly to the well-thumbed section where the stubborn equation dwelled. The instant she saw the printed line, her mind wrenched the equation, clear and distinct, from the alphabet soup of her memory. She moaned in disappointment; she had known this equation very well.

Jeri knew she would receive one of the best scores in the class, but she wanted to have the top score—or, barring the solo top score, to share a tie with another perfect 100 percent. She knew now that the best she could expect would be a 98 percent, a very good score, but she knew there were at least two other people in the class who strived for perfection. Medical schools had very demanding entrance requirements, and it didn't take many forgotten equations to eliminate a person from consideration.

"Damn, I knew that equation." Jeri spoke the words softly over the cold steering wheel, feeling hurt and amazed at her lapse of memory, her unfocused eyes staring blankly at the breath-fogged windshield. She closed the book with a gentle, reverent slowness and paused to gaze fondly at the familiar cover. She stared at the book for what seemed like a long time, feeling the heaviness of its mass in her lap and the chill of the binding on her thighs, before pushing it gently back inside the pack.

She unzipped the small outside pocket of the backpack and removed a metal Band-Aid can. Holding the metal box with both hands, she applied pressure to the lid with cold thumbs until the top opened with a metallic pop. Inside were two hand-rolled cigarettes. She put one of them between her lips, closed the can, and put it back in the pocket of the pack. Unconsciously, with the fluidity of autonomic motion, she simultaneously pushed in the dash lighter and released the emergency brake. She pulled out of the Fort Lewis parking lot with a lighted marijuana cigarette between her lips. She smoked the joint alone as she began the drive to the Ram Restaurant and her afternoon shift as a waitress.

She had not worked at the Ram for most of the week preceding the biochemistry final. She had worked hard memorizing the material, had stayed away from alcohol and had gotten plenty of sleep. She had also smoked pot at the end of each day. She believed it relieved the pressure of academic competition, and it helped her fall asleep. Donna had been a big help in this regard. When she received a delivery of very strong California grass, she had insisted that Jeri take a small Baggie full. She had argued that since Jeri had been so sharing when she had pot, she was obligated to return the favor. Jeri had objected at first, but Donna had simply shrugged and left the fat bag of green buds on top of her dresser. When Donna had left her bedroom, Jeri had held the bag in front of the vanity mirror, smiling at the reflected perfection of the plump Baggie. It had looked so clean and full, so complete and heavy, that Jeri had rolled several joints immediately, thinking she would soon find a way to repay her friend.

She had studied very hard for the biochem final, spending twelve to sixteen hours each day working on the rote memorization necessary to do well in the subject. Jeri hated memorization and the work had been dreadfully dull. Thankfully, she was not one who waited until the last minute to study. She had always been the turtle type; the hares always seemed to run out of time.

She deviated little from routine when she reviewed for a big test. She started each day at six in the morning, sitting at her makeshift desk in her room at Donna's apartment, drinking strong ginseng tea to bring her awake. Sometimes eating toast to stop the morning cravings, she studied at home until it was time to leave for school. She normally arrived at the library before opening time at eight, usually seeing the same group of tired-eyed overachievers at the entrance. After spending the morning in her favorite cubicle in the physical sciences section, pangs of hunger would drive her to the Student Union for a tasteless meal of granola bars and juice. Then it was back to the library until the sun went down. The darkness signifying dinner, she would return to the Student Union for a few pieces of pizza or a folded paper bowl of cheese nachos. With dinner finished, she would study in her cubicle, immersed in the work, until the library closed at ten. After returning to the apartment, if it was sufficiently quiet, she would organize her study notes. Finally she would relax, get high and go to sleep.

It was not unusual for Donna to have company over, the music playing at the apartment-dweller maximum, a decibel level that drifted up and down as the tolerance of neighbors in nearby units varied. But the neighbors were usually included in the small group of the people that came over to smoke pot and listen to music, and they would play it loud while watching the late movie with the volume turned down. On most nights like this Jeri would be pulled reluctantly into the party, and she would drink some wine and smoke some pot before going to bed.

But during this last week before finals, Jeri had wanted to work especially hard on the biochem. She knew she would need to put in some nighttime hours at home, and she had asked Donna if she could keep the parties to a minimum for a few days. Donna had agreed without hesitation, explaining that she only had people over to be polite. She said she liked keeping her apartment clean and that the hard-partying kind of people usually made a mess, burned holes in things, and generally showed a lack of respect for other people's personal property. Donna promised that if Jeri needed the apartment quiet for a few days, she wouldn't allow the usual club-house atmosphere. Donna had kept her word. During the week prior to Jeri's biochemistry exam the visits to the apartment had been hushed and businesslike.

When people did come over, Donna would only let them stay for short periods, fifteen minutes or half an hour. They visited quietly, passing into the apartment with a few hushed words, Donna greeting them with a smile, or a hug, or occasionally a kiss. They would sometimes be a fellow food server at the Ram, sometimes an old friend from another job, or sometimes a friend of a friend. They would smoke some of Donna's pot and talk about the weather or skiing. Finally, in an awkward, risky, and uncomfortable parody of business, money would be given to Donna and a ziplock bag would be given to the guest. The people never stayed very long, only long enough to buy some of Donna's popular California pot.

Jeri had been aware that Donna sold pot almost as long as she had been living with her. She didn't feel that Donna did it to make money; it was her way of returning a favor or helping a friend. In the circle of friends that Jeri had joined since the breakup of her marriage and her move into Donna's place, drugs were a normal part of life. The purchase and sale of drugs were necessary components of the possession of drugs, and the possession of drugs was a necessary prerequisite to getting high. Getting high was the thing that drove the machine, the friend-to-friend mechanism of drug trafficking in their small, intimate community of shared drugs.

This circle of good young mountain people was not a group of television-style, gun-wielding, profit-seeking drug dealers, but it was a circle of drug traffickers nonetheless. Jeri had drifted into the group without thought or restraint. She had continued to work hard at school and to maintain a high standard of responsibility at the Ram Restaurant. She received A grades in her advanced classes in biochemistry and physical chemistry, and she continued to make a living at the restaurant, earn and save money, pay her bills. She functioned in every outward way she had before she had become part of the unorganized group, but she now smoked marijuana every day, drank alcohol almost every day, and snorted cocaine when it was offered, although it was far too expensive for that to be very often.

She had found she enjoyed the conflicting effects of marijuana and cocaine as they competed for her consciousness, her mind working fast, yet playfully slow. As she drove from the slushy parking lot after her biochem exam, the joint between her lips, this was the feeling she experienced; the feeling of conflicting drugs, one a depressant, another a stimulant. During Jeri's week of marathon study, Donna had helped in another way. After one of the hushed visits, Donna had come into Jeri's room with a tiny packet, a homemade envelope that Jeri recognized as the type used to carry coke. She had traded some of her popular California grass for it and had given it to Jeri as a gift, to help her stay up and study. Jeri had been using the cocaine during the week before the biochem final, adding long hours of study that had never been possible with ginseng tea. She had been more than nervous at the exam; she had actually been a little shaky.

Leaving the parking lot, with the smoke of the joint filling her lungs, she began to regain the difficult balance, the perfect feeling, promised by the use of multiple, conflicting drugs. She drove somnambulistically out of town, out of Colorado and into New Mexico. She arrived at the outskirts of Farmington, New Mexico, as if in a trance, her mind basic, blank, and calm. She slowed to below the twenty-five-mile-per-hour speed limit and studied each of the old buildings as she passed. Her drive had not been planned, but somehow it had not been unexpected. As she drove through the outlying area of the town, she noticed its negative aspects, the rundown condition of the neighborhoods she passed. It caused her to compare this town to the little mountain town where she lived and went to school and worked. The soft concept of work solidified into the hard reality of the Ram Restaurant; she was stunned by the sudden realization that she had forgotten to go to work at the Ram. Quickly, the drive became tedious; the pleasant shadows of late afternoon changed instantly to the threatening darkness of early night. She was exhausted after too many drug-aided hours of study, and now she was getting very tired. She turned her car around, making a U-turn in the middle of a deserted four-lane street. The lights of the city faded in her rearview mirror and she felt a strong desire for home. She drove out an unfamiliar stretch of dark desert road, the stars becoming brighter as the road became darker.

Cresting a small hill, a bright beacon of white fluorescent tubes shone into the night. Far down the road—a long, straight road that glistened cold and razor gray in the reflected light—gleamed a brilliantly lighted but seemingly abandoned gas station. She drove down to the lonely lights, her car very slow for the long road, the radio searching endlessly for a station. The gas station was a cube of native rock architecture, a whitewashed leftover from the 1950s with hand-painted signs and a gravel driveway. New pumps and a small grocery store indicated that progress was, at times, pulling the station grudgingly into the future.

A teenage Navajo girl was at the cash register; perfect skin and a shy dimpled smile showed her young age, but her large body made her seem years older. Jeri avoided conversation with the girl because she still felt high and obvious to the world. She paid twenty dollars for gas and bought some fruit and juice for the drive back up the mountain.

Her mind still foggy with pot, she pumped the gas and looked out across the lonely country, increasingly more visible in the brightening moonlight. It stretched out in an endlessly sparse repetition of small rocks and thin brush, the ground still dappled by the glistening white remains of the last low-altitude snowfall. A slight stirring of the cold, silent air filled her nostrils with the strong chemical smell of the gasoline, and as though she had breathed smelling salts, it helped her refocus on the small task of filling the tank. She hung the fuel nozzle on the pump and chanced to look across the brightly lighted islands and into the rock building. The fat young Indian girl smiled her beautiful, lonely, dimpled smile and waved, her image framed by a large plate glass window. Jeri waved back as she got in the car, feeling a sudden need to be on her way. She fumbled with the emergency brake and gearshift and almost stalled the engine. Coaxing the car out from under the white lights in a series of bumpy jerks, she pulled onto the two-lane highway with relief.

She drove away from the gas station until the first small rise in the road shielded her from the strong lights. There, she pulled her car to the side of the road and stopped. With the hand brake engaged and the transmission in neutral, she pulled her green backpack from the backseat and unzipped the pocket. She took out the Band-Aid can and from it retrieved a square paper packet made from the slick pages of a photo magazine. The packet was a rustic study in the Japanese art of paper folding; the intricate folds produced a tight rectangular envelope that was ideal for the transport and recovery of cocaine. The crisp flap tended to quick, brittle movements, so she opened it slowly, careful to avoid sudden snaps of the paper that would eject the precious drug from the handcrafted envelope.

When she had it open, she found that the once finely ground powder had been fused into a thin, brittle cake by time and pressure. Using a short length of plastic tube cut from a McDonald's drinking straw, she broke the cake into a more workable form; then, putting the straw into one nostril, she inhaled a rough mixture of fine powder and irregular flakes deep into her sinuses. The abrupt presence of the foreign substance deep inside the delicate breathing passages caused a reflexive need to sneeze. She resisted the autonomic requirement with a rigid-spine effort of will, closed her nose with the thumb and first finger of her right hand, and painfully coughed the air her body had intended her to sneeze. Her eyes watered, and she could feel the next sneeze response already at the edge of her self-control, but the drug quickly anesthetized the thin membranes of her sinuses and the sneeze response was attenuated. She sniffed the drug farther into her sinuses and tasted the alkaline tartness at the back of her throat. She found a slightly used tissue in the glove box and wiped the tears from her eyes. She dabbed at her nose, but did not blow; instead, she continued to sniffle the drug ever deeper into her head.

The long drive back up the mountain to Durango was made surrealistic by her exhaustion and the cocaine-induced acuteness. She entered a trancelike state of mindless vehicle operation. She watched the turns as the car moved through them, knowing that it was she who directed its course, yet she was not conscious of the method of that direction. The drive became a visual on a wide screen, her seat at the steering wheel the best in the theater; she watched as the car was propelled through the barren flatness of the desert, then up and into the forest. Eventually, after clips of time without duration, she found herself back at the Ram Restaurant, neatly parked, with eyes wide and engine off, an empty orange juice bottle between her thighs.

She pushed her way from the car, swinging the door hard into one of the yellow-painted steel posts that supported the neon hotel sign that invited passersby to stop and enjoy the warm comfort of the Ram Restaurant. She walked to the glass entrance doors with her gloves dangling from elastic bands clasped to her coat sleeves. She was riding a wave of relief that flowed from the end of another difficult finals week, yet she knew that she had again let down the others at the Ram Restaurant. She hoped that she would have the strength to explain without making excuses. She had done wrong, and would accept responsibility for her lapse.

She walked silently to the hostess podium and made eye contact with the manager of the restaurant, a pretty middle-aged woman with stiff, short black hair and soft brown eyes. Jeri loved this woman and her husband, a tall, thin cowboy who ran the resort's engineering department. The two were surrogate parents to many of the young people who worked at the resort and were far from home. They always seemed to have the time to listen or to help out. The couple had never had children, and Jeri thought they enjoyed helping the young resort workers because of it. The couple gave of their time generously: running errands, playing chauffeur, and offering soft, strong shoulders on which many of the young people had shed tears of misery and of joy. Jeri's eye contact made the older woman's face burst into a wide smile.

"Hi, Jeri. How'd it go in your chemistry final? I just know you did well." She continued to smile her loving smile as she waited for Jeri to answer.

"Oh, I did OK—but I forgot a simple equation." Jeri stumbled over the words, unable to believe that there would be no mention of her dereliction of duty. She felt she had betrayed this sweet woman who had given her so much, but the manager was acting as if nothing had happened, as if her absence had not been a rejection of trust, that it did not matter that she had been absent, that it had not lessened her in some important way.

Jeri knew by the exacting principles of her own upbringing that she was a slacker; worse, by not showing up at her appointed and agreed-upon time, she was a liar. She should be punished or, if not punished, ostracized by her co-workers, but the others seemed to accept her failure without judgment, even without notice. She was stunned by the possibility that all she had been raised to believe about duty and responsibility was somehow untrue. She knew from her own success at school that it was true in many ways, but she also knew that some of the others at the restaurant were happy in their irresponsibility, happier in many ways than she had ever been. She waved a confused farewell to the manager and wandered without predetermination to the Sheep's Head bar.

Inside, behind the shining bar counter, stood the big bartender—Donna's odd boyfriend. He seemed, to Jeri, to be waiting for her to arrive. He was standing quietly behind his station, leaning forward, his arms were extended to the bar, the large weight of his upper body supported through the arcs of his outstretched arms. His head was slightly cocked to one side as if accentuating his ability to hear. His perfectly combed gray hair rested thickly over his ears. His immobile gray eyes smiled gently. His mouth was a single flat line extended emotionlessly between mustache and beard. He showed no hint of judgment or contempt, no twitch of condescension. His body contained no movement, no coiled strength, no threat.

For an instant, Jeri was reminded of Donna's cat as he patiently waited for small birds to blunder too close for safety. She sensed that this encounter with John was to be different; not only was she there without Donna, but he seemed poised for the meeting, prepared in some unknown way. She trusted the older man, yet she knew him to have dangerous knowledge, primitive experience. She walked slowly up to the bar, carefully measuring her step, wanting not to stir the predator from its tall cover. She maintained eye contact with him until she was fully seated.

"Damn, John. You look like a gargoyle hanging over the edge of a gothic cathedral." She felt her confidence coming back now that the mass of the bar separated them.

"The better to see you, my dear." He spoke as he smiled with his entire body. His eyebrows pulled up, his hair jerked back, his arms drew away from the bar to an invisible position behind his back, and his body moved up and down as he rolled his weight on the balls of his feet.

"I think you may have hit the nail on the head with the wolf metaphor, *Big John*." She plopped her large purse on the bar with a dramatic pantomime of immense weight. She also smiled.

The bartender went to his well and began to shovel ice into one of his stainless-steel blenders. "You know, Jeri," he said, sounding slightly bored, "I don't know where that 'Big John' tag got started, but I would like you to call me by my name." He looked up from his well to make eye contact with her, and she immediately felt a connection with the man she had never had before. His eyes changed suddenly from gray to blue.

"OK, no problem. John?"

"That is perfect. Now, let me make you a drink to cut the dust, no pun intended, and bring the old biological clock back to normal space-time."

A theatrical wave of his arm to turn on the blender resulted in a deafening mechanical roar. The blender screamed for half a minute while Jeri watched the man working behind his bar. He cooled a large glass in his ice, spinning it with one hand with an impatient expression on his face. After several spins, the glass came quickly up to the bar and he carefully rubbed a fresh lime around its lip before inverting it in a rimmer of sugar. His hands disappeared in a blur of motion; whisking the blender can from off the motor with one as he simultaneously switched off the power with the other. In an instant the room was silent. Jeri could hear the wood breaking in the fireplace across the room as it burned, a soft snapping that sounded loud now that the powerful machine was silent.

"This drink is full of juice," he said, looking at her as he poured the pale red drink into the waiting frosted glass. His eyes did not drop to the glass while he poured. "Full of citrus and cranberry and ice, and most importantly for you, I think, lots of vodka." Still without a measuring glance, he poured the last of it from the blender can, the final trickle filling the glass to just below the sugarcoated rim. He deliberately placed the drink in front of her, careful to center it on a tiny square bar napkin.

"This is the antidote you need."

"Antidote? Why do you think I need an antidote?" She sipped the drink through the straw without lifting it from the napkin. It was tart and sweet like some exotic fruit, and so cold that tiny crystals of ice were forming as it traveled up the straw to freeze her tongue. She could not taste alcohol at all. "Mmmm, this is really good, John."

"I thought you might like it. You look like you will be up for a week."

"Really, you can tell?" She reflexively reached for her eyes with both hands, touching the puffy tissue below them gently with the tips of her fingers. She felt a wave of panic as she realized she had been very high while she drove through parts of two states. She slumped on her stool as she envisioned being stopped by the New Mexico Highway Patrol; a failed sobriety test and an arrest for drug possession were just what she needed to fill out her resume.

"Don't worry, Jeri, I'm an expert at this sort of thing. It's a bartender thing, part of the job. You should avoid getting behind the wheel of a car, though, especially after a couple of those." He glanced down to the drink. "But you're in luck. I was just cleaning up before you came in. I will join you for a quick drink and chauffeur your dilated eyes home. In return I ask only that you provide me with a small measure of what you have been using to poison yourself." He turned his back to her. Walking to his station, he tapped his knuckles on the bar. Ice and glass rattled together sharply as he continued to speak. "I heard you had a big test today. Is that why you got high and missed your shift?"

His directness startled her. She had been silently asking herself very similar questions, only her own hadn't seemed to cut as close to the truth. She began to answer before she had fully formulated her reply.

"I don't know. I finished the test, got into my car and just started to drive. I drove all the way to Farmington. I didn't even think about work until it was too late."

"Like I said, don't worry, you work too hard anyway." He positioned himself across from her, with one foot up on the beer cooler, his weight leaning through his elbow to his knee, a barrel glass of anonymous brown fluid in one hand and a cigarette in the other. "But it will pay off for you, Jeri. I know it will." He lifted his drink in a mock toast before taking a long sip. "There are a lot of people who can make a go of life using their wits and their looks. It's easy, why put out extra effort?" He took a drag from the cigarette and shook his head. "But you know, these same people could do so much more if they had the drive to push themselves into getting an education, the discipline to work hard toward a goal. Drive like you have, Jeri. You are a very special person and I am honored to drink with you."

Jeri wondered about the new openness the big bartender was showing. She had always thought of him as cynically secretive, observing but not participating. Unless, of course, she realized, he was setting someone up for one of his convoluted practical jokes. She wondered if that was what he was doing now, setting the stage for some raucous comedy with her as the buffoon. She imagined herself standing wide-eyed, a cream pie speeding sloppily into her face. The image caused a moment of mirthless appreciation that dissolved into a barren carelessness; she no longer cared if she was the target of some thoughtless joke. She realized with slack surprise that she felt empty and valueless, unworthy of embarrassment. She judged her life devoid of meaning and her essence sterile of sensitivity.

Exhausted but not sleepy, she mused on her life, viewing the world through eyes made wide with dilated irises; then the hard, loud sound of the blender caused her head to snap tightly back on her neck. She had been staring unconsciously at the rows of bottles standing at the ready on the narrow, brightly lit shelves of the back bar, and her eyes struggled to focus as she turned to the sound. Mercifully, he was not facing her or seeing her zombielike performance as he worked. His eyes were rigidly aligned with the blender, watching only his fingers on the machine's power switch.

The squealing metallic crushing ended and she watched him pour another of the pinkish drinks into a tall frosted glass. He picked up her drink with one hand and his own glass, already refilled, with the other, before he came back to her end of the bar. She followed his movement as he placed the new drink in front of her. It didn't seem possible that the first drink was already gone. She couldn't calculate how long she had been drifting, but it didn't seem that enough time had passed to have finished her drink and for him to have made her a new one.

"It may be none of my business, Jeri, but it seems to me you are as low as I have ever seen you." He smiled sadly, with one corner of his lip curled higher than the other, and the eyebrow on the same side of his head pulled up into a gray question mark.

"None of your business, huh? You seem to be doing all right. Who drank my last drink?" The dull humor of her question made her chuckle. "I am in a weird mood, aren't I?"

"Not at all, not for someone who is finishing finals week. I'm locking this place up. Enjoy your drink." He put his drink down next to hers before moving away to finish his side work. He replaced and locked the night panels over the back bar inventory, and as he worked, he told her a stupid joke over his shoulder. It made her laugh. When he was finished, he poured their drinks into Styrofoam cups and put the glasses into the empty sink with hollow-sounding clunks. "Now let's get out of here before someone comes in." They walked together, the bar between them, toward the door. At the end of the bar he came closer to her and put his arm lightly around her shoulders.

The restaurant was closed and deserted as they passed through it on the way to the outside doors. They stopped at the coat rack to get John's jacket and Jeri helped him put it on. They left their coats unbuttoned and did not bother to put on their gloves. Outside, the sky was overcast and the air was cold and refreshing, but not bitter. They stood close together as he unlocked the passenger door of his old four-wheel-drive van. She had ridden in it before and thought it an incongruous remnant of a decade long past, but fortunately the curtain behind the front seats was closed and she couldn't see most of the tacky interior. The van warmed up quickly, and they drove out of the driveway without mishap on the frozen surface.

At 550 John turned right instead of left, toward the mountain and away from town—away from the apartment Jeri shared with Donna.

"Hey, I thought you said you were going to drive me home."

"I did," he said as he turned toward her, smiling. "I just didn't say whose home."

Ted had never been to Hawaii, and he hadn't planned to go on this trip either. He had been thinking about returning to a quiet, tropical place just south of Puerto Vallarta, but Tony's generosity had made the trip to Hawaii easy, and it had satisfied his preference for someplace tropical. The destinations had seemed equivalent, irrelevant. The sudden accident at the SENGS site and his subsequent reevaluation of his life had filled him with a longing to get away, to recuperate somewhere far from the industrialized, technological culture of LA. He had wanted only to leave Los Angeles as soon as possible, to go someplace where he could forget about nuclear energy, drug overdoses, and jumpers. Tony was a big fan of Hawaii, often describing it glowingly after his trips there. He said it was the best place in the world to go to get away.

Since the flight from LAX to Honolulu was over five hours long, Ted had decided to upgrade to first class. He normally flew economy, and occasionally business on long flights, but he had discarded any justification for thriftiness, wanting to make the best of Tony's gift. When he had called the travel agent to change his flight reservations, she had been surprised that this was to be his first visit to Hawaii. Her voice had been full of vicarious pleasure as she talked about the state, and she had been very pleased with the quality of the accommodations.

"It's an oceanside suite at the Moana Surfrider Hotel in Waikiki," she had told him. But her happy statement had been the first time Ted had heard that he would be staying in Waikiki, and he had been disappointed. His impression of high-rise Waikiki was one of the reasons he had never vacationed in Hawaii. When he had asked if he could go to another, less populated island, the travel agent had explained that Tony's trip was a package and could not be changed. Hearing his disenchantment, she had quickly reassured him about the beauty of Waikiki, explaining that it was usually the first place people visited, and that the sun and the sand and the views were exceptional. She had been especially excited about the hotel, saying it was a part of Hawaiian history and one of the best in the world. He had resigned himself to Waikiki, and they had finalized the arrangements.

During the flight, the rear of the giant jet was overfilled with passengers. He took a walk around the plane after the in-flight movie and was astounded by the number of small children that were aboard. The large economy compartment was active with the rustling of nervous movement and the whining of disturbed babies. Many of the smallest seemed to be without their own seats, perching on top of obviously uncomfortable parents. There was also, in one area, the sickening smell of vomit. He returned to the first-class cabin after one turn through the rear of the plane and he did not leave it again for the duration of the flight.

The plane made a wide turn as it glided toward Honolulu International Airport, and he could see the city below as the big jet banked. Hundreds of high-rises were crowded together on a narrow strip of light tan sand. A friendly flight attendant saw him looking out the window and leaned over from the aisle to point out the Diamond Head crater. The bowl was dotted with buildings and rows of military vehicles. The flight attendant explained that the air traffic control center was based in the caldera. The overhead view of the volcano was unspectacular and unfamiliar. Ted wondered why it warranted the obvious pride shown by the Honolulu-based flight crew.

They landed on a long runway that had been constructed offshore, on the once living reef of the island. The Reef Runway was far from the main terminal, and a ten-minute taxi was required for the pilot to commute to the gate. When they had finally stopped and the Jetway had been extended, Ted stood without haste to pull his carry-on bag from the overhead storage. He was the last person in the small forward compartment to arrive at the exit. There, the friendly flight attendant stood blocking the departure of the surging economy passengers, giving the forward cabin priority. The faces of the people crowding out from the rear section looked exhausted and impatient.

He exited the Jetway into a glass boarding room crowded with people waiting to board other flights. They formed a narrow gauntlet of colorful clothing and expectant faces amid a clamoring babel of conversation. Although the terminal held the usual mob of surging passengers common to any airport, it was tangibly different from others he had known. The open-air walkways, with sweeping views of blue skies and green mountains, were brushed by a pleasant tropical breeze. Another difference was the way most of the travelers were dressed. Almost all the men wore flowered shirts, and many of the women wore tight T-shirts or tops exposing bare midriffs. Obviously tourists, most wore shorts, exposing deathly white or recently sunburned legs, and more than a few heads sported comical straw hats that bobbed above the crowd. The necklaces of colorful, aromatic flowers were ubiquitous.

He exited the terminal by passing down a short escalator to the ground floor baggage claim area. Just outside the security zone were dozens of people waiting to meet the new arrivals. Their dark skin, exotic dress, and colorful flowered hats indicated they were members of the local hospitality industry; tour company banners and welcome signs waved over their heads, printed in more languages than Ted could identify. Beautiful young Asian girls wearing muumuus and holding armloads of flowers stood in the midst of the confusion.

To his surprise, among the crowd of paid greeters Ted spotted a hand-printed sign that shouted his name with a comical stutter of penmanship. A woman held the sign in one hand and a flower lei in the other. She noted his recognition of his name with a smile. Evidently well practiced in welcoming strangers, she walked straight to him and stood on her toes to place the necklace of purple-dyed flowers over his head. She wore a simple sleeveless dress with a pale flowered print. Her light brown hair was straight and parted on the side, shiny clean and recently combed. He guessed her to be somewhere in her late twenties or early thirties.

"Hi, I'm Shawna Howard," she said. "I work with Century 21. I'm a friend of Tony's. He asked me to meet your flight." She seemed adolescently awkward, apparently unaware of her own femininity. Her skin was tanned in a way that implied she spent much of her time outdoors, and her body appeared strong and athletic. The cotton dress ended halfway down her thighs, but was not seductive. She did not wear stockings, and dirty white open-toed sandals flapped on her feet.

"Tony thinks of everything, doesn't he?" The flowers were damp and felt clammy around his neck, so he removed them as they walked, wondering if the purple dye would run on his clothing. As she led their way from the terminal he spotted a large plastic trash bin with the word *mahalo* printed in block letters across its front. He was tempted to drop the lei in it, but the woman seemed sweet and innocent, and he didn't want to hurt her feelings. He decided he would keep the flowers until he got to his hotel and lifted the wet necklace back around his neck.

He carried his two checked bags and the woman, Shawna, took his carry-on. They walked from the air-conditioned coldness of the building to the warm day and bright sunlight outside the baggage claim doors. Ted was astonished to find that, in spite of the glaring sunshine, it was raining lightly and a magnificent rainbow arched across the sky, so near it seemed impossible. A rusted and threadbare Cadillac limousine was waiting for them at the curb. It had a yellow taxicab sign on its roof and a smiling heavyset Hawaiian standing beside it. The driver also wore one of the ubiquitous flowered shirts. Watching the driver place the bags in the trunk, Ted did not notice Shawna entering the passenger's compartment. When he saw her there, he was a little surprised, but not uncomfortable, and he joined her on the wide backseat of the car. Once they had taken to the road, the driver turned his head slightly and said, "Aloha," over the back of the front seat. They were out of the airport and driving down the Nimitz Highway when he offered his "visitor" conversation.

"Have you been to Hawaii before?"

"No, this is my first trip."

"Vacation or business?"

"Vacation, I suppose. I really don't know what I should call this. A retreat, maybe."

"I think you'll like the Sheraton. It is one of the most famous hotels in town. One of the first on Waikiki. Very posh."

"Only the best for Tony's friends," the woman said happily. "Tony said you were going to stay a week." She was smiling at him, but he couldn't tell if she was being dryly seductive or simply friendly. She was sitting erect in the sagging cushion of the limo seat; her knees and lower legs showed the faint scars of a person who enjoyed her sports. Her cotton dress buttoned down the front and she wore no slip. Her small breasts strained at one of the chest buttons and a hint of white bra was visible where the light material pulled apart.

"That's right, a week."

Ted couldn't believe it. He could not believe he had been set up so cleanly. He did not want to become involved with a woman on this trip. He did not want to fall in love. He did not want to have a friend. He did not want to get laid. Tony was a great guy, but if this thing was what it appeared to be, a setup, Tony had misjudged him. Yet the woman was not being overt. She seemed unaware of the sexuality she exuded. Ted realized there was no way for him to challenge the situation; if he accused her of being involved in some contrivance, she would surely turn out to be some innocent relative of Tony's wife. It had been a long, tiring flight and his defenses were down. He decided he would try to relax and not look at her. There was no reason to speak of it.

"He asked me to do a computer search on some properties for you. I have some printouts here if you want to go over them. I'll need a day or so to schedule showings."

Ted took the blue and red legal-sized folder from her. Inside were several pages of computer-generated listings, a map of Oahu, some tourist brochures, and a complicated-looking booklet entitled "Understanding Lease Hold Ownership."

"I'm very tired. I think I just need to get checked in to the hotel and take a nap."

"Take a look at those comps when you can, we don't need to start looking right away. Oh, look. That is Aloha Tower to our right.

There are lots of good restaurants there. You'll have to let me buy you dinner after we do your business." As she spoke, she pointed out his window without leaning across his body. Her voice had a happy, musical lilt that made her sound foreign, exotic. During the rest of the drive into Waikiki, Shawna supplied a running tourist-guide monologue of the passing sights.

The hotel was in the heart of the city. Shawna explained that the Waikiki district was part of the city of Honolulu, but isolated from it culturally. Unless they worked there, the locals rarely visited. The hotel had an easily missed white façade with an old Hawaiian-style veranda. The driver turned in to a compact circular driveway that led from Kalakaua Avenue, the wide one-way street that ran parallel to the beach, and parked in front of a broad set of steps. Several young men in high-buttoned white uniforms ran from behind the bell desk to meet the car. They had the car doors open and were collecting the luggage before Ted could ask about the cost of the ride. He spoke to Shawna over the flutter of activity their arrival had stirred.

"Shawna, how is this being paid for?"

She walked closer to him so she could speak in a low, drolly conspiratorial voice. "The car is included with the hotel, but the driver expects a tip. Them too." She looked at the bellmen. Ted knew the conventions of tipping and usually tipped well, but Shawna's whispered explanation had made him feel that she thought him cheap. He knew that to overtip now would only make him feel worse. He gave the driver a five-dollar bill, and it brought a smile to his face.

"Much mahalo. Have a good visit," the driver said as he walked around the car, wiggling his thumb and pinkie at them. "Aloha." He got into the car and drove away. When Ted turned back to the hotel, one of the bellmen was waiting with his bags piled on a cart at the top of the steps.

"This way, Mr. Johnston, to check in." He began to push the cart into the hotel.

"Well, my car is in the garage," Shawna said. "I'm very glad to have met you." She held out her hand to shake and Ted took it.

"Yes, nice to have met you, too. Thank you for meeting my plane." Their handshake communicated nothing. It was not awkward and it did not linger.

"No problem. I'll call you in a couple of days, after you have had a chance to relax. Good-bye." She turned to the bell kiosk and waved. "Mahalo, guys. Aloha."

Ted watched her quick stride as she walked away, unable to decide what he thought about her. She walked down the broad sidewalk, her simple dress pulling tight across her narrow waist and round hips, and disappeared into a throng of Japanese tourists. He walked up the steps, crossed the veranda and entered the old-fashioned lobby.

It was an open room with large, warmly colored carpets on a hardwood floor. The decor made Ted feel he had gone back in time to the nineteenth century. Across an atrium the room opened onto a courtyard, and across the courtyard was the ocean. Surfers were riding the long, low waves into the beach. The activity did not seem extreme, but relaxed and effortless, a simple trip down a blue and white escalator.

He registered before walking back across the lobby and down another set of broad white wooden steps into the hemispherical courtyard. The area was dominated by a single giant tree, its canopy a leafy green ceiling high overhead, its trunk and limbs thick and massive as gray stone. He walked under the tree, past the pool, to the beachside bar. White glass-topped tables with big sun umbrellas flanked a round bamboo bar with a grass roof. He looked down the narrow beach as it curved to his left and saw the familiar, yet new to him, sight of Diamond Head. This view of the crater, familiar from countless TV and movie exposures, was genuinely beautiful. The waitress greeted him by saying aloha, and he replied by saying it for the first time, feeling slightly silly and phony. He drank his scotch and soda slowly, watching the boaters and surfers and beach people.

When he finished the drink, he signed his name to the check and walked back inside the hotel. He felt relaxed and tranquil as he rode the elevator up to his room. He wanted to call Tony at his office before he left for the day. He knew he was up to something, but he couldn't tell if it was a romantic setup, or if he expected him to do property inspections during the trip.

The small suite had a separate bedroom with a single king-sized bed, a sitting room with a narrow lanai, and a very large bathroom with elaborate fixtures. The view from the sitting room lanai was spectacular, a 180-degree span of Waikiki Beach with Diamond Head crater at one end. He took the phone with him onto the lanai, sat in one of the two deck chairs and called California. Tony was waiting for his call.

"Ted, how was your flight? Did Shawna meet you, OK?"

"It was fine. Yes, I met Shawna. What the hell are you up to this time? Are you trying to set me up with a date?"

"Ted, I'm surprised at you. Shawna is just a business associate. I just thought it would be nice if someone met your plane. Your first visit should always be met with a kiss and a lei." He chuckled nervously.

Ted ignored the tired double meaning as he watched the dinner cruise ships leaving for the outer bay waters. Shawna had said they would troll slowly, serving up heavy doses of food, drink, and the famous view of Waikiki.

"Come on, Tony. You better come clean. She's going to call me in a couple of days. She thinks I'm here looking for a house or something. If you don't tell me, I might not be nice about how I tell her I'm not."

"OK, OK. Here's the deal. She has a half-dozen multiple families I was going to take a look at if I came over. I thought you wouldn't mind letting her give you the island tour while you checked them out. I probably should have told you about it, but it isn't important. If you don't want to have a private tour guide for a day, just tell her to wait for us to come over."

"No romantic setup?"

"Hell, no. But we did think it probably wouldn't hurt you to get to know her a little. She is a very good person, and believe me, she is not on the make. She's as safe as they come: an engaged born-again Christian."

"Why do I get the feeling this is all for my own good? Like exercise or penance or something. I hope your wife hasn't taken an interest in my miserable life."

"Look, just enjoy the beach for a few days. Then, if you want, spend a day looking at the properties. If any of them seem worthwhile to you, we'll come over and take a look ourselves. If not, you saved me a lot of trouble. OK?"

"OK. I just hope she doesn't try to convert me."

"Not Shawna, she is strictly the personal relationship type. If you don't have a relationship with God, she will feel sorry for you, but she won't apply any pressure. You'll like her, believe me."

"Hell, Tony, I already do."

They finished the conversation discussing a few details about the properties Tony had lined up. It didn't take long, as the concept was very similar to properties they had purchased together in Southern California. After they said their good-byes and ended the call, Ted dialed room service for a drink. He faced the traveler's evening quandary; he was tired and willing to stay in the room with a room service burger, but at the same time excited by the prospect of the new adventure waiting outside.

He had begun to study the television and the incorporated radio system when there was a knock on the door. The bellman entered pushing his luggage cart, and a room service waiter followed close behind. The waiter, holding the drink chest high on a polished stainless-steel tray, walked across the sitting room to the writing table and placed the glass there. Ted signed the check and the waiter left, saying mahalo as he slid by the baggage. The bellman put his bags in the closet, hanging his garment bag on the rail, before explaining the electronic panel that controlled the lights, television, radio, and air-conditioning. When Ted refused his offer to unpack his baggage, he backed out of the room with a bow. The bellman had waited for Ted to make his way upstairs before delivering the baggage. It was obvious he hadn't wanted to deprive the new guest of his demonstration, or himself of a chance for a gratuity. Ted gave him a good tip as he went out the door.

"Mahalo, sir," he said. "Just give me a call if you need anything."

Ted took the drink into the bathroom and stripped for a shower. He wondered, as he luxuriated in the cool water, if he would have the energy to go downstairs to the dining room for dinner. It was six p.m. Hawaii time, but his biological clock was telling him it was hours later. Not late for a man with nothing to do, but he had had drinks on the plane and more here; that always made him a little tired until he had something to eat. He stood in the shower drinking the scotch, facing away from the water as it massaged his back, thinking he should get out and see the town. He had not been out since the night Mary had overdosed herself. That had not been his fault; she would never have let him prevent it.

He could hear the radio clearly; an energetic rock-and-roll song was beating insistently from the bathroom speaker. The rock music and the cold water had an energizing effect on him, and when he finished his shower, he unconsciously began the ritual of shaving and dressing for a night out. He wasn't sure how to dress. Shawna had said that a flowered shirt was the local equivalent to a business suit, so he didn't think a coat and tie were in order, even if he could stand wearing them in the warm climate. He settled on some tan slacks and a blue polo shirt.

He went down to the beach bar for another drink and carried it across the courtyard to the quiet open-air restaurant. He liked to start a stay at a new hotel with visits to the bars and restaurants. He liked to meet the people working food and beverage and give them tips. It was always handy to have the people who made the food and the drinks remember you. He recalled several occasions when he had been able to squeeze a cold sandwich from a restaurant long after it had closed. That wouldn't happen if it was the first time the help had a chance to meet you.

The food was good and unpretentious, the safest kind for a hotel restaurant to serve. He ate pasta and drank water. The Hawaii tap water tasted as good as any of the bottled waters popular in the California market. He told the middle-aged Hawaiian waitress that the water was so good someone should start exporting it, and she surprised him with a frown. She seemed inexplicably irritated by his innocent comment, saying Hawaii didn't have enough water to ship it out, that Hawaiians had to keep something for themselves. It was his first encounter with the Hawaiian desire to save what little was left of their devastated kingdom. But when she picked up the bill and saw her tip, she smiled broadly, her anger about the water apparently forgotten.

"Mahalo, sir, come back again before you go home," she said with the characteristically musical accent.

"You'll see me around, I'm sure."

Ted wandered under the huge banyan tree toward the lobby and the Kalakaua entrance. At the bell desk, he asked where a grown-up should go for a night out in Honolulu and the group of idle bellmen answered simultaneously, their mixed voices and strong accents making it impossible for him to understand a word. Then they argued quietly with one another, excluding him from the discussion. Their final consensus was Restaurant Row or Aloha Tower.

"Let me ask you this," Ted said, starting to have fun, "what does it cost to get a car to drive you around this town?"

"What do you want to spend? My sister's husband has a limo and tonight he is just being a taxi. I could call him on the car phone. He would go with you tonight, show you where to go. Not for much."

"How much is 'not much,' my friend?"

"Not much. You'll see."

It turned out to be 150 dollars for the night, or at least until Ted became tired and went home. The car was another of the aging white Cadillac limousines that were ubiquitous in the city. He gave the bellman a good tip before getting into the car with his brother-in-law.

The driver introduced himself as Junior, and spoke almost entirely in a dialect Ted would later learn the locals called pidgin. He was understandable, but sometimes he used phrases or words that seemed only to have meaning due to the rich hand and body language that accompanied them. His voice was powerful, but not deep in tone. He was serious about his driving and only rarely turned his head away from the road to speak into the passenger compartment. He seemed to take great enjoyment from the act of driving, and he spoke few words to disturb his pleasure.

Junior was a big man. Not big in a human sense of the word, he was big in the sense used when discussing geology or shipbuilding. He had walked around the car to open the door, and Ted had noticed that although he seemed to be moving slowing, he was not. It was an illusion of size; the kind experienced when a large jet is seen from the ground and seems to hang motionless on the air. His gait was characterized by the size of him and by the rolling stride that transferred weight from side to side as he stepped. He wore tan slacks, a pink aloha shirt, and an impossibly large pair of inexpensive rubber flip-flops. They drove east, toward Diamond Head, down Kalakaua Avenue, with Junior driving carefully and Ted gawking out the window. Thousands of tourists were flowing, a human tide, in both directions on the wide sidewalks.

"Restaurant Row, yeah?" The statement was clearly a question, and Ted understood it, but he was intrigued by the musical quality of the speech. He rewound his mind's recording of the sentence and played it back to himself. It was beautiful to hear and wonderfully economical with words. Ted felt the question asked again, but it had not been vocalized.

"That's what the guys at the hotel said. I really don't know. What do you think?"

"Good deh. Dinner, yeah?"

"No, I already had dinner. I'm just looking for where the people go, you know, nightclubs."

"Yeah, yeah. I know. Still early, you know. Ten, eleven best." He raised his massive arm, lifting his hand off the steering wheel to look at his watch. "Only nine now, brah, best place open late. Where you want go now?" He asked himself the question, obviously wondering where he would recommend. "I know, by Aloha Tower, nice place, on da water, outside, Honolulu people go deh *pau hana*." He spent one of his rare glances over the back of his seat. Ted felt uncomfortable and very far away from him sitting in the back of the car, flanked by empty liquor decanters and the inactive electronic control panel. "You know, *pau hana?* Get togeddeh, after work."

"That'll be fine, Junior. Let's go there and park. We can have a drink and decide where we'll go next."

"You want I park?"

"Sure, you can have a drink or something to eat. You can try to explain this town to me."

"OK, boss."

The bar was on the second floor, overlooking Honolulu Harbor. Completely outside, including the staircase from the ground floor dining room, the entire lounge area was covered with sailcloth awnings. A sweet breeze drifted from Sand Island across a narrow strip of water. The clientele was very much like that found in thousands of other after-work bars in hundreds of other American cities. The difference was again the dress; it seemed that a banker's business suit consisted of slacks and an aloha shirt. There was, of course, also a racial difference; most of the patrons could trace their lineage to Asia or the South Pacific. The beauty of it was their apparent lack of interest in the differences. They walked up to the wooden bar and ordered—Ted another scotch and Junior a Coke.

Ted turned to face the small lanai and leaned back against the bar. He recognized these strangers. They were the young people who worked in a city: bankers, lawyers, brokers, accountants. He knew them and he understood them; he had, after all, been through it himself. He was glad he had passed through the period, only now he didn't have a period of his own. He frowned and took a long drink of the scotch. When he brought the glass down from his mouth he noticed that Junior was looking at him, and it seemed that he was smiling approvingly.

"Dey got 'ono pupus heah." Junior passed the plastic table tent to him.

"Ono pupus? Will I like it, Junior?"

"Pupus food. Snacks. 'Ono is good."

"Sounds perfect. Which one should we get?"

"Mix plate da best: teri steak, fish, squid, French fry. Dat's da kine."

When the pupu plate arrived it was clear that Junior was hungry. He tried to get Ted to eat, but Ted replied that he had eaten a big dinner at the Moana. The most Ted could do was taste the different meats and offer his approval. None was wasted. While Junior ate, Ted had another drink. It was ten thirty when they left the outdoor bar. At the top of the stairs, Ted took another look around; the young professionals, their happy-hour numbers thinning with time, were so confident they seemed brash, even arrogant. Had they never experienced a loss? Could they not see the reality of the world? Ted frowned and shook his head as he turned back to the stairs. Junior was watching him carefully from below.

"Dem yuppie boys don't know nothin', brah. Just make-believe. Hear 'em in my taxi all da time, cryin' deh blues." Junior did not believe these people held all the answers either.

The first club they visited was in the center called Restaurant Row, a concentrated linear arrangement of restaurants on the ground floor of business buildings. There was a cover charge and Junior volunteered to stay outside, but Ted wanted the big man to keep him company.

"Hey, Junior, we're in this together. Come on, I'll buy you a drink."

"OK, brah, let's go. I know da bouncer, brah." He led the way past the line of people waiting to pay their cover charges and approached the Hawaiian doorman, who was dressed in a black tuxedo. He was almost as big as Junior, but he wore the formal dress easily. He stood next to a table at the door where a local girl was taking the money, using his great bulk to discourage any reluctance to pay. Ted watched as they shook hands in the Hawaiian way and greeted each other profusely. He listened as they conversed in the thick dialect of the island, speaking of relatives and jobs and past acquaintances. They seemed to talk for a very long time, extending this friendly opening conversation far longer than seemed necessary. Yet the two big men were comfortable with the long period of superficial talk. They were obviously not in any rush to finish, and they remembered and spoke and laughed beyond anything Ted had ever experienced. Then they ended it with another handshake, and Junior led Ted past the girl collecting the money without stopping. "My auntie's neighbah," Junior said, "dey go da high school togeddeh."

Inside the club were the usual loud music and spilled drinks. The club operated on the tired disco motif, only with new music. Ted had seen it before, and had seen it done better, but he had never seen a clientele having a better time. It was much too loud to talk and much too crowded to find a seat. Ted gave up on the club when the bartender, on whom he had been waiting, ignored him and left the bar abandoned. He turned to Junior and screamed over the pounding music, "I've had it. Let's get out of here before I start making a scene."

"OK, boss. Let's go." Ted followed the huge body through the crowd, reminded of a running back following a pulling guard through a hole on a football field, or a soldier behind a tank on a battlefield. At the door the big man turned to Ted, looked down into his eyes and said, "I know da place, brah."

They parked in an overly full asphalt parking lot in front of a small wooden building. When they entered the club, Ted was assaulted by the music and the women. Several stages jutted into the room, and on stage more than a dozen young women danced nude. The men in the room were a mix of international sailors, Japanese tourists, local construction workers, and the senseless, unexplainable, unidentifiable drunks that were always hanging around this kind of bar.

Junior led him through the crowd of men and dancers to the bar on the far wall of the strip club. They each had a small five-dollar draft beer and watched the dancers from a safe distance. The young women were uniformly beautiful, had slim figures, and represented most of the more common races. Ted found himself watching a Polynesian woman who seemed little more than a teenager. Her facial features were angelic and her skin unblemished. Long, thick black hair fell heavily down her back. She seemed out of place crouching and spreading her legs to any drunken man with a dollar bill. She really wasn't dancing. She simply walked back and forth looking beautiful until a dollar bill was raised in her direction. Then she would walk to the money, move gracefully to her knees, and lean forward into the leering upturned face. Pressing her breasts against the bill, pushing them together with her palms, she would take the dollar between them. After one these efforts, when she stood up and lifted her arms to pull back her hair, Ted noticed that she had undergone a poor breast enlargement procedure.

Ted was washed by a sudden tide of disgust; not with distaste for the scars or the ill-fitting implants, but with abhorrence for the need of the already perfect girl to artificially enhance her breasts. He turned from her to find Junior watching him, not the girls, apparently waiting to see how he would react to the environment. Ted pushed his unfinished flat beer away and jerked his head toward the door. Junior moved from the bar, leaving his glass untouched, to lead the way through the crowd toward the exit. Ted slowed near the beautiful Polynesian girl to drop a ten-dollar bill on the stage below her, and for a moment she didn't seem to recognize it as a tip. It had not been shoved lewdly into her garter or pushed face-first between her breasts. Outside again in the clean, cool air of the Honolulu night Junior spoke to him.

"*U'i nani* dancers, deh, brah," the big driver said, and Ted understood him to mean they were beautiful. "Come and go, except da girl. Local girl, brah, from Wai'anae. Smokes da crack, brah."

"It's a goddamned epidemic. I just left someone on that path, back in LA."

The next stop was a bar on the Honolulu end of Kalakaua Avenue, on the edge of Waikiki. Junior had noticed it was getting close to midnight and had mentioned that it might be late enough for the club to be full—it opened at ten and closed at four in the morning. Junior explained that it was a favorite of Honolulu dwellers as well as young tourists from the mainland. The music was deafening, the repetitious urban-style beat pounded at the ears mercilessly. They walked up a flight of stairs to another, much smaller room, one side of which was walled in glass. The entire room overlooked the downstairs dance floor. The atmosphere was hot and humid, but the sound level was less head splitting. Couches near the windows were already swarming with patrons drinking and staring down through the glass to the dance floor.

The two men pushed their way to a tiny bar in the farthest corner of the room. Four or five stools stood at the bar and people were trying to sit on them. Drinkers, surging to be served at the little bar, continually leaned into the people on the stools, pressing them sideways like small boats at a dock during a heavy tide. When Junior pushed up to the bar, the bartender leaned across it with his hand outstretched to the big limo driver turned nightlife tour guide.

"Junior, brah, what brings you out in the nighttime? I thought all you do now is work."

"Dat's it, brah, no time to party. Just work." He turned to indicate Ted. "Dis guy's from da mainland. I been takin' 'em around, you know. He's OK."

"Yeah, yeah, it's cool. You want something to drink?"

"Couple a beeh, bucket ice." The bartender returned with two bottles of Bud and two Bloody Mary glasses full of ice. Ted followed Junior's lead and poured his beer over the ice. Ted had put a ten-dollar bill down on the bar, but the bartender pushed it back at them.

"It's OK. This one's on me."

They both said thanks, and Ted pushed the ten into the small shelf on the back edge of the bar.

"See dat, he's a good guy." Junior smiled as he nodded to the bartender. He picked up the large glass between his thumb and index finger as if it were a shot glass, and Ted wondered how much alcohol it would take to get the big man drunk. He knew it would be much more than a few beers.

They moved away from the bar and closer to the windows overlooking the dance floor. The thick glass vibrated with every thump of the bass beat, rattling ominously in the mountings. The ground floor was packed densely with the crowd, and the transition between the dance floor and the table area blurred as the dancers mingled among the tables. The music was very fast and the dancers were dancing fast with it. They all seemed in their very early twenties, possibly late teens. They danced in an uninhibited, spontaneous free-form fashion, tied more to the music than to any partner. Most of them were sweating profusely, their hair wet and stringy. There was a band playing on a low stage, crowded together into a space barely big enough to hold them, and they too were jerking rhythmically to the music and sweating. The bathrooms were situated at the flanks of the bandstand so the people using them were forced to traverse the most crowded part of the dance floor.

They drank their beers and watched the club below them: the band, the dancers, the onlookers, the people struggling to get to the restrooms. Then, without a word, Junior started toward the stairs. Ted knew without asking that they had stayed as long as they were going to stay. On the way out, Junior said hello to a bartender working the ground floor bar, and then they were on their way to another club. Ted realized that Junior was starting to take control of the evening, which was just fine with him. He didn't know the town or the people, and it was becoming clear that Junior knew both well. Their next stop was back at Restaurant Row. Junior parked the limo in the valet parking driveway, and the valets said hello and shook his hand with the Hawaiian handshake that reminded Ted of a secret society. Ted offered to pay for the parking, but Junior smiled and said, "Don't worry, brudda, it's OK."

Back inside the complex, in the courtyard between the towering office buildings, it was relatively quiet. They walked to a kiosk-type bar in the center of the courtyard, with the clear tropical sky overhead and the cool, clean air around them. The circular bar was tiny, but tables and chairs around it held many people relaxing quietly. The high-energy party people were all inside one of the loud clubs of the complex. Here people could talk. Ted noticed that there was an engagingly high percentage of female customers sitting together, socializing in pairs or in groups of three or four.

They sat down at the bar, but the bar stools, being made from the steel seats of scrapped farm tractors, were not particularly comfortable. Still, Ted liked the quiet ambiance of the bar and was glad that Junior had selected it as a stop on their tour. The bartender was preoccupied with a conversation he was having with two pretty young women seated at the other side of the circular counter and he took what seemed to be a very long time to serve them. When he came around to their side of the bar to greet them, he was smiling and obviously didn't think he had slighted them.

"What can I get you guys?" he asked happily. Ted answered by ordering his usual scotch and soda, but Junior surprised him when he switched from beer.

"I think I'll have a vodka martini, straight up," he said, his pidgin accent gone.

"Gee, Junior, that's quite a change from beer," Ted commented, as he leaned over the bar to watch the bartender mix the drink. He seemed to enjoy making it, taking his time to find the proper glassware, mixing it with exaggerated theatrics, shaking it over one shoulder. "You know, Junior, I didn't even know they made those things anymore." He turned to the big man, and for possibly the first time since Ted had met him, he was not smiling.

"I have a tendency toward the past. Sometimes I think that is all I have left. The past and memories." Ted was a little drunk, jovial and obtuse, but Junior's transition to grammatically correct English stunned him into sobriety. Before Ted could get his head organized to question the big man, it was evident that he was opening up in a special way.

"Once, my family was very strong here. We were farmers, here." He paused with the look of one who thinks he has not been understood. "I don't mean here in Honolulu. I mean here, under this building. My family grew taro, and they had a fish pond down by the water. Things were different then—there were many

Hawaiians then." He stared at Ted without anger or censure, but the look made Ted feel embarrassed. He didn't know why, but he felt guilty of some ancient wrongdoing. "Do you know the story of Hawai'i, Ted?" Ted was shocked by the sound of his own name; it was the first time the big Hawaiian had spoken it.

"Until this conversation, I thought I did. But now, somehow I know I don't. But I have a full drink, and I'm listening."

"It's really a short story. A story of a weak country in a very strategic global location. An agrarian culture, without even the basics of metallurgy, faced with the colonialist nations of the industrial revolution. It was no contest, really. The world hardly noticed the conquest." He raised his martini glass, the delicate stemware lost in his powerful hand, and Ted was reminded of a doting father holding a tiny cup from at a daughter's miniature tea service.

"The history books dwell on the end. It was a very short, bad, regretful end. But the part that seems to be forgotten is how long our king kept the wolves at bay, playing one against the other. He was very good at it. Unfortunately, no one lives forever, and his lineage was not up to the task of keeping the modern world at spearpoint."

Ted couldn't believe the man was telling him these things. He was just a drunken, radioactively poisoned castaway. He couldn't fathom what Junior had seen in him to justify dropping his façade of pidgin English to begin a conversation of meaningful, nonconfrontational self-exposure.

"The businessmen were responsible, but the local U.S. military was the muscle. It happened, it had to happen. The only thing is..." He paused to take another sip from the dainty stemmed glass. "We were not the kind of people who knew how to resist it. We had fought our wars, one clan against another, one island against another, but we really didn't realize that, at that moment in time, it was the moment to fight to the death for our culture. It is almost gone now, here on O'ahu. The Hawaiians were just not prepared to resist a major world power. War was a symbolic thing for us, not like for the Vietnamese or Koreans—those cultures have been at war for thousands of years. They were hardened by their locations before global politics ever noticed Hawai'i. America rolled over the Kingdom of Hawai'i, and no one even noticed. Now I drive a cab.

Once, I could have said that I was of royal blood. Funny how the world is, isn't it?" He tipped the tiny glass back and the martini was gone. When he turned back to Ted, his big smile had returned.

"Shit, is dat da kine? You listen, too, brah. Tink da night over. I drive you back now, yeah?"

Jeri awoke with a start, frightened and disoriented. John was sitting on the edge of the bed in which she was lying, squeezing her shoulder in one of his huge hands. He pulled his hand away when she jerked her throbbing head up from the bedding.

"Hey," she mumbled as she grew more awake, "where are we?" She realized that the shoulder he had pinched to awaken her was bare and she pulled the bedclothes up to her neck.

He was extending a large glass canning jar to her; it was apparently full of water and ice. "Have some water, Jeri. It will make you feel better."

Jeri propped herself up on her right forearm and took the water with her left hand. The frigid glass was almost painful to hold, yet in her dry throat the water was simply cool and wet. She continued to drink until the water was gone and the ice rattled into her nose.

He took the glass and stood up; he was wearing blue jeans and a green plaid flannel shirt. He reached into his chest pocket to remove a small plastic bottle of aspirin. He placed it carefully, but obviously, on the nightstand before leaving the room.

Jeri collapsed back on the bed, turning her face to the shiny black satin pillowcase. It reeked of stale cigarette smoke. She was miserable: her head ached, she felt sick to her stomach, she had awakened in a bed clothed in tacky black sheets, and she was having trouble remembering details from the previous night. She heard tap water running somewhere nearby, followed by the sound of a glass of ice being filled with water. She lifted the satin top sheet surreptitiously, self-consciously, and found herself naked beneath it.

She remembered more of the night before; they had driven up the highway from the restaurant for a few miles before turning onto an unpaved side road. The road had wound narrowly into the woods, with a lively stream flowing along her side of the van. She remembered they had been laughing and joking with each other when they stopped on a small bridge made from the metal frame of a railroad flatcar. He had stopped the van in the middle of the one-lane road as it crossed over the stream. The bridge had no side barriers, and she remembered that they had smoked a joint together, sitting on the edge, dangling their feet inches above the splashing current. He had kissed her there, sitting on the edge of the bridge, and she had kissed him back.

They had finished the drive to John's mobile home without Jeri saving any memory of the trip. She did remember stomping up the wooden steps and her surprise at the warmth that greeted them at the door. Inside, they had watched late-night television, sitting together on a playpen living room set upholstered in dark brown velour. They had had more to drink and had smoked more pot. Finally, still overstimulated by the cocaine she had taken earlier, she had accepted the tranquilizer John had offered. He had taken one too. They had settled in to watch television, sitting close, with his arm around her shoulders. She remembered kissing him as if it was a memory of the movie they had watched on television. They had kissed, and the kissing had led to the inevitable progression of his hands on her body. She remembered that she had not really wanted to have sex, but she had just been too tired and wasted to object. When it had come time for her to disagree, to tell him to stop, she had simply been too disinterested to make the effort. She remembered being led from the living room by the hand, with her vision obscured through a sleepy fog. Then, in an instant of horror followed by rising nausea, she remembered being an intoxicated participant in drowsy, mechanical sex.

The heavy sound of his walking approached, the gentle tinkling of ice adding counterpoint to the bass beat. She forced herself to sit up in the foreign bed and pulled the sheet across her breasts. When he pounded back into the room, Jeri recognized that the floor sounded hollow in the familiar mobile home way.

"There are aspirin next to the bed. Here's some more water." He smiled down at her with an open, friendly face. "You know, these jars hold thirty-two ounces. I wouldn't chug too many of them. You could have an embolism or something. I'll be out in the living room if you need me."

She watched him carefully until he was all the way out of the room. His plaid bulk plugged the doorway when he passed through it. She followed his journey from her by listening to the heavy footfalls pound ever more quietly away.

The childproof cap of the aspirin bottle proved highly effective; she struggled to remove it, the hard white plastic cutting into the soft skin of her thumb. She finally found success by wrapping the cap in the corner of the satin sheet and pulling with the full force of hangover-weakened limbs. The cap popped off into the knotted black sheet and the bottle flew in the opposite direction, trailed by a hail of white pills. She swept up a handful and poured them back into the bottle before pulling the sheet over the rest. She took two of the aspirin, despite the stubborn instability of her stomach that cautioned her to wait for some Tylenol. They felt large and chalky as she forced herself to swallow, her eyes tightly closed, her head tilted back. One of the pills stuck to her dry throat, and she feared she would gag and begin to throw up. Gulping more of the icy water caused the impression of the un-swallowed pill to go away, but a bitter medicinal taste remained in a part of her throat that the water would not rinse.

After taking the aspirin, she surveyed the room. The smallness of it surprised her; it was no more than twelve square feet and was crowded by the king-sized bed. The walls were covered with dark paneling, and the single window was hidden behind very thick curtains that blocked any light from entering. Her clothes were draped over a wooden chair that was wedged into a corner of the room where a tiny half bathroom peeked through an open door.

She listened for the sound of his footsteps before leaping up from the bed and to the chair. She yanked her panties and bra from the pile and put them on quickly, watching the door for him. Her jeans and blouse followed the underwear; her heavy white socks and boots were not, evidently, in the room. She edged sideways through the narrow space beside the chair to the bathroom. Once the door was closed and locked, she partially undressed to relieve her demanding bladder. Sitting, she stared directly into the mirror over the sink, only a foot or two away. She was so colorless her skin seemed gray, except below her eyes where it was dark and puffy. She felt physically and emotionally ill.

When she was finished, she noticed that the bathroom was surprisingly clean. The sink and toilet were shiny, the mirror was unspotted, and a pile of neatly folded hand towels waited on the molded plastic countertop. She wondered who was doing his housework, hoping it wasn't Donna. She leaned over the sink to wash her hands and face, frowning at the bags below her eyes in the mirror. She dried with one of the clean towels, balled it up, and threw the soggy wad on the linoleum floor, next to the commode. She left the bathroom and the bedroom without looking back at the unmade bed.

Her own footsteps produced the familiar empty pounding as she walked down the narrow hallway to the living room. The dimly lit hallway was covered with the same dark wood paneling she had seen in the bedroom, crowded with indistinct photographs of nameless friends and esoteric memories. At the end of the depressing passage she exited into the slightly remembered living room of the night before.

John was half sitting and half leaning on a wrought-iron bar stool; his long legs were extended straight from his hips and his ankles were crossed. His bulky upper body flowed backward with astonishing flexibility, concealing most of the small counter of a portable service bar. One of his hands grasped a Bloody Mary that rested on the bar, the other relaxed, palm down, on his thigh, a smoking cigarette between the first two fingers.

"Hey, kid. How do you feel this morning?" He raised the cigarette to his mouth and inhaled deeply. "Care for a Bloody Mary?"

"No thank you, I couldn't stand it. Where are my boots?"

He motioned with the cigarette toward the big sofa set. Her boots and socks were on the floor there. Jeri only wanted to be out of this dark tribute to the day sleeper, to be free of the stale smell of old cigarette smoke. She wanted to see the light, to feel the sun on her face, to breathe the clear mountain air. She needed to sleep and then to think. She was having trouble believing that she had become entangled in this embarrassing situation.

"I just want to go home and get some rest before work." She sat down to put on her boots. "Can you give me a ride to my car, please?"

"Absolutely. I've been waiting for you to get up." He leaned his head down to the glass to sip off the top inch of fluid before lifting it to his mouth. He continued to drink until only discolored ice remained. "No celery. Bloody Mary is just not the same without celery." He stood slowly, unbuckling his pants immodestly to tuck in his shirt. He seemed to realize what he was doing, and turned away as he readjusted his belt. "Come on, I'll take you back to the Ram."

He walked over to her, and as she stood she felt his hand move to the small of her back, gently guiding her to the door. Shocked by the familiarity of his touch, she moved quickly forward to minimize the pressure.

When he opened the aluminum-framed door, the brilliant white light of day crashed into the dimly illuminated room. Jeri was instantly blinded by the brightness of the light, but the pressure on her lower back kept pushing her onward through the doorway. She turned her head away from the light, trying to help her eyes adjust by focusing them back into the room. As she passed through the doorway, eyes directed to one side, holding her hand like a shade over her brow, her last vague perception was of a black tripod and video camera standing sentry near the door. More than any other lapse of memory, she was the most disturbed by not being able to remember seeing the video equipment by the door when they had entered the trailer the night before.

Outside on the wooden porch, she stopped to dig through her purse for her sunglasses as John pushed the metal door noisily closed, rattling the knob to verify that it was locked. She put on her sunglasses while walking down the four steps to the wet ground. She used all her willpower to avoid thinking about the video camera, or her inability to remember critically important periods of the night before. She let him guide her to the passenger's door of the van and waited impatiently as he unlocked it. Once they were seated inside with the engine warming, John turned to her as he removed his own sunglasses.

"I'm sorry about last night, Jeri. It's all my fault. I shouldn't have brought you here. I don't know how we ended up doing what we did. Believe me, I never thought that was going to happen. Not ever. You are one of the most wonderful women I have ever known, and given another chance—knowing about you and Steve, I mean—I would have pursued you like a dog. But I guess you know I'm in love with Donna. We just sort of made a drunken mistake last night. I'm sorry."

"Yeah, I'm sorry, too. Poor Donna."

"Jeri, I'm not going to tell Donna—or anyone else, for that matter. I hope you will forget this ever happened. Chalk it up to too many drinks, too many drugs, and too little sleep. It was nothing. It never happened. OK?" He turned back to the steering wheel before shifting the van into gear.

Jeri could not make sense of the events of the night before or of the morning as it had unfolded so far. Her head ached and her stomach was light and threatening. She couldn't remember how she had let herself wind up in John's bed, and she didn't want to think about it. She wanted to forget the incident, to black it out of her mind, to erase the incomplete, foggy memories like some corrupted file on a computer disk. It was done; she had betrayed Donna, and worse, she had betrayed herself. She just wanted it to be over.

"Yeah, it never happened," she said sarcastically.

The trip seemed to take hours as she fought feelings of nausea and self-disgust. She sat stiffly, with her hands in the pockets of her coat. She tried to make her body small as she sat in the big captain's chair, wishing she could become invisible, hiding behind her dark glasses, enduring the interminable ride. She wanted to believe that there had been some extenuation for her actions, that there could be some absolution found for her guilt. She struggled with her memories, trying to mitigate the fact that she had lost some valuable part of herself before passing into a drug-induced coma in a strange bed. She wanted to believe that she was the same person she had always been: intelligent and strong and beautiful. But she was becoming aware, for the first time, that she was different; she was less than she had once been.

In this moment of perception, she realized she was lost, adrift in frightening currents of self-degeneration. She had somehow lost herself after Steve left, lost her essence in a flood of new experiences. The night with John, the drugs, and the alcohol were all newly encountered facets of herself. She felt dirty and ashamed, contemptible and cheap. When they pulled up behind her car, she rushed to open her door and get out, ignoring John's feeble attempts at farewell. She left the van behind without looking back, hearing it drive away as she unlocked the car door.

She was miserable as she drove home, her shame amplifying the pain and nausea of her hangover. She parked in the street outside the apartment and climbed over the mounds of icy snow piled at the curb. She felt marked and obvious as she walked, every movement of her body awkward and stiff. She wanted to run up the path to the apartment, but she forced herself to walk, resisting the overwhelming desire to hide.

She pushed disjointed memories of the night before from her mind as she climbed the steps to the tiny covered porch. Then, as she fumbled with her keys, trying to recover normalcy, she looked to the brass mailbox mounted beside the door. It was stuffed to overflowing. There were many bills, some for Donna and some for her; grocery store sales flyers, sloppily printed on poor grade newsprint; and an official-looking letter from the School of Medicine, University of California, Irvine. Her purse fell unnoticed, spilling its contents across the damp floor of the portico. Her heart pounded and her breathing stopped as she tore the letter wildly from the envelope.

"Congratulations! Ms. Singleton,…The admissions committee is pleased to inform you…Your acceptance…contingent upon completion of…"

Jeri exploded with happiness and excitement; she couldn't finish the letter because of the shaking of her own hands. Then, in the next instant, she realized that she was screaming at the top of her lungs, waving the letter above her head, jumping up and down in the foyer of Donna's apartment.

Ted got up late the morning after his nightclub tour with the enigmatic Hawaiian. He awoke refreshed. The sluggishness caused by crossing too many time zones too fast had been defeated by the only efficacious treatment: long uninterrupted sleep. He showered quickly and dressed casually, putting on shorts, a loose-fitting polo shirt, and canvas deck shoes without socks. He breakfasted in the beachside cafe of the hotel. It was a typical hotel buffet, with the usual heavy American dishes, made unique by the addition of many traditional Japanese favorites: rice, soups, noodles, and fish. He assumed it to be a concession to the Japanese tourism on which Waikiki depended. He spurned the ham, bacon, eggs, and potatoes, and enjoyed the taste change offered by the Japanese diet. The light dishes were excellent, perfect for the first meal of the day. Thinking he might adopt the tradition, bring the idea of noodle soup for breakfast home with him, he suddenly realized he didn't have a home any longer.

After breakfast, he wandered out from the hotel and walked down Kalakaua Avenue. He window-shopped the upscale stores on the avenue and browsed through the cheap tourist trinkets at the International Market Place, eventually finding himself on a street called Lewers. It was busy with wandering tourists and street-side hawkers. Sidewalk vendors were passing out flyers, thrusting the sheets into reluctant hands, and selling everything from T-shirts and tanning oil to dinner cruise tickets and submarine rides.

Lewers Street was lined with a half dozen hotels that were all named the Outrigger; only a second designation, such as Tower, Reef, or Waikiki, made them identifiable from one another. In front of one of these touristy cookie-cutter hotels, he stopped at an outdoor activity desk and rented an open Jeep for the day. The rental agent, who was dressed like a beachcomber in long cutoffs, a tank top, and a raggedy straw hat, was loud and animated. When Ted gave him his charge card, he became very helpful, loading him up with brochures and maps and advice. He explained that most *malihini*, newcomers, made the circuitous drive around the island, and he marked the route on the map of Oahu, cautioning him against going further west than Kapolei.

"They don't like *haoles* out there, my friend," he said.

The trip started with a drive down Kalakaua Avenue, with Waikiki Beach on the right side and Diamond Head Crater directly ahead. It was a beautiful day, sunny and cool, and Ted began to think that the Hawaii trip had been a good idea. The narrow road around the ocean side of Diamond Head rose gently higher and the view became spectacular. He stopped at a turnout to watch windsurfers skipping over the waves toward the shore; the brightly colored sails contrasted beautifully with the incredibly blue ocean. The water was the blue he had only seen in movies, very different from the green Pacific of the California coast. Farther out on the horizon was the hump of another island. He unfolded the map of the state on the hood of the Jeep, trying to compare the location of the distant island to his vantage point on Oahu. He decided it must be the island of Molokai.

He spent the rest of the day driving, stopping frequently to take in the beauty of the less populated areas of Oahu. He thought often about the driver of the night before, Junior. He was a puzzling man; a happy-go-lucky, pidgin-speaking local guy on one hand, a well-educated, erudite thinking man on the other. He had said he would have been royalty, and Ted wondered what it would be like to be part of a dethroned royal family. He had only been in Hawaii one day, and already he was learning about the Hawaiian sovereignty movement.

The Hawaiian people wanted their country back, and some were still spitting mad about the American seizure of their land over a hundred years before. Junior had warned Ted to be careful about some parts of the island, places where the Hawaiians had become illegal squatters on their own lands. He had warned, "There are some angry people out there. Better watch yourself, *haole.*" While still in the crowded tourist area of Waikiki, Ted had wondered how dangerous it could be, but during the drive around the windward side of the island, he saw the lonely beachside campsites of the Hawaiians, homeless in their own homeland. On these beaches he did not stop.

He drove all the way across the north side of the island to the part the locals called the North Shore. It was a beautiful drive, but rather long and without much to see or do. He stopped at a casual restaurant in Haliewa for a late lunch; it was crowded with tourists, canoe club rowers, surfers, and townspeople. The food was simple but good. Adjoining the dining room was a souvenir shop with the usual worthless stuff tourists find impossible to do without. The drive back across the center of the island became much more interesting as the two-lane road passed through wide expanses of cultivated pineapple. It was after six when he dropped the Jeep off at the tattered rental lot on Beach Walk Street.

He was beat. The long drive in the open Jeep, with the sun and the wind burning his skin, had drained him. When he started the walk back to the hotel, he realized that his jet lag had returned. He walked the few blocks to the Moana with diminished interest in the tourists or the attractions that beckoned from the doorways and sidewalks along the way. He crossed the lobby to the elevators without slowing to view the ocean or the courtyard active with music and dancers, and he walked the hallway to his room oblivious to the thick carpets and the tropical wallpaper.

He realized the next day that he had entered his room and had passed through the sitting room without noticing the new basket of fruit on the table. He had dropped onto the bed without caring that it had been turned down or that a mint lay on the pillow, and had fallen immediately into a deep, exhausted sleep. He also realized the next day that as he had fallen asleep, still clothed in shorts and shirt, he had not noticed the emphatic blinking of the telephone's red message light.

He awoke in darkness at five the next morning and saw the blinking message light while still lying in bed. He called the message desk from the bathroom phone to find that Tony had called the previous afternoon, while he had still been driving around the island. The message lacked detail, including only Tony's name and phone number. At first he wondered if he had somehow missed a showing with Shawna, but when he thought about it, he knew she had not attempted to schedule a meeting.

It was still too early in California to get Tony at his office, so he ordered coffee, juice, and toast from room service. He showered and dressed while he waited for his order to arrive. The casual tropical garb allowed him to finish dressing in fifteen minutes; the simple breakfast didn't arrive for forty.

He ate out on the lanai, enjoying the early morning view of Waikiki and reading the *Honolulu Advertiser* that had been slipped under the door of his room. He read the business section carefully, studying the thick real estate insert, trying to understand the intricacies of the local market. When he was finished, he checked the time—it was six thirty, eight thirty California time—late enough, he thought, to call Tony at his office.

The connection had a long echo delay that made speaking over each other's words inevitable. The receptionist at Tony's office was completely flustered by the failure of the long-distance system and couldn't adapt to the delay. He finally hung up and called back. The second connection sounded as if they were across the room from each other. She was maddeningly quaint in her interest of the Hawaiian weather, her banal questions heightening his impatience. Eventually she was satisfied and put him through to Tony.

"Ted, I'm glad I finally got through to you. Your cell phone number keeps giving me a 'no service' recording. Have you heard the news about Shawna?" His voice was strained.

"No. I haven't seen her since she dropped me off at the hotel. I've been expecting her to contact me here. I haven't turned on my cell phone since I got here. I'm sorry. What's wrong, Tony?"

"She's...had an accident. We're taking the noon flight and should be there by three or four your time. We'll be checking in at the Sheraton. I asked them to put us on your floor."

"Damn, Tony, what's happened? What can I do?"

"I want you to be near her. She has family there and that should be all she really needs, but I want you to be near her until we can get there. Anything she or her family needs, Ted. You understand?"

"Sure, only what's happened? Where is she?"

"She is at the Queen's Medical Center, in intensive care. She and her fiancé were walking down the beach on Magic Island last night and were attacked."

"Jesus, that's right downtown."

"Yeah, but still not pacified territory at night. They must have thought they could talk their way out of trouble."

"Are they all right?"

"No…they were tortured and…and raped for hours. She may not make it, he is already dead."

Ted realized he was standing straight, his back rigid. The muscles in his legs and arms were tight and hard. He tried to relax but could not. His grip on the phone receiver was causing a dull pain in his fingers, but he could not loosen his hold.

"I'll leave as soon as I get changed. If there is any trouble with checking in, just move in here. I'll leave instructions at the desk. God, I can't believe it. She was so gentle."

"Is, Ted. She is gentle. Be there for me, until I can take over."

Inside the Queen's Medical Center Ted felt out of place. A stranger to the island and to the injured woman, he felt he was an impostor, a phony, mimicking concern and sorrow for someone he had met only once. The small waiting room near the intensive care ward was filled with the family and friends of Shawna and her now dead fiancé, Larry. Their faces were blank and strained from lack of sleep and shock. Ted tried to identify himself to several of the people waiting, but he was unsuccessful; it was as if he were an invisible, soundless article of furniture. He would speak to a person face-to-face and the person would not comprehend him. Finally, he decided he would simply wait, without anyone understanding he was only a friend of a friend. And as the hours slumped away, the waiting group separated into two family camps, one of which, the fiancé's family, gradually dwindled in number as they slowly accepted the reality of his death.

During the wait Ted gradually learned more about the two lovers and the tragic, grisly end of their love affair. He listened to the somber conversations in the waiting room and read the sensational account of the crime that had been printed in the *Honolulu Advertiser*. The crime, it appeared, had already been solved. The vagrant and intoxicated perpetrators had been found quickly, wandering nearby; still in possession of the couple's credit cards, the criminals had confessed readily, providing horrifying details of the ordeal.

Shawna and Larry had been friends since childhood, growing up together and attending the same church. They were both devout Christians and successful businesspeople. She was a hard-working real estate agent and he owned a school for the blind. He was, in fact, legally blind himself. Their wedding date was less than a month away, and they would never grow closer to it. Their calm, giving lives had collided violently with another world, a brutal world of cheap handguns and drugs, gangs and knives.

The couple had met at the beach during the afternoon, intending to enjoy the sunset at Magic Island in the early evening. The cooling dusk was still warmed by the setting sun when they happened upon a group of three young men from an obscure South Pacific island. The three men were poor and alienated, intoxicated on alcohol and crack cocaine, accustomed to violence and death. When they saw the beautiful woman and the almost helpless man, they saw opportunity. But they didn't, at first, have the courage to attack. They blocked the couple's escape, but did not close in on them. They taunted them, at one point knocking Larry's cell phone from his hands when he tried to summon help. They spoke to one another of the sexual acts they would like to perform upon Shawna, being careful to speak loud enough for them to hear and understand. They repeatedly bent over, arms around each other's shoulders, in some mad parody of a football huddle, then broke apart to feint an attack. Then, when the protective light of day was gone, they did attack. The blind man was stabbed in the chest and held down by one of the attackers while the beautiful, innocent woman was stabbed in legs and arms with shallow slices intended to produce pain and terror. She was dragged off and raped by each of the three, but the attack didn't stop at that. She was again sliced, threatened with immediate death, and forced to accept oral and anal penetration, while only a few yards away one of the attackers had his hand inside the open chest of her fiancé and then his penis inside his rectum. The attack went on for hours, with terror and pain being some foul nourishment for the fiendish violators. Finally, with their lust for power satisfied and their bounty of hate dissipated, they had left the two good people for dead, naked and bloody on a Waikiki beach.

They were found by the morning beachcombers as the sun's protection returned to Magic Island. Shawna was near death from loss of blood and the man she loved was gone forever. They both had been rushed to the Queen's, but Shawna's fiancé had never had a chance; he had been cold to the touch when the paramedics arrived at the scene. Shawna also should have died from the shock induced by the many shallow knife wounds, but something inside her had fought for life. And although she had been near death many times during her first hours in the hospital, her subconscious will for life would not allow her body to surrender. She had held on long enough for medical technology to have the chance to save her.

Tony's wife was one of Shawna's oldest friends, a member of her extended family. She had been called by another friend, one of Shawna's cousins, soon after the families began to gather in the intensive care waiting room. Tony and his wife had booked the first available flight out of LAX, and Tony had left the message while Ted had casually lunched at the North Shore.

Ted watched the shocked family members clinging to one another, drawing strength from their intimacy, and punished himself with an indictment of absence. Whenever people needed him, he was busy, selfishly out of touch, seeing to his own comfort. He had been making love the night he could have saved his brothers, he had been drunk and jealous when he should have prevented Mary from taking the drug overdose, and he had been selfishly worried about time when the lonely jumper had delayed his trip to Santa Monica. Now he sat in this confined, windowless room that smelled of fear and fatigue and hate, waiting for any chance to atone for his inadequacies.

He remembered his brothers, and the time they had spent together in high school while still in their teens. His younger brother had always seemed drawn to the extremities of teenage life, bikes and drugs and rebellion. His older brother had been the conservative one, the one with the job and the good car and the homecoming queen girlfriend. Ted had been in the middle, somehow always the truce maker and the negotiator, linking their worlds, cars and beer to motorcycles and pot. He knew he could have saved them, had he been with them that night, but instead he had chosen to be with the love of his teenage life. When it counted, when he absolutely needed to be there for his brothers, he had been in the back of their mother's station wagon with the seats turned down, a sleeping bag opened into a makeshift bed, taking the virginity from a girl whom timing and circumstances would ordain that he never speak with again.

It had been after the city championship. Ted and his younger brother had starred in a last-minute victory: Johnston to Johnston for forty yards and a touchdown with three minutes left in the game. Their older brother, a year out of high school, had watched from the stands with their proud mother and father. It was a night that began with success and glory and pride; it would end in a nightmare of drugs and violence and death.

He remembered the anguish the deaths of his brothers had caused his parents. His mother had died from the loss, wasting away in less than six months. The doctors had said it was cancer, but Ted knew the cancer had only come because of her broken heart. His father had tried to be strong, as he had always been, but as his wife withered away he had become increasingly depressed. The day after his mother's death, Ted had found his father in the garage, hanging by a long extension cord from the wooden rafters of the roof. He could never forget the image, or the way he had screamed and screamed as he tried to lift his father's weight in his arms.

"Ted, are you all right? You look worse than Shawna's mother. Do you need a glass of water?" Tony shook his shoulder gently as he spoke.

His question brought Ted back to the present, back from his intolerable memories, and he sighed with the release from the pain. He realized he had been pulled into his own private hell by the ambiance of the waiting room, the whispers, the tired eyes, the stench of fear and despair. He had seen the couple circulating through the room—consoling, hugging and offering drinks of water, coffee, or soda—without being aware it was Tony and his wife. He was the last patient of their private triage.

"No, of course not. I'm fine, but the family is…They are devastated. I really couldn't help them. They didn't even recognize I was here."

"You helped, Ted. You were here for us, not for them. We couldn't have endured the flight if you had not been here. You were our connection with this room, with the pain and the grief. Looks to me like you might have done your job too well. You, my friend, are a mess."

Although Tony seemed to be trying to lighten his mood, the explanation only amplified Ted's feelings of guilt. Tony had managed to be there for this family, even when he was physically thousands of miles away and totally out of touch while over the Pacific Ocean. Ted was stunned by the wisdom: being there when needed meant more than physical presence.

"I was glad to help. I just wish I could have done more. I seem to just have drifted off into a dream world."

"Ted, you need sleep. Why don't you take off and go back to your room. If we need you to come relieve us, we'll call. But I don't think that is going to be necessary. Shawna's out of the woods and Larry's family is beginning to realize that he is gone." Tony helped him up by lifting on his elbows.

"OK, Tony. Call me if you need me. I am just a little drained."

Ted regained his composure as he walked from the hospital. It was all too insane: the sudden break from normalcy, the senseless violence, the families with the cardboard skin tones. He struggled to understand what had happened, and why he was involved. He wondered if he was some kind of lightning rod for disaster, a jinx that attracted the evil that flowed below the thin veneer of life. Events were carrying him along to some inevitable end; he could feel the inertia of the outwardly random moments, and he was terrified by the sensation.

He left the front of the Queen's Medical Center through a well-manicured garden, crossing the busy street to a small park where giant banyan trees grew. Their mammoth branches covered immense areas of earth, their roots descending from the branches to form new trunks wherever they made contact with the ground. Ted noticed that nothing could grow in the perpetual darkness beneath the thick foliage of the trees. Although beautiful, they seemed similar to weeds; impressively large weeds, but still creeping and spreading and devouring all about them with their growth.

Suddenly he was tired of Hawaii. He was tired of the tropical vegetation and the blue water and the clear, cotton-ball-cloud-spotted sky. He was bored by Japanese tourists and the slow pace and the Hawaiian sovereignty movement. He was offended by the Waikiki bars filled with California college students on five-hundred-dollar vacations. But most of all, he was revolted by the meaningless destruction of a happy, gentle, innocent couple; disgusted by the clash of cultures that had fermented into random violence, brewed from the grains of poverty, alienation, and drugs.

He caught a cab on Punchbowl and rode back to the Moana. It was late afternoon, and the business workers were taking their short commutes across town; even Honolulu had its share of traffic congestion.

In his room, he pulled the curtains on the picturesque view and the murky shadows of twilight replaced the shiny sea. He called room service to get something to eat: a sandwich and two Chivas Regals, neat, with club soda on the side. He drank one of the drinks straight, chasing it with a long drink of soda. He mixed the second, messily pouring a little of the soda into the glass of whiskey. He tried to eat the sandwich, but it tasted like sawdust. He managed to force half of it down before placing the round cover over the remainder. He turned on the television and the hotel channel filled the air with melodic Hawaiian folk songs, the awkward falsetto sounding strangely like an Americanized version of Chinese opera. He found the high-pitched singing artless and irritating and switched the TV off. He sat in the dark, silent room completely awake and completely sober, wishing he was neither. He called room service for two more whiskeys, and when they arrived, he searched his shaving kit for the over-the-counter sleep agent he kept there. He took two of the pills, washing them down with scotch and soda, and sat on the edge of the bed waiting to be tired.

Across the narrow room he could see the image of himself in the dresser top mirror. He looked like the cardboard faces he had seen at the Queen's. He lifted his glass and toasted himself—he really knew how to vacation. He decided he would wait until he could talk to Tony, but then he would change his flight to return early to the mainland and Los Angeles.

The thought of California depressed him further; there was nothing left for him there, it was just where the return ticket would take him. He leaned back onto the softness of the bed and closed his eyes, holding his drink on his lap with both hands. He realized that the sleeping aid was beginning to produce its effect and he sat forward, placing the drink on the nightstand. He sat on the edge of the bed for a long time, very near sleep, his head resting in his hands, his elbows on his knees.

Finally, he stood up and took off his clothes, tossing them into his open suitcase. The suitcase reminded him of the dog-eared envelope from his travel agent's office. He went to the bag and rummaged in the side pockets until he found it. He broke the seal for the first time and pulled out the contents: the prepaid ski trip to Durango, Colorado. Clean white snow and cold mountain air; maybe Durango would help him forget Honolulu. He had experienced enough of it to last him a very long time.

Mardi Gras

What makes mankind tragic is not that they are the victims of nature, it is that they are conscious of it. To be part of the animal kingdom under the conditions of this earth is very well but as soon as you know of your slavery the pain, the anger, the strife – the tragedy begins. We can't return to nature, since we can't change our place in it. Our refuge is in stupidity, in drunkenness of all kinds, in lies, in beliefs, in murder, thieving, reforming in negation, in contempt – each man according to the prompting of his particular devil.

—Joseph Conrad, Letters to R. B. Cunninghame Graham
1897–1898

Her sleep had ended much earlier, with a jolt into sudden wakefulness. Confused at first by the dark forms around her, she had been unable to resolve the hulking shadows with her expectation of her room at the apartment. Disoriented by the unanticipated surroundings, she had attempted to roll out of the bed in the wrong direction, pushing clumsily into the heavy sleeping form beside her. Then, with the touch of him, and the smell of him, the chaotic moment that sometimes comes at the end of sleep had collapsed into a kaleidoscopic instant of realization. Becoming fully cognizant of herself and of him, she had remembered that she was in his room at the Iron Horse, as she had been each morning for almost a week.

She had kissed his bare shoulder hard, but he had not stirred from his deep sleep. Disappointed by his lack of response, but unwilling to wake him, she had dressed quietly in the chilly gray twilight of morning. Downstairs, she had rekindled the smoldering coals of the fire before adding two big logs. The orange flames had quickly lapped up the split faces of the wood, and she had slid the hearth screen closed with as little of the scraping noise as possible. Then, as she stood watching the fire grow, she had been seduced by coffee cravings.

On her way outside into the silent, cold air that remained after the late-night snowfall, she had opened and closed the front door quietly to avoid waking him. Gingerly, with thoughts of hot coffee tempting her to go faster than was safe, she had walked along the freshly shoveled but icy sidewalks to the Ram Restaurant. As she had hurried, balancing herself on the slippery walk with outstretched arms, she had breathed the sharp, pure air deeply and had exhaled huge, long-lasting columns of steam.

When she had returned to the room, carrying a big Styrofoam cup of the freshly brewed black liquid in each hand, she had found him still in bed, sleeping boy-like, with his knees high in a fetal position. Taking care not to wake him, she had sat on the bed. Sipping her coffee while he slept, she had studied the intimate details of his face and upper body with self-conscious anonymity.

During the long, silent minutes of inspection she had gradually become aware of imperfections—lines and scars and blemishes— that she had not noticed before. He seemed little more than a stranger, a being from some alien world of cities and business and wealth. She wondered how, after such a short time, her feelings had grown so strong. She had felt strong feelings before, for Steve, but that was after an entire marriage.

He was older; the lines around his eyes betrayed years in the sun, years she could never share, years spent with other women in that other world. Yet she felt a compelling sensation of oneness with him, an overwhelming emotional affinity. She imagined the devotion of an attached twin joined in some critical way to a sister, who if separated would surely perish. He was, she thought, like some magic bullet, created only for her. She worried that she was losing control of herself in the strength of her feelings for him. And as she sat on the bed next to him, she asked herself how she could have gone out to him so completely, so terribly fast.

He had slept the deep, refreshing sleep of a mind without apprehension. His waking, when it finally came, was gentle and slow. Captivated by the pleasant fantasies of the night, he resisted wakefulness, but burgeoning consciousness brought awareness of his new reality and he embraced it. Life had become eminently more fulfilling than any insubstantial dream. His existence had recently been transformed.

She was astonished that it had been only a week since they had met. It seemed impossible that their time together had been so short. Her memory was already filled to overflowing with images of him and of them together. She remembered the moment they had met, skiing up on the mountain. She had believed him to be yet another Texan looking to get laid on his ski vacation, and had scolded herself for not paying more attention on her way to the lift. They had arrived at the chair at almost the same time, without another person on that part of the mountain. She had thought he had adjusted his speed to cause the meeting, and she had dreaded the inevitable come-on. But instead, he had seemed surprised and somehow subdued. He had watched her for a long time, hiding behind his dark glasses, but he hadn't seemed to be leering at her. He had seemed quietly isolated and mysterious. His body language had indicated that he was not going to speak, and she had wondered if he would board the chair up to the summit or take the lower trail back to the chalet. Then he had reached up to his face with his ski pole still held in his hand, and his glasses had dropped to dangle around his neck, exposing his dark eyes. They had been shockingly sad and shy.

Their meeting had been a rendezvous of chance, a serendipitous pairing at a surrealistically deserted chairlift station. The methodical machine had seemed to operate without human guidance or intervention, with no lines and no wait, not even the usual bundled-and-gloved attendant. They had arrived together after completing their separate runs; converging slowly, they had skied across the hard, flat snow from different directions. He had been unprepared for the encounter and disinclined to approach her, reluctant to make the obvious suggestion that they ride up the slope together. He had first studied her from behind the small anonymity of his sunglasses, fearing rejection, searching for hints of hesitation or aversion. Then he had spoken to her, and she had boarded the double lift beside him.

"Shall we ride up together?" he had said in a halting, almost stuttering voice, and she had known it would be all right to ride with him. She had even been pleased when he had asked. Then, when she had nodded and moved to the chair, his eyes had changed, filling with pleasure and confidence, and that too had pleased her.

They had spent the day together, skiing and getting to know each other. She had discovered him to be intelligent and interesting; he was vastly experienced compared to herself, yet reticent and shy about his past.

Deep contentment filled him as he recalled that first day together, on a mountain devoid of other skiers, skiing and riding lifts through the silence. They had become comfortable with each other as they had challenged the first run, stopping briefly to discuss and select each new path before proceeding. Initially, their discourse had been impersonal discussions about the mountain and the terrain. But as the day continued, they had shared long, quiet conversations, traveling suspended over the lonely white slopes, revealing information about themselves. They had lunched on cheese, French bread, and icy, crisp white zinfandel at the Powder House, midway between the summit and the chalet. After spending most of the day together, they had sat close on the old resort bus as it bumped down from the mountain to the Iron Horse Inn. He had become a guest at the resort a few days before, disjointed from his old life, his memories, and his doubts; she had been scheduled to work there, waiting tables in a dining room without diners.

She remembered their second day together: waiting impatiently for his call, and her excitement when it came; their trip in her Toyota up to the Tamarron resort, where they had shared a slow, romantic dinner; and surprisingly, how easy and comfortable it had been to stay with him on that night of their first real date.

He remembered his fears before their first nervous night together. He had been afraid that, in private, he would prove to be another man than the one she had met on the mountain. But his fear had been baseless. He had been relieved to discover that the intimate element of their relationship would be as good as, possibly superior to, the public aspect of their friendship. And as the first full days of their love affair cascaded through his memory, he was overwhelmed with the wonder and impossibility of it. Still, he lay without moving, savoring the sweet conflict between the aching need for her and the sublime comfort of muscles well exercised and a body well fed and rested.

It had been another long day, the day before, skiing while the sun had permitted, then dinner and dancing afterward. They had returned to the room late, after the last bar had closed, planning to resist the biological need for sleep and return to ski the mountain early in the morning. But once they had fallen asleep, their bodies had prevailed, and they had slept late.

Looking down at his sleeping form, trying to convince herself she was still in control, she tried to dismiss her feelings as a flash infatuation, something that most women had experienced before they turned twenty, but she was not convinced. She sat on the edge of the bed for long minutes, silently willing him to come back to her from the distant solitude of sleep. She finished one of the two cups of coffee and was removing the white plastic cover from the second when he stirred.

Then, in an instant of sudden clarity, an experience that reminded him of the acuteness felt just prior to an accident, when the inevitable was helplessly accepted, he became aware of her nearness. He knew she was there without opening his eyes. He felt her presence as a tightening in his solar plexus, a painful, lonely knot buried deep in the center of his chest. There was invariably a change in him when she was near; her proximity always produced a physical response. Sometimes it was cool and gentle, refreshing, even life-giving; sometimes, like now, it was hard and sharp and demanding, a feeling of lost time and lost opportunities, of lost love and lost hope. He opened his eyes and she was there, sitting on the edge of the bed, her eyes pulling him up, out of himself and in to her. He heard his voice as he spoke; it seemed somehow inadequate, dwarfed by the heavy feeling active in his chest.

"Hi there," he said softly. She thought he sounded like a little boy who had been discovered in some secret mischief. A thrilling wave of euphoria washed over her; the lonely time, the time when he was away in sleep, was over. He had awakened slowly and peacefully, looking directly into her eyes. She handed him the coffee and tried to say something witty. But she felt out of breath, as if she was speaking into a gentle wind, and her words were being consumed by the breeze.

"Welcome back," she said, as she offered him the Styrofoam cup. Her sweet voice was an airy breeze winnowing smoothly over him, separating him from sleep, making him glad to be awake. "The road is closed," she continued. "It started snowing last night, after we fell asleep. It stopped for a while, but they say it's snowing like hell up on the mountain."

"No skiing today," he said.

"It's almost ten."

"I'd better get up and face the new day." He pulled himself up into a sitting position, leaned back against the cold stucco wall and received the outstretched cup of coffee.

"I'm not too sure you should. I've been up over for an hour and there really isn't that much going on out there, you know." She smiled with her beautiful blue eyes. Blonde brows slightly raised, head cocked a little to one side, she placed a joint between her naturally pink, full lips.

At that moment, with her sitting on the edge of his bed, still in her bulky down vest, smiling over the hand-rolled cigarette, he knew he could not prevail in a philosophical argument but he must resist her. He must resist the overwhelming desire to please her; he must somehow protect her from the dangers of the world without the appearance of fatherly guidance. He knew that in a frontal disagreement he must lose the point, and he knew that she was too intelligent to be manipulated. But the drugs—he must find a way to deflect her from the drugs. He knew it was easy for him to come across as pedantic; he also knew that if he did, he would be remembering the mistake from an unknown, lonely future without her. And a future without her was a prospect that filled him with despair.

He watched her blue eyes as they squinted into the hot flare of the butane lighter; the squinting caused the skin at the corners of her young eyes to wrinkle prematurely. The familiar smell of pot drifted to him, mixed with the powerfully musky lure of her exhaled breath. He knew that before he would lose her, if he was forced into a choice, he would meekly surrender to her will. When she offered him the joint, he reached out and took it. She had power over him he could not, would not, diminish; yet he knew he must parry her influence if he were to survive to protect her. He was compelled to protect her. He knew the dangers of the world outside this pleasant little lodge. He knew about science and expensive cars and beach-side houses. He understood the allure of money and the culture of drugs. He had belonged to the club of science and industry, and had paid for his membership with a contaminated body and a mind without hope. He knew she was attracted to the very past that had driven him to this small town in southwest Colorado, and that without that past she would probably never have given him a chance to know her. He understood her need for the new and the modern, the cool and the avant-garde, but he must try to keep her protected from the terribly sharp edges of that world. More importantly, he must not lose himself in her needs; if he did, they would both begin the slippery run that led to personal disaster.

She watched him as he took a carefully small hit from the joint. His life had been a storybook success tale; he had lived and worked in the real world. He had competed in that world and had won. She admired him for that, but he seemed to think of it as some shame to be forgotten. She knew that he disapproved of pot, and she knew that the only reason he was smoking now was to make her happy. The knowledge pleased her as it tweaked her guilt. She knew they would stay in the room all day getting high and making love; with the chilling snow outside the room and the warm fire inside. That was the important thing, the love that had ignited between them. She watched him as he placed the joint in the ashtray; his unenthusiastic hit had let the cherry die. She knew he was playing with her, letting the joint go out so it was just that much harder for her to get another hit, but for some reason she perceived it as an act of love by a little boy. She leaned over and kissed him lightly on the lips.

"Asshole."

"What? It went out." He pulled her down and kissed her, at first to avoid the need for further explanation, but the kiss quickly lost all reason or motive. Conscious of his own early morning muskiness, he ended the kiss and pulled them both up to sitting positions. "I'm going to take a shower and brush my teeth." He threw the sheet and blankets back and the sailing bedding landed across her legs. He stood quickly as she struggled to free herself from the tangle of bedclothes. The cold morning air pinched chill bumps on his naked body as he scampered downstairs to the bathroom.

"What's the matter? Embarrassed about a little manly stink? You city boys are such wimps."

He squirted a cylinder of green paste onto his toothbrush before stepping to the shower. Leaning into the tub and shower to turn on the hot water, he could feel the cold from the icy tiles passing into him through his feet. He went to the sink and began to brush his teeth, studying his reflection in the vanity mirror, waiting for the water in the shower to get warm. He judged himself to look old: his face was becoming lined, and he had a few white whiskers in his unshaven beard. He turned away from the sight to find steam rising from the shower. He stepped in and adjusted the heat. He preferred the water slightly hotter than cold—tepid. He stood facing the shower flow with his eyes closed as he continued to brush his teeth. The warm water on his face and shoulders was soothing and hypnotic, sensuous and luxurious. Suddenly the warm water became very hot and he stumbled back with a yell. He bumped into her; she had silently entered the stall and was leaning around him, increasing the flow of hot water.

"Hey, big boy. Don't knock me over." She stood up to regain her balance after his behind butted her in the head. The water was finally warming up; he always set the temperature too cold.

"Not so hot, you'll burn us." Foamy spit ran down his face as he spoke, and he looked silly and cute. He held the toothbrush near his mouth, but he seemed to have forgotten he still had it. She reached up and took it from him, then put it in her own mouth, keeping her eyes steady on his. She pulled the brush across her teeth in a few exaggerated strokes, tasting the spicy mint flavor, and then put it back in his mouth. She carefully brushed his front teeth before pushing it into his cheek.

"Mmmm, not bad. Move over, I'm cold," she said, as she pushed her way past him to stand under the full flow of the now scalding water. He stepped to the rear of the stall, reaching around the curtain to toss the toothbrush into the sink. He watched her as she let the water spray onto the top of her head, her eyes closed. The steamy water rushed down her face in a multitude of wet blonde rivulets. He found himself sexually stimulated as he watched the water flowing over her slim body. Her closed eyes somehow caused an exciting sense of voyeurism. He reached out with both hands and enclosed her waist gently. Her eyes opened, and he was once again stunned by their blueness, amazed as only a person from a family of dark brown-eyed children could be. She collapsed into him with her forearms in front of her breasts, clenching her small hands under her chin. Her eyes would not let him go; soft and inviting, they held his own gaze with an ancient instinctual power. He pulled her waist tighter to his own, wanting her to feel his excitement, wanting her to feel the power and the submission of his need.

She could see his desire for her in his boyish brown eyes, and his need for her fired her own need. She could not move her focus from his face, a face shining with lust and love and need. The strength of his arms and hands, as he pulled her closer, increased her need for him. And as she leaned against him, she realized with surprise that he was ready. She pulled her arms from between them to clasp her hands behind his neck, and the coolness of his torso pressed tightly against her breasts. She pulled down hard on his neck and his hands became tighter around her waist. She felt herself lifting, as if weightless, into the flow of the shower; she didn't know whether she was pulling herself up or if he was lifting her. They turned a little as she brought her legs up, clasping them around him. The hot water flowed down between their two bodies, and the wall tiles of the shower felt suddenly cold against her back. He kissed her wet face and lips, and he tasted the stimulating essence of her mouth. He was lost; all ability to control his desire was gone. He needed her as he had never needed another human being. He pulled her legs up to lift her onto him and let her slip back, deeply down. Lost in the moment, she was unaware of when or how it happened, but she found herself upon him, her arms around his neck and his arms under her legs. He heard a small moan emanating from low in her throat and felt an answering moan from deep in his own. He kissed and kissed, unable to stop kissing her. She moaned and he moaned, the shower flowing hot between them.

Ted was bent down to the fire, ready to put another piece of wood on the flames, when Jeri bounded down the stairs from the bedroom. Dressed in jeans, a turtleneck, and her down vest, she jumped playfully to the floor of the living room, momentarily tucking her feet up and to one side as if she were taking a ski jump. Jeri was a dynamo of youthful energy and childlike exuberance, even in the morning after a long day of skiing and a late night of drinking, even immediately after very physical sex. She landed at the foot of the stairs and smiled at him.

Intensely beautiful, she carried her beauty carelessly and without vanity. She was as quick intellectually as any person he had ever known, and she had used the gift wisely, performing the years of hard work needed to establish her intelligence, to be accepted to an outstanding medical school. But more than her beauty or intelligence, there was a tenderness about her that penetrated to the raw part of his personality, illuminating the darkness there with her own brilliance. It was as if he had been waiting for her his entire life. He knew at that moment that he loved her, that she could ask anything of him and he would be helpless to refuse, that he would abandon his past and his future to spend the next few moments with her. He followed her glance down to his hand holding the log, ready to be added to the fire; his arm was still stretched outward and downward in awkward pantomime, the action forgotten.

He had left their common shower first, running naked across the cold living room floor as he dried himself. Pulling the fluffy towel diagonally across his back, rubbing the rapidly cooling water from his body with brisk shivering strokes, he had rushed to the warmth of the fireplace to finish drying in the radiant heat of the inviting fire. The quiet flames still licked up between the logs Jeri had added to the fire while he had slept.

The image of her stopping on her way out for coffee, thoughtfully adding a log to the previous night's embers so he could rise to a warm room, had overwhelmed him. The ache in his chest, almost gone after the shower, had flared up and he had needed to fight an impulse to go back to her. Reminded of the long-gone Labrador puppy that inhabited bittersweet memories of his childhood, he had realized he must avoid being a nuisance with his love and had silently warned himself to resist his relentless need for her. Enduring his sudden loneliness, he had listened to her finishing her shower: running water, something dropped with a hollow plastic sound, water valve squeaking, and finally the tub enclosure opening and immediately closing. Then she too had run across the cold room to the fireplace, one bath towel around her body and another wrapped around her head.

After drying together in front of the fire, they had raced to the bedroom, ascending the narrow staircase on the run, the damp bath towels around their bodies growing cold and uncomfortable. Separating at the top of the stairs, they had moved to the little spaces in the impersonal hotel bedroom that had become their personal spots. He had dressed over his open suitcase where it rested unpacked on a folding stand next to the empty dresser. She had sat at the rustic hotel vanity, leaning into the mirror to apply her makeup.

It was then, as he had watched her put makeup on her naturally perfect face, that he had first realized that with Jeri, for the first time since his early, awkward experiences with women, there were no memories of other encounters, no sexual déjà vu.

He had dressed casually, selecting jeans and a baggy wool pullover sweater. Then, leaving her alone to get ready, he had gone downstairs to wait. He had passed the time poking at the coals in the fireplace, stirring a small flame back to life. He was reaching to place another log on the grill when she had appeared at the head of the stairs. He had stood watching her, wood outstretched to the forgotten fireplace, as she had bounced downward toward him.

Jeri felt happy and clean and full of energy. She leaped over the last two stairs, pretending she was skiing. Ted was putting more wood on the fire, as if he was planning to stay in the room. She wanted to go out for a big breakfast and then get outside, to do something fun, to take a hike or play in the new snow.

"Are we staying inside?" She tried to keep her own desire to go outside out of her voice. "We can call room service. The menu is on the TV." The idea of staying in the small suite, possibly watching daytime TV while they waited for room service, leaned heavily on her buoyant mood. But if that was what he wanted to do, she thought, the great outdoors could wait until after breakfast. She felt sure he would want to go out for a walk when they were finished, maybe down to the river or along the highway to Durango.

"What do you want to do?" He put the fresh log back on the wood pile. "Is it nice outside?"

"It's great outside." Her expectations soared. "And there is a cool little breakfast restaurant in town. If we get there fast, we can catch them before they close. They're only open in the mornings and they are not very good businesspeople. If the snow is good for cross-country skiing, they might close early. Sometimes in the summer, if the trout fishing is good, they don't open at all. I hate that. They make the very best hash browns." She skipped toward the door and Ted met her there, encircling her with his arms. They kissed, leaning into the comfortable bulkiness of their coats hanging from hooks on the inside of the door.

"Jeri, you're always so happy. First thing in the morning, stone sober and razor straight, you're as happy as a kid on Christmas morning. I can't understand why you smoke so much pot."

"So typical of the older generation. You all had your fun, now you're all judgmental about what we do to have fun."

She knew immediately that this comment would hurt him; she regretted having said it as soon as it was out. He didn't answer, and her words seemed to hang in the air, echoing in her ears. But damn it, he was condescending sometimes. It had made her angry that he wanted to control her habits, and she had felt an instant of uncontrollable recalcitrance, as if she was listening to a disapproving parent or a controlling husband. But the feeling passed quickly and she was at once contrite. She knew that he worried about the difference in their ages, and when he had angered her, she used the knowledge to hurt him. He was watching her quietly, obviously waiting for the next attack. She smiled meekly before giving him a quick peck of a kiss.

"I'm sorry, Ted, that wasn't fair. It's just that I feel so strong now. No, strong is the wrong word. Independent, maybe, and like I have to get on with life, as if I'm late getting started. There is a magnificent world out there waiting for me to arrive, and I've been here." She waved toward the room with a small, one-handed gesture, but she meant Durango and Colorado. "I've been trapped in a life I got by accident, only now I have control, and I want to experience it all. Do you understand? I want to have fun, and I want to learn, and I want to explore everything about the modern world. Does that make any sense? Am I being selfish or childish?" She pulled him tighter, pressing her lips and nose to his smooth, warm neck. He smelled of soap and shampoo and aftershave.

"No, it makes perfect sense—to me, anyway. I thought about the very same things a lot before I met you, until I wound myself into tight little emotional knots. There is an incredibly attractive world out there—a wonderful, civilized, technological world filled with nuclear energy, pharmacology, intercontinental air travel, e-mail, and every other good thing that has advanced our culture since the Stone Age. Only it's all delicately balanced in some mystically intricate way with pollution, industrial accidents, the loss of privacy, drug dependence, and all the other things that eat away at the individual as the culture advances. It has become, in my mind, an intellectual minestrone soup."

"Are you saying that technological advancement is a bad thing?" It didn't seem possible that someone like Ted, who had been involved in science and technology for so long, could think the Stone Age was better.

"No, Jeri, I don't know what to think. That's my point. It's just that I think people can be hurt as a culture advances." He could see in her eyes that she didn't understand. "Look, take polio as an example. Until society cleaned up the drinking water, it didn't exist. The kids gained some immunity from the bad water. When cities advanced to a certain point, polio exploded into the population."

"But medicine, technology, cured polio. You can't think that we were better off drinking bad water, with dysentery and cholera and parasites."

"No, of course not. But sometimes we are able to develop technologies we don't fully understand. Take nuclear energy. The electricity is a good thing, a necessary thing, but the technology is inherently dangerous. And if we want to maintain our culture we don't have any better choice. Fossil fuels will damage us as surely as nuclear."

"That's what I mean, we can't avoid going forward, it's our nature. Science must find the answers to the problems that pop up along the way. Science and technology are the cure, not the disease." He was quiet, and she felt she had made her point. "Well, what do you think?"

"I think I'm hungry." Ted knew it was useless to argue a point he didn't understand himself. He wanted to end the conversation that reminded him of the past and return to the happy present with Jeri. "Let's go get some breakfast, OK?" He broke their embrace to reach for his coat and then leaned back to kiss her softly. "Jeri, for the first time in my life I am happy. Money and parties and the fast life never made me happy, so I may not understand everything you're feeling, but I understand that I am happy when we are together, and I won't do anything to jeopardize that happiness." He stepped back from her far enough to pull his coat around his shoulders before he opened the door. "What was the name of that breakfast place where we're going to eat? I'm starving."

"I don't know that they have a name, other than 'the breakfast restaurant,' I mean." She pulled her Levi's jacket over the down vest. "But I do know that they grate the potato directly onto the grill when they make hash browns. And the grill is just opposite the little counter so you can watch them cook." She followed him outside, listening for the click of the lock as she pulled the door closed behind them.

Jeri drove her Toyota station wagon south on Highway 550, happy the glistening black pavement was dry by mountain standards. Ted sat in the passenger's seat watching her, the Animus River valley passing behind her profile as if she were embedded in some motion picture derivative of a Norman Rockwell painting. When they entered the little tourist town of Durango, Ted's movie analogy grew into true fantasy; the western façades of the storefronts merged colorfully into the imaginary cinema backdrop, and Jeri's silhouette became the twenty-foot-high close-up of the young star. In his mind, he added worn clichés as comical narration to the scene, a ridiculous overdubbing in simulated surround sound: city mouse, country mouse; small-town girl conquers the big city; absolute power corrupts absolutely. The last phrase was too incongruent to avoid chuckling, and when he did, Jeri heard him. She turned briefly from the road to face to him, with an unspoken "what?" on her smiling lips. Ted felt the warm, hard ball in his chest and leaned over to kiss the question lightly from her lips. She let him take the quick brush of a kiss without resistance, but wouldn't let the question be avoided.

"No, you can't get off that easy. What made you laugh? I saw you looking at me just before you laughed. Tell me what it was about me that you found so funny, Ted." She was nodding toward the road with self-assurance, knowing she had caught him in what should have been a covert act.

"It really wasn't anything about you that made me smile; it was my own poor command of the English language." He watched as the nodding transformed into a slow cynical shaking, her smile still bright. "No, it's true, but I will tell you the important part of what I was thinking. I was imagining you in the starring role of a vast old movie. You know, the beautiful young heroine from the pastoral outback. Maybe a Southern belle on a plantation, huh? Anyway, you were the star of the big screen, in a movie with this beautiful place as the set." He motioned to the row of picturesque buildings, each one a simple poem of local architecture written in redbrick or brightly painted wood, standing, as they had after a hundred winter storms, behind a tall white barricade of icy, snowplow-molded snow mounds.

"Pastoral outback, huh? I think you lived in LA too long. Watched too many movies." She turned abruptly in to one of the diagonal parking places that lined the street and the car bumped to a stop in a mound of snow. "No time to think about it now, we're here." She turned off the ignition, yanked up on the emergency brake, then leaned over to place her hands behind his neck, pulling his face close to her own. "I know where we should go. Buy me breakfast and I'll take you to a magical place, a place that will feed your soul." She kissed him.

After a very large western breakfast, they left Durango, heading west on Highway 160 with Jeri doing the driving. As they left the quaint old mining town, Jeri pointed to the side of a large hill that loomed heavily behind the narrow gauge railway station. "See that big hump on the slope? That's where they cleaned up the radioactive tailings left over from the old smelter. I understand it kicked up quite a lot of dust when they did it."

"It was right here? Right on the edge of town?"

"Yep. That old smelter and the train bringing ore down out of the mountains made this town. Only silver and gold are a little different to work with than uranium. Who could have guessed, huh?" She smiled sweetly as they passed the snow-covered hillside.

"Where did they take it? The radioactive waste, I mean."

"Not far enough, I guess. People are still complaining about it. It's a joke, really. They wouldn't let them move it for years because they thought the process would scare off the tourists. No matter that every little breeze blew the stuff down on Main Avenue. Now they complain about the stuff not being far enough away. Not properly sealed."

"In the fifties, during the big uranium rush, no one ever imagined the mess we could make of things, I suppose. A little bit of that stuff goes a long way. I know." Ted was reminded of his own personal radioactivity and shuddered. "I'm glad it's under a layer of snow, cleaned up or not."

They drove over a small pass before dropping down out of the tree-covered mountains and into wide, rolling farm country. The beautiful brown and white high country was dotted with farmhouses and barns; the well-maintained, two-lane road was only a small incursion into the natural charm of the perfect land. As they drove through it, Ted watched as Jeri handled the car. She drove with an intense, but seemingly directionless, purpose until they reached the entrance to Mesa Verde National Park.

"This morning, when I went out for coffee, I was trying to think of a good place for us to go today. My friend at the front desk suggested the cliff dwellings, but it didn't really interest me until you started talking about the evils of technology and the pastoral life again. This place fits right in with the pastoral existence and what it really means."

She drove into the park through a forest of stumpy, brush-like pines, passing the visitors' center and the ugly assemblage of condominium-style hotel rooms without a glance or a word. She drove the narrow road quickly, undistracted by the many turnouts and photo-op stops, until she finally slowed her pace and stopped near a small wooden sign that read: Sun Temple. They left the car, with the doors unlocked and the windows down, to walk the short distance to the temple. They were, apparently, the only two human beings on the mesa.

The temple had never been finished, but even incomplete, Ted found it impressive and beautiful. It was located at the apex of a Y-shaped canyon, overlooking the three legs of the fissure and the distant plains beyond. The sun was nearing the horizon; a large, cool, yellow orange disk, so filtered by the failing day near them that they could look at it with unprotected eyes. But its light was still bright where it landed high on the rock outcroppings miles away across the valley. A cold wind blew up the vertical canyon walls and swirled its way into and under their clothing. They stood in an embrace, faces cheek to cheek, the wind blowing into their bodies.

"They were a wonderful, technological people, the Anasazi. They lived up above their world in stone high-rises when London was still a stick village." Jeri spoke as quietly as she thought possible without her words being lost to the cold wind. "Living in cliff houses that were built high above this canyon, an impenetrable fortress retreat, they probably farmed up here, on the mesa. They maintained a vast trading network that brought them goods from as far away as the Pacific Northwest and Central America. Then, long before Columbus learned how to sail, they simply disappeared."

The wind seemed to pick up speed, creating an oddly coinciden-
tal dirge through the short trees that were growing in the center of
the ruined temple. Ted was subdued by the beauty and loneliness
of the site. "What could have happened to them?"

"No one knows for sure, but there are plenty of guesses. One
of the less romantic theories is that the more warlike peoples to
the north, the Apache or Navajo, drove them out. Not much evidence for that, though. The best theory is that there was a great
drought and they simply ran out of the things they needed here on
the mesa: wood for fuel, game to hunt, water to grow corn. Sort of
a mini environmental crisis, you know? And when the institutions
that had always worked for them failed, they cast them aside. They
abandoned their society and their religion because of the failure
of their priests, their science, to predict the drought and to protect
them from its effects. The theory is they stepped back from their
high level of technology and simply faded into a simpler way of
life. A more pastoral way of life, Ted. They disappeared without a
trace into the mountains that had once been their dominion." She
pulled back from him far enough to look directly into his eyes. She
felt cold where their bodies had been together, but she wanted to
see if he understood her point.

"Jeri, are you saying that if they would have just stuck with it a
few more bleakly dry planting seasons their technology would have
prevailed and they would still be here? Is it so simple, is all progress
good, and is all technology progress? What about the radioactive
waste we passed on the way up here?"

"You know, Ted, sometimes you sound like the damn Unabomber.
Do you believe that bull about technology destroying the world?
Want to return to the old days, Ted? This is the old days." She waved
to the ruins. "A few dry years and they gave up."

"The Unabomber! Hell, I hope not." Ted was forced to laugh
at himself. She had found an excellent way to disarm him while
she made her point. "Jeri, I don't think the problem is as black and
white as that maniac thought, and I don't think it's as black and
white as you make it either."

"Another theory is a lot more romantic, you know." Her voice
contained the familiar edge that he recognized as a warning he
was about to be teased. "And it should be easier for a guy like you

to accept. Being a person who would like to go back to the simple way of life, I mean." She was smiling and he knew he was about to be had.

She pulled herself against him, her cold chest more at home in his warmness. "Aldous Huxley wrote about people like the Anasazi. He called them peyote eaters, and he thought that they had some mysterious ability to perceive some greater truth of existence."

"Peyote, Jeri?" Ted realized she had switched gears. She had made her point about the benefits of technology, and she was now going to use some still unknown logic to justify the use of drugs.

"Now, just listen for a minute," she continued. "Huxley believed that they existed less in the sensuous world, the world of sight and sound and touch, and more in a world of insight and intuition and mind, the world of perception. He thought they had less cultural bias, that their ability to acquire knowledge of the universe was limited only by a mental filtering process he called the reducing valve of perception." She laughed happily as she looked into his face. "For that matter, he thought the same thing about us. As we became civilized, the reducing valve narrowed, and we became less and less able to collect the intuitive information. Finally our entire technological culture was doomed to the life of a blind man in an art gallery."

"Sounds a little like Peter Pan, never wanting to grow up."

"Exactly." She pushed back from him gently, holding him only by his elbows. "It is like Peter Pan. That is what happens to us, Ted, a gradual loss of innocence. We grow into tightly controlled think-ing machines, without the capacity for creativity or radical change."

"Maybe they just ate too much peyote and forgot to water their corn," Ted teased, trying to sidetrack her logic.

"No, really. We grow too conservative and can't accept anything out of the ordinary. We stop being able to fly."

"OK, I think I know what you're trying to say. Not too long ago I read a book about nuclear physicists and the life they lead. The author said that all the big breakthroughs in physics come from young people. There was a quote from—who was it? Pauli, Wolf-gang Pauli. He complained that he had lost his creativity because he knew too much."

"Yes. That's it. All the real progress comes from the insights of people free of the rigid boundaries of old science. We don't need to go back, Ted, we need to go forward, beyond the old science."

"I don't know about that, Jeri. But I do know that much of what we call progress is incomplete, technology without principles. Our technological ability to destroy ourselves has overreached our ethical and moral ability to control our impulses to do so."

"OK." She spoke very quickly, as if she were close to the end of her argument. "Maybe we need to clean out the old reducing valve. We, you and I, us as a civilization, try desperately to glean meaning from all the information we find bombarding us, but sometimes that information is not enough. We need to use our perception to find the answers we need to form new theory."

Ted stood holding her silently for long moments, watching the shadows grow and move into the canyon. He turned back from the darkening valley to Jeri's face; she was smiling sweetly, but with an air of triumph. She leaned up to him and kissed his lips. When he opened his eyes after the kiss, she was watching him, a great happiness shining on her face. Then she slowly raised a hand-rolled cigarette to a position between their faces.

"Got a light?" she asked with a giggle.

"Is that what all this philosophy has been about? Pot?"

"Well, I've never even seen peyote, this will have to do."

"OK, Jeri," he smiled in defeat, "but you have to let me have the last word." He waited until she agreed with a nod and a shrug. "Maybe these people drugged their reducing valve and disappeared because of it. Maybe their consumption of peyote put them at a reproductive disadvantage when competing with other more practical neighbors."

"Yes, or it had nothing to do with perception or peyote or technology. Maybe they just gave up, Ted."

He realized she meant his own surrender, his own rejection of his prior life, and he realized she was right. Science and engineering were part of him; to reject them would be to reject himself. He watched her as she lit the joint with the skill of one who has performed the task on the windiest mountain slopes. She took the first puff and handed the joint to him.

"OK, Jeri, you won the debate. But know this, I love you. And no matter how preachy it sounds, I have been there, and I will try to dissuade you from this culture." He gestured with the joint to indicate he meant drugs. "I really don't have much to lose anymore, but you have a great future and I'm not going to let this destroy you."

As he spoke, Jeri pulled herself closer to his chest, her eyes turned up to look into his down-turned face, the joint momentarily forgotten. When he had finished speaking, she seemed to be thinking about something else.

"You do?" she asked.

Jeri's awakening started deep within a pleasant yet unremembered dream, a dream that had left her with wispy feelings of positive self-worth and primal fulfillment. Then the residual contentment of the dream slowly dissipated into the confused, insecure feeling of waking in unfamiliar surroundings.

Ted watched her face in the first moments of waking—it was flushed with a soft, childlike contentment. Then, the babyish softness twitched from some real or imagined irritation and she jerked reflexively.

She raised her head a few inches, wondering where she was, and the movement made her uncomfortably aware of lost warmth. Unable to focus, she dropped her face back into the soft warmness, abandoning any effort to see, and with her first comfortable breath she became infused with the musky, sweet, man smell of his body.

She seemed frightened at first and opened her eyes blankly as she pulled away from him, but before he could lean over to kiss her forehead, she had again closed her eyes and dropped her head to his shoulder.

The feel and the warmth and the smell of him brought back the contentment of the dream. She reached across his chest with her arm and pulled her face deeper into the soft, clean, odoriferous spot where his arm joined his shoulder, breathing him in. She nuzzled gently against him, as would a loving cat.

"A guy could get used to that," he said. His voice surprised her, but not enough to interrupt her feline caresses.

"Promises, promises," she answered into his armpit, as she continued to cuddle against his body.

"I'm hungry. How about you?"

"I guess." She became aware that they were lying on top of the bed, where several hours before, exhausted, they had collapsed without undressing or turning down the comforter.

The round-trip to Mesa Verde had been long and uncomfortable in the small, poorly heated, compact station wagon. The return trip had degenerated into an unsuccessful search for hot, sweet coffee drinks, highlighted by an adventurous visit to the microscopic town of Mancos. They had been told by a convenience store clerk that the only bar in town was the local VFW, and when they pounded on the locked door it had opened to the sound of an electric buzzer. When they stepped inside, they had been presented a long, surrealistic view down the length of a smoke-filled bar: old white faces made motionless by their unexpected entrance, tobacco-coarsened voices silenced in mid-conversation, even the ubiquitous smoke seeming to have frozen into a wispy white gauze. No coffee drinks in Mancos. They had stayed long enough to have a beer and a quick game of pool before continuing their return trip to Durango. Finally having finished the journey back to the hotel, they had walked, cold and stiff, to the warm room, where they had unintentionally fallen asleep on top of the bed, with the television droning as it flickered in the growing dusk.

She lay her cheek on his chest as he encircled her with his arms and pulled her tightly to him. She felt secure and satisfied as he kissed the top of her head. She turned her face up to him, and they were once again lost in each other, making love without awareness of the world around them. She felt time as disjointed moments, instants of sudden pleasure or harmless pain; the passage of time became discreet instants, without duration or chronology. Their lovemaking led them through the familiar stages of passion and sweat, tenderness and chill, until finally they bathed together under the hot shower, carefully washing each other's backs, a human interpretation of the loyal grooming of paired birds.

They had dressed much too lightly in the deceptive comfort of the room; once outside, the unexpected cold forced them to return for their heavy coats. Running the short distance to the Ram Restaurant, hand and hand, supporting each other through the slippery spots on the sidewalk, laughing and yelling, their voices hushed by the deep snow covering the parking lot. Then, stumbling happily into the main building, their laughter suddenly too loud, the warm air inside burned the skin on their faces and hands.

Famished, they ordered hugely from the red-meat-dominated menu, receiving special attention from Jeri's friends waiting tables in the trophy-head-decorated dining room and preparing the food in the modern kitchen. They ordered too much food and were unable to finish. Jeri requested doggie bags, and Ted teased her mercilessly for her waste-not husbandry. The meal finished and the check paid, they sat at the table with only the red candle centerpiece, their coffee cups, and the paper doggie bags interrupting the white flatness of the tablecloth.

"You know, Jeri, now that I think about it, a little brandy might be nice." Ted sipped the last cold drops of his coffee.

"Yes, that might be nice." She turned to signal the young waiter who was standing next to the server station, waiting for them to leave.

"No, Jeri, let the guy go home. Let's go into the bar. It looks kind of romantic in there, dark and quiet. And there's a big rock fireplace we can sit next to."

"It's kind of boring in there, Ted. Joey won't mind if we have a drink here." She turned again to the young man at the server area and motioned to him to take possession of the doggie bags. She could not stand for the good food to go to waste, but she didn't want Ted to tease her anymore about taking it back to the room. He began to walk toward their table.

"I know he'll do it for you, Jeri, but you can see he wants to get out of here. Let's just go into the bar." Ted began to stand.

"All right, Ted, only let's not stay too long. We can always go into town, if you want." Jeri loathed the contact with John. She had managed to keep this moment at bay since she and Ted met. She knew that he had been to the bar, and he may even have already met John, but she dreaded the moment when the two of them would realize their common connection through her. The thought of them doing the old-boy thing together, with her sitting quietly to one side, began to make her nauseous. She stood awkwardly in response as Ted rose from the table. They walked across the room toward the bar, and Ted wrapped her arm around his, holding it uncomfortably away from her side. She walked reluctantly beside him as they entered the dark bar, the skin on her cheeks growing hot with premature embarrassment. An icy tear of perspiration formed under her blouse and ran down her side, trickling from her armpit to her waist.

Ted felt contented. He was satisfied and rested from the afternoon nap, and his stomach was full from the meat and potatoes dinner. He was with the woman he loved, and he was beginning to believe that she loved him too. The bad times in Los Angeles seemed very far away as he led the way into the little lounge. Walking arm in arm with Jeri he felt complete, the comfortable warmness of her arm against his side adding to his feeling of wholeness. They entered the lounge and he led her to two stools at the empty bar.

She didn't know how she was going to get through the next few minutes. It was bad enough that they were here, but Ted had pushed her right up to the bar, pulling out a stool so she had to sit. She sucked in her breath and willed herself to stay calm.

Ted leaned over to watch the activity of the bartender. He was busy chopping or slicing something, his head turned down to the low counter. Either he hadn't noticed their entrance, or he was deliberately avoiding them. Finally, he looked up from his work and smiled down the length of the long bar top. He walked toward them with the patient gait of one that has walked the same ten feet thousands of times. His smile seemed to Ted to be too nondescript, too lacking in personality, as if it were a tiresome part of his tiresome job. Ted thought his eyes looked cynical and old, as if he had spent too many nights in too many bars. His hair and beard were gray, but he was tall and muscular. Yet he seemed to be out of shape, dissipated from some earlier, more solid form. Dorian Gray: the long unused image, from a book he had read his freshman year in college, came to Ted's mind. It was a story about a handsome man with an overdrawn karma account. When the passion bills finally came due, Dorian turned old and ugly. The literary template seemed to fit in a slightly overweight, middle-aged way, and Ted couldn't help but smile. The bartender stopped across the bar from them and extended his hand in greeting.

"Hi there, Jeri. How are you doing tonight?" He grasped Jeri's hand limply. "And you must be Ted. How are you? Glad to meet you." He shook Ted's hand with the strong grip of a bricklayer. "What can I get for you folks?"

"Rémy Martin, a cup of coffee, and a tall glass of water." Ted was beginning to enjoy the ambiance of the bar. He looked around the room as he heard Jeri ordering.

"Just a glass of white wine, please." She didn't look up to John's face when she ordered. She couldn't. He had asked for their order as if nothing had happened between them. That's what he had said the next morning: "This never happened." Did he think she could just forget everything? Had he been able to put it out of his own mind?

There was a small stage set up on the side of the room opposite the blazing fireplace. On the little stage, behind a miniature grand piano, sat a female singer who played the piano and sang quiet love songs. Her voice was low and smooth and sad as she sang an old Beatles song. She appeared to be unaware that the room was empty, her attention firmly on the keys of the piano and the music book mounted above them. When the song ended the room was instantly plunged into an ear-ringing silence, an emptiness that gradually filled with the popping and snapping of the fiercely burning fire. The quiet reminded Ted of the snow that blanketed the mountains, muffling the night. The singer closed the piano and organized her sheet music before leaning down from the bench to switch off the power to her equipment. She stepped around from behind the piano, forced to turn sideways to negotiate the small confines of the little stage. She seemed lonely and far away as she came down the few stairs and into the lower level of the room. She stopped at the jukebox, reaching behind it to turn on the power. It came slowly back to life with the accelerating groan of a country-and-western ballad.

She wore her brown hair in a curly round ball that looked soft as it bounced with each of her energetic steps. Ted was surprised by her petite stature, as her low voice had carried the strong, even power of a larger source. She possessed a full and curved yet well-proportioned figure that deceptively masked her small height until she was very close. Clear brown eyes and a dimple that flashed easily added charm to her rustic talent. She sat down one stool away from Ted and ordered an orange juice by calling to the bartender at far end of the bar.

John brought all three drinks at the same time, serving the singer last. Jeri took a gulp of her wine and watched as he made introductions. "Ted, this is Windy Lee, the best entertainer in this part of the country. Windy, this is Ted, Jeri's boyfriend." He paused and looked back her way. He seemed to be acting completely normal. "You know Jeri, don't you, Windy?"

"Sure. Hi, Jeri. Good to meet you, Ted. Where you from?" She was obviously accustomed to fraternizing with the clientele. Ted liked her in spite of the seemingly artificial interest.

"I'm homeless. Jeri's showing me around a little."

"Lucky you, huh?" She turned to Jeri. "How are you doing tonight? We don't see you out much after the sun goes down."

"No, I generally don't go out much. Too busy, I guess." Jeri tried to sound calm and natural. "But I'm on break from school for a while. How has business been tonight?" Jeri looked around the empty room, hoping she hadn't said the wrong thing. She didn't know the singer well, but she had seemed nice the few times she had served her lunch.

"Don't ask! It has been like this all night. You know, I play this empty room every winter. I don't know why the resort bothers to book entertainment. The skiers either go into town to party or go to bed right after dinner."

"No, not much nightlife at the Iron Horse Inn," Jeri agreed.

"How long have you worked this club?"

"Well, I don't actually work in the bar. I've been working in the restaurant for years. Mornings mostly."

"Sure, I've seen you there. I eat just about every meal in the restaurant while I'm here, although with my hours, I don't eat that many meals before noon."

"I was off today," Jeri said, and felt embarrassed that her statement didn't really fit with the conversation. There was a moment of silence that seemed to beg for someone to say something.

"Hell, this goddamned snowstorm has everyone staying close to home," the gray bartender said. "The bus couldn't even get through to the mountain today. The morning waitresses made a mess of my bar getting pissed-off Texans drunk before lunch." He wiped the shiny, clean bar hard as a means of punctuation. Ted realized he wasn't as old as he had first looked; his silvery gray hair and white beard had rushed ahead of him toward old age. He seemed to be blaming the snow and the closed road for the lack of customers, as if by the damning the weather he could absolve Windy Lee of any responsibility for the empty room. He looked directly at her when he continued to speak. "It happens every time they close the road. Might even have to close up early." He flashed an uninhibited and flirtatious grin at the singer.

"Well, give me a drink, then." The singer shoved her glass of orange juice across the bar with a smile of perfectly straightened white teeth. "If I don't have to work, I might as well play. Right?" She smiled separate dimpled smiles for both Jeri and Ted. They nodded agreement as John went to make her new drink. As Windy Lee told them stories of other towns and other bars where she sang, the big bartender emptied the ice from his station and poured hot water down the drain.

Jeri watched John doing his side work as Ted discussed life in California with Windy Lee. John was ignoring her, pretending that nothing had happened. She felt the embarrassment and anxiety drain from her, and she was able to sip her wine slowly. It was much easier than she had thought it would be. He poured himself a cocktail, and after taking a long, practiced drink, placed it on the stainless-steel counter near the triple sinks where he was washing glasses. She stared at her reflection in the mirror behind the bar and watched John in her peripheral vision as he placed the open bottles into the night cabinets. It hadn't been difficult at all; if he could forget it, she would too. She tipped her wine up and finished it. Maybe she had made too much of it. They had been drunk and high, and it had just happened. She turned to Ted and he was looking at her with concern. He obviously knew she was upset.

"Are you OK, Jeri? You seem a million miles away." He put his arm around her shoulders as he whispered to her. She forced a smile and handed him her glass.

"Sure, I was just thinking about something. How about another glass of wine?" She could see by the change in his face that he believed her. She felt a little guilty at her half-truth, but the feeling left when the quiet of the room was torn by the happy peal of Donna's voice.

"OK, what the hell is going on here? Don't tell me you're closed already." She was across the room and sitting on the stool between Ted and Windy before Jeri could assimilate the new dynamic her arrival had created. "I deserve a drink for driving on a night like this. Black ice everywhere."

"And a drink you shall have, madam," the bartender's voice boomed back. "What will it be? Hot or cold?" He walked to a point opposite Donna, reached across the bar and took both of her hands in his. Donna's small, chill-reddened fingers disappeared into the big man's beefy white hands as he rubbed them. "Not wearing your gloves again, I see. Little girl needs her gloves clipped to her jacket sleeves."

"Hot. Hot and strong." She looked to the brandy and coffee on the bar in front of Ted. "What is that you're drinking? Coffee?"

"Yes, and brandy," Ted answered.

Donna began a survey of the drinks. "And Jeri's into her white wine,"—she turned her head to the singer's glass—"and Windy Lee is drinking—juice or driver? Driver, I think. And the bear behind the bar is drinking, what else, Jack Daniel's." She turned back to Ted and stared directly at him. "I'll have the coffee and brandy."

Jeri wondered what she would do next. Ted might be in for a surprise or two now that Donna was in the room.

"Coming right up," John answered, as he walked to the other end of the bar to pour the coffee. Donna never lowered her gaze from Ted's face.

"So, you must be Ted, the lover." She extended her hand. Ted gave her his hand and she shook it hard three times, as young people will if they are not quite comfortable with the art of shaking hands.

"And you can only be the roommate," Ted said.

"Correctomundo, big boy. Although my roommate isn't coming home much lately." She leaned from the bar to speak behind his back to Jeri. "Cute. Sure you don't want to trade?" He felt Jeri throw a punch at Donna across his shoulders. "Well, I didn't think so." She turned to Ted. "Puritan upbringing, you know." She leaned forward, lifting herself off her bar stool, forearms on the bar, and yelled down its length to the bartender, "Hey, down there, how about that drink?" She turned back to Ted, laughing. "Just can't get good help these days."

Ted couldn't resist laughing himself. Donna's sudden appearance, and her good humor, had triggered an elevation of the mood in the bar. He had sensed a strange tension in Jeri since they finished dinner, and her discomfort had begun to impair his own self-satisfied feelings. But Donna's arrival had lifted the atmosphere in the bar and seemed to release Jeri's strain. As he laughed, he felt the warm breath of Jeri's laugh, soft and damp at the nape of his neck, and in a moment he felt her arms going around his shoulders from behind and her cheek pressing to his ear. He reached back to her, resisting the natural mechanics of his elbow, to place an awkward forearm around her waist. Holding and being held in this way, he regained the confidence that had been fading in the dim light of the dark bar. He found himself once again looking directly into the happy face and glowing eyes of Jeri's roommate. She was quite pretty; dark hair and black eyes contrasted dramatically with the unblemished whiteness of her skin. Very dark lipstick, too inky to be called simply red, caused her mouth to look large and sensual.

The bartender returned with her coffee. "As usual, my dear, you've arrived just in time. Jeri and I were beginning to feel left out of tonight's California travelogue." He placed a brandy snifter in front of her and poured.

"You won't find much interest here." Donna's comment seemed angry and short.

"Ah, Donna, where would you be without Californians and Texans to blame for all that is wrong with Colorado?" The bartender smirked as he poured, shifting his eyes to Windy Lee as he spoke. Ted noticed a conspiratorial wink and realized that the man was deliberately baiting Jeri's roommate.

"Oh no, we couldn't do without Texans and Californians. Without them there would be no traffic, no tourist shops, no pollution. I hate them."

"No jobs, no money, no place to live." Windy Lee spoke with anger in her voice, and Ted saw the unmistakable expression of satisfaction on John's face. Donna's posture tightened and her heavy lips pursed together. She stared across the bar at the bartender without answering the singer's comment.

"Please, John, cut it out." Jeri had managed to put the memory of her night with John out of her mind. Ted's love and Donna's friendship had been unchanged by John's presence. Even John's attitude had seemed the same as it had always been. But she knew that John had somehow instigated the conflict between Donna and Windy, and the knowledge brought back her fear and discomfort. "Please don't cause trouble." She found herself looking directly at John for the first time. There was an instant of repentance in his eyes, and she knew it was not there because of the dissention he was orchestrating. Then it was gone and his face transformed into that of the jocose bartender.

"Oh, Jeri, don't be a spoilsport." He turned away from her and looked at Donna and Windy Lee, who by this time were both sitting stiffly and staring into their drinks. "I love these spirited growth/no-growth debates. Gets the mind working, you know."

"No, John, you just like causing trouble," Jeri said. As she spoke, Ted felt her grip around his shoulders tighten and the muscles of her waist get hard. He wanted to enter the conversation with a witty comment that would defuse the moment, but he didn't understand the stress around him and feared his intervention could make things worse.

"Trouble, spirited debate, what's the difference, as long as we do something to break the monotony?" The bartender took a sip from his drink and put one foot up on the metal sink. He seemed to try to make eye contact with Jeri, but she turned away.

"As long as you are not the one at the ass end of the joke," Jeri said, also sounding angry now.

"No, now that is not correct. I would rather be the object of the joke than to have a boring monotone droning through the room."

He held his eyes on Jeri for only a moment more before turning to Donna. "Hey, wake up. Have another drink, this one is on me."

"Don't tempt me," Donna said quietly, as if trying to control her voice. "This coffee would be a nice addition to your beard." She turned to Windy Lee, who was still looking into her glass. "Windy, I'm sorry, I forgot that you were originally from California. I've only known you from working here, and I've always thought of you as a local. I just got carried away, I guess."

"Hey, I shouldn't be that easy to rile. If I hadn't wanted you to like me, you could never have gotten me going." Windy Lee seemed sad and alone, transformed from the lounge singer with the please-all personality to an orphan in the rain. She took a drink from her screwdriver and smiled sweetly at Donna. "John, make mine to go. I want to try to get up before the train comes back from the mountains tomorrow. That damned whistle wakes me up every morning. I don't know why they blow it right outside my room, anyway." She stood up to put on her coat. The bartender added ice to a large Styrofoam cup and nearly filled it with vodka before topping it with some orange juice. Windy Lee finished her first drink as she stood behind her abandoned bar stool, dressing for the lonely, cold night that was waiting for her outside, slowly putting on her coat, gloves, and stocking cap. She took the Styrofoam cup in a gloved hand and smiled. "So long, see you tomorrow, John. Nice meeting you all, see you soon." She waved forlornly as she left the warm bar with the blazing fireplace.

Ted felt sorry for her at first, then remembered the wink that had passed between her and John. He wondered what game they had been playing and how it would be resolved.

"Shit. I really messed that up." Donna sounded embarrassed as she spoke into her brandy snifter.

"It wasn't you, Donna. John set the whole thing in motion." Jeri reached around Ted to touch Donna on the cheek, using the same hand with which she had earlier punched her friend in the shoulder.

Ted didn't know what to think about these people; they seemed simple at first, yet they were mysteriously intricate. He had not even had time to finish two drinks and had already passed through a full range of emotions: from angst to happiness, then hilarity to pity.

He thought about the bartender's comment about boredom, wondering if their small-town existence caused them to create an endless stream of mind games for entertainment.

"Oh, come on, you guys," the bartender said. "You all look like you just lost your best friend or something. It's her own fault, you know. Windy is just too damned sensitive for her own good." He walked around the end of the bar, went across the room to the now silent jukebox, and began dropping coins into it. The sound of the change clunking into the machine made Ted realize how quiet it had become in the empty bar. The bartender punched numbers without looking at the listings, and the room filled with upbeat modern rock. Ted watched him as he came back to the bar, and just before he sat down next to Donna, John smiled at him and winked.

"Hey, kid. Really, if I had known how that one was going to turn out I wouldn't have started it. Sometimes I just don't know when to quit. I'm sorry." He was looking directly into Donna's depressed face as he spoke, but when he finished he turned to face Jeri and Ted. "And I apologize to you two also. I went too far. I didn't think this one would get so political."

Donna laughed, then said, "Political. I've been called a lot of things, but political is a first."

"Why, baby, you were a regular Ralph Nader." He reached out to put his hands on her forearms.

"Oh, shut up and get me another drink." She was smiling as she pulled her arms away from him. "Who the hell is Ralph Nader anyway?"

"You know, we should all have another one." He stood rapidly, his subtle agility contrasting with his large mass.

"You better make mine a Chivas and soda or I'll never get to sleep tonight," Ted said, pushing his coffee cup from in front of him. He realized the mood of the group was light again, the incident between Donna and Windy past, the energetic music revitalizing the three remaining at the bar. The bartender was back at his station, putting ice into Styrofoam cups, when Donna leaned forward to call to him.

"You are an asshole, you know. I don't know why I hang around with you. Make mine a white Russian." Her voice was loud, competing with the music, but it didn't sound angry. She was once again in a buoyant mood.

"He is an asshole, Donna. You're too good for him," Jeri said. She spoke to Donna between drinks of wine. Ted saw that she too was starting to loosen up.

"What did the old bear do to you?" Now Donna seemed happy, as if asking someone to retell a funny story.

But Jeri was shocked by the question, a fleeting fear of being discovered racing through her mind. Then she realized that Donna's question was innocent. Her secret was still safe.

"Oh, nothing unusual." Jeri stood up as she spoke, moving to stand between the two bar stools where Ted and Donna sat. "Just manipulating people, playing one against the other. You know, the usual." She was standing so the three of them were shoulder to shoulder, holding her wine with both hands in front of her.

"You bet I know, he's located all my buttons," Donna said, looking down the bar to the bartender.

Ted listened to the two women without fully understanding them. He wondered about the lonely singer going out into the snow and hoped that she had not driven, that she had instead taken one of the area's few taxicabs. The bartender brought back four large Styrofoam cups, identical to the one the singer had taken, and Ted accepted they would continue their night without her. Ted was becoming drunk, and the play that had been performed earlier was gradually losing importance. Jeri and Donna seemed not to notice the new drinks as they talked and laughed together, and the bartender continued his work closing up. Ted finished his snifter of cognac, pushing the glass into the narrow lower shelf of the bar, before grasping the white cup that had been placed in front of him. He leaned one leg purposefully against Jeri's hip, comfortable in the contact, with the rest of the party around him secondary to being with her.

He was taking his first drink from the cup of scotch when the phone rang. John looked up from washing glasses long enough to reach back to the wall-mounted phone and answer it. He braced the receiver on his shoulder, leaning his head sideways to hold it, and continued to slosh glassware through the three sinks as he talked. Ted watched him and tried to hear his conversation, but the music, the ongoing conversation beside him, and the motorized brush in the sink made the room too loud. As the bartender spoke, a sly smirk passed over his face. He smiled as he washed, and laughed out loud several times before turning off the brush and holding the receiver out to Donna.

"It's for you, dear, I'm afraid." He handed her the phone, a serious expression on his face. He quickly moved to the other end of the bar where he busied himself with locking up the liquor cabinets below the back bar. This time Ted could hear more of the one-sided conversation.

"Yes? Really? That shit. The whole thing? I should have known I couldn't trust you two…I'll kill the old fart. Sure, we'll be over in a little while. Good-bye now." She walked behind the bar to replace the receiver with the indifference of one who had performed an action many times. She stood motionless, staring down the bar at John, but he would not look up from his work. Finally, she shook her head and returned to her seat beside them. She took a drink from her Styrofoam cup without speaking.

"Well, who was it?" Jeri asked, concerned that something was wrong.

"It was Windy Lee. She's waiting for us to go over to her room." Donna took another drink. "She was in on it. That shit got her to help him set me up." She looked down the bar to where John was carefully keeping his distance. "Don't worry, you gray-bearded old man, I'll get you when you don't expect it. You can come back over here."

"No way." Jeri stood up and looked down the bar at the smiling bartender. "He never lets up."

Ted at last understood what the singer and the bartender had been doing. He turned to Donna; she was shaking her head slowly and seemed to be having trouble stifling her own laughter.

"Yes," she said with a giggle, "Windy Lee is wondering where we all are." She smiled broadly and then tossed her coaster, Frisbee-style, down the bar at John. "She's waiting for us to come to her room and party. They really got me this time."

The bartender quickly finished locking up the liquor, and they left the lounge through the rear exit, each holding a Styrofoam cup. Outside in the cold night, they stood shivering in deep, new snow as John locked the door from the outside. Ted hugged Jeri from behind as they waited, resting his chin on the top of her head. He was surprised by the quiet beauty of the night. The sky had cleared, exposing brightly coruscating stars in the black mountain air, and the snow around them glistened in the glow of neon lighting, as if it were seeded with multicolored chips of glass. They tramped single file across the silent courtyard, placing their feet in the deep holes John depressed knee-high in the new snow, their low laughter muted in the hush that lingered in the wake of the snowstorm.

Windy Lee was staying in a complimentary room at the hotel. When they went inside, Ted saw it was a duplicate of the one he had been sharing with Jeri for almost a week. The bedroom was upstairs in a loft; the living room and bathroom were downstairs. A tiny kitchenette faced out from the back of the room and a large fireplace filled the space next to the door. Jeri and Ted sat together in a deep-cushioned sofa facing the fireplace while John stacked logs in it. He carefully built a tepee-shaped structure with the wood prior to lighting a little block of commercial fire starter at its base. Donna hovered over his shoulder supplying unwanted advice. Windy Lee turned on a small portable stereo and classical music filled the room. She shuffled through her ample supply of compact discs, apparently looking for a suitable recording for her little party.

"Well, I've got classical and jazz. Let me know if you get tired of this and I'll swap out the disc." She dropped heavily into an easy chair that was upholstered with the same Navajo print as the sofa. "I think the cold drains my energy. But that fire should warm this place up in no time. Thanks for starting it, John. I can never get the damn thing to light."

The fire began to blaze with an excited series of small explosions. John and Donna sat next to each other on the stone hearth, with their legs extended straight into the room and their bodies pressed intimately together from shoulder to feet. Jeri felt happy to see them together, unaffected by anything she had done. She leaned closer to Ted and he put his hand on her leg. Everything was going to be OK. Everything bad was in the past. She wondered how Windy felt about being the only single person in the room and spoke to her, wanting to begin a conversation that did not depend on the two couples. "How long are you going to be playing here, Windy?"

"Tonight was the last of it, I'm leaving tomorrow. Back to New Orleans, it's Mardi Gras time." She seemed to remember something and her face paled. "John, the road to the airport won't be closed, will it? Do you think I'll get snowed in now that this storm has hit?"

"No, I don't think the roads will be that bad by tomorrow—not bad enough to close, anyway. These Colorado highway guys are real heroic about clearing off the snow. Too damned heroic, really, they keep getting themselves crushed under avalanches. But 40 East out of Gallup, New Mexico?" He sounded ominous and powerful as he stared into Windy Lee's concerned face. "Now that little stretch of road can get to be a little tricky this time of year, through Oklahoma and Arkansas." He directed his eyes toward Ted in a disarming man-to-man connection as he finished his ominous warning. Ted noted that all the macho disappeared from the John's voice when he spoke to him; a faint cushion of passivity had quietly embraced his words. Ted reevaluated the big man. *He's probably a damn good bartender*, he thought, *a regular human chameleon—must be great for tips.*

Windy Lee crossed her legs and took a showy sip from her Styrofoam cup. "I wish you could come to Mardi Gras this year, John. Everyone else is going to make it. Besides, I hate the idea of taking that long flight alone."

Ted couldn't resist the impulse to look at Donna. Surely, she would become jealous of the implied history between the singer and the bartender. But she appeared undistracted by the historical reference or the remembrance of mutual friends not present.

"Now, Windy, I've done the Carnival thing too many times to be interested, and I've got a good thing going here in Durango." He raised his arm from his lap and draped it around Donna's shoulders for emphasis.

"You could take me with you," Donna said. She now seemed interested in the conversation, but spoke with the defeated tone of a person exhausted from long discussions without progress. "We could go if you wanted to go. You're just bored with it because you've done it so many times. Well, I've never been to Mardi Gras and I'd like to go. I might just catch a plane, too."

Ted felt Jeri lean forward, apparently very interested in the conversation. He turned to face her. She was listening silently to Donna's tired argument, but her eyes were glimmering with excitement.

"Donna, it's just a bunch of drunken, boring kids," John said, removing his arm from around her shoulder.

"Yeah, like me," Donna answered angrily.

"I'd like to go to Mardi Gras," Jeri said quietly. Her voice seemed soothing and gentle to Ted as she spoke, but it caused both John and Donna to jerk upright. Their simultaneous movement seemed comical, almost choreographed.

Jeri had surprised herself. She heard herself saying the words and stopped. The idea of Mardi Gras had seized her before she remembered the situation with John. She wanted to see the famous Carnival in New Orleans, but she had not intended to invite herself on a trip with John. She turned to Ted and he was staring at her, apparently waiting for her next statement. "I mean, if someday Ted and I could go it would be great. You always see it on the television and it seems like so much fun." Ted lifted his eyebrows and cocked his head in a way that indicated he didn't care one way or the other. She began to feel that her mistake would pass and no one would notice.

"See, John," Donna said with great excitement in her voice. "We can all go. You and me and Ted and Jeri."

"Oh shit." John's voice was filled with the dread of an outgunned opponent. "Please, Donna, don't start again."

"Come on, John," Windy Lee said. "You know it will be fun. Everyone is expecting you. I talked to Angie on the phone the other day and she said they have booked a big suite at the Sonesta. And I have a free room there until my gig is over."

Ted had been watching Jeri as the others had been speaking. She seemed excited, her eyes were wide, and she was sitting on the edge of her seat. She was looking at him with anticipation, waiting for him to speak. He didn't care about Mardi Gras or staying in Durango; he only wanted to be with Jeri, and she had just voiced a desire to go on a trip to Mardi Gras. He realized that had he not met Jeri, he would have already left Durango. If they had not met, he would have drifted alone to some other town where he would be drinking himself to sleep, trying to forget his past. But Jeri had changed him, healed him. Their relationship was the only good thing in his life, and after a single short week with her, he knew he would follow her on any quest she could define.

"I'd go." Ted spoke the words before he realized he had an opinion. "Here or there, I'm a sure bet to drink too much," he added.

Jeri let out her breath. He wanted to go. If Ted wanted to go with Donna and John to Mardi Gras, she would go too. As long as she was with him, she knew she would be happy—and safe. It would be better if they went alone, but Donna was her friend, and John seemed to have forgotten everything. If it could be like earlier, in the bar, it would be all right. She would just have to forget everything too. After all, she would be with Ted, not with them. He was still looking at her, and she knew he would do whatever she decided. He was so good to her. She loved him.

"OK, Ted. I guess we're going to Mardi Gras."

In an instant Donna and Windy had pulled Jeri up from the sofa and were hugging her. They erupted into the simultaneous speech patterns only comprehensible by other women—all talking and all listening at the same time. Ted thought it a wonder of female physiology; the outgoing information did not seem to interfere with the incoming. They were standing in the center of the room discussing dress requirements, food, and partying; their faces together in happy comradeship; their feet, at times, lifting off the floor with excitement. Ted could see John intermittently through the dancing legs, facial portraits between the randomly parting curtains of denim. He was staring at Ted with an unhappy grimace obvious through his thick white beard. When he spoke, Ted was surprised at the clarity of his deep voice over the staccato conversation above.

"This is not good. These trips always turn out bad."

"When does Mardi Gras start?" Ted didn't believe any vacation was inherently bad; they became, he had found, what the vacationer made of them. He was committed to the trip, and the excitement in the room was making him feel happy about it. Mardi Gras had always seemed unique to him. He was intrigued by the hundreds of thousands of strangers who came together, abandoning their inhibitions for a short time before the beginning of a religious period of sacrifice and atonement. Until this moment, the closest he had come to Mardi Gras was when he heard about it on the eleven o'clock news after it was over.

"Damn! I'm not going to be able to talk you people out of this, am I? And all this new snow will be going to waste while we stand in the rain in New Orleans." He shook his head and took a drink. "Well, technically, it has already started, but it won't get going really hard until the parades get everyone out into the streets. Fat Tuesday, that's the last day." He looked at his watch and counted on the fingers of his other hand. "That's ten days from tomorrow. There's nothing like it in the United States, Ted. But let me tell you, they will eat these cherries up down there. Windy is strong, she can take care of herself. But they shouldn't go." He gestured with his cup to Jeri and Donna.

"I don't think we can stop them. Do you?"

"No, and that is just too damned bad."

Eventually, their initial excitement dissipated, the three women sat back down. Ted listened while the others talked about New Orleans and Carnival. John seemed to have accepted he couldn't dissuade Jeri and Donna from making the trip and began talking about logistics, becoming more involved with the trip as he planned it. Windy Lee explained she would be singing at a hotel on Bourbon Street that had become an annual rendezvous point for a dedicated group of Carnival revelers. John, it appeared, was one of the original members of the group. But it was another couple, one that now lived in New York, which did the most to perpetuate the perennial party. John had met them while tending bar on Bourbon Street years before. The New York couple made yearly reservations for a large suite at the hotel and the party group would just show up. Windy Lee assured them that the New York couple deliberately reserved too much space because they expected the loosely confederated group to headquarter out of their suite. Windy was adamant in her rejections of Jeri's reluctance to intrude. She insisted that in each of the prior years the rooms had filled with strangers—or worse yet, gone unused.

"Besides," Windy argued, "this year I even have my own complimentary room." Windy was convincing in her assurances that there would be plenty of space for everyone.

"Are you sure that we wouldn't be barging in on your friends' party?" Jeri asked, obviously uncomfortable about showing up without an invitation.

Ted listened carefully for the answer. He knew from sour experience that few things could be more disagreeable than being an unwelcome guest.

"Listen, little girl." John's voice overwhelmed the rest of the conversation. "This is truthfully one case where the more the merrier really applies. These people always get too much space because they never know who will show up. That's why a lot of the people in this krewe do show up. They know they can decide to go at the last minute and not have to fly out of town the same day they get there. Like Windy said, the rooms fill up with street people anyway, might as well be people everyone can trust. Besides, I never heard anyone turn down an offer to help pay. You won't be a charity case, if that's what's bothering you."

Before Ted finished his big drink, it had been decided: they were all going to meet at Mardi Gras in New Orleans. Since Windy Lee had a singing engagement at the Royal Sonesta, she would fly out in the morning, on schedule. John and Donna would make the long drive in his van, and Ted and Jeri would follow by air. John worked out the timetable of their arrival so that the van trip would be comfortably finished before their plane arrived; three days seemed to be the trip John had in mind. If Jeri and Ted arrived four days after the van left Durango, the others would easily be settled and John could pick them up at the airport.

Ted looked over to where the three women were sitting at the little dining table, talking and playing cards. Windy Lee was trying to light a cigarette as she spoke, but the rapid movement of her lips prevented her from holding it steady in the flame of her lighter. She stopped talking for a moment and the end of the cigarette flared, then glowed red. She blew the smoke out of the corner of her mouth with practiced proficiency, aiming at an imaginary spot on the high ceiling. Ted noted disgust in Jeri's tired eyes, directed at the cigarette but not at Windy Lee. Jeri hated cigarettes but never blamed the smokers for the smoke. She seemed to believe that cigarettes were an independent evil, and that the smoker was not a willing accomplice. As he watched, Donna looked at Jeri with the arched eyebrows of inquiry. Jeri shrugged and nodded approval. Donna reached into her purse and produced a joint. When she reached for Windy's lighter, the singer smiled and immediately put out her cigarette.

The five of them stayed in Windy Lee's room until very late playing mindless card games. The snow started again and stopped as they played cards and talked about their upcoming trip. Windy wrote down the details of the hotel in New Orleans and said she would call ahead to inform the New York couple of their plans. John laughed and joked that the New Yorkers would probably try to book more rooms. Ted promised to call John with the flight itinerary as soon as he had made the reservations in the morning. Then finally, with the hint of dawn coming in the loft windows, Jeri and Ted collected their things to leave. At the door John shook Ted's hand tightly as he intimately squeezed his biceps with his left hand. The women exchanged hugs and light kisses all around, and Ted hugged Windy and Donna in turn, placing dry kisses on their cheeks. He noticed that as John hugged Jeri, she turned her head away from him, making even the most innocent peck of a kiss impossible.

Then he was alone with Jeri, back out in the snow. They walked side by side, their bodies touching from where Jeri's shoulder tucked under his arm to where the effort of stomping through the new snow pulled their hips apart. It was snowing again, but the flakes were tiny, their frequency sporadic.

"Ted? Do you think they'll get snowed in tomorrow?"

"I'm just a tourist, you live here. Why don't you tell me?"

Jeri lifted her head from where she had been leaning against his chest, looked up at him and said, "No, they'll get to New Orleans all right." She stopped to face him. "I'm just a little afraid, that's all. I was wondering if it's a good idea for us to go in with them. They could decide they don't want us to intrude on their party. I mean, everything that seems right at night doesn't always sound so good after the sun comes up."

"Especially when you're stoned the night before."

"Exactly. That is what I was thinking. We should give them another chance to decide—in the daytime."

"You are a damned intelligent lady. Do you know that?"

"You just say that when you're trying to take me to bed. But to answer your question, yes, I suppose I do."

They made the final part of the walk under the awning that ran the length of the building. Teenage boys were unloading firewood from a truck that was parked in the courtyard between the two rows of rooms, placing a small pile at each door.

"Hello, guys," Jeri said as they walked by them. They all called back to her happily, answering her by name.

"It's damn late. Tomorrow is shot for sure." Ted spoke as he fumbled with the key, his fingers thick and slow from the cold. The door finally opened and Jeri pushed him into the dark room from behind, both of her hands squeezing his butt.

"Oh, I don't know about the day being wasted," she said. "What could be better than a day in bed with me?"

They undressed quickly and crawled between the ice-cold sheets, snuggling close to keep warm. The feeling of Jeri's hot, smooth skin against his chest and the cold bed linen around them made him pull her tighter to him.

"Ted, are you sleepy?" She spoke into his chest without looking up, and he realized she was asking if he wanted her.

"Yes, Jeri, I'm sleepy. How about you?"

"Very sleepy," she said. They held each other without moving and soon they were both asleep.

Ted and Jeri are lying on long beach chairs, basking in the sun—bathing suits, sunglasses, and oiled skin. Ted watches Jeri and himself from the outside, as if from some point beyond and above the moment. The usual resort paraphernalia litters the white sand near their chairs: beach bags, books, drinks in plastic cups. They are quiescent; if not asleep, then dozing at the fuzzy edge of sleep, the hot sun burning down on them through a cloudless blue sky, their hands linked between them.

Then, with his next breath, he sees them hiking along a coastal trail, still in their swimwear and plastic slippers, walking high on a sandy bluff above the wide beach, the ocean a friendly warm blue at their flank.

Abruptly, with excited looks around her as if to verify her surroundings, Jeri stops walking and drops to her bare knees in a foot of undisturbed snow. Apparently satisfied with the location, she bends forward from the waist, probing the snow carefully with her bare hands, examining its frozen depths for some undeclared and unseen objective. Then she digs frantically, using her small hands roughly to scoop snow from the shallow hole, exposing the outline of an icy trapdoor. She uses her soft palms to scrape the sharp ice from the wooden door until one soft hand hits hard on the frozen blackness of a cast-iron ring. She works fast, both hands sweeping the snow away from the iron handle. Then she turns her face up to him, cheeks and nose reddened by the cold.

"I need to go down," she says imploringly, as if begging for his help.

Startled by the snow and her urgency, Ted lifts his eyes from Jeri and discovers he is with her on a narrow mountain path—just an icy shelf on the edge of a snow-encrusted, rocky cliff. Snow is all around them, on the ground and falling hard in weighty, dry, icy-popcorn clumps. The mild ocean sounds are gone, overwhelmed by the loud whistling of an arctic wind. Turning back to Jeri he finds that she is dressed in the elastic tights worn by mountaineers.

"No, Jeri, everything was fine, don't go!" he yells to her, his voice small and muted in the screaming blizzard.

"Listen to me, I have to go, no choice," she calls back to him. She sounds distant, but he can see the determination in her eyes.

Confused and helpless, Ted watches as she jams both hands through a disk of ice that has formed in the metal ring. Then, grimacing with the effort, arching her body back against the weight of the thick door, the frozen seal of ice cracks. She pulls the door up and lets it fall heavily backward with a crushing flop into the snow, a cold square of empty blackness remaining in its place. Without delay she extends one Spandex-coated leg into the frightening darkness. Ted notices a red nylon belaying harness is strapped tightly around her thighs and waist, and a blue mountaineering rope is laced through the metal fittings of the harness. The rope stretches to a huge pile coiled next to the black pit. Ted is surprised to see that the coil of rope is almost covered with powdery snow, as if it had been waiting next to the shaft for some time. The layer of snow makes it impossible for Ted to see the length of the rope; only a few of the coils are completely visible above the whiteness. He looks up, refocusing his eyes on Jeri and the black shaft as she begins to free climb down the sheer interior face of the abyss. He watches as her tormented face passes from sight, her blue eyes begging silently for help as tears turn to ice on her cheeks.

Suddenly he understands the situation; no time for discussion or logic. He plunges his hands through the snow to the blue coil and pulls it free. Positioning the rope across the wide muscles of his bare back and shoulders, he broadens his stance and braces his rubber beach slippers deeply in the snow. The icy rope scorches immediately taut across the skin of his back. He guides the rope up one naked arm, across his shoulders and back, then down the other arm and into the pit. He leans back against the weight, pushing his swimsuit-covered buttocks against the sharp rock of the cliff. From down in the pit he hears echoes of Jeri's voice.

"On belay!" A clear, emotionless command.

And at the command, Ted allows the razor edge of the rope to cut across his back. The snakelike cord spirals up from its coil on the ground, traces a painful path around his body and disappears down the menacing dark shaft.

"Line! More line!" echoes from the blackness.

He plays more of the rope across his straining back as she journeys deeper and deeper into the icy nothingness. Yet the sound of her voice seems clear and sharp as it drifts up to him with commands.

"Line, I'm going down, deeper. I need more slack." The rope sliding painfully across his raw shoulders, he wonders why she makes him suffer so greatly. Surely she doesn't need to go into this cold, lonely blackness. But silently, submissively he belays line across his abused back. Deeper and deeper she descends, the blue rope pursuing her, her voice tragic in its insecurity and need. "Line, more line."

Ted notices blood flowing from the deep burns in his shoulders, running thickly down the rope and into the pit. The red liquid oozes down the line as it snakes around his arm, trickling down the rope as it slides into the darkness. He follows the flow of blood without remorse, aware now that this was something that needed to be done.

Without warning, the weight of the rope lifts from the deep gash it has carved across his back. Then the painful rope burn is also gone, and in a timeless instant the rope itself has vanished. Then the snow and the pit and the mountain cliff are all gone and only Jeri is left. Standing dry and happy in the warm sun, a few millimeters of white untanned breast peeking from under her colorful swimsuit top, she looks intimately into his eyes. She reaches up to him, encircling his neck with her clasping hands, and pulls herself close. Her body held tightly next to his, her face pressed hard against his ear, she whispers, "I love you."

The sudden, sharp noise of the aircraft's cabin speakers awakened Ted instantly, and his hands snapped from the unread magazine in his lap. The intercom stuttered into a loud, annoyingly familiar, static-garbled weather report from the pilot. Years of flying had given Ted the habit of wearing little foam earplugs, the kind commonly used at industrial sites, while trying to sleep on airplanes. But this trip he had been afraid that Jeri would find the practice an eccentric indicator of aging, like the big black plastic sunglasses, the ones with wide side panels, sometimes worn by old people. The earplugs remained in the outside pocket of his carry-on bag.

"It's a balmy sixty-one degrees in New Orleans with intermittent light rains at this time. We are about ten minutes ahead of schedule and will be landing in about fifteen minutes. Local time is four fifty-five, if you need to reset your watch. We hope that you have had a pleasant flight with us and hope you will join us again very soon. For those of you staying on in New Orleans we wish you a Happy Mardi Gras."

Ted looked out the window to find the sun floating close to the horizon and the plane flying low over heavy, thick white clouds. Gray shadows chased them across the tops of the clouds as the plane's graceful attitude of flight changed to the precise, mechanical stiffness of landing. The flaps whined powerfully as they extended and the wing changed from the convex shape of a sea bird slowing to land to the hard metal calculus of aerodynamics. They descended into the white layer, and the clouds were so thick that the tip of the wing disappeared intermittently. He glanced over to Jeri as she dog-eared the page of the paperback she was reading. Then she bent gracefully to the floor near her feet to stuff the book into the canvas bag that was doubling as an overnight travel case and gigantic purse. She looked up to him and smiled, and for an instant he remembered the strange dream from which he had been awakened. He attempted to recall the details of the wildly disjointed dream, wondering about the dramatic changes in climate and the odd episode of mountaineering. He found he could recover some of the images, but the meaning and importance of the dream, so clear while he had been experiencing it, escaped him.

"You could sleep anywhere, I think," she said. Jeri had watched him sleep between attempts to maintain interest in the mystery novel she had brought for the fight. But the book's plot seemed complicated and slow in the excitement she felt for the trip. She had wondered how he could sleep during the adventure of the flight and with the anticipation of the Mardi Gras. She had ordered a glass of wine and had pretended to read as she watched the activity in the cabin.

"A carefully cultivated ability it is, too. I'm ready for this sinful city now. How about you?"

"Sure I am, but then I'm still young and strong." She leaned her shoulder playfully into his and he looked down at her with mock anger. Buckling her own seat belt, she checked his lap to make sure he was buckled in. *He is so conservative,* she thought, *he hasn't removed his seat belt once during the entire trip.*

"Well, yes, I suppose I am cavorting with a mere child, but only in an intellectual sense, I'm afraid. You are over the hill physically, you know." The plane was in the final glide path, falling toward New Orleans and the Carnival and a hotel suite full of strangers.

"What? Over the hill?" she objected, punching him hard in the shoulder. He was surprised by the pain and laughed as he tried to lean away from her, but he was trapped in his seat.

"Sure, I read it somewhere. It's all downhill for ladies like you after the age of sixteen or so, whereas men only begin to mature in their thirties." He grinned at her, still leaning away, rubbing the pang in his shoulder.

"Nonsense. What scientific journal printed that, *Playboy* or *Hustler*?" She reached down and straightened her clothing as she spoke. "Ha. Thirties? Your bodies may get old, but I don't think you guys ever grow up." She was looking down at her lap, pretending to be insulted, but he knew she was playing with him. He leaned over and kissed her on the cheek, and she smiled without looking at him.

She looked across him and through the small window. The plane broke through the bottom of the cloud layer and she saw that they were very low. A flat, wet swampland—bayou, she supposed—was racing past below; a vast shining surface of standing water, it was discolored with green algae, spotted with the bright bodies of white birds, and broken by the sparse growth of tall, skinny cypress trees. She leaned on Ted to get closer to the tiny window, her face almost touching the glass. She loved to fly. It symbolized, in some abstract way, the modern high-tech world to which she aspired. Ted flew; for him it was a necessary thing. But she lived each flight as if it were the destination, the reason for the trip. They passed an elevated highway, and a big teal sign that was level with the plane as they flew by announced: To Baton Rouge. She took his hand in her own, wanting to share the high excitement of the landing with him. But he didn't seem to appreciate the moment, dropping back into their silly conversation as if nothing was happening.

"Jeri, my love, when I was your age, all I cared about was whether Navy beat Army in the next football game. I hope I've matured a little since then." She smiled, but didn't seem to be listening to him. He realized she had put him on the defensive. "OK, Jeri, quit teasing or I'll let you hold your own hand when we land."

"Bull!" She drew his arm into a coil of strong, slender arms. "I've read about this city, and I'm going to know exactly how to find you every minute during this trip."

He leaned over and kissed her on the head just as the motion of the plane changed to that of a very fast, but slowing, ground vehicle. The engines raced loudly in reverse as the pilot struggled to slow the massive machine on the wet runway, and he felt Jeri's grip on his arm grow tighter during the few moments the procedure was still in doubt. Then the plane slowed to taxi speed, and she gradually released his arm and the breath she had been holding. The plane stopped and she released him altogether. In a way, it seemed to Ted, she had enjoyed her momentary fear. The experience had made her seem very alive and happy.

"Come on, let's see if we can find our luggage," she said.

"I hope ours didn't go to Alaska." He was trying to make a joke, but she was too impatient to appreciate it. She could feel him standing very close behind her, in the narrow aisle of the aircraft. He rested his hands on her shoulders as she watched the other impatient passengers rustling in the aisle, intimate in an unexpected way as they waited for the doors to be opened.

"Do you think they will remember to pick us up?" Jeri asked when he removed his hands to recover his carry-on from the overhead compartment.

"Who knows? If not, we can always take a cab."

"Do you think they will still want us to go in with them on the room?" The tightly packed passengers began to slowly deplane.

"I don't know, Jeri. But the worst case is that we play around here until we get tired, then we get back on a plane for Colorado. Everything will be all right."

As they made their way forward from the Jetway, Ted could see the grandness of the terminal. He was reminded of a European cathedral; the ceiling above them was very high, supported by towering steel arches that curved gracefully down to an expanse of majestic windows, and the wall in front of them was adorned with a magnificent mural of festively colorful Mardi Gras images. Their walk through the terminal ended with a short trip down an escalator to the baggage claim area.

On the way down the escalator Jeri saw John and Windy Lee walking through the glass doors on the far side of the baggage claim hall. The big bartender was wearing a gigantic yellow T-shirt that proudly proclaimed *Coors* in red script, a pair of baggy tan corduroy cutoffs, and a pair of rubber flip-flops. Windy was a little less casually dressed in jeans, a red turtleneck sweater, and a lightweight white blazer. "I see them, Ted." She waved her arm above the crowd and John waved back happily. The big bartender engulfed Windy around the shoulders and changed their course through the dense throng.

"Hello, Jeri!" John yelled over the bobbing heads as he used his large mass to blaze a path through the crowd. "Excuse me, sir!" His voice had taken on an obviously phony Southern drawl, "I'm a-comin' through thar." The accent seemed to Ted to be a poor cross between Colonel Sanders and Yosemite Sam. But John used the deep, powerful, resonating voice generously, and the crowd began to part. The milling passengers turned openly to the sound, as if they expected a performance from a street musician or jazz dancer, mobbing themselves even tighter to make room for the expected performance. But when they turned to see that the source of the theatrics was some exile from a San Diego beach, with silver gray hair and beard, they seemed disappointed. As soon as John and Windy Lee had pushed through, the original confusion pressed back into their wake.

When they shoved their way out of the crowd Jeri knew that Carnival had started. They looked as if they had already been partying, and she couldn't wait to join them. John sounded silly and drunk as he faked a Southern accent, and Windy seemed to be pushing him through the crowd from behind. She looked for Donna, but she didn't seem to be with them. She had a sudden vision of Donna riding a Mardi Gras float, dressed in an old-fashioned gown, and she felt impatient to get out of the airport.

Ted extended his hand, and John greeted him with a knuckle crushing handshake that grew into a quick, awkward hug.

"Welcome, Colonel. As you can see, these Yankees have us outnumbered this time." Ted had tried to affect a Southern accent, but it broke up halfway through his statement.

"Yes, sir." John's accent was more practiced. He was energized, exuberant in a way Ted had not seen him before. "But you and I, sir, and these two fine examples of Southern womanhood, are more than a match for any five hundred beer-befuddled Northerners." Jeri and Windy Lee hugged each other like old friends. Jeri was obviously also very excited, but not in the same wild-eyed way as the big bartender. When John hugged her in greeting, Ted noticed that her reluctance to physical contact, the reticence he had noted in Durango, was gone. She hugged the big man in return, and they even exchanged a small peck of a kiss. Windy embraced him as would a long-lost lover, kissing him hard on the lips, her mouth wet and slightly open.

"Ah, you two have arrived just in time," John said. Jeri could tell by his voice and his eyes that he had been drinking hard, but he was also animated in a way only speed or coke could produce. "This has turned out to be a great Mardi Gras. You two are the last couple coming into town. Everyone has been waiting for you."

"Where's Donna?" Jeri asked. She had the feeling that Donna was doing something exciting, experiencing Carnival without her.

"She's waiting out in the van," John answered. "She gets embarrassed when Windy and I start playing our games. She has no theatrical timing, you know."

"Let's get a drink," Windy said as she took Jeri by the arm. "The luggage will take forever to get here. This way, the closest bar is upstairs." She pulled Jeri into the crowd, grabbing her carry-on bag as they walked. John and Ted followed as Windy Lee set off through the airport, looking for the nearest bar. The two women talked excitedly as they walked a few feet ahead.

John turned to him and said, "You know, I was afraid of this trip, but now I think we are all going to have one hell of a Mardi Gras. You bet, wait until you see the rooms: Bourbon Street side, second floor. Hell, when I first got there I didn't even ask if there were beds or shitters. Not much sleep in store for us anyway. Too close to the action. Don't let me forget to remind Donna to stop for some garbage Mardi Gras beads. We've got to have lots of them to throw off the balcony. It's funny, but during Carnival, the least valuable plastic beads become precious if someone throws them from a float or a balcony. Yep, this is going to be one Mardi Gras to remember, you wait and see, Ted."

Windy and Jeri led the way into the bar, congratulating each other for having found a place to get a drink. Ted thought it probably wasn't too difficult a task in pre-Lenten New Orleans. As the men followed them into the open-front airport lounge, John smiled to Ted and said, "The only thing better than walking behind a woman is sitting on a bar stool next to one, and the next best thing to that is sitting on a bar stool alone."

They stood close to the two bar stools the women had chosen, but did not sit down themselves. The women seemed oblivious to their presence as they talked of things that had passed since they had last met. Ted turned his back to the bar and leaned against the rear of Jeri's stool. She moved forward to make room for him, but a lean was all he needed after the long, confining flight.

"I really need a drink!" John bellowed. "You ready, Ted?"

"I might be coerced into taking a little medicinally myself."

"I think another Daniel's might go down real easy."

"Yeah, well, this will be my first of the day, and the first one tastes like drinking grapefruit juice right after I brush my teeth. Puckers me right up."

Jeri turned a little to put her head on Ted's shoulder; although she still remained sitting forward, her face was momentarily in the men's arena.

"What puckers you up?" she asked.

"Scotch. Makes me cringe to drink it," Ted said.

"Bullshit. You drink more than anyone I know!" She started to turn back to the bar.

"Jeri, I'd like you to meet John. John, this is Jeri. Now I don't drink more than anyone you know."

"Hey, Ted, it's not my fault, you know. It's an occupational hazard. Just like black lung for coal miners, only they have a stronger union." The gray-haired bartender made the statement without a hint of insincerity. Ted wondered if this was yet another joke from the man's extensive repertoire. Windy Lee turned around, her head over one shoulder, her body twisting at the waist.

"Is he giving you that workmen's compensation for drunks rap? Sometimes I think be even believes it himself. Once he had a drunken social worker convinced that retired bartenders should get booze stamps." She used the moment of laughter to pass back drinks with a smile. Across the bar, the bartender was already setting up another round of drinks—including one for himself. He was smiling at the jokes without entering into the conversation. He leaned into the back bar and raised his drink to his lips, nodding his thanks to Windy Lee as he did so. Ted realized that Windy had bought the bartender the drink, but was surprised at the uninhibited way he was drinking it in an airport bar.

"A worthy cause it would be too," John said to the young bartender as he toasted him with a wave of his second drink before finishing it off. He leaned his arm around Windy's shoulder to place his empty glass on the bar. "You know, Donna is going to be scratching mad if we don't get out of this place," he said to Windy.

"You're right!" Windy stood as she spoke, and Ted had to step back to give her room. "Let's get out of this airport before we decide to fly somewhere."

Ted noted that both Windy and Jeri had left their second drinks almost untouched when they left the bar. They would be good party companions during the coming festivities. Outside the bar John took the lead down to the baggage claim area.

The claim area was very small and the low ceilings seemed to press down on them. Jeri felt incarcerated by the room and a little claustrophobic. At the baggage carousel Ted held her in his arms until a bell rang and the luggage began to appear. Jeri wanted to get out of the confining airport and into the Mardi Gras, and she wasn't about to stand behind the mob and let someone else fight for her bags. She moved to the front of the confusion, pushing with the best of the others. She laughed when Windy Lee pushed in next to her, and the two of them jostled happily with the crowd.

Ted noticed that several other baggage carousels had begun to operate, and the number of people in the claim area was multiplying rapidly. The crowd near their carousel thickened as Jeri and Windy rummaged through the madness of mostly drunk and usually rude travelers. But soon they returned from the chaos with all four of the bags. Ted felt slight feelings of inadequacy for letting the women fight for his baggage, but also felt powerful and special for having had them do it. The four of them stood for a moment around their small pile of baggage, the closeness of the crowd pushing them in undesired directions. Jeri looked up at him happily; he could see her pride at having obtained the bags. Then a highly piled baggage cart passed close behind her, the corner of a bag clipping her in the back of the leg.

"Hey!" she called after the offender, before turning back to speak to him. "This place is getting dangerous. Maybe we should get out of here."

"Exactly," John said. He smiled to Jeri deviously as he drew Windy close to him. "Well, Windy, are you ready? I think you're looking a might peaked." The thick Southern accent had returned.

"I don't know, John." Windy was smiling, but she looked unsure of herself. "The last time we tried this, if I recall correctly, it didn't turn out too well. Remember? Police? Angry mob?"

"Oh, Windy, a slight miscalculation in timing, I assure you. Something like that could never happen twice." He produced from the pocket of his cutoffs a shiny chrome police whistle. "Do you think I should chance the whistle?"

"No, John, not the whistle—that would be sure to get us put in jail." Windy's face was serious while she spoke, shaking her head.

"Damn, it really gets their attention." He frowned as he pushed the bright nickel-plated whistle back into his pocket. "All right, woman, here we go!"

"Wait." She took off her jacket and handed it to Ted. "This always works better when they can see some skin." She untucked her sweater and pushed one corner under her bra, exposing her midriff. "OK, ready as I'll ever be."

"Grab those bags, Ted, and pull in close. We've got to be out of here before they know what hit 'em."

Jeri helped him collect their baggage and they waited for what would happen next. John bent over slightly to hide the source as he affected yet another voice, a voice that had no regional clues or informalities, a TV newscaster's voice.

"Make room there! Give the poor girl room to breathe!"

Instantly, the people around them stood in silence, stunned into immobility by the powerful call of authority. Ted followed John's big-eyed gaze to find a sick-looking Windy Lee. The color was leaving her face, and large hard veins had formed in her neck. Her eyes rolled back to expose only the white portions, then she fell in a round-heeled arc toward John. He scooped her up from behind her knees and under her arms like a limp rag doll. Her head fell back on a sickeningly flaccid neck, swinging sideways, her eyes still open and white. Ted felt John's knee kick him in the butt as he carried the stricken singer out through the parting crowd. Ted and Jeri followed closely behind them, carrying their bags as they trotted in the big man's wake. They quickly passed out of the claim area, the airport guards neglecting to check their baggage claim-checks.

Outside, Windy Lee had a miraculous recovery. She leaned up into John's arms, bringing her face near his neck. She looked back to them and winked suggestively before leaning into John's neck and biting the soft skin there, pulling it out in her bared teeth for them to see. John dropped her instantly, but she landed on her feet with astonishing dexterity.

"John and I did a skit like that in the very first joint we worked together," Windy said to Jeri as she skipped to keep up with John. "You two picked it up pretty quick. The last time we tried it someone wanted to give me CPR. It was so stupid it was funny."

John grabbed one of the bags. "Let's go, Ted. I don't want to give 'em any time to think about our little show." There was a mixture of fear and mischievousness in the big man's gray eyes as he rushed ahead.

"Yeah, not much sense of humor around airports these days. It sort of takes the fun out of traveling." Ted was trying to keep his tone light, but he didn't want any trouble. Trouble in an airport meant federal charges. Jeri didn't think the effort had been worth it. She didn't think they had really saved that much time. John just liked to play tricks on people, even if they didn't make any sense.

Parked awkwardly in the parking structure was John's van, side door rolled open, Donna sitting on the floor, her legs dangling over the side. She stood when she spotted them coming her way.

"Where the hell have you been? I've been sitting here alone for an hour." She was directing her question to John, but she glanced over to Windy Lee as she spoke.

"Late flight," John answered tonelessly, as he began to toss luggage into the back of the van.

"Bullshit, John, you stopped for a drink. Didn't you?" She turned back to Windy Lee. "I told you we should make him stay in the van, didn't I? He can't stand to walk past a bar."

"It wasn't his fault, Donna, I wanted to stop. I had been feeling faint." She raised the back of her wrist to her forehead, pretending to be dizzy.

"You two really did it? I can't believe it." Donna turned to Jeri. "Did you see them?"

"Sure did. Windy deserves an Oscar." Jeri wanted to put the airport behind them and climbed into the van. Windy and Ted followed her through the side door. John and Donna entered through the driver and passenger doors.

Ted was amazed by the inside of the van. It was half barroom and half bedroom. "Well, this isn't your ordinary delivery truck, now is it?" He watched John as he fiddled with buttons and switches from his seat behind the wheel. Dials, gauges, stereo system, and telephone lighted up in sequence. It was like a huge, shiny child's toy. Finally the engine started and the van pulled away from the curb. Windy knee-walked to a small wet bar and began to put ice into Styrofoam cups. They were identical to the ones used at the bar of the Iron Horse Inn.

"Anyone want a drink? Anyone but you, John. You're cut off until we park." Windy's voice was harsh and loud as she yelled over the road noise and the stereo.

"Just give me a plain soda, Windy. I can wait until we get this boxcar through all those one-way streets." John called back over his shoulder, turning his head briefly away from the road.

"Make that two, please," Donna said, as she turned sideways in her seat to face the windowless rear part of the van. "I can wait too. It's going to be a long night." She looked directly at Jeri and smiled broadly. Ted could see that the two young women shared a special excitement for the trip. Jeri leaned forward and put a hand on Donna's knee. Donna took the hand in both of her own, and they seemed to communicate without words as they stared at each other. Windy Lee knee-walked between them carrying two of the big cups.

"Plain sodas for the pilot and copilot. How about you guys?" she asked Jeri, assuming she would order for both of them. Jeri glanced to catch his eye. He shrugged.

"Sodas for us too," Jeri said. Her voice was animated and happy. "Do you need some help?"

"Naw, I've got it covered. But this is some party group. Plain soda all around and hold the lime." She moved to the wet bar as she spoke, shuffling awkwardly, her arms waving for balance. "Hell," she said while she filled more cups with ice, "I'm going to have a screwdriver. Just as a matter of principle."

Jeri didn't like the back of the van. It was dark and had a damp, musty smell. When everyone had a drink, she crowded forward between the front seats to look out from the dark interior and watch the scenery speed past. The road was lined with brick apartment buildings and an occasional ramshackle house, the front yards of which were dotted with cars of questionable serviceability. The apartment buildings and rundown homes approached quickly, stood depressingly alongside for an instant, and then shot out of sight behind the van to become fading memories. The highway was posted liberally with gambling theme billboards: Harra's Diner, Four Seasons Sun Rooms, Landmark Motor Lodge. In a half hour the van, riding high on an elevated superhighway, had drawn abreast the city of New Orleans, a giant gray hump dominating the skyline.

"What's that?" Jeri pointed out the windshield at the hump.

"That's the Superdome, my dear!" John looked over at her as he drove. "They say it almost got blown down during the hurricane. But it's all fixed up now."

"You mean it's right downtown? Seems like they would have put it outside the city."

"Hell, lady, it's practically inside the French Quarter."

Ted too began to feel the excitement of the adventure and glanced away from the windshield to look at Jeri. She was alight with energy and happiness, and the longer he looked at her, the happier he became. Finally, he leaned over and placed a light kiss on the side of her neck. He was surprised when she turned to face him and the light peck he had planned turned into a vigorous, emphatically sexual encounter of long duration. He was stunned that she would kiss him so sexually when the others could see. It didn't seem like her. He tried to pull away, but she seemed reluctant to let him go. At last he broke the embrace and looked into her eyes. She didn't seem aroused. He realized that the kiss had not been in spite of the people near them, it had been because of them. She had been making a statement that he belonged to her. It made him feel good, desired and loved. He squeezed the knee he was holding and winked what he hoped said, "Later. Wait until I get you alone." She smiled and put her hand down to hold his. He turned to John, who had been busy weaving the van through traffic and seemed not to have noticed them kissing beside him.

"Hey, John. These vans really work, I see. Didn't even take an hour."

"Don't worry, I'll get us down there. People tend to give a van room when you push them."

"No. What I mean is what one of these things does to a woman. It's great." Jeri pushed him lightly in the forehead before turning back around to look out the windshield.

"Yeah, sometimes it works like that and sometimes it don't. Just have to keep a good high turnover in women to be sure." This time it was Donna's turn to shove. Only she didn't spare her strength. The van lunged suddenly toward the bumper-to-bumper traffic beside them. The line of cars parted immediately and the van passed through them, decelerating unmolested down the Claiborne Avenue off-ramp. "Thank you, dear, as usual, your timing is perfect. This isn't exactly the off-ramp I was planning to use, but it will do. We'll be on Canal Street in just a few minutes."

"If you weren't driving, you would have gotten a whole lot worse than a little shove," Donna threatened.

John looked over his shoulder to Ted while he slowed down at the end of the off-ramp. "Ain't she beautiful when she gets pissed? I try to get her that way as often as I can just so I can look at her."

"Bull. You're just an old tease and you know it."

"Yes, dear."

Jeri wanted to be near the windshield so she could see outside, but she made sure Ted was beside her, between her and the driver. They were standing on their knees between the two captain's chairs as the van moved slowly down Canal Street. All five of them were pushed forward toward the windshield trying to see. They watched the people and studied the large business buildings, pointing and sharing their discoveries. The day was overcast and gray, and the grayness permeated the old buildings, but it seemed to Jeri that the people on the streets overwhelmed the grayness with their freshness and color. They were crowding the sidewalks, a sea of varied-colored people and clothing, some dressed in the dark suits of business and others garbed in the vivid, nonsensical costumes of tourism and Mardi Gras. They slowed into a traffic jam. A small parade was moving madly from a cross street and a crowd of pedestrians blocked the road. Jeri was elated by the sounds of the Carnival coming in through Donna's window.

Windy Lee was so close behind them that Ted could feel her breasts against his back. He shifted closer to Jeri to make room for Windy to move forward, next to John. Jeri slid into the big chair with Donna, and her friend moved over to make room for her. Ted found himself next to Windy Lee, on their knees between the chairs. They were all watching the insanity in the streets just outside the van, when Jeri turned to him and planted a kiss on his grinning lips.

"I'm so happy we came, Ted. Thank you so much. I've always wanted to come here." Before he could answer she was leaning across Donna's lap and out of the passenger's side window, calling and waving to the crowd that followed the parade, now passed.

"Hell," John said to Ted, "I hope I can get to the damned hotel. This place has already gone berserk." John was not complaining; he was glowing with happiness. "You know, these are my kind of people." He turned off the engine as some merry drunks formed off in the windshield, plastic cups in their hands. Ted turned to Jeri in time to see her pulled out through the open window, laughing uncontrollably. He moved up into her vacant place beside Donna, prepared to go to her aid, but he found her just outside the window, dancing wildly with a half-dozen masked Mardi Gras cartoon characters. She came back to the window, still laughing, but wearing a plastic Popeye mask. Ted couldn't help laughing; the vision of her beautiful body and lovely hair joined to a Popeye face was ridiculous. The thickest part of the crowd had, by this time, moved along with the parade, off Canal Street and into the French Quarter. Jeri was leaning in through the window looking at them, cocking her head back and forth. John finally spoke to her.

"Now listen, Popeye, get back inside so we can get out of here before that parade comes back, or another one blocks off the way to the hotel."

Jeri opened the door and squeezed into the seat on the other side of Donna. She hated to leave the crowd of people partying in the street so she leaned out through the window from inside the van. They again started down Canal Street as the way began to clear, but at an incredibly slow pace. She almost fell out the window when the first streetcar she had ever seen passed dangerously close, with the conductor ringing his bell emphatically to warn them out of his path. John seemed oblivious to the warning and turned up the volume of the stereo. She raised her mask a little to take a sip from her drink; an icy, pink, sweet drink in a clear plastic cup.

"Where did you get that?" Ted asked.

"Chuck bought it for me. They were selling them through a window back there. This city is great." She lifted the mask to the top of her head, but did not take it all the way off. She pointed down the middle of the wide street to the famed New Orleanian streetcar as it clanged noisily away from them. It was overflowing with the drunken revelers of the holiday, screaming heads and waving arms protruding from its green body as it turned suddenly to the right and left Canal Street. Donna seemed to read her mind and spoke first.

"We have to ride the trolley cars, John." Donna sounded like a child as she begged.

"Streetcars, Donna, streetcars. We will do everything, I promise," John soothed. "We just need to get everyone settled. It's going to be a trick to get to the hotel. The police barricade off Bourbon Street when the sun goes down. Our hotel is on Bourbon, but the parking lot is a few blocks away. I hope we can just get unloaded and let a valet park this thing. I'm getting tired of driving. Hell, the valet will unpack the van if we give him enough green—that is, if we want to take a chance." He turned to Ted and raised an eyebrow knowingly. "One time when I came down here the parking lot attendants at the Marriott were stealing the cars right and left. Only the best ones, mind you. They definitely went for the expensive ones. I talked to a guy who lost a new Mercedes. Told the attendant to get it one night and it was gone. The guy was heartbroken."

"I think we can unpack ourselves, if that's what you want."

"All I want is to park this boxcar and get out into the streets." He slowed to a stop in the right-hand lane. "I'm going to ask someone who looks sober how to get to the Sonesta." A pair of blue-shirted patrolmen stood on the corner, talking happily to a group of wildly drunken teenage girls. John inched the van forward and stopped beside them. "Officers? Officers?" He called across Ted and the two women crammed into the passenger seat beside him. One of the policemen looked up and walked around to John's side of the van.

"What can I do for you, sir?" He was looking into the van, at the gauges, the gaudy instrument lights, the women, and the Styrofoam cups. When John spoke to him, he redirected his attention to John's face.

"We have a room at the Royal Sonesta, but I'm afraid we can't get to it. I was wondering if you could tell us the best way to get there."

"I can. Turn left on Burgundy and stay on it until you get to Saint Ann Street. Take a right on Saint Ann and go down to Royal. Go up Royal until you get to Conti and take a right. Stop before you get to Bourbon and walk the rest of the way. They'll park for you."

"Thanks a lot, Officer."

"No problem. But by the way, we're easygoing down here, but it is still not legal to drink and drive. I suggest you park this van as soon as possible."

"Sure thing, Officer, and thanks a lot."

The policeman nodded with thin lips before returning to the corner where his partner waited. As he walked away, John pulled the van forward. "These guys are the greatest. As long as you don't get violent, they cut you a mile of slack. Just never get violent." He turned to Ted and smiled cynically. "No use arguing with the guy over a plain soda. Eh, Ted?"

He inched the van forward and took a left turn onto Burgundy Street. Their progress slowed almost to a stop as pedestrians seemed to zoom past them. Delivery trucks and private cars partially blocked the narrow street. Ted realized that it had been designed and built hundreds of years before the first automobile was invented. John continued to edge forward, zigzagging his way between obstacles.

The street was churning with human activity. The storefronts on each side of the one-way street were bursting with the tiny stores that sold souvenirs and T-shirts to the masses. The tourists walked down the sidewalks and into the street, drinking cocktails in plastic cups. Policemen, though numerous, seemed to be relaxed and happy to be at work. After nudging the big van forward for twenty minutes, a distance that could have been walked in five, John pulled the van to the curb in front of the valet parking area of the Royal Sonesta Hotel.

Jeri knew the Royal Sonesta had been an old hotel before she had been born. She had been told that it was one of the best places to stay while visiting the French Quarter of New Orleans, but she was not prepared for the customer-oriented Southern elegance that was carefully fostered by the hotel employees. A doorman wearing spectacular green livery guided them into the hotel, opening the glass doors for them, inviting them inside with a sweep of his white-gloved hand. Colonial French architectural techniques flavored the immaculately maintained brick and wood construction, but the ambiance of the hotel throbbed with the energy of the modern American South. Tall arched windows fronted the wild Bourbon Street side of the lobby, and a wall of French doors led to a sidewalk cafe beyond it. The lobby was busy with tourists and hotel guests, but when compared to the chaos that reigned just outside the glass doors, it was a quiet retreat. Anticipation of joining the crowds outside filled Jeri with excitement, causing her heart to beat faster.

John, Donna, and Windy Lee had rushed away to the elevators as soon as they had entered the lobby, laughing and joking back to them, even as the doors slid closed. She and Ted had walked hand in hand through the teeming lobby to the registration desk. As they waited in line at the check-in counter, the quaint beauty of the hotel and the sensuous excitement of the street made her want to scream. The building energy within her brought a rush of romantic fulfillment. She pulled Ted's arm closer to her, gripping his biceps hard with both hands. She looked up to find him smiling down at her. He brought his other arm across his chest and patted her hands, resting his hand on hers. They stood very close to each other, their arms tightly interlocked.

"Not bad, so far, huh?" He nodded his head at the lobby as he spoke.

"It's great, Ted, thank you so much. I can't wait to see our room."

"The pleasure's all mine, dear, but I'll be glad just to get a room. I know what Windy said, but it makes me nervous when I don't make the reservations."

Jeri felt a wave of anxiety wash through her body. She was suddenly worried that they would not be able to stay as they had planned. The thought of going back to Durango without having experienced the end of the Mardi Gras party made her feel gloomy and unhappy. She felt Ted's grasp on her hands tighten.

"Don't worry, Jeri. We've got a room. I didn't mean to throw cold water on your excitement. In another life I was the type that always wanted to take control of everything." When he finished speaking, he leaned down to kiss her. Physically and emotionally ready for a deep, romantic kiss on the mouth, Jeri bowed her neck and closed her eyes. Presenting her face to him, she felt his lips touch her forehead lightly. She was surprised and disappointed. She immediately opened her eyes to find him watching her face. He smiled and kissed her again, but this time on the lips. She pulled him close with all her strength, kissing him deeply. She felt his mild resistance break, and he kissed her back. The kiss did not end quickly. Finally, he pulled himself a few inches away from her, but she saw reluctance and love in his eyes. He glanced away to the registration desk and his face filled with embarrassment. She looked to the desk also; the clerk there was watching them, a knowing smile on his face.

"You are very hard to resist, Jeri. But we're at the front of the line. Don't you think we should check in?"

She watched the flowing crowd outside the windows and the busy people inside the lobby as Ted went through the formalities of checking them into a room adjoining the party suite. A uniformed bellman led them to a nearby elevator, pushing a brass luggage cart in front of them. Even the elevator seemed to be from a bygone era; it was tiny and airless, yet elegantly detailed with antique brass fittings and smoky old mirrors. The bellman led them down the narrow second-floor hallway. She could feel the old wooden floor give under their feet as they walked, and she bounced a little to accentuate the sensation. The lighting in the hallway was dim and yellow, but to Jeri's surprise, not in the least depressing. It seemed that the heavy red carpet and the flocked velvet wallpaper were slowly consuming the artificial light as soon as it shone from the Victorian sconces. The bellman stopped in front of a nondescript wooden door. Aside from a brass number tacked to its surface, it was identical to all the doors they had passed in the hallway.

The room was very small, dominated by a four-poster bed with a frilly canopy. The bathroom was tiny and just a little overused; the white porcelain was a shade nearer beige, the wallpaper bore a few too many moisture spots, and the tub and shower combination hinted of a European retrofit. But Jeri was ecstatic; she loved the room. They were finally at the Mardi Gras. The bellman concluded his short presentation by pulling open the thick flower-print curtains to reveal white wooden French doors and a narrow wooden balcony. The intensity of sounds from the street below increased immediately. Muted through the glass of the French doors, a background of loud music and crowd noise was sometimes overwhelmed by sudden cheering from the street and hysterical shrieks nearer the room.

There were people outside on the balcony; the occasional passing of a quick figure, the sporadic screaming of female voices, and the frequent peals of uncontrolled laughter brought them into the room. The bellman was looking expectantly at Ted, with his hands on the double handles of the French doors. "Would you like me to open the doors, sir?" he asked.

"No." Ted fished a tip from his pants pocket. "I think we can get them open when we need to. We might want to get settled first."

The bellman took the bills with a little bow from the waist.

"Thank you, sir. Let us know if there is any way we can help." He spoke as he walked back to the hall door, counting the money on the way. Once he had closed the door behind him, Jeri looked to Ted with amusement.

"Well, sounds like we won't be far from the action."

"Yeah, we might have to get another room—in Biloxi—if we ever want to get any sleep."

A sudden pounding interrupted Ted as he spoke. They both looked to the only door the bellman had not explained. The loud pounding grew and an unintelligible yelling began in muffled accompaniment. Ted walked to the door opposite the bed and placed his ear against it to listen. "Damn, I think they are calling our names." He reached for the knob and smiled back at Jeri. "Are you ready for this? I think it's the gang from Colorado." He held the knob, but did not turn it. The pounding and yelling increased to yet another level.

"Hell yes, that is why we're here, isn't it?"

Ted turned the knob and both Windy Lee and Donna tumbled into the room, laughing and screaming, drinks spilling on themselves and the carpet. Ted watched as the old-girl network joined in a football huddle hug, jumping and spinning in rapid circles, the drinks continuing to spill. He passed by them, through the two doors that separated their bedroom from the rest of the suite.

The adjoining suite looked like the living room of a small apartment. The area opposite the doorway was occupied by several sofas, some matching chairs, and several coffee and end tables. The room was split-level; near the door to the outside hallway a single step led up to a kitchen and breakfast counter. Over the small kitchen area was a loft bedroom. Opposite the kitchen, on the side of the room that faced Bourbon Street, were two sets of French doors identical to the set in their bedroom. These were both wide open to the balcony. There were a half dozen people outside, calling down to the street and throwing things to the crowd. The living room was almost empty; a single male form sat on one of the sofas. He was facing away from Ted, hunched over the coffee table. He soon leaned slowly back from the table, drank leisurely from a cocktail, and, still facing away from him, stood deliberately from his seat. The man paused for a moment, watching the people outside. Then he seemed to sense Ted's presence and turned to face him.

"Ah, you must be the rest of our Rocky Mountain contingent," he said. He walked carefully around the furniture, a large glass in one hand and a fat cigar in the other. "Windy and Donna have not shut up about you two since they got here."

He was tall, six foot three or four. He was wearing a white polo shirt; his heavily muscled and deeply tanned arms defined Ted's quick first impression. His hair was cut very short and he wore a neat mustache of the same length. Round, gold wire-rimmed glasses, perfectly positioned high on his sharp nose, gave him a scholarly look that contrasted mildly with his muscular physique. He walked across the room to Ted, a smile that seemed a knowing smirk exposing large white teeth. He put the cigar into his mouth and extended his right hand.

"Sam Williamson." He spoke with practice around the smoking cigar. Ted took his hand and shook it; his handshake felt deliberately limp, as if to say: "I don't need to show you how strong I am with my shake, it should be obvious."

"Ted Johnston. Nice to meet you. Are you the person I should thank for getting us a room on such short notice?"

"That would be Angie. She works miracles like that all the time. Angie, my wife, is out on the balcony somewhere. The girls are out showing their tits to the mob, and when Angie gets wild enough to do that, it incites the rabble. Very impressive, believe me." He did not seem bothered by the cigar smoke when it wafted up to his eyes, but he released his grasp quickly and recovered the cigar from his mouth. The crooked grin returned to take its place. Ted didn't know how to answer the man's comment about his wife so he didn't reply. They just stood staring at each other. He was beginning to feel uncomfortable with the man's lazy stare when Jeri, Donna, and Windy Lee loudly entered the room.

"I see you two studs have met," Windy Lee said as she walked quickly past them. She continued across the room to the sofa and sat in the same spot the big man had occupied when Ted had entered. She leaned forward to put down her drink before turning her head over her shoulder to continue speaking. "You know, we shouldn't let these men spend this much time alone, you know how they like to brag to one another." She bent over, out of Ted's line of sight, but obviously down to the surface of the coffee table. Jeri had moved close to him, putting her arms around his torso, pressing her head into his shoulder.

"I'm not letting this one out of my sight with you two alley cats prowling around." She lifted her face to be kissed and Ted felt an unembarrassed need to kiss her. When the kiss was over, he noticed that Donna had also moved to sit on the sofa. Soon after Windy Lee sat back, Donna leaned down to the unseen coffee table. Sam Williamson was still standing watching Ted and Jeri. Ted was surprised and a little miffed by the man's frank examination of Jeri, but before the feeling could grow into anger the open inspection turned back to Ted.

"Quite a party going on, Ted. I hope we don't do anything that makes you feel uncomfortable." Sam spoke softly, his eyes narrow, watching Ted closely.

"I wouldn't worry about that, Sam, but I do draw the line at going to jail. I'm better at bailing other people out than actually being incarcerated."

"All the better, we may need a good phone man before this is over. Do you need a drink?" He waved the cigar at the small kitchen on the upper level. "We have just about everything you need in the kitchen."

"Why not? I probably do need a drink. It is Mardi Gras, isn't it?" Ted put his arm around Jeri's shoulder.

"That it is, Ted, that it is." Sam waved his cigar one more time as he turned back to the center of the room. He walked around the furniture to the sofa as Ted and Jeri moved to the kitchen.

The counters were covered with the cork-lined plastic trays used by hotel room service workers. They held empty, partially emptied, and yet unopened bottles of alcohol. Strangely small, the hotel bottles looked like the larger, commonly available versions, but they seemed half or three-fourths the size of the liquor store variety. One of the two sinks was filled with blue plastic bags of ice. The bottom of the stainless-steel sink was lined with empty bags. The ice in several unopened bags was slowly melting away, diminishing into yet more blue plastic sink liners. As Ted filled two plastic cups with ice, Jeri stood behind him, her arms wrapped around his waist. He could feel her head and her breasts against his back; her affection made him feel comfortable in the new environment.

Where he stood, leaning over the sinks, he had an easy view over the breakfast counter and into the living room. Windy, Donna, and Sam were sitting next to one another, drinking and talking with their backs to him. Occasionally, one of the three would bend over to bring his or her head close to the top of the coffee table. They were snorting drugs. He assumed it was cocaine, but he realized it could be methamphetamine or even heroin. It could be anything, really, any white powder that human beings would form into long, thin piles and inhale through tubes rolled from common paper money. Ted was reminded of his past and his dead brothers and Mary Peralta. This scene had been played out so many times with him in the audience that he was not shocked or surprised or even upset. It just seemed to be part of life, another dangerous part of living in the modern world. He watched them a little longer before returning his attention to the plastic cups of ice. He reached for the small bottle of scotch whiskey as he looked over his shoulder to Jeri.

"What would you like to drink? Seems that they're well stocked. They have Stoli, if you want it." He felt her arms loosen their grasp around him and her body pull away from his back. He felt suddenly cold where her warmth had been.

"That would be good, with Seven Up. Do they have Seven Up?"

"Yep, right here with the rest of the midget bottles." Ted made the drinks without looking fully around to Jeri, afraid he would find her watching the drugs. When he finished the drinks and turned to face her, she was staring over the breakfast counter to the coffee table and the three people sitting in front of it.

"Let's join the party, shall we?" She took her drink, stood on her toes to kiss him lightly, then moved away to the living room. Ted hadn't answered, but she sensed that he had followed her. She wondered if he was ready for this party, hoping he would not be upset. She squeezed onto the sofa next to Donna; they all shifted over to make room for her. As soon as she sat down, Donna handed her a smoking joint. She took a long hit, knowing Ted would be watching. When she was finished, she looked up to offer it to him with her eyes. He declined with a diminutive shake of his head that she knew only she noticed. She passed it to Windy instead. He sat in a chair that faced them at a ninety-degree angle, the glass coffee table extended lengthwise from him.

He was watching her. It made her feel self-conscious. But she wanted to get high and there was more coke in front of her than she had ever seen. She knew he wanted her to decline the coke, but she also knew he would not be angry; he would be disapproving, but not angry. He put his drink down on the corner of the table, and as she leaned over and inhaled one of the lines she could see him watching her. She leaned her head back, using her free hand to hold her nose tightly closed, struggling not to sneeze. When the sneeze had passed, she remembered she still held the tube; she placed it back on the glass surface of the table. Sniffling, she blinked away the moisture that had formed in her eyes. When she thought about Ted watching her she felt again self-conscious, embarrassed. She looked back up to him, blinked away a tear and hoped he would understand. She smiled at him through her watery eyes, hoping he would have a good time.

"Care for a line, Ted?" Sam Williamson asked very quietly.

"No, I'm OK for now, Sam—maybe later," Ted answered, feeling he had spoken too quickly, thinking he had sounded too sure of his response. Becoming suddenly aware of his hands, they felt large and awkward; he picked up his glass to give them something to do. Without tasting the scotch, he took a long, slow drink. He wondered where this Mardi Gras trip was going to take them, him and Jeri. He hoped they would be safe—that they would someday be able to laugh about it as part of their dangerous past. He was feeling very much outside the group when Sam Williamson's wife came into the room from the balcony.

"Is this all you're going to do this vacation, Sam? Hell, you could do this in Manhattan." Her voice was very powerful but not shrill. She had walked into the room as she was speaking, stopping in front of the coffee table, facing Sam and the three women who were bunched tightly together, shoulder to shoulder, facing the drugs. "Just look at you people. That can't be very comfortable."

Ted was definitely not looking at the four on the sofa; he was looking at the woman who had saved him from his lonely exclusion from the drug camaraderie. She was short, as short as her husband was tall, five foot one or two. She was wearing tight black pants and a long-sleeved, lightweight red turtleneck. She was standing with her weight shifted to one leg, her hands on her hips, tapping the weightless leg in front of her in playful displeasure. She was smiling broadly; Ted could see that behind her dark red lipstick, her teeth were imperfect. Her thick black hair was very straight, cut to her chin and curled under in an attractive, shiny wave. She had big brown eyes and a somewhat large and hooked nose. But her most dominant, most noticeable feature was the size of her breasts.

Ted was astounded; he wondered if it was an illusion brought about by slightly larger than normal breasts placed on her small frame or if she was truly a wonder of magnitude. He felt his glance linger a moment too long and quickly brought his eyes up to her face. He found her watching his eyes, a knowing grin on her lips.

"Well, Sam, are you going to introduce me or are you too drunk?" She walked to the chair opposite Ted's, at the other end of the table. She crossed her legs when she sat down, dropping her hands into her lap. Ted felt that she had been staring at him as she had been speaking.

"Angie, this is everybody. Everybody, this is Angie." Sam raised his glass to the small woman and took a drink.

"I'm afraid that may be as good as we get this time of the evening." She leaned out of her chair and extended a tiny hand to Jeri. "Hi, I'm Angie Williamson, Mr. Manners's wife." Jeri found her voice warm and soothing after the phony anger she had shown toward Sam.

"Hi, I'm Jeri Singleton." Jeri felt slightly intimidated by the meeting. She had thought of nothing but getting high since she had entered the room. Now she felt some doubt that she could speak coherently. "This is my boyfriend, Ted Johnston. Glad to meet you."

"Me too. Windy and Donna have told me so many good things about you. And let me tell you, girl, when Windy Lee says another woman is nice, that person is nice." She turned to Ted, "Glad to meet you, too, Ted. I hear you're some kind of a wandering playboy, escaped from California. That true?"

Jeri was fascinated by the woman's presence and by her heavy New York accent. She was such a little woman to have such power over people; in moments she had taken over the room and all those within it. Jeri liked her instantly.

"Hardly, just trying to stay close to Jeri," Ted said. He seemed to be deliberately trying to avoid looking at her. The avoidance led

Jeri to study the woman more closely. She was not a young woman and not beautiful in the accepted way, but she was seething with sexual energy. Her outfit was outrageously tight and her bust was so big it seemed she would burst out of it at any moment. Jeri immediately wondered if she had undergone enlargement surgery, but hoped she had not. Boobs that were naturally that big were a little embarrassing, but phony ones of that size were simply grotesque. Then she realized it didn't matter; she liked Angie and would do all she could to become her friend.

"Well," Angie said, "you sure can pick 'em, Ted. This lady is one beautiful woman. They would be falling all over her in New York."

"They fall all over her wherever she is, only she doesn't seem to notice."

Jeri was feeling very self-conscious by the conversation. She knew she was attractive, but she never thought it was a big part of who she was. She was beginning to feel the power of the coke she had ingested, and her wit, dulled by the pot she had smoked, began to return.

"Hey, folks, this is me, in the room with you? Can we change the subject, please?" Jeri pushed herself up from her seat, smiling at Angie. "Besides, Ted likes me for my mind, don't you, Ted?"

"That's right, Jeri." Ted stood up too, following her lead. "That and your money."

Jeri saw a change take place in Angie. The happy, dominant woman seemed to shrivel in front of her eyes. The power and the energy drained from her face and she seemed, during that moment, older and less sure of herself. Jeri didn't know what had happened, but she felt that moving away from the living room would help.

"Hey, what were you doing out on the balcony? It sounds like half the town is downstairs." She picked up her drink and stepped from behind the table, pulling herself fully upright, throwing her shoulders back. "I'm ready to find out what Mardi Gras is all about." She spoke directly to Angie, hoping she could communicate her empathy and willingness to be friends. The effect was as instantaneous as the deflation that had drained the other woman's face seconds before. The powerful, attractive, sexy Angie was back in the instant.

"We were teasing the crowd, Jeri. Throwing doubloons and beads and, if one of the horndogs performs satisfactorily, showing a little tit." Angie spoke as she led Jeri to the French doors, and Jeri let herself be led. Then Donna and Windy Lee were by their sides, and the four of them were moving through the doors out onto the balcony.

"Don't let her kid you, Jeri," Windy Lee said. "It is impossible for Angie to show a little tit. If you get what I mean." They all laughed, including Angie, as they walked through the doors onto the balcony. And as they stepped outside a loud cheer came up from the crowd below.

"Not bad for the ego, eh, Jeri?" Donna was by her side screaming in her ear. "This is better than getting high."

The old wooden balcony was narrow, feeling slightly unstable beneath Jeri's feet. Below was Bourbon Street, paved, it seemed, with upturned faces. The people in the street, mostly men, were waving and yelling up at them.

"Watch this," Donna screamed again as she leaned over the railing. She shimmied her breasts at the mob and the roar from below redoubled. "Hell, and I don't even have big tits. Got to love it." Jeri couldn't help enjoying the excitement of the animalistic adulation.

Ted and Sam watched from the threshold of the French doors. Ted felt good about the way the four women had taken to one another. It reminded him of college parties he had not remembered for years. Only his concern about Jeri and the coke tempered his good feelings.

"They are something, aren't they?" Sam asked.

"They remind me of when I was in school. All charged up and ready to party, like a bunch of sorority girls."

"That's Mardi Gras. Pretty much trashes the inhibitions. Gets worse, too. Couple of days of this and we'll all be dancing naked in the streets. But watch yourself. This is not a safe town for a guy to run around naked. The natives in this neighborhood just love a bare behind." Sam again used his glass as a pointer as he gestured to the world outside the room.

"What do you mean, the Mardi Gras crowd?"

"Yeah, them too. But it's all year. This district, they call it the Quarter, is almost all gay. The farther you go from Canal, the worse it gets. They say there are some wild bars below Saint Ann Street. We were out that way last night and teenage boy hookers were thicker than flies. It's funny, you go walking down Bourbon and it's all lights and music and people, then you walk past Saint Ann, and the street lights are dimmer and farther apart, and the music fades behind you, and the boy-hookers come out of the woodwork. One block and you're in another world. Of course, Angie wanted to go into one of their bars. I'm glad I wasn't drunk enough to go."

"Well, to each his own, I guess."

"You said it, Ted. That is just about the theme of the Mardi Gras, to each his own. That's good, right on target." Sam looked down at his empty glass and rattled the ice. "I need another drink. Can I get you one?"

"Yeah, I guess I might as well get into the spirit of this thing." Ted's cup had been empty since he had been sitting at the coffee table. They walked back through the living room to the kitchen with Ted following his muscular host.

"What do you do, Ted?" Sam asked as he walked, still facing away from Ted.

"Well, that's a good question. I had my own business in Southern California, but I ran into some...difficulties and decided to give it up."

"Business is tough, believe me I know it. Go ahead, sit down." He motioned to the stools at the breakfast bar as he rounded the counter into the little kitchen. "Worse, if it's a family business." He was grabbing handfuls of ice with his bare hands, packing it into two glasses. "What are you drinking, Ted?"

"Scotch. Glenlivet, I think."

"Ah, another scotch drinker. We're going to get along just fine, Ted. I think I'll have the same thing." As Sam made the drinks and talked, it seemed to Ted that he was less drunk than he had seemed earlier—when Angie had been in the room. "Great room service here, no problem getting bottles of booze. They charge a ridiculous price, but... You know, I bet they're charging us by the shot, even though it's in the bottle. That's quite a scam."

"Can I help? I mean, I'd be glad to buy another bottle."

"Hell, Ted, that wasn't what I was saying, you'll have plenty of chances to pick up the check before this is over. Besides, Angie is so loaded that even I can't count it. We couldn't spend it all if we tried. Her dad keeps making it too damn fast." The sounds of the glasses and ice seemed to take on new furiousness. Sam shrugged and smiled across the counter, putting the two ice-filled glasses between them. He tipped the bottle of scotch above each glass as he poured the drinks. "There I go again, Ted, starting to sober up, I guess." The drinks finished, he offered one to Ted and took the other. "Here's a toast." He held his glass up and Ted followed suit. "A toast to all the broken-down football players in world, to all the operations, and all the scars, all the nights without sleep and all the pain pills, all the hidden limps and all the metal parts." He tipped back his drink, and after a series of large gulps it was gone. Ted took a big drink too, but his glass was still almost full when Sam began to make another for himself. He seemed to be drifting into a drunken, yet cocaine buoyed, monologue.

"You know, I used to play halfback for the Saints once upon a time. Not much good at it, I guess, special teams mostly. Not very good for money, but great for partying and picking up girls. I met John in a bar here on Bourbon back when I was still playing. Now that guy can pick up women. Well, at least he could then. He seems a little uninterested these days. I think he is starting to grow up, as they say. Good thing, too. If you think he is wild now, you should've seen him then."

"So you were a pro football player? Every red-blooded American male's fantasy. How long did you play?"

"Like I said, I didn't play much after college. But the Saints pretty much used me up in three years. Let me go before camp started the fourth year. Can't complain, I had a good time. Sure beats peddling stocks for a living."

"You're a stockbroker now? In New York?" Ted found this career almost as glamorous as playing pro football.

"Yeah, I work for Angie's father. He owns his own firm, offices in New York, Boston, and Honolulu. Not a big firm by the standards of The Street, but a good size for a private company."

"Is that how you met Angie, through work?"

"Ha! No, it's the other way around. We met up at Syracuse. Talk about college days. We dated on and off, mostly off, the whole time we were there. But then I was chasing everything in a skirt so we were bound to get together occasionally, especially since she had already made up her mind to marry me. I never gave her much of a chance, but she never gave up. Hang around Angie very long, and you'll see—when she wants something, she usually gets it."

"She does seem to be a strong woman. Jeri likes her, I could see it the minute they met."

"She's strong all right. She followed our college team all over the country, hanging around, trying to see me. Only, in the beginning I still thought I had a chance at a big career, big pro contract and retirement into broadcasting. She came down here when the Saints picked me up. I wasn't that interested in her, but she was always right there with John and me. Yep, the three of us cut a swath through this town in those days, the good times, and she was there at the end when I needed her. I suppose, finally, she was just there, she just grew on me. Then, when they didn't pick up my contract, it seemed like settling down into a big Jewish investment banking firm was the next best thing. She's OK, she still puts up with a lot of my shit."

"You got that right, handsome." Angie had appeared at the end of the breakfast counter. "What nonsense is he telling you, Ted? I hope he isn't boring you with old football stories." She moved around the counter into the kitchen next to Sam. "Don't believe anything negative, Ted. He could have been a contender, except for his undying love for me." She hugged him from the side and he smiled, wrapping his arm around her small shoulders.

"See what I mean about always being there?" Sam squeezed her shoulders as he spoke. She pulled away from him and began to search the countertop.

"Is there any champagne? I'm ready for a drink." She spoke as she turned to open the door of the small refrigerator.

"Call room service. We need ice too." Sam started to pull the empty plastic bags, dripping, from the sink. He tossed them to the floor near the overflowing trash container. "And tell them we're ready for maid service, for Christ's sake. I don't know what there waiting for. Do we all have to leave the room for them to dump the trash?"

"OK, I'll call, but put your stuff away." She motioned to the cocaine on the living room table before turning to Ted to continue speaking. "Last night the little shit they sent up with booze sat down and lined himself up."

"Hell, Angie, it's Mardi Gras. I told him he could have some." Sam shook his head, laughing, before moving into the living room. "He did make a glutton of himself, though," he called back to them as he collected his box of drugs. "That black sombitch kid would probably still be here if Angie hadn't chased him off."

Ted listened absently to Sam as he watched Angie make the call to room service. She was definitely a powerful and likable woman. He wondered about their relationship and Sam's obvious problem with working for her father. Then he felt gentle arms moving around his waist from behind him. Happy to have Jeri back close to him, he leaned back into the embrace and felt a warm kiss on his neck.

"Hey, what's going on here?" The voice was Jeri's, and she wasn't standing behind him kissing him on the neck. Ted stood up so fast that the stool on which he had been sitting tumbled out from under him, clattering to the floor. He turned around to find Windy Lee behind him, smiling broadly. "Damn, Ted. Aren't my girlfriends safe around you?" Jeri said as she laughed at his confusion. She walked over and kissed him. "Sorry," she said, her lips still touching his.

As Angie hung up the phone, she said, "Listen, Ted, you've got to watch your back around here. Once they get started, the practical jokes these people play can get pretty vicious."

"Practical jokes? Who plays practical jokes?"

Jeri recognized John's voice. She turned to the sound of the voice to find him still outside the room. She couldn't see him, but the affected Southern drawl was coming clearly through another set of double doors. John was calling from a second adjoining room, a room that was connected to the suite in the same way as the room she occupied with Ted. She was impressed by the size of the suite the Williamsons had booked. A dozen people could stay in it without discomfort. She was still hugging Ted around the waist. He looked down at her and she smiled up to him.

"Sorry, Ted, we couldn't resist," she said softly. At first she thought he might be mad, but he smiled down to her and she knew he accepted being the target of Windy's small joke.

"There will be no practical joking without me." John's voice again echoed into the room, but this time the accent was English. He jumped into the room, landing heavily on one knee. He was wearing the costume of a Shakespearean jester: shiny multicolored silk shirt, red tights, floppy silk cap with long conical extensions tipped with small bells, and pointed shoes with upturned ends and more bells. He looked ridiculous. His large size and gray beard simply did not fit the ideal of the court jester. He was followed into the room by a short handsome man in jeans and a sports jacket. John leaped again, landing hard on the other knee, with both arms spread wide from his body in over-accentuated dramatic gesturing, the bells on his fleur-de-lis jester cap ringing brightly.

"What's a drunken man like? Like a drowned man, a fool, and a madman. One draught above heat makes him a fool, the second mads him, and a third drowns him." Finished with his speech, he stood up and walked the rest of the way into the room, jingling as he moved.

The handsome man who followed the jester was smiling a white toothy smile as he watched John put on his performance. He had dark hair that was carefully combed back from his forehead, brown eyes that shined happily, and a heavy five o'clock shadow that looked like shaving wouldn't do much to lighten it. Jeri thought he seemed a little shy as he moved slowly through the doorway. Then a loud screech pierced the air of the room. Windy Lee continued to scream as she ran to the new man in the sports coat. She jumped up on him, thrusting her legs around his torso, and kissed him frantically. John walked to the kitchen, holding one of the pointed ends of his cap in one hand, shaking the bell at its end.

"Well, what do you think? Not a bad costume for Mardi Gras, is it?" John was speaking directly to his friend Sam Williamson.

"Not bad, John, but it's not Fat Tuesday yet," Sam said.

"Well, I wanted to try it out. You know, get into the mood of the thing. How about a drink?" He was leaning over the counter next to Ted, inventorying the bottles near the sink. Angie moved across from him, inspecting his costume for a few moments before speaking.

"I love it, John. Fits your personality perfectly." She was smiling broadly at him.

"Well then, how about that drink?"

"I don't know. You look like you're already in the third degree of drink. Drowned."

"I am only but MAD yet, Madonna, and the fool can look after himself." He rang the bells on the ends of his cap fiercely.

"OK, what will it be, clown?"

"A little Jack Daniel's would hit the spot right about now."

"Yeah, Shakespeare or not, you're still a hick at heart. Coming right up. On the rocks OK?"

"Perfect, Madonna." He turned to Ted and Jeri. "I see you two are making friends with everybody all right. These people are hard not to love." He took his drink and turned his back to the counter. He watched Windy Lee mauling the new man and laughed.

"That good-looking Italian over there, getting dry humped by Windy, is Sal Benito. He's the best classical guitar player I've ever heard. He's playing to an empty room over at the Bourbon Orleans. As you can see, Windy likes him."

They were all meeting downstairs in the coffee shop for breakfast at nine. Jeri had stayed up partying until after four and
had managed less than four hours of sleep. After roaming
the streets and bars in the French Quarter until after midnight,
their group had returned to the suite at the Sonesta. There, on
their balcony over Bourbon Street, partying suspended over the
wild melee below them, they had agreed to get up early. They had
planned a trip by streetcar up Saint Charles Avenue to see one of
the biggest parades of the long Carnival schedule. When Ted had
awakened her with gentle shakes, her body had felt drained and
weak, but she had not found it difficult to get out of bed. Her biochemistry remained altered by the cocaine of the night before. Late
in the night, after everyone else in their group had staggered off
to bed, she had found herself alone with Donna and John. Sitting
between them on the living room sofa, he had taught them how to
use more cocaine to wake up alert after a night of partying. They
had both done several lines just before going off to their rooms
to sleep. The foggy memory of sitting close to John, their thighs
touching intimately, his arm occasionally around her waist, had
been unnerving. She had forced the distasteful memory from her
mind and occupied herself with getting ready for the trip uptown.

When the elevator doors slid open, the organized chaos of the busy lobby engulfed them. They were running late. Ted had been impatient while he had waited for Jeri to shower and dress. She had gotten up quickly when he had shaken her, but she seemed dazed and slow. He understood the way she felt; he was tired and achy, his own hangover making him disinterested in the planned outing with the party group. He had drunk too much again the night before, but it was difficult not to; they had done little else but party since they had arrived. He looked at his watch to check the date and was stunned to see they had been in New Orleans less than two days. It seemed like a week and they weren't even halfway through it yet.

Everyone else was already there, sitting on a long wooden bench outside the coffee shop. The place was a madhouse of activity. Every table was full, and the waiters and waitresses and busmen were rushing back and forth between the dining room and the kitchen. A harsh rumble of jumbled conversation, jingled silverware, and rattled plates reverberated from the room. Their group was crowded together with the rest of the people waiting to be seated. Jeri recognized the symptoms of hungry customers; they seemed impatient and angry.

"This doesn't look good," she said quietly to Ted. He turned to the bench seat where John and Donna were seated.

"How long is the wait? Did they say?" he asked.

"Yeah, they said ten minutes about twenty minutes ago." John stood up and pulled Donna to her feet with him. "Let's get out of here."

"I'm with you, big guy." Angie stood energetically, turning her face down to Sam. "We can eat on the way. We'll be here all morning if we stay." She reached down to her husband and touched his cheek with the palm of her hand. "Come on, Sam, I'll buy you breakfast."

"Some place with a bar, I hope. I need a Bloody Mary." The ex-football player pushed himself slowly off the bench. "And none of this health food shit. I need something substantial in my stomach, no sprouts." He pulled himself up next to Angie, putting his arm around her shoulders. Then he smiled at them.

"Yes, dear. High grease, high cholesterol coming right up." Angie nodded her hello to them as she started to lead the way out of the crowded waiting area. "He thinks I'm a good cook as long as everything we eat is on his doctor's forbidden list," she joked as she walked by them. "How about a pizza, dear?"

Jeri took his hand and they followed the New York couple out of the coffee shop. They walked out through the glass doors leading to Bourbon Street with John and Donna trailing behind them. The loud, murmuring, people sounds inside the hotel were replaced and superseded by a cacophony of bar hawkers, delivery trucks, and Dixieland jazz. His nose was invaded by the spicy smells of Creole cooking and the rancid smells of gutter excrement, and his sight was overloaded with the multicolored decorations and costumes of Mardi Gras. His hangover receded, and he found himself excited to be there, experiencing the old city and the famous Carnival for the first time. He turned to Jeri; she was looking up at him, her face happy and animated.

"Mardi Gras," she said, skipping forward from him. "Mardi, Mardi, Mardi Gras." She pulled his hand as she skipped, singing the made-up song. He was forced to jog or walk with long strides to keep up with her. She pulled him along the crowded sidewalk, her silly song parting the crowds and creating smiles. They caught up with the Williamsons in less than one of the French Quarter's short blocks. Ted felt slightly embarrassed at being pulled along the busy street, but when he saw the many men on the street staring at Jeri with longing eyes, he also felt proud to be on the end of her arm. When she was alongside Angie, she stopped her performance and began to walk normally.

The morning was cool, but the clear sky promised a warm day. Jeri was energized by the atmosphere of the French Quarter the moment she passed through the doors of the hotel. The street and gutters were very wet, puddling in places, with the early morning, garden-hose cleanup performed by storefront vendors adding to the residue of the night's rains. But the sidewalks on both sides of Bourbon Street were bursting with activity. Jazz music came to her from one direction and country music arrived from another. Across Bourbon, jammed with small delivery trucks, their exhausts making an oily stink, the storefront businesses trickled out onto the sidewalk. A young bartender with stringy long hair leaned out from the window counter of a closet-sized take-out bar. A tiny shop was hidden behind a multitude of T-shirts, its windows draped and doorway blocked with them. Asian employees, wearing red shirts and red hats, worked at a fast-food stand under a huge yellow sign with Takee-Outee printed in black, imitation Chinese characters between grinning slant-eyed caricatures. A man in bib overalls was spraying a fire hose on the white wrought-iron furniture of a silent open-air nightclub. The storefronts beckoned to her on an animal level, called to her to come and enter, to experience and spend.

"Angie?" Jeri was short of breath after her skipping rush down the street. "How many times have you come to Mardi Gras?"

"Wow, Jeri, we've been coming for years." Angie smiled up at her husband. "We lived here once, you know. Sam played running back for the Saints."

"Really! So that's why you're so huge. My brother would be ecstatic, he loves football." Jeri did not care very much for the game, but she wanted to be supportive, to acknowledge their interests.

"Hey, this big body takes a lot of fuel. Let's find somewhere to eat, OK?" Sam patted his stomach, speaking with an artificially deep voice while deliberately distending his belly.

"OK, Fridge, how about right here?" Angie turned abruptly into a corner doorway and Sam followed quickly behind her. Ted was surprised by the big man's agility as he matched his wife's sudden change in direction. Inside the doors, a pretty young hostess led them upstairs to the dining room of a second-floor steak house. Ted trailed behind Jeri as they trudged, single file, up the narrow staircase, his legs feeling heavy from the previous night's drinking and lack of sleep. He raised his eyes from his feet when Williamson yelled a hoot of joy from above him. Looking around Jeri, he saw there was a breakfast buffet set up at the top of the stairs. A long table crowded with food extended to each side, beyond his limited view up the stairwell.

"That sounds like Sam found something to eat! Get a move on, you guys," John bellowed from behind and below. "Don't give him a chance to eat it all before we get to it." Ted felt Donna's hands on his butt, pushing him up the stairs and into Jeri.

"Hey," Jeri shouted back down the stairs, "hold on down there, you're going to push me into the food!"

The hostess led them to a narrow second-floor balcony where small tables lined an elaborate wrought-iron railing. They walked past several of the tables as she led them to the far end of the balcony. In the corner, a single large table was set for four diners, but a busman was adding two additional place settings. Tall cardboard menus held to her chest with one arm, the hostess pointed to the table with the open palm of her other hand.

"Will this be OK?" the hostess asked happily. "We could get you a larger table inside if you want to wait." Jeri thought the restaurant must be a good place to work. She was reminded of her friends back at the Ram and realized a good work environment made it natural to act happy to customers.

"Wait? No way. This is just perfect," Sam answered, turning away from the table, edging his way past them. "I'm going to the buffet. Let the waitress know, OK, Ted?" He was gone the way they had come before Angie had a chance to sit.

"He must be very hungry," the hostess said with a laugh.

"He is always hungry," Angie said. "Could you bring us some water and coffee, please?" Angie spoke to her as the others milled around the table, finding places to sit. The hostess distributed the menus as the busman brought the coffee and water. Before he had filled the last glass, their waiter approached the table with a pad of checks and a pen held ready. Jeri approved of the efficient division of work—things were getting done quickly and none of the workers seemed flustered or behind. It gave them more time to be polite.

"I see the gentleman has decided on the brunch buffet. It's a great choice, but you can also order off the menu if you'd like." He looked around the table, holding his pen to the checks.

"I'm going to have the buffet myself," John said quickly as he stood to go for the food. Jeri looked around the table to see what the others would do. They all got up with the clear intention of following John to the buffet tables, and she did too.

"Everyone for the buffet, that's easy," the waiter said. He put his ream of checks into the front pocket of his white apron and pressed his back against the redbrick exterior wall of the building to let them pass. Ted followed the rest of the group through the balcony and into the restaurant where the buffet was waiting. As they entered the room, Williamson passed them going the other way. He carried two plates piled high with so much food that Ted wondered if he could really eat it all.

They ate a comfortably slow breakfast, and Ted's headache gradually disappeared. John and Sam went back for more food several times. Jeri and Donna ate large New Orleans-style breakfasts of eggs, grits, and smoked sausages. Jeri even tried a plate of biscuits and white gravy, but she didn't seem to like it. The two big men split the plate of biscuits between them. Ted avoided the more regional fare, sticking to a plate of bacon and scrambled eggs with country potatoes, forgoing the grits. Angie drank juice and ate cottage cheese with a plate of fresh fruit. After finishing his final plate of food, John lifted his video camera. He recorded each person in their group from his seat, baiting them with teases to produce entertaining responses for the audio recording.

Jeri felt her stomach tighten as the camera swung in her direction. Her mood, so buoyant and happy moments before, became heavy and depressed, the unwanted photography making her feel obvious and exposed. She stared helplessly into the lens without smiling or acknowledging the bartender's banter. Then the cold eye of the camera panned away from her, and John was leaning over the banister, taking shots of the crowd in the street below. As the others were picking at the remnants of the meal and sipping their coffee, Angie reminded them of their plan to go uptown to the Garden District by streetcar.

"Why do we always have to take every antique train in every old city, Angie?" Sam scolded her with a wide smile, apparently in a much better mood with his stomach recently filled.

"Sam thinks the streetcars, and the cable cars in San Francisco, are just old versions of the subway. He doesn't see their beauty or the history." Angie leaned her shoulder into Sam, her eyes squinting into crow's-feet from her wide smile. Ted noticed the dark areas in the back of her mouth again and wondered why she didn't have something done about her teeth.

"Oh, I can see the history all right, but it belongs in a book, not under our bottoms. Those things are always slower than walking, and you're lucky if you can find one that isn't already full." Sam leaned backward, away from Angie, turning to face her with dramatic emphasis. "Maybe me and John and Ted should stay here in the Quarter and keep our eyes on things."

"Oh no, you don't." She pushed him on the chest with both hands. "Leave you alone on Bourbon Street where every other doorway leads to a bar? No way, Sam, you would be trying to pick up every tourist in town. You're coming with us."

"Hell, Angie. I'll have John and Ted to chaperone me. What could go wrong?" Sam seemed to Ted to be teasing her without reason. He didn't seem to have real interest in being separated from the women. Ted hoped it wouldn't come to a vote; he had no desire to spend his day with the boys while Jeri was off sightseeing.

"What could go wrong? I'm not even going to answer that one, Sam. Get up, were going uptown." Angie stood to go, and Williamson stood with her, smiling. "And Jeri, don't let these two corrupt your good man. They are basically no good, and their bad sides tend to come out when they're together."

"I'll remember that, Angie," Jeri answered, as they were all rising from the table. "Although, they are all basically no good, aren't they?"

"Yeah, but some are worse, believe me."

They walked up Bourbon Street toward Canal Street, the taller, more modern buildings of the business district looming in the background. They window-shopped many of the Canal Street stores as they walked; through the glass, Jeri priced antiques, luggage, cameras, and a huge array of electronics. As they crossed Canal, Angie pointed out the grandstands that lined the sidewalks, informing them that they had tickets to the stands in front of the Marriott for Fat Tuesday.

They joined a small eclectic crowd waiting for the streetcar in front of an athletic-clothing store on the ground floor of an old bank building. There were many who were obviously Mardi Gras tourists, but there were also local people who seemed to use the old streetcars for commuting to work. Jeri watched two old black women, trying not to be noticed. They were similarly dressed in heavy work shoes, white socks, stockings, long dresses, sweaters, long coats, and oddly shaped hats, and carried unopened umbrellas. One was very dark-skinned and wore the cheap plastic rimmed glasses available on drugstore racks. The other was rather light-skinned with many dark raised moles around her eyes. They talked loudly to each other, using such a strong local dialect that Jeri was unable to follow the details of their conversation. But they seemed to be chatting about the weather and the coming Mardi Gras parades; they never discussed the work from which they were apparently commuting home. She liked the old, strong women. She wanted to go to them and join in their conversation, but she felt too different, too young, too rich. She watched them as they boarded a streetcar, struggling with their packages and their umbrellas and their aged legs. The streetcar had been almost full when it had arrived at the stop and only a few people were able to board. The same was true for the next one, but the third had room for all those remaining at the stop. Angie led them up into the car, stopping to drop coins into an old coin box next to the conductor.

The inside of the car was old but very clean; the metal surfaces of the ceiling and between the varnished wood of the windows were painted bright white. Small cardboard billboards covered the headliner above the windows. Bare white light bulbs were screwed into sockets in the ceiling. The six of them took the first three rows in the front of the car, sitting on the hard wooden benches that had been treated in a way that allowed the natural wood color and grain to be preserved. The conductor pulled an overhead cord, ringing a happy-sounding bell, and with the whine of a heavy electric motor the streetcar began to move. The windows of the car were all slid up and the air came inside with a friendly breeze.

They first joined traffic on Canal Street, heading toward the river, but as soon as they passed the block that the bank building occupied the car turned to the right, starting on its never-varying route uptown through the business district. They stopped again to pick up more passengers almost as soon as they had made the turn off Canal. After the new riders boarded, the car was still relatively uncrowded, providing John with room to move from one side of the car to the other depending on the video recording opportunities.

They passed through a concentration of high-rise office buildings to a large roundabout where the streetcar navigated slowly through the heavy automobile traffic, bell ringing. Angie pointed to a place where the Saints had kept offices when Sam had been a player; although Jeri tried to follow the direction of her finger, she couldn't decide which building Angie was trying to point out. The conductor told them that the traffic circle was called Lee Circle and pointed to the statue of Robert E. Lee standing on top of a single tall gray column. The circle was ringed by temporary grandstands similar to the ones on Canal Street, only these were painted with the bright yellow and deep purple of Mardi Gras. The grandstands were already crowded with people waiting for the parade. The car man explained that the streetcars would be delayed during the parades, and if they were in a hurry to return downtown, they should make other plans for their return trip. Jeri wanted to see the parade. She didn't think they would be going back until it was over.

Ted looked from one to another of the party group on the streetcar. John was taking video pictures from either side of the car, moving from side to side, crossing the aisle with the excitement of a teenager. Sam sat on the wooden bench behind the driver, his body turned to the car. One of his big arms rested on the windowsill, and the other extended on the back of the bench behind his wife. He was staring at Donna. Ted followed his eyes as they moved slowly up her legs, stopping at her breasts, lingering there for uninhibited moments. He seemed unconscious of his surroundings, of his wife by his side, of Mardi Gras outside the streetcar. Angie was joking with John about his video camera, seemingly unaware of her husband's obsession with Donna. Ted didn't realize that he too was staring until Jeri nudged his shoulder.

"Hey, what's up," she said as she pushed him. His attention broken, he turned to her. She slid her body closer to him so she could speak quietly. "It's not nice to stare, Ted."

"I'm sorry, I've been drifting off." He put his arm around her as he brought himself into the new conversation. "I must still be tired. This constant partying has drained me, I'm afraid."

"John wants to get off and watch the parade, what do you think?" Her face was very close to his own, and her breath smelled sweet as he breathed it.

"Hell, Jeri, I don't care. I'm with you, let's tie one on. We're not driving, are we?"

"Nope. But I was counting on you as our steadfast bastion of reason and sobriety." She kissed him lightly on the lips before turning to John, who was again changing sides of the car. "John, do you want to get off here?"

"That's right. I wanted to get off at the traffic circle." He reached up and pulled an old dirty cord that ran the length of the car. A loud buzzer sounded, and the conductor operated his foot pedals and levers to slow down for the next stop. They filed out from the old car onto the manicured grass of the center median of Saint Charles Avenue.

The streetcar rumbled off with the conductor clanging the bell to mark the passage. Jeri turned her head several times to look both directions up and down Saint Charles. The day was shining and bright; she would have guessed it to be from the middle of summer, but the grass of the median was browned by the coolness of winter. She felt a pang of regret as she watched the cheerful streetcar rattling down the tracks without them. In the distance beyond it she could see another car coming slowly their way, its single headlight shining brightly. She held Ted's hand as they followed the rest of the group across the street to the sidewalk on the far side of the wide divided boulevard. Apparently with a specific location in mind, Sam and John led the way on the sidewalk, backtracking for a short distance, creating a swath through the many people waiting to see the next parade.

They entered a white building designed with attention to the pillared architecture of the old South, passing through a single very tall glass door. Inside was the small bar of a quiet Italian restaurant. Sam and John were already ordering drinks when she followed Ted through the glass door. They sat up at the bar and a handsome middle-aged Italian host approached them. He was wearing a gray suit and an energetic tie with purple, green, and yellow diagonal stripes. He went to each of the three women in turn, attaching small Mardi Gras pins to their collars. Each pin was made from purple and green feathers; a golden plastic cast of the happy and sad masks of the old theater, a ubiquitous symbol of Carnival, was nestled in the colorful plumage. After carefully pinning them, he kissed them each in a friendly but masculine way on the lips.

"A small gift for the Mardi Gras, my ladies," he said as he pinned Angie. He kissed her and moved on to Donna with the next feather brooch. "On Saint Joseph's Day I would have roses for such beautiful ladies, but during Carnival I must make do with these small tokens." When he kissed Donna, she put her arms around his neck and tried to kiss him back, but Jeri could see he kept the kiss the same light and friendly brush of the lips that he had given Angie. He moved over to Jeri, smiling at Ted as he passed by his place next to her at the bar. "I hope you all have a very happy and safe Mardi Gras," he said to her, as he attached the pin to the neckline of her knit shirt. She felt anticipation, even eagerness, for the kiss that would follow, but she was slightly disappointed in its dry, clinical nature. "Happy Mardi Gras," he said to them all. Then he left the bar to go back to his place at the door, ready to greet and pin the next female guests to arrive.

"Hey, ladies, snap out of it, would you?" John's loud voice interrupted the moment. "What do you want to drink? Watch out how you fall for that Southern gallantry, Donna. I saw you try to slip him the tongue."

"Bullshit, John. I was just being polite." Donna answered happily as she turned away from him. She raised her eyebrows and winked pointedly to Jeri. "I wouldn't want to do anything rude to the locals, you know. What are you going to have, Jeri?"

"I don't know, maybe a local drink." She turned her attention to the tuxedoed bartender. "Does New Orleans have a favorite local drink?"

"Yes, miss. We have several: Sazerac, hurricane, gin fizz. New Orleans is famous for drinks and drinking."

"I'll try a hurricane," Donna interrupted, sounding adventurous.

"Me too," Jeri said. She had been thinking about the first, somewhat odd-sounding drink, but Donna's enthusiasm had swayed her. Sharing the experience of the new drink would be fun. Jeri leaned forward from her stool onto the bar, placing her weight on her forearms. Donna, sitting on the other side of Ted, was doing the same. They watched the bartender making the drinks; two of them were juicy red and in huge, gracefully curved glasses, the others went into the usual, conventionally small and stubby glassware. The bartender brought the drinks over, placing the tall red drinks in front of Donna and Jeri. She was happy that the red drinks in the beautifully curved glasses were the hurricanes.

"Be mighty careful with these hurricanes, misses, they have an awful lot of alcohol in them," the bartender warned them as he served the tall drinks.

Jeri sipped her drink through the long straw and found it to be sweet and fruity. The taste of the alcohol was almost covered by the flavor of the drink.

"Wow, this is good." She looked back to her friend. "What do you think, Donna?"

"I could get blasted drinking these things. I can't taste the alcohol at all," Donna said, before she took another long drink through her straw.

Angie squeezed between Ted and Donna, pushing her way into the conversation, her breasts pressed together between her upraised forearms, her wine held under her chin with both hands. She leaned forward, her breasts resting heavily on the bar, and put down her wine.

"Hey, let me have a little taste. I haven't had one of those bombs in years." Angie seemed playful and happy. Jeri pushed her drink toward her just as Donna held her long straw up to her lips. As Angie sipped through the straw, her eyes grew large and her lips pulled up into a smile.

"The hell with wine." She pushed her glass of wine to the far edge of the bar. "Bartender, make me one of these, please."

Ted found himself in the center of the women's drink-tasting process, Jeri on one side and Donna and Angie on the other. He watched them with interest as he drank his unblended scotch. They seemed so childlike in their actions. Even Angie seemed like a schoolgirl, except for her breasts spilling all over the bar. The bartender had been staring at her so hard that Ted had thought he might fall down on his face as he walked back to his well. He stood from his stool and walked, drink in hand, to where the other two men were seated.

"Hey, Ted. Those hens drive you out down there?" John turned on his stool to face him. "If they drink too much of that stuff we'll be carrying them home early."

"Well, you might say I thought I might find more suitable conversation at this end of the bar," Ted replied, facing the other men.

"This is a great spot to wait for the parades to pass," Sam said. "Nice quiet restaurant, good food and good drinks. No crazy kids spilling beer down your back." He turned back to the bartender as he spoke, motioning for him to return. "Hey, you don't have any cigars behind the bar, do you?"

"Yes, sir. We sure do." The bartender brought out a wooden humidor and presented the cigars. Sam selected a handful of what seemed to Ted to be the largest and darkest.

"Not a bad selection you have there. Do you smoke?" Sam asked the bartender as he turned to offer them each a cigar. "A good selection behind the bar usually means the bartender is running a little side business." He smiled conspiratorially at the bartender.

"That would be the night man. I don't know anything about cigars. And no, I don't smoke them myself."

Ted didn't normally smoke either, but the male camaraderie building at their end of the bar tempted him to join the others in the small ceremony of clipping the end and lighting up. He held the large cigar up to his mouth and puffed on it furiously, unable to tell if it had taken the light.

"Easy there, Ted. Don't want to hurt yourself or set off the fire alarms." John teased him in a friendly way as he held the lighter for him. They stood at the men's end of the bar drinking men's drinks and smoking cigars while their women sat at the other end of the bar drinking sweet red drinks while laughing and telling stories.

Angie was telling a funny story when Jeri noticed how the bartender was watching her. No, not her, he was watching her cleavage. She nudged Angie with her elbow and raised her eyebrows to indicate the man. Angie didn't even turn to look at him. She just laughed.

"You just notice him, Jeri? He hasn't taken his eyes off of them since we got here." She laughed again. "I guess I still got it." Jeri and Donna laughed too.

"And it looks like he wants it," Donna said.

"Let him look, I don't mind a little attention from a handsome young bartender." She straightened her back, pushing herself forward, turning toward the bartender. Donna released a shrill peal of laughter as she pretended to hold her glass down on the bar.

"Don't, Angie, you're going to knock over our drinks." They all laughed at Donna's joke, and the bartender turned away at last. When they had calmed down, Donna stood up and looked around the bar.

"I wonder where the bathroom is. Now I've got to take a pee."

They left their drinks on the bar and went to the restroom together. As they passed the men, the air was full of the smelly smoke of cigars. Jeri was surprised to see that Ted was smoking one too. She looked at him, trying to show her displeasure with a frown.

After they were finished, Angie led the way out of the bathroom. Jeri started to follow her, but Donna grabbed her arm.

"Jeri, wait, I've got something for us." She reached into her pocket and took out a square of folded aluminum foil. "I brought this all the way from home. I wanted to wait until the right time." She began to unfold the foil carefully.

"What is it?" At first Jeri had thought Donna had brought some coke along, but she was acting as if she had something very special. She was curious, but uncomfortable in the public restroom. She moved closer, looking into the foil wrapper as Donna opened it. There were two pills inside. They looked like aspirin.

"Ecstasy, one hit each. Today is perfect. Here." She picked up one of the pills and put it in Jeri's palm. Jeri looked at it for a moment and then looked up to her friend.

"I don't know, Donna. I've never tried X, I don't know how I'll react to it." The organic structure of the molecule formed in Jeri's mind. It was a derivative of methamphetamine, but it acted on the mind differently, increasing neural transmitter levels—serotonin and dopamine. It was supposed to make a person feel more sociable. Some people said it was like love, if it was the real thing, but the street drug was usually just speed spiked with LSD. The thought of being on an LSD trip in public made Jeri feel frightened. "I don't think so, Donna, not today."

"It will make you feel good. Not loaded or drunk or anything. Just high and good. This isn't some of that shit with acid in it. It's the real thing—pure. But we shouldn't drink too much, that will spoil it."

Jeri had been curious about Ecstasy since she had first heard the stories about the way it made a person feel, but she had always been afraid of the purity, afraid of taking something unexpected.

"Don't worry, Jeri. I had four. I took the other two back home. It's the best." She put her hit into her mouth and swallowed it without water. Jeri trusted Donna's knowledge of drugs; she was an expert on street chemicals. And she had already tried it, so it must be safe. Jeri turned on the cold water, pulled her hair back and took the pill, washing it down with handfuls of tap water.

They had not finished the cigars or their first drinks when the parade made its way up Saint Charles to a point outside the restaurant. The well-dressed Italian host came back into the bar to inform the customers that the parade had arrived. If they wanted to see the parade, they should make their way outside. Ted was happy to have an excuse to leave the cigar. They added a second round of drinks to the bill and settled up with the bartender. They walked outside carrying plastic cups, as were most of the spectators watching the parade, and pushed slowly toward the curb.

Jeri was sipping her new drink, a plain orange juice, when a cascade of plastic-bead necklaces came down on the crowd. She felt something small but very hard hit her in the head and she ducked. She bent her head away as another shower of trinkets, thrown from the passing float, landed around her. There was an immediate rush about her feet, and she spilled some of her juice when she was violently pushed aside. Sam moved close to her—so close she thought for a moment that she felt his hand on her behind. She looked up into his face. He was reaching to her shoulder, a huge belly laugh bellowing from his throat.

"Here, Jeri. You've caught some beads." He plucked a strand of Mardi Gras beads from her shoulder, untangling it from the ends of her hair. He lifted it over her head and gently lowered it around her neck. He looked directly, immodestly, into her eyes and touched her cheek with the back of his hand.

"All these people scampering around on the ground, and these beads almost went around your neck. You must be a very lucky girl, Jeri." His eyes held hers for a moment, his gaze, powerful and sexy, immobilizing her animal-like.

She turned to find Ted standing behind her; wanting to be closer, she moved back toward him. She felt someone crawling between their legs. A stranger was picking up doubloons at her feet. She tried to step away from him but Donna was beside her, bending over to pick up the plastic coins. She lost her balance, bumping hard into the top of Donna's head. Donna went over backward, landing softly on her rear end, her hurricane splashing onto the crawling drunk who had started the string of events.

"Hey," Donna screamed through her own laughter, "quit shoving, Jeri. Get your ass out of my face." She sat on her bottom in the middle of the sidewalk, looking up at Jeri, still laughing. Jeri handed her juice to Ted and bent down to help her up.

"I'm so sorry, Donna. I didn't mean to…" Another shower of doubloons rattled to the pavement, and Donna was off on her hand and knees after them.

"Come on, Jeri, help me get some of these!" Donna screamed again. And without thinking, Jeri went after the red and green plastic with a fury, picking the coins up with both hands. When her hands were full, she picked up the empty plastic cup that had once held Donna's hurricane and began to fill it with the coins and necklaces. When no more of the souvenirs were near them on the sidewalk, the two women stood, looking at each other greedily. A moment of embarrassed silence between them was punctuated by screams and hugs.

"Heads up, you guys, here comes another float." It was Angie. She had pushed through the crowd to get close to them. "Let me show you how a lady does it." She turned to Sam, handed him her drink, and put her arm around his neck. "Come on, Sam, let me up."

Sam put both of the cups into his left hand, holding them from the rims, his thumb and first finger dipped inside the drinks. He reached down with his right arm and engulfed Angie's hips with his forearm and hand. A single effortless lift and Angie was up on his wide right shoulder. He passed up Angie's hurricane and took the puffing cigar from his mouth with one sweeping motion. Angie sat on his right shoulder, left arm around his head, left hand holding her drink. With her right hand, she lifted her blouse and bra up over her breasts to shimmy vigorously at the oncoming float.

"Hey, mister, throw me something!" she screamed above the roar of the crowd. The costumed men riding on top of the float had been waving to the crowd as if it were a faceless, lifeless mass, throwing souvenir throws at measured, calculated intervals. Then one spotted Angie and pointed at her. The slow monotonous waving and routine distribution of the throws ended with rabid recognition of Angie's efforts. Doubloons, beads, plastic cups, and small figurines arced from the float, raining down on Angie and the area around her. Angie pulled her blouse back down to catch the beads and cups while they were still in mid-flight, dropping some of the treasure down to Jeri and Donna standing below.

The crowd around them went wild as the bountiful manna fell around the Williamsons' feet. Those lucky enough to have been close to them acquired vast plastic fortunes in minutes. Drinks were downed or spilled and necks were adorned with beads.

A second float motored slowly past, and Angie repeated her performance with an identical result. She placed bead necklaces around Sam's neck as soon as she had untangled them, and soon his throat was buried up to his chin with the plastic jewelry. Before a third float drew near enough for the riders to reach them with their throws, Donna had climbed up on John's shoulders. She sat with his head between her legs, her hands holding his forehead for balance. When the float came close, she followed Angie's lead, lifting her clothing above her breasts. The plastic bounty continued to be directed at their small group, and the crowd surged to recover that which was misdirected or had by some chance made it to the ground.

Then Jeri turned to Ted and asked if she could get up on his shoulders. His cup held only ice and Jeri's juice was almost empty, so he leaned down to drop them in the gutter. Jeri climbed on his back before he was ready and he almost fell over. Laughing as he told her to wait, he squatted to let her get on. Then, hoping he could do it, he strained his legs to push them back up. Sitting on his shoulders, with her legs around his neck, she caught the throws and cheered wildly at the floats, but she did not imitate the method of her two friends by exposing herself. He recognized the jealousy he felt and was surprised by it. But he didn't want her to expose herself. He didn't want anyone else to see her. The next float did not follow immediately behind the last, and a gap in the entertainment lengthened. The three women on top of the men's shoulders became the object of the mob's attention. Slowly at first, but gaining in volume quickly, a chant rang up from the crowd.

"SHOW YOUR TITS! SHOW YOUR TITS! SHOW YOUR TITS!"
Angie and Donna were quick to oblige the mob, flashing brief exposures of their anatomy. But the chant did not diminish. They had seen their breasts; it was Jeri they wanted to see.

"SHOW YOUR TITS! SHOW YOUR TITS! SHOW YOUR TITS!"
The chant became a deafening roar. The crowd was chanting and surging up and down in unison, a bodiless pumping of arms in synchronization with the chant.

"SHOW YOUR TITS! SHOW YOUR TITS! SHOW YOUR TITS!"
Jeri turned to Donna and Angie, embarrassed to show herself to ten thousand strangers. She tried to scream to Donna, but she couldn't hear her own voice. She looked down at Ted, but he was facing forward, toward the throng. She wondered if the crowd could become violent, if it were as mindless as it appeared.

Donna and Angie, waiting and watching so that they could do it in perfect synchronization, raised their tops simultaneously, baring their breasts for a moment, showing them to the feral mob. The crowd cheered for a few seconds, but soon the chanting drowned out the cheers.

"SHOW YOUR TITS! SHOW YOUR TITS! SHOW YOUR TITS!"
Only now they were pointing at Jeri, disinterested in the other two women, demanding that she join Donna and Angie in the exposure, demanding that there be no flower left unpicked. Jeri felt immense pressure to do it. It was a flash, a second of nudity, yet she worried that she could be arrested for indecent exposure, and she couldn't push herself to do it. Angie was bobbing up and down on Sam's shoulder, smiling at the crowd; she didn't seem to have any opinion about whether Jeri did it or not. But Donna was motioning to her, pointing to her shirt and nodding.

"SHOW YOUR TITS! SHOW YOUR TITS! SHOW YOUR TITS!"
the crowd roared.

Jeri reached down to the bottom of her blouse and a cheer rose from the crowd. She slowly raised her shirt, and the cheer became an explosion. She raised her shirt above her bra, flashing her pretty lace underwear for a moment before pulling her blouse back down. The cheer became a chorus of rumbling boos before returning to the chant.

"SHOW YOUR TITS! SHOW YOUR TITS! SHOW YOUR TITS!"

The pumping fists were in perfect cadence to the chant. The unknown faces smiled up from all around her, yet the sound of the horde was evil and mean. Her heart was pounding and she was afraid, but the smiles and the attention felt good. She looked around one last time for an angry policeman. Then, satisfied that she could do it without being caught, she reached down and grabbed her shirt. The clamor of the crowd increased to unbelievable levels. She teased them for a moment, holding the bottom of her shirt and the front of her bra in her hand, feinting moves up and down. They became wild with watching her. The next float was passing down the street, throwing things to the multitude, but they were not interested; they only wanted to see her do what they demanded she do. She teased them again, realizing that they wouldn't care about her boobs; they just wanted her to bend to their will. She lifted her shirt and bra up to her collarbone, holding them up there for a long time before pulling them back down.

The muted sounds from below, Bourbon Street reborn to another day of Carnival, passed easily through the old glass of the closed and locked French doors. The sounds of voices and laughter and music penetrated the thick drapes without definition, only the most sharp or loud sounds remaining recognizable. Jeri rolled over in the soft bed with lazy difficulty, the thick comforter becoming trapped beneath her as she moved. Finally, she faced the doors, lying on her side, head propped up, with one arm under her pillow.

Sunlight beamed in narrow cylindrical shafts from sources at the extremities of the drapes, filling the room with twilight. A tall plane of light split the overlap in the center of the drapes, bisecting the room with a bright new surface, a narrow rectangle teeming with shiny floating particles of dust, projecting a brilliant vertical line on the opposite wall. She felt happy and comfortable, in spite of a small hangover. She wanted the drapes and the doors to be open, but she was too comfortable to move from the bed. She sighed.

"Are you awake?" Ted asked quietly from behind her.

"Yes, I guess. What time is it?" She felt and heard Ted moving to view the clock radio on the nightstand.

"Eleven, a little after. How do you feel?"

"OK, I have a little headache. How about you?"

"I have a big headache. I need to drink some orange juice and eat something. Are you hungry?" He put his arm over her body and moved closer to her, pulling himself into contact with her from her shoulders to her feet. She pushed back into the soft warmness of him and reached back awkwardly to his legs with her free arm.

"You feel good. I think my headache is going away." She rolled back to face him, and he was waiting for her. He kissed her softly, mouth closed, on the lips before moving his kisses to her neck and ear. She felt suddenly warm and tried to kick the heavy comforter off the bed. Ted completed the task with a roundhouse wave of his arm, flinging the bedding from the bed. It flew to the floor, flapping at the edges like a matador's cape. She felt him above her, on his hands and knees kissing her on her neck and breasts. He paused for a moment to reach behind her head, pulling the pillow more fully under her head and neck, then continued to kiss her. He kissed her eyes and her hair and around the edges of her ears. He kissed her softly on the lips and hard in the mouth. He kissed her long and gently on her neck and nibbled at the tips of her breasts.

Ted felt a powerful need to please her. Jeri's happiness had become the only thing in the world that mattered to him. He couldn't isolate the moment it had happened, but he knew that he had surrendered himself to her. Sometime since their first dinner date together he had lost the will to refuse her anything. It frightened him. Not for himself, but for her. He should be doing a better job of protecting her. He knew he should force her to pack her bags and push her onto a plane. He should demand that she stop taking drugs. But his fear of losing her was too strong. He had no chance of stopping the momentum of her lifestyle; he could only hope to deflect the course of the passage. If he could protect her during the most dangerous part of it, she was bright enough to realize on her own that bad things didn't just happen to other people. She would eventually realize the truth of life and hunker down to protect herself. He wanted only to be with her when she did.

He felt so good that she dared not move. Occasionally she was able to touch his hair with one hand or hold the hard muscle of his upper arm with the other, but he seemed always some place beyond her own caresses. He was moving her forward and upward as his kisses moved down her torso and stomach, his gentle hands touching her breasts. Then he was lower yet, and with a sudden cool then warm rush, she knew he was making love to her. She lost herself in the sensual pleasure of the act, unable to restrain herself from the selfish satisfaction of being pleased. She held his head by the hair with both hands, pulling him into herself, wanting only the pleasure. Her body reached its final plane of gratification and began to produce waves of satisfaction that pulsed through her body. She held his head, wanting to kiss him but unable to let him stop making love to her. Then she felt the waves subside, and she began to feel pain. She pulled his face up from her and leaned forward to look at him. He smiled as he moved up to lie beside her, and she kissed him hard on the mouth, a final, gentle wave filling her as she held his face to her own.

Then she realized what he had been doing. He didn't want to be with Donna and John, or the Williamsons. He hated the way they partied, the pot and the coke—he didn't even know about the X. He was here because of her. He had sacrificed his strongest beliefs to be with her. But he had said that he would keep her away from drugs. Had he given up on her? No, that wasn't it. He was risking everything to help her, and she had been unbelievably selfish. No more; she could be as good and giving as he could. She was good; she didn't need to get high to be happy. In an instant she realized that he had won; she was his and she wanted to be his. She didn't need the other.

As they kissed, she wrapped her arms around him tightly and rolled to bring him onto her. He moved his legs between hers. He felt wonderful and perfect inside her, but it was Ted she wanted to be pleased. She hugged him and said his name over and over. Then, when he was finished, he lay spent with his weight full upon her, but he did not seem heavy. They lay together for a long time, with him upon her and still inside her. His breathing gradually slowed down, and the pounding of his heart on her breasts became more difficult to feel. Finally, he pushed himself up on his hands, pulling back from her chest, his eyes on her eyes.

"I love you, Jeri," he whispered.

"I love you, too, Ted," she said. He kissed her again and began to roll himself off her. She held him and pulled him back above her. "Let's stay here all day, Ted. We'll just stay in bed and play." She tried to pull him down to her, but he was too strong.

"No way, Jeri. You brought me all the way down here to see the Mardi Gras, and that is just what you are going to do. Besides, I'm starving. Get up and take a shower before your girlfriends barge in on us." He muscled himself free of her grasp and got out of bed. She felt mildly abandoned by his refusal, but he was right, it was Mardi Gras time right outside their windows. She got out of the bed and walked to the drapes. She peeked through the crack between the two curtains just as the sound of running water began in the shower. It was a beautiful, bright day with a blue cloudless sky. She felt wonderful and impatient to go outside. She ran to the shower and joined him inside the tub enclosure.

"I'll wash your back if you wash mine," she giggled as she pushed him from under the spray.

"Deal. Only let me get the soap out of my eyes, will you?"

They had just finished dressing when the familiar pounding on the connecting doors began. Jeri was still in the bathroom putting on her makeup when he opened the door. Angie looked around his shoulder and into the room.

"Wow, Ted. This place is dark as a tomb. Why don't you let some light in here?" She walked across to the drapes and threw them open. A burst of light blazed into the room. "And while we're at it, we might as well get some air too." She opened the French doors, and the sounds of Bourbon Street became close and immediate. The sweet smell of clean fresh air, recently washed by the rain, filled the room.

Ted hadn't realized how stuffy it had become inside. The study flow of recycled, air-conditioned air had kept the temperature comfortable, but the air had become stale and musky. He followed her through the doors out onto the balcony. The day was spectacular: sunny and bright like summer, yet cool and breezy like fall. The delectable scent of the brisk new day encouraged him to take a deep breath; it felt cool and rejuvenating in his lungs. They walked to the railing together and looked down into the street. It wasn't as crowded as the night before, but there were still many people walking the daytime streets, sharing the right of way with cars and delivery trucks. Many were already drinking from plastic cups. He was amazed at the fortitude it took to get up and party again after the near riot of the night before.

"Damn, they get started drinking early, don't they?"

"Sure do, that or they never stopped from last night. It's a twenty-four-hour party down here this time of year." She answered him with a dimpled smile in a perfectly made-up face. "Matter of fact, Sam and John are making Bloody Marys next door right now. Better get one before we go out to breakfast."

"No, I don't think I need one this early. But breakfast sounds great."

"I'm surprised, Ted. I've heard nothing but what a hard-driving partier you are, and you've turned out to be quite human." She placed her hand on his forearm, resting it there for a long moment. "We're going to Brennan's for breakfast. Plenty of time for drinks later."

"Hi, Angie. How are you this morning?" Jeri said as she joined them at the railing.

"Just fine, Jeri. How about yourself?"

"I'm wonderful." She took Ted's arm and wrapped it in her own. She looked up to him, then kissed him on the cheek.

"Watch out, Jeri. You two are making us married folk look bad." Angie smiled at them both sweetly. "Come on, let's get out to breakfast before Sam and John get too sloshed. I was just telling Ted that we have a reservation at Brennan's for breakfast. They say Brennan's is the restaurant that invented eggs Benedict. I don't know if that's true, but it's a nice place. Why don't you two get your stuff and meet us next door when you're ready."

"I'm ready. How about you, Ted?" Jeri said, holding up a large straw purse.

"Just let me get the key and lock up, and I'm ready to go." He untangled his arm from her and turned back to the room. "You go ahead over, Jeri. I'll be right there."

Ted closed the French doors to the balcony and locked them from the inside. He retrieved their room key from the dresser top and hung the Maid Service sign on the hall side doorknob. He closed the hall door and took a last look around the room to see if he had forgotten anything. Then he went through the connecting doors to the Williamsons' suite, pulling the door on their side of the pair closed, realizing there was no way to lock it from the Williamsons' side. He wanted it locked, but that would mean leaving their room from the hall door and knocking at the suite to be let in. He knew that would seem strange, so he reluctantly gave up on the idea and joined the others.

They were all in the kitchen area. Sam and John were in the kitchen making Bloody Marys. Angie, Donna, and Jeri were sitting on stools at the breakfast counter. Windy Lee and Sal Benito were standing very close to each other at the end of the counter. Each of them had a Bloody Mary in front of them, but it seemed that only Sam and John were actually drinking. As Ted walked up to the counter next to Jeri, John handed him a reddish brown drink, a large stalk of celery protruding from the surface. Ted took the drink and set it on the counter next to the one in front of Jeri.

"Hope you like 'em spicy. I think we got a little carried away with the Tabasco," Sam said, after taking a drink from his own reddish brown drink.

"Naw, we didn't. These are perfect for Carnival. You've got to have extra Tabasco during Carnival." John tasted his drink and smacked his lips.

"Let's get out of here, shall we?" Angie said. "I'll buy you a real Mary over at Brennan's." She made the comment to John as she stood.

"Brennan's? Haw! A good Bloody Mary is not complete without celery. That string bean they use just can't compare with a fresh cut stalk of celery."

Jeri thought he was objecting to the move to the restaurant, but he tipped up his glass to drain the contents before moving from behind the counter to take up a position behind Donna. Sam took a sip from his drink, but put it down almost full. She could see it was too spicy for him. He took the celery from it and also walked from the kitchen, taking crunchy bites from the stalk as he walked.

They left the room as a group, several separate conversations continuing as they rode the small elevator down to the busy lobby. As the doors opened, the sights and sounds of Mardi Gras invaded her consciousness; they beckoned to her even as she struggled through the crowd of people pushing to get on the elevator.

Outside, on Bourbon, the sidewalks were full of Carnival revelers pushing in both directions and spilling out into the street.
Angie had Sam by the arm as she led the group to Bienville Street,
where they turned toward the river and their goal of eggs Benedict
at Brennan's. Wandering on the streets were already a few people
in costumes, and John made a disappointed comment about not
wearing his.

When they arrived at the restaurant, they found the foyer small
and crowded. The hostess greeted them pleasantly and offered
Ramos gin fizzes to pass the time during their wait. The hostess was
an attractive woman in her forties. She was dressed in a long blue
evening gown, and Jeri understood how different this breakfast
would be from the ones she had served at the Ram Restaurant back
in Durango. She explained that the drinks were a tradition in New
Orleans and were the proper start to a traditional, leisurely ante-
bellum breakfast. Only Sam and John had drinks, but they each
ordered a Bloody Mary, not the fizzes. John took one sip and began
to explain why his recipe was superior to that of the bartender on
duty. Eventually, they were led through the restaurant to be seated.

The central courtyard was more old redbrick and white-trimmed
French doors. The French doors lined the side of the courtyard,
standing open to the inside of the restaurant. Large trees and air
ferns filled the space. Wrought-iron furniture and fine violet table
linens completed the relaxed yet busy ambiance. They were led
all the way into the back of the restaurant to a small dining room
called Bacchus. Inside, two tables had been brought together to
accommodate their group. Ted found himself seated between Jeri
and Angie, their conversation passing intermittently across him.

When the menus arrived, Ted couldn't believe the prices. They
were so high it was comical. He tried not to smile, but Jeri exhaled
a sharp gasp. The gasp broke the silence, and everyone at the table
laughed or made some sort of joke about the prices. Angie laughed
as she leaned forward to speak around him.

"Don't be too shocked, Jeri. You don't have to worry about not
having enough to eat, but at Brennan's they think fifty dollars for
eggs Benedict is a bargain."

"Well, I might just have a glass of water," Jeri said.

"Yeah, I'll split an order of toast with you," Donna called down the table.

"Nonsense," Angie called over the joking. "Everyone must have eggs Benedict. I insist." And that was that. They watched quietly as Angie waved the waiter to the table. He stood respectfully by her side as she ordered. "Everyone will have the oyster soup Brennan, followed by the eggs Benedict. No, make that eggs Hussarde. Then the sirloin and mushrooms. And then, of course, we must have your bananas Foster."

"Yes, ma'am. And would you care to have a nice chardonnay with the soup? Possibly a cabernet sauvignon or a merlot with the steak?" The waiter was still furiously writing their order on the check as he asked about the wine.

"Yes, that would be nice. Chardonnay and cabernet, two bottles of each." She reached for the wine list and scanned it quickly. "The Napa Ridge chardonnay and, let me see, the Wolf Blass cabernet." Ted was again impressed by Angie's power and worldliness.

"Right away, ma'am," the young black waiter said as he backed away from her.

Jeri found herself staring at Angie, her mouth open. She turned to Donna and found her friend as wide-eyed as she felt. Donna blinked twice, shook her head and smiled at her.

"I guess we won't need to eat for a while after breakfast," Donna said with a happy laugh.

"Well, Donna," Angie answered, "you have to have a healthy meal before you eat the bananas Foster. A person could make a meal of that. Believe me, I have." She laughed at herself and smiled to Sam. Jeri noticed he was watching her approvingly.

"Maybe I'll finally get a decent meal, Angela." He reached into his lap, repositioned his napkin and smiled broadly at her.

John spoke down the table to everyone and to no one in particular. "Hey, that street we walked on to get here, Bienville? It's named after the original city engineer. He was ship's engineer on one of the first ships that arrived here. He's considered something of a technological genius around here. He figured out a way to get the city's storm drains—the French Quarter, anyway—to drain into the river. Only the river level is higher than the drains. You see? He saved the Quarter from every big hurricane that has ever hit this town."

"Gee, John, you're a wealth of trivia, aren't you?" It was clear Donna was having fun teasing him; even as she leaned nearer to kiss him.

"No, really, that kind of stuff is fascinating," Ted said.

"Yeah, Ted has some very strong opinions on technology and the industrialization of society. He believes we're all victims of technology." Jeri had picked up Donna's teasing, shifting it to Ted.

"Really, Ted? I understand you were a nuclear engineer in another life." Angie had spoken much louder than was necessary for his place next to her. He hadn't planned on broadcasting his past to this group of party makers; they just didn't seem to be interested. But with Angie's comment the table came alive.

"No way, Ted. Nuclear engineering? That was the little company you had out on the coast?" Sam was leaning over the table from his spot opposite Angie. "I think you've been holding out on us, Ted. Let me buy you a drink. Not enough good old, honest mendacity in this world today."

"Oh boy, a nuclear engineer who agrees with the Unabomber Manifesto," John bellowed down the table. "This is going to be an interesting Mardi Gras." Everyone, including Ted, burst into laughter.

"Now boys, just because you were a couple of phys ed majors, you mustn't be jealous." Angie's voice was sweetly unctuous as she barbed the two big men. "Just because Ted believes the plague of mankind is industrialization, and just because he has a full knowledge of nuclear energy"—she paused—"doesn't mean he has to be a Unabomber. We can still have a wonderful Carnival"—she paused again—"if we don't get blown up first, that is." She had quieted the table with her first remarks, but the last of it resulted in a renewed outpour of laughter. Ted knew he would be the object of more joking, but he didn't mind. It was a good group, they meant no harm.

"Ted, Ted, defend yourself." Windy's voice came down the table. "Don't let these city folk get away with this."

"Well, Windy, I'm afraid they've caught me red-handed. What can I say?" He looked at his watch dramatically. "But we do have time for breakfast before my suitcase takes out the city of

New Orleans." More happy laughter erupted from the table. "Now I know why they made us sit in the back. Much too loud for civilized society."

"Seriously, Ted, do you really believe we should all live in dirt burrows in Texas?" Sal was speaking with the level tones of someone who genuinely expected a straight answer. When he spoke, the rest of the table grew gradually quiet, anticipating Ted's answer.

"No, Sal. I don't believe in anything that nutcase tried to do. He believed we all need to return to some preindustrial existence, that we must abandon our technological inventiveness. But our inventiveness is what defines us as a species. We can no more abandon it than we can reject speech or thought." Ted turned to Jeri, smiling at the way he had been goaded into making a speech. She smiled back at him, a playfully upturned corner adding to the smile's perfection.

"What I mentioned to my faithless friend here is that modern life can be very dangerous for the individual. It's great for the culture—you know, pyramids and agriculture, jet planes and hospitals. But the individual is faced with ever-increasing risks."

"Holy shit, I told you this was going to be an interesting Carnival," John said loudly. "I need another Bloody Mary." He raised his glass into the air over his head and rattled the ice fiercely. Ted was relieved by the commotion John had caused at the other end of the table as he ordered drinks. The group had grown quiet during his too-serious statement. He didn't want to be the wet blanket for this party because it was too important to Jeri.

He watched her as she played with Donna and John. They were involved in a slapstick decision-making process, deciding between a Ramos gin fizz and a Bloody Mary. She was so beautiful and happy it made his stomach light and his breath short. When Carnival was over it would be time to approach her with a plan to move to California together. She could continue her plan for medical school at U.C. Irvine, and he could try to put his business back together. It wouldn't be so bad living in LA if he could do it with Jeri. His eyes drifted around the table, and he found Angie watching him closely. He forced his thoughts back to breakfast and tried to put on his party face.

"You know, John," Ted said, "if you guys can get someone's attention, I think that I could drink one too. I've become much too serious for this kind of trip."

"You think so?" Angie asked, her voice directed softly to him. "I'm going to get you alone before this is over so we can talk. I might have a good time after all."

The food came to the table in a long series of deliveries by several of the waiters and busmen. They ate slowly, joking and telling funny stories. Ted realized that, aside from Angie, no one at the table had paid any attention to his too-serious speech. When the breakfast was finished, the waiter rolled a table-side cooking cart over to them. Next to a large flambé pan were dishes of seasonings and bottles of rum and banana liqueur. Large bowls held piles of bananas and mounds of vanilla ice cream. He lit the Sterno burner under the pan and mixed butter, sugar, and cinnamon in the pan. As he simmered the sauce he began to tell the history of the recipe.

"When Chef Paul invented this dessert in the 1950s, no one had any idea how popular it would be. He just had some extra ingredients, local ingredients, and he made up the dish using them. Now the way I make the Foster is the health food recipe." He spoke jauntily as he caramelized the sugar. Everyone at the table listened as they watched. "Butter from the thinnest cows and brown sugar from the smallest plantations and healthy potassium from the bananas and fiber from the grain used in the alcohol." He added the bananas to the sauce, slicing them quickly in his hands. "You know, the best part of this is when you add the liquor." He poured the two varieties of alcohol on top. Then, with a quick tip of the pan, he ignited an eruption of fire that reached above his head toward the ceiling. The flames subsided quickly, and he finished the dessert; removing the bananas and placing them on dishes of ice cream before spooning the sauce on top. "You know, back in 1974 there was a waiter who flamed his bananas right under the intake to the air conditioner, and the flames went right up the vent. The fire went up to the attic. Where they used to store the Sterno? And, well…the restaurant was closed for six months. The good news is they hired the waiter back, and I haven't had a problem since." He yelled the last line of the joke, and they all laughed.

Jeri couldn't believe that she was eating the wonderful dessert when minutes before she had felt completely stuffed. Even Ted was spooning the stuff up, between groans and moans of approval.

When the check came, Angie insisted that breakfast was her treat. She overruled the objections around the table with a dismissive wave of her hand, stating that they had all been her invited guests, explaining that she had picked the restaurant and the meal as well. Jeri glanced at Ted; she could tell by his body language that he felt uncomfortable about letting Angie pay. He squirmed in his seat and looked around the table at the other men. In sole possession of the check, Angie ignored the loud resistance of the others as it grew weaker, and finally the waiter took the little tray and her platinum card.

As they left the crowded restaurant, a new wave of hungry customers was flooding through the doors. They pushed their way through the throng and out onto the street. Angie led them, a scattered formation of ever-changing couples or groups of three or four, on a leisurely walk through the French Quarter. They walked down Chartres, making slow progress as they window-shopped and stopped for drinks. It was cool and sunny. The air was filled with the fresh smells of the river and the recent rain. The spicy, smoky, sweet smells of the many busy restaurant kitchens and open-front sidewalk eateries flavored each delicious breath. Their walk took them into a great area of sidewalk vendors, street musicians, open-air art galleries, eccentric face painters, and drunken Mardi Gras revelers.

On one side of them was Jackson Square, a large parklike court between old redbrick multistory buildings. A tall statue of Andrew Jackson riding a horse stood in the center of the square. Opposite Jackson Square was the Saint Louis Cathedral, an ancient but still functioning Catholic church. Inside the cathedral, Sunday Mass was being celebrated, and the sounds of organ music and frail singing floated through the open doors. Ted looked inside the cathedral from out on the steps. The interior was as dark as twilight; only faint yellow candlelight illuminated the few worshippers within.

"Not much of a turnout, is it?" Angie asked him from his side. He turned to her voice to find her also gazing into the church. They were alone on the steps; the others were nowhere near.

He looked back to the square to see if he could find them. John and Sam were across the street next to the wrought-iron fence of the square, drinking from plastic cups and tossing change to grade-school-age black boys who were tap-dancing on the sidewalk. He didn't see any of the others.

"No, not too good, I guess. Must be the Mardi Gras." Ted answered Angie as he surveyed the crowd in the square.

"They went to get their faces painted. Sal has a friend that sets up on the other side of the square. They shouldn't be too long, but we can catch up if you want."

"You didn't want to get face paint?"

"Plenty of time for that, Ted. They'll be washing it off before we go out to dinner tonight. Besides, I wanted to go with you."

"Want to take a look inside the cathedral?" Ted wondered why she had decided to follow him. By this time, the other three women would probably be having much more fun than she was.

"No thank you. You gentiles enjoy depressing yourselves too much. Looks awfully dark in there, no telling what ancient ceremony is taking place. I wouldn't want my disbelief to spoil the invocation."

"Yeah, or mine either. I fell out of the fold a long time ago. No use tempting fate." Ted put his arm around her shoulders and led her down the steps toward the street and the two men on the other side. They walked past the kids dancing on the sidewalk to move next to the two big friends.

"We thought for a minute you two were going to convert," Sam said.

"I told you they wouldn't have the nerve." John laughed as he spoke, then dug into his pocket and pulled out two dollar bills. "Here, take this and get on your way. We're not giving you any more money. Better find some other suckers." After giving the boys the money, he made an exaggerated motion to chase the happy dancers away.

"We didn't want to bring down the wrath of God by despoiling the holy place with our presence," Angie said as they began to walk, without discussing a move, to the other side of the square. They walked slowly past street people who were selling and performing, entertained by their energetic commerce of taking money from the tourists in the crowd. They meandered through the square, always moving toward the face painter and the rest of their group.

They found the others sitting on bar stools in the open front of an elevated sidewalk bar. They faced the square with their legs visible below a narrow counter, their drinks resting on top. All four of them wore colorful designs around their eyes and down their cheeks. Sal was the first to spot them as they made their way through the crowd.

"Hey, over here. Up here." Sal's voice was powerful and distinctive above the murmur of the crowd. They walked up the steps and into the bar where Sal sat with Windy, Donna, and Jeri. They turned from their perch overlooking the action to face them.

"Come over and have a drink, you guys," Windy said.

"My friend is just outside if you want to get your faces painted. That's her down by the fence." Sal motioned over his shoulder with his plastic cup.

"No, no paint, but I'll have a drink," John said.

"OK, but only one drink, John. You and Sam would sit inside some dark bar drinking all day if we let you." Angie put her arms around the two big men's waists and pulled them together. They weaved easily toward her like playful kids; she looked tiny between them. They found more bar stools and squeezed together at the counter to have a drink and watch the people go by.

Tourists and locals of every race and type walked below them: old white-skinned tourists with baggy shorts, striped shirts, and camera necklaces; young people with long hair, jeans, and rock-and-roll T-shirts; black-skinned people with British accents and large plastic bags bursting with recent purchases; Asian people with cameras and unintelligible speech patterns. All these varied people had come for Mardi Gras and were passing three feet below them. It was a continuous parade of humanity, happy and sad, rich and poor, drunk and sober.

They finished their drinks and joined the migration toward the river. Crossing Decatur Street, they walked past the Café Du Monde to the levee. Wide concrete stairs led them up the side of the levee to a viewing area on top, the Mississippi River flowing slowly past below. From there they could see the panorama of the brown river, up and down in both directions. The sedulous river churned with the navigation of large oceangoing freighters and tankers, tug boats and barges, and the inevitable red and white paddle wheelers. It was teeming with activity on its surface and on its shores. Windy and Angie pointed a telescope up and down the river laughing at the people they caught unaware of their observation. John and Sam each assumed the role of tour guide, pointing in every direction as they explained the business on the river. Ted stood with Sal a little behind the sightseeing as the self-appointed guides were barraged with questions from Jeri and Donna.

"What is that cafe down there? What kind of food do they serve? Do they have a bar?" Donna asked John. He laughed and started to answer, but Sam seemed to push him aside with his voice.

"That is the world famous Café Du Monde, Donna. All they serve there is coffee and doughnuts, chicory coffee and beignets, that is. They have been doing it for a very long time, since the days of the French, I think. I remember when all the waiters were respect-ful middle-aged black men. Now they are all Asian or Indian or some other hard-to-understand immigrant—women, too. It's just not the same ambiance, ordering your chicory coffee and beignet from someone who can barely speak English. We'll go over there for some coffee some morning."

"Oh, Sam," Angie said. She and Windy were back from the tel-escope and were leading the big men back down the stairs. "You can be such a racist sometimes, dear." She pulled Sam by the hand toward the square. "Let's head back to the hotel. At the rate we've been going we won't get back until dinnertime." They restarted their unorganized walk through the narrow streets of the French Quarter, only this time they had a goal, the Royal Sonesta Hotel on Bourbon Street.

Jeri found herself walking beside Angie as they walked up Saint Anne Street toward Bourbon. The sidewalks were bursting with people, and they were often forced into the dirty gutter where food wrappers and plastic cups swirled around their ankles. When they were almost to Bourbon Street, Angie stopped in front of a sidewalk bar; its tattered green French doors were open to the street along the length of the business. Loud disco music blared from the bar, over the sidewalk and into the street. She tossed her head in an obvious message for Jeri to look inside the dim bar.

"Check it out," Angie said. "Do you think we can get the boys to go inside?" Jeri tried to make out the shapes inside. Couples were sitting intimately at small tables, others were dancing on a floor of blinking colored lights, another pair was leaning against the bar in full embrace.

"Are you kidding? I've never seen those guys pass up a chance to drink." But Jeri was aware that Angie thought this bar unique. She squinted in an ineffectual attempt to see more clearly into the darkness. Suddenly it became clear, everyone inside was a man. All the couples were men, both partners. It was certainly a gay bar.

"Still think we can get them inside?"

"I don't know. Ted is pretty liberal, but John might make a scene." Jeri was beginning to want to go inside and see what it was like.

"John? He is a pussycat. It's Sam that's the problem. He is one of the world's best haters. He hates all minorities and most religions. He really hates gays."

"Well, maybe we shouldn't try to get him inside, huh?"

"Come on. It would be good for him. Besides, there is safety in numbers. Maybe being with all of us will mellow him out some." Jeri followed Angie's look back down the sidewalk. The rest of their group was approaching quickly. "Come on, Jeri, let's go inside and order a drink. Maybe they'll follow us." Angie took her by the arm and pulled her through the open doors. They walked across the dark room to the bar. Angie sat down next to the embracing couple; they were too preoccupied with each other to notice their arrival. The bartender approached them quickly and cheerfully asked them what they would like to drink. Angie turned to Jeri with a blank look.

"Hell, I don't know. Jeri, what should we drink?"

"Beer, I guess." Jeri was watching the sidewalk as Ted, Windy, and Sal walked through the French doors. Behind them, Donna was walking between John and Sam, her arms entwined with both of them. She appeared to be leading them in their unsteady walk. Sam was speaking, his head bobbing for emphasis. John was alternating between listening intently to his friend and glancing down at Donna's face. Donna occasionally raised her eyes from the sidewalk to smile happily up at the tall men as they walked. Jeri could see that the two men were feeling the many drinks they had consumed during the day, and they followed the others through the old green doorway without looking around or noticing their surroundings.

"Beer it is. Bartender, two beers, please. Small ones."

As the bartender left to draw their beer, the rest of the group filed into to the room and took up bar stools down the almost empty counter. Ted walked past them to sit on her other side. Sal and Windy sat next to him, and Donna led her two drunken bookends beyond them to sit at the far end of the bar.

"Jeri and I are having beer, what do you want?" Angie called down the bar, her voice raised above the loud music. Sam continued to tell his story, and Donna and John were listening attentively; the three of them were in a separate world as he spoke. The others nodded or shrugged in noncommittal, no-opinion approval of the order. The bartender arrived with the first two beers and placed them in front of them.

"Six more beers, please." Angie took a hundred-dollar bill from the front pocket of her jeans and placed it on the bar. The bartender smiled as he picked up the bill with both hands, tilting his head to one side as he went for the beer. "Well, Jeri, looks like we did it. I'll bet you a buck that we drink these beers and leave before Sam finishes explaining how he could have won the Sugar Bowl. If we're lucky, he won't even notice the people around him, and we can tease the hell out of him later."

Jeri watched the trio at the end of the bar carefully, so carefully that she did not notice Sal watching her. She brought her eyes back to find her beer and saw him staring at her with a wry smile.

"Quite a town, New Orleans, isn't it?" Sal asked her. His smooth, deep singing voice made the question sound sweet and important.

"It certainly is. A regular hub of the alternate lifestyle." He exploded into laughter, a laughter she had not seen him enjoy since their meeting. She had thought him a strangely serious and silent man for a one who made his living as a professional entertainer.

"Jeri," he said, as he regained his composure, "I have never heard it put quite so succinctly. You are quite right. The Quarter is a hub of alternate lifestyles. And what about you, what brings you here to the Quarter?" He was smiling, but Jeri felt that he was genuinely interested in her answer.

"Oh, I don't know how to explain it. I grew up on a farm, miles from anywhere. I always wanted to experience the world. I read about the Mardi Gras and I suppose I always wanted to go, but it's more, really. I love all cities. I love the buildings and the trains and the multilane highways. I love flying away to a new one, and I love the people I meet when I'm there. Cities seem so energized, part of the future, the cutting edge of everything new and exciting. And I suppose I imagine that someday I will become part of it." As she spoke to him, Sal nodded his head and looked into her eyes softly. She realized that he was a very good listener, but she wondered if he really understood anything she was saying or if he was simply being polite. As she finished her explanation, Sam Williamson bellowed from the far end of their group.

"Angelaaaaaaaaaaaa! Don't order anything else, we are leaving."

Jeri turned back to the trio at the other end of the bar. Sam was walking stiffly toward Angie; the muscles on either side of his jaw were throbbing intensely, as if he were grinding his teeth viciously. John and Donna followed him, walking arm in arm. Donna was giggling nervously, and John was exaggerating a wide-eyed look of fear. Sam walked to a point opposite Angie where he stopped and stared into her face, his eyes squinting with anger.

"Angie!" he yelled. "Nice going. I don't suppose you have noticed how many faggots there are in this bar? Let's go." He kept his eyes focused on some spot inside her skull as he screamed. Jeri noticed that the couple on the other side of Angie had separated as the screaming started. The older man and teenage boy had stopped kissing but remained standing close together, their near arms still wrapped around each other's waist. The older man seemed poised to speak, and Jeri hoped desperately that he would not. The animal rage imprisoned behind Sam Williamson's eyes appeared to be on the verge of some terrible escape. She wished that they would leave; more, that they had never come inside. Jeri hoped that Angie could neutralize the rage long enough for them to get outside. Then she watched helplessly as the older man pulled himself free from the younger and stood up straight.

"Hey there, that's no way to—"

Before the man could finish his sentence Sam punched him in the middle of his face. The blow had been thrown without warning, an effortless snap of his big left arm. The man crumpled to the floor instantly, with his friend bending over in a vain attempt to stop his fall. Jeri found it difficult to believe what she had seen.

"Now are you happy, Angie?" Sam's voice was lower but still filled with fury. "Is this what you wanted?" He turned and stormed out of the bar without waiting for an answer. John and Donna followed immediately behind him. Sal led Windy out through another set of open French doors, trying, it seemed, to avoid appearing part of Sam's entourage. When Jeri turned back to the fallen man, Angie and Ted were kneeling by him, one on each side. The teenager was standing behind Angie, looking down in confusion. The older man was shaken, but aside from a small drop of blood hanging from one nostril, he seemed unhurt. They helped him stand, and Angie handed him a paper bar napkin.

"Are you OK?" Angie asked, as she steadied him by holding one of his arms in both of her hands.

"Leave me alone, bitch." The wounded man pulled his arm free, wiped his nose on the sleeve of his shirt and inspected the blood. "Shit! Goddamned butch son of a bitch." He looked quickly around the bar and then turned to look at his friend for a few moments, indecision on his face. Finally, he wiped his nose a second time on his sleeve and walked out of the bar without looking back. Angie turned to the teenage boy in confusion.

"Aren't you going to follow him?" she asked.

"Why should I?" He spoke with contempt as he turned back to the bar. "I don't know him. He's just a guy. But your damn friend cost me a hundred bucks. He was going to give me a hundred bucks."

Angie looked to Ted and back to Jeri. She seemed first bewildered, but her expression rapidly changed to anger. She reached for her pile of money on the bar and pushed it to him.

"Here, this is almost a hundred, and you won't even have to do anything for it." The boy's disappointment evaporated into a wide smile.

"Thank you, lady, thanks a lot." He scooped up the money, put it into his front pocket, and he too walked out of the bar.

"Here," Angie said to the bartender, as she dug again into her pocket. She pulled out another hundred-dollar bill and handed it to him. "Sorry to have caused a scene. We didn't intend to make trouble."

"Yeah, right." He took the money and walked away from them. After putting the bill into a brass spittoon next to the cash register, he called back to them. "But you're cut off, you better leave."

"Sure, we're going," she called back to him. Then, facing Ted and Jeri, she spoke more softly. "Come on, you guys. We're getting off easy this time." She pulled Jeri by the arm so hard that Jeri felt her elbow pop. The three of them walked quickly out through the nearly empty room, the couples on the dance floor still standing immobile, watching them go. Jeri felt very large and obvious as she let herself be led from the bar. As they stepped into the sunlight Angie spoke angrily, without turning to face her or Ted.

"That little whore, all he cared about was the money. Men. They are all alike, even the ones that seem so different. Let's see if we can catch up with the rest of the crowd." She finally turned back to them as they crossed the street. "Did you see Sal and Windy slinking out like a couple of whipped dogs? I can't wait to find them."

Jeri was standing next to Ted on one side of the tall café table and Windy Lee was with Sal on the other. Each of them was drinking from a large glass of beer. They were downstairs in Desire, the sidewalk oyster bar of the Royal Sonesta.

After leaving the suite to get something to eat, they had followed Sal's recommendation to go for peel-and-eat shrimp. He had assured them that the meal would be casual and fast, but most importantly, delicious. He had ordered ten pounds of the shrimp and Jeri had thought the amount absurdly large, arguing that two or three pounds would be plenty. Sal had smiled knowingly, placing one hand on her forearm to reassure her, but had used his knowledge as a local New Orleanian to override her objections. After they had ordered the boiled shrimp and draft Dixie beer, the waitress had returned to cover their table with newspaper, leaving two big tubs of red cocktail sauce in the middle of the sports section.

The beer had come quickly, and they had stood around the chest-high table sipping their beer and discussing the strange fight in the gay bar earlier in the day. Windy was the only one of the four who had known Sam Williamson longer than a few days, and the others had bombarded her with questions. Jeri had seen her impatience growing as she had answered them, and had not been surprised when she had abruptly ended the discussion.

The conversation had then turned to music and the two singers' careers. Jeri had found it a pleasant change of topic.

The waitress soon came back to their table with a tray mounded with packets of saltine crackers. She poured them into a heap, inverting the tray over the table. Sal divided the mountain of crackers into two roughly equal piles, pushing them to opposite edges of the table, almost upsetting the tubs of cocktail sauce during the process. He tasted the sauce that had splashed on his knuckles, and then dipped his index finger into one of the tubs. He sucked the cocktail sauce from his fingertip with a loud smacking sound and sneered.

"That sauce is just catsup. It's definitely going to need a good spike of horseradish." He took a drink from his beer before following the waitress to the oyster bar. He returned quickly with another tub, but this one was piled high with white paste. Proclaiming himself to be the premier mixer of shrimp cocktail sauce, he stirred the horseradish into the red sauce with a cocktail fork, tasting it occasionally for bite. A few minutes later a young black man in a white chef's uniform and a tall paper hat brought out the steaming and dripping shrimp. He tipped a huge stainless-steel colander on edge and the hot, wet shrimp poured into a massive pile on top of the newspapers. Some of the scalding shrimp tumbled to the perimeter of the table, and Sal brushed them back toward the center before they could fall.

"I told you ten pounds would be too much," Jeri screamed as she stepped back from the cascade. She was delighted by the steamy, spicy smell and the creepy, alien appearance of the shellfish. The shrimp came complete with all their members: heads, eyes, feelers, legs, and shells. They were hot, red versions of their former selves, and aside from being boiled were in the same condition as when they had been captured. "But how do you eat them?" she said, laughing. Sal took one of the shrimp and showed her the fast, but certainly not dainty, method of decapitation and leg amputation. Then he demonstrated how to peel the shell from the crustacean in a single piece and how to pull the black vein from its back. When he finished, he dunked the shrimp in the cocktail sauce and ate it. During his demonstration, Windy had been plowing through the shrimp, creating a pile of discarded legs, heads, and shells.

"If you don't just jump into this, Windy will eat all ten pounds," Sal said.

Ted took a drink of his beer as he watched Jeri dismember a boiled shrimp with gusto. She represented, he thought, the perfect juxtaposition of youth and beauty to intelligence and capacity. She was the perfect woman, and he had the opportunity of a lifetime. He was not going to waste it; he was not going to lose her.

He reached for a shrimp, pulled the head and legs from the body, and the shell seemed to fall free as if by magic. He dipped the shrimp into Sal's sauce before eating it. Squeezing the tail with his thumb and first finger, he sucked the last of the meat from the tubular husk. The shrimp was marvelously fresh and firm, and the spicy cocktail sauce complemented the mild flavor of the fish. He ripped the cellophane from a package of saltines and ate the two crackers in quick succession—one bite apiece. When he lifted his beer he found he needed another, but Sal was already calling to the waitress for another round. He drained his glass through his horseradish-abused palate and looked around the table. They were all eating the delicious shrimp as fast as they could peel them. He watched Windy and Jeri pulling shrimp apart and eating happily. Then he realized that standing there, at a small chest-high table with his new friends, shelling shrimp and creating a huge pile of their dismembered bodies, he was enjoying shrimp as he had never known they could be enjoyed. He worked as vigorously as the others to dismember the jumbo shellfish, shelling and eating them rapidly. He stopped only to stuff saltines in his mouth or to slosh beer down his throat.

The first fifteen minutes after the shrimp had arrived had been devoid of the usual conversation, their mouths too full to speak, but soon their hunger was dulled and the conversation began again. Ted was washing down some crackers when Windy wiped her lips and hands on her napkin and tossed it back to the table.

"John has been talking about this kind of shrimp for weeks—back in Durango. I'm sorry he missed this," Windy said, before she tipped back her beer and emptied the glass.

"He'll have other opportunities, Windy," Sal answered, as he too wiped his hands. "I wonder where those two got off to."

After the fiasco in the gay bar Sam had taken off down Bourbon Street. He had walked with such large, quick strides that he had pushed through the crowd at a rapid pace. John had left Donna behind as he had jogged to catch up with him. When the rest of the group had finally mustered in the lobby of the Royal Sonesta the two big men had disappeared. They had waited upstairs in their rooms for the remainder of the afternoon, but the men had not returned. When Sal had suggested they go downstairs for shrimp and beer Angie had declined to leave the room. Donna had insisted she stay behind with her, but it had appeared to Ted that she did it reluctantly. Angie had made light of staying behind, making a joke about wanting to stretch the room service envelope. But her joke had failed to break the tension. When the foursome had left the depressing atmosphere in the suite, Ted had felt feelings of relief and of guilt.

As he continued to eat shrimp and crackers, he looked to Jeri to find her nibbling the large tail of one of the shrimp without actually eating it. She was watching him eat with a smile.

"Like those 'bugs,' don't you, Ted?"

"Seem to be OK to me. You seem to have developed an intimate relationship with that one." He nodded to the tail on which she was gnawing. She pushed it back in the cocktail sauce and licked it suggestively.

"This one does have something special." She put it in her mouth and sucked it from the last section of shell remaining at the tip. Finished, she tossed the husk into the pile of waste pieces, and she too began to clean her hands and face. "But alas, it is gone. And I'm stuffed. You are going to have to eat that last pound of shrimp by yourself, Ted."

"I wouldn't be so sure of that, Jeri," Sal said, looking toward the street. "Here they come now."

She followed his eyes to the door. Sam and John were coming into the oyster bar. Their arms were bulging with boxes and bags, packages of plastic and brown paper. They were both smiling as they approached the table. The anger that had destroyed the afternoon had, evidently, been forgotten.

"Ah. You all have been reading my mind." John dumped his burden under the table and began pulling the legs off shrimp without an invitation. He stuffed one in his mouth while he was still speaking. "Where are the girls? Upstairs?"

"Oh shit, don't tell me Angie is upstairs pouting," Sam asked, as he too unloaded under the table. "I need a beer, dear." He spoke to the waitress who had arrived to distribute the four beers previously ordered.

Jeri had watched the two men as they had walked into the bar. And in hindsight it was obvious that they had not been alone, but since she had not been expecting anyone else she had not noticed her. It wasn't until the men had pulled up at the table and unburdened themselves that she became aware of a third person: a young light-skinned black woman. She too stopped at the table and dropped packages underneath.

Ted realized the new girl was very beautiful: she had large almond-shaped black eyes, high cheekbones, unblemished skin, full sensual lips, and long wavy black hair. Her makeup was almost imperceptible. She was wearing a short, tight black evening dress. Her stature was small and very thin, the dress accentuating her model-like figure. He forced his eyes from the girl and looked to Jeri. She was staring at the newcomer with open-faced amazement. He looked to Sal and Windy and they too were expressing themselves silently. Sal was studying the contents of a tub of cocktail sauce, stirring it slowly with the small oyster fork, and Windy was looking directly at the black girl with unbridled hostility in her eyes.

"Well, everyone, let me introduce Tara." Sam reached around the girl's shoulders and pulled her up to the table, squeezing her to himself before leaning down to kiss her cheek. "Tara, these good people are Sal Benito from here in New Orleans and Windy Lee from Colorado. They are both singers—entertainers like you." He used his free hand to point to them as he pulled the girl against him again, though more roughly this time. He kissed her again on the cheek, and Jeri thought she seemed to bend her neck and shoulders away from him slightly. It seemed an unconscious indication of fear. "And this other happy couple is also from Colorado. They are intellectuals, I think, but they seem to be fun."

Ted realized that in spite of the clear eyes, precise speech, and controlled way the ex-football player was acting, he was very drunk, and judging from the dilation of his eyes, Ted assumed that he had also taken a great deal of cocaine. Ted continued his inventory of faces to find John still eating shrimp. He seemed to be deliberately avoiding eye contact with the others.

"Just what is this, John?" Windy spoke harshly as she yanked on the bartender's arm. She appeared unwilling to let John pretend that nothing was wrong.

"Hey, Windy." He pulled his arm free of her grasp. "Let it be, would you? It's really not any of our business, is it?"

Ted could see that John was as drunk and high as Williamson. His eyes were red and tired-looking, yet alert. His pupils were dilated too, and this made his eyes rather wild-looking.

"Calm down, everybody, Tara is just another Mardi Gras trinket," John said, as he tossed a shrimp head into the pile of shells. Then he reached under the table with his fishy hands. "Like these doubloons and beads." He pulled a big blue plastic bag up to the table and reached inside. He pulled out a shrink-wrapped package of Mardi Gras beads as big as a small bed pillow. "Now we have something good to throw to the crowd." He pushed the package of beads back into the bag and fished around until he found another, smaller bag of colored plastic coins. He ripped the top off the bag, and some of the doubloons spilled out onto the table and fell to the floor. As John struggled to push the open package back into the larger bag, both he and Sam burst into edgy laughter. No one else at the table joined them. Once he had the spill contained, he scooped some of the doubloons from the top of the sticky newsprint and held them out across the table. "They go wild for these things. Just a little plastic with 'Happy Mardi Gras' on it, and they will kill each other to get it." The plastic coins were protruding between his fleshy fingers, like a drunken parody of some old treasure movie.

Sam laughed uproariously at John's statement, while he pointed to the plastic coins spilling from the other man's hands. Jeri didn't know what to think. Sam seemed on the verge of hysterics. Then he stopped laughing, looked around the table at coins strewn around its base and pushed the girl away from him.

"Pick 'em up, will ya, Tara?" He pushed her again, a little too hard in the small of the back, as he spoke. She seemed to crumple a little under his small violence. Then she bent her knees politely and went to the floor to recover the coins. She still had not uttered a word.

"This is bullshit," Windy almost screamed. "Don't do it," she called to the girl, who was now busily picking up the coins at their feet. "Don't let him treat you this way." Windy walked around the table to stand next to the girl.

"No, it's OK, miz." The beautiful young girl spoke softly from the floor, her round face turned up to Windy. She was smiling sweetly, trying to make light of the degradation. "I really don't mind. Really, miz." She turned back to recovering the coins. Her thin body curved demurely into an S shape as she balanced herself on the toes of her high heels, her knees together and close to the floor, but not touching it. Her lithe waist bending easily, she reached for the coins with one hand, depositing them in a neat cylinder she formed in the fingers of her other hand.

"Now that is hot!" Sam said behind Ted's down-turned head. He looked back to the voice, and Sam was staring down at the girl with obvious excitement. "Hell, John, get that bag back out and drop some more." He began to laugh again.

"Don't you dare, John," Windy warned, as she too bent down to the floor and began to pick up the doubloons. "I'll bust your balls for sure."

"Yeah, right. Promises, promises." John was also watching the girl picking up the plastic coins beneath the table. Ted couldn't tell if he would dig into the bag for more coins or not. Neither of the men seemed rational. He was about to move around the table to help the two women when the sour atmosphere was broken by the arrival of the two newly ordered beers. With beer glasses in hand, the two big men cheered immediately. Sam even became magnanimous.

"Hell, ladies, forget those things. We bought five thousand of the damn things." He waved his glass at the bulging bags under the table, and some of the beer slopped out onto his leg.

"Come on, Tara, get up. Can't you take a joke? You too, Windy, get out from under there." He didn't seem to be having as much fun degrading the new girl once Windy had joined her on the floor.

"Almost have them all, Sam." Tara's sweet, soft voice was still happy and upbeat as she stood up to the table next to John. "Here, John, open the bag so I can put these inside."

"You guys are out of control," Windy Lee said as she stood. She was still very angry. She dropped her coins into the bag and moved around the table to stand next to Sal. "If you keep this up," she said severely and directly to John, "you are going to get arrested or something."

"Oh, Windy, it's Carnival, for God's sake. Try to have a little fun." John spoke as he crumpled the top of the bag into a roll, sealing the coins inside. He reached under the table and recovered several more of the packages. "Let's get out of here. I want to go up to the room and take a shower."

"Good idea, we need to get these bags upstairs or we'll lose them." Sam was answering John, but he was looking at the girl—Tara. "Hey, babe, go pay the check, OK?" He snapped a wide blue rubber band from a large fold of paper money he held in his hands. Peeling off a hundred-dollar bill, he was poised to give it to the girl, but he stopped and looked to Sal Benito. "How long have you guys been here, anyway? How much do we owe?"

"I don't know, a couple of rounds, ten pounds of shrimp. We can get it ourselves." Ted thought Sal was trying to avoid becoming an accessory to the rudeness of the New Yorker. He joined him in reaching for money.

"Hell with that. I want to get out of here." Sam turned back to the girl with his hands still on the thick fold of bills. Jeri noticed that the girl was staring at the money—oblivious to the world around her, waiting for the bill to be peeled free.

"Here, Tara." He slowly removed a second hundred-dollar bill from the wad and handed them both to her. "Pay the bill and give the kids a good tip. OK?"

"Yes, Sam. I sure will." She took the two hundred dollars and turned to the oyster bar. "I'll be right back," she said with a genuinely happy face.

"See, Windy. Everything is just fine. Tara is very happy. Let's get this stuff up to the room." Sam bent down to pick up packages from under the table. They all reached down to help pick up the bundles.

They were standing next to the table, all holding some bag or another, preparing to move to the lobby elevators when Tara returned. Jeri watched the men in the restaurant follow her with their eyes as she walked back from the cashier. She was wearing a very tight and very short black dress and black high heels. She held a tiny black purse under one arm at the end of a long, narrow shoulder strap. She seemed very sophisticated. When she got back to them, she stood quietly next to Sam. She made no attempt to offer Sam his change, and Sam showed no indication that he expected her to do so. Instead, she took one of the bags from him and smiled brightly, waiting to be led away.

"Sam?" Windy asked firmly. "You're not going to bring her upstairs, are you?"

"Sure, Tara is part of our krewe now." He hit the girl playfully on the behind with a plastic bag. "Aren't you, Tara?"

"Anything you want, baby, anything you want." She pushed her body closer to his and stood on tiptoe to kiss his down-turned face. Sam kissed her and then raised his eyes to the others at the table.

"Tara found us at Harrah's, losing our asses at the craps tables," Sam said. "The minute she joined us our luck changed. She made us a lot of money. I'm not letting her go now." He kissed her again. "Come on, Tara, there's someone I want you to meet."

"Just lead on, Sam, honey," she said. Jeri was stunned by the revelation that he planned to bring the girl up to meet Angie.

"OK, let's go. I can't wait to get cleaned up." He pushed Tara forward with another bang on the backside with the bag, and the two of them began the walk to the elevators. John shrugged his shoulders at the four stunned people still standing mutely around the table of dismembered and eviscerated shellfish.

"John, he's your friend. You have to stop him from bringing her upstairs." Windy had blocked the path the gray-haired bartender had taken away from the table. The two of them stood face-to-face, their hands occupied with packages.

"Now, why is that, Ms. Windy Lee? Have you decided what Sam will or won't do? If so, why don't you just go stop him yourself?" John's voice tailed off at the end of his question. Ted watched as his expression changed from angry to contrite. His eyes focused on Windy for the first time and his voice became calmer. "Listen, Windy, I've been with him all day. And he has calmed down quite a bit since Angie led us into that bar. I haven't seen him that pissed off since the old days. Frankly, I think we all got off easy on this one.

Tara did a lot to calm him down. I knew she would as soon as I spotted her. He hates to be manipulated."

"What about Angie?" Jeri had found her voice and joined the discussion. "What will Angie do?"

"Well, I don't really know, little girl, but Sam says she is going to like Tara. Now folks, can we please go? We won't be of any use standing around this smelly fish." He stepped slightly to one side, with a movement intended to break the standoff with Windy. She opened her stance to let him go by and followed mechanically behind. Sal joined her as she passed him. He too was holding a large plastic bag in one hand. He put his arm around her waist, and they walked out of the oyster bar together.

"Shit! I'd kill the bastard," Jeri said to Ted, astonishment in her wide eyes and consternation on her tight lips. Ted noticed a hard dimple had formed in the middle of one cheek. "And did you hear? John is the one who found her."

"You've got to admit that this isn't a dull group."

"Dull? Damn, a bar fight and a—whatever, all in the same day? Nothing like this back in Colorado."

"No, nothing like this very many places, I'd say."

"Is that—is she a prostitute, do you think?"

"I don't know, but she seems to fit the part, doesn't she?"

"Come on," Jeri said, pushing him forward toward the lobby. "I don't want to miss anything. Let's catch up with them before they get to the room. I want to see how Angie handles this."

Ted let Jeri push him through the lobby to the elevators. They rode up in an otherwise empty elevator, alone for the first time that day. He wanted only to go to their room and lock the connecting doors to the suite, to lock out the rest of the group and the argument that he felt sure would ensue. He wanted to close the drapes to the Mardi Gras and be alone with Jeri for a long nap, but he knew that none of those things would happen because Jeri wanted to be near the action. He also knew that he would follow her into the suite to watch the embarrassingly public display of what should be very private passion.

They entered the suite from the hallway door, Jeri still carrying a plastic bag of Mardi Gras paraphernalia. She expected to enter into the midst of a tragic argument; instead, she found the others ringed around the little kitchen counter rummaging through the contents of the other packages.

"Come over here with that, Jeri," Sam called across the room to her. "We're trying to see just what we bought."

They walked over to the counter and Jeri tossed her bag up on top of a pile of feather-fringed masks, magic store novelty items, Mardi Gras beads, doubloons, toss cups, T-shirts, hats, and assorted crepe-paper streamers and banners. She couldn't believe what she was seeing; even Angie was sifting through the pile, although somewhat halfheartedly. Tara was standing in the kitchen, next to the refrigerator, drinking a glass of water. Sam inverted the last bag, and more of the same type of cheap party favors poured down onto the pile.

"Too bad we couldn't find any fireworks. But this will do us just fine, I think." Sam had turned to Angie, who was standing by his side. "Come on, Angie, I brought someone I want you to meet."

"Yeah, I saw you brought home a stray. I hope you don't intend to keep it."

"Oh, Angie, she just wants to party with us. You'll like her. You'll see." He turned away from Angie and spoke to Tara. "Hey, Tara, this is Angie, and Angie, that is Tara. She helped John and I shop for all this party stuff. Believe me, Angie, we were lost when she found us."

"Oh, I bet she is quite the party girl. Do you like to party—Tara, is it?"

"Yes'm, Miz Angie. I love to party." She was looking directly into Angie's eyes, with a sweet, shy, little-girl smile on her face. She held the water in both hands in front of her small breasts. Angie stared at her for a long time without saying anything. The activity in the room and over the party toys seemed not to diminish, but Jeri felt a strong feeling of expectation in the air.

"You're good," Angie said finally. "No wonder this dog brought you home. He is such a whore." She turned away from the counter, walked over to the sofa and sat down. She raised a glass of wine from the glass table and took a sip, staring out the French doors and across Bourbon Street to the balcony of the hotel rooms that faced their own. Jeri followed her to the sofa and sat down next to her.

"Are you all right, Angie?" Jeri asked.

"I'm fine, Jeri. I'm used to it." She spoke with affected toughness in her voice. Jeri felt an answer would break her façade, so she simply placed her hand on her knee and nodded.

"He's trying to teach me a lesson. Showing me what a big manly stud he is. I guess it's my own fault for taking him into that gay bar, but I didn't think he would go off this way. He's trying to show me that I was getting too big for my britches, and he is going to punish me by humiliating me. He is such an asshole. Just once I would like to get even with him." She turned to face Jeri for the first time, and Jeri could see that her eyes were full of moisture. Jeri felt her own eyes begin to well up.

"Don't you dare do it, Jeri. I can handle this. Just don't you go weak and girly-girl on me. I can tough this out, I've done it before."

Jeri turned away and wiped her eyes quickly with the tips of her fingers. "Hey, that wine looks good. Mind if I get myself some?" She stood up next to the cocktail table and looked down to Angie, forcing herself to smile.

"Sure, Jeri. I'm sorry I didn't think to offer you some. It's in the refrigerator. Why don't you bring it back over here? I could use a refill too."

"I'll just do that. It's about time I consumed something nicer than stale draft beer. And I want a glass. I'm sick of the chemical taste of those plastic cups."

"The glasses are in the freezer compartment," Angie called after her.

Jeri walked to the kitchen to get the bottle of wine. The new girl was standing in front of the refrigerator door as she walked toward her; she dreaded the need to ask her to move. Jeri could see the expression of contentment and happiness on the girl's face as she approached her. She seemed happy to have been invited to the suite and to be part of the festivities. Then she noticed Jeri's approach and her expression changed to one of street-smart wariness, and as Jeri continued toward to her, she seemed poised to defend herself.

"Don't worry, Tara. I'm just going to the refrigerator for a bottle of wine." As Jeri spoke, Tara stepped away from the door.

"I don't want to make anyone feel bad, miz. But Sam and John, they invited me to come up, you know." Her tone of voice was apologetic.

"Hey, it's not my affair. I hardly know most of these people." Jeri opened the refrigerator and reached inside to get the already open bottle of white wine. "Just one thing, Tara."

"Yes, miz."

"You see that one over there?" Jeri pointed to Ted with the bottle as she spoke. Ted waved back and smiled, without understanding the meaning of Jeri's gesture.

"Yes'm, miz."

"Don't go anywhere near him. I'm not from New York, and where I come from we don't share. Understand?" Jeri hoped that she looked as stern and forbidding as she was trying to appear. She opened the freezer and took out two frosted wineglasses. As she closed the door, Tara was waiting to speak.

"Yes'm, miz. You have a very nice husband, miz, and I won't cause you any trouble." The girl was extremely respectful, almost submissive in her mannerisms.

Jeri was happy that she had made her point about Ted, but she felt something for the young prostitute—a basic, primal feeling. As she turned away, beginning the short walk back out to the sofa, she finally recognized it to be a feeling of camaraderie. In some surprising way, Jeri felt that in another reality she too could have been forced into relying on the minimal resources of a woman: her body and her beauty. She was terrorized by the concept of selling her body to strangers for money, but she could, in some superficial way, understand how it could happen.

When she sat down on the sofa next to Angie, her loyalties were not as clear as they had been when she had stood from the same place only minutes before. She placed the two cold glasses on the tabletop, holding them by their long stems. The moist air swirled in the icy glasses, and steamy weather fronts were created in microcosm within them. The steaming air welled up out of the glasses as she filled them with the wine, overflowing the rims in thick, white, lethargic waves.

"Did you talk to her?" Angie asked, as she lifted her wine to her lips, her eyes forward, her focus directed toward the revelers on the balcony across the street.

"Not really, I had to ask her to move."

"Yeah, sure." She sipped her wine thoughtfully. "I bet you told her not to fuck Ted."

"I'm sorry, miss, but we don't seem to have any record of your application." The gray-haired clerk smiled broadly, safe behind her high counter and small window, but Jeri thought she recognized the wary look of one experienced with identifying fraudulent paperwork. Her faded blue eyes peered narrowly over thick reading glasses with hemispherical lenses, a thin gold eyeglass chain hung heavily from each side of the tortoiseshell frames. "If you would like, I can give you a new application." She bent slightly behind her computer terminal, reaching for some unseen pile of forms. "It is a little late to apply for this term, but perhaps next—"

"No, you don't understand. I've already been accepted."

"I'm sorry, miss, but you will have to go to the end of the line until you have your paperwork completed," the registration clerk said. Only she was changed; she had dark eyes and hair and wore a tight sweater over large breasts. Someone pushed Jeri from behind and she lost her spot at the window. As she continued to be pushed father away she glimpsed the clerk watching her and shaking her head sadly. The line became a mob of pushing and thrusting face-less forms. Jeri thought she saw Ted; he was calling to her from across the crowd, but she could not make her way to him, and then he was gone. Suddenly she was awake, breathing rapidly, terrified of the dream and unsure of her surroundings.

She got up as quietly as she could and traversed the unfamiliar room to the bathroom, using her feet and hands as feelers in the darkness. She sat down carefully, feeling for the seat so she wouldn't have to turn on the light. She felt herself drifting back into sleep and the lines at the registrar, and she forced herself to full wakefulness, unwilling to rejoin the confused terror of the dream. She knew she should move back to the bed, but the move seemed too much to attempt. Then, sitting alone in the bathroom, she realized that she was still a little drunk or dingy from a hangover. Yes, she realized, she was hungover, and her head began to ache the moment she accepted the fact that she had drunk too much wine the night before.

She stood and pushed the door slowly closed, listening as the latch clicked quietly. She felt disoriented and clumsy as she blindly rubbed her palms over the wall, searching for the light switch. She felt the plastic toggle just as she was losing her equilibrium in the darkness. Her eyes shut instantly—automatically, but the white light converted her eyelids into bright pink lampshades as it forced its way painfully through the thin skin. Massaging the sockets, she rubbed her closed eyes with stiff fingertips to block out the brightness. Sharp, crusty remnants of sleep ground from her sticky lashes as she rubbed. Gradually, she let more of the light energy pass between her fingers, and she grew more accustomed to it, using squinting eyelids as a final, somewhat ineffectual defense against the brilliance. She rummaged through her makeup case until she found the bottle of aspirin she needed. After a frustrating struggle with the childproof cap, she washed two of them down with a plastic cup full of warmish tap water. As she finished drinking she realized that the cup was still sealed in a tight plastic sanitary film. She tossed the cup into the trash bucket and reached for the bathroom doorknob.

Her mind still cloudy, she opened the door moments before turning off the light. For an instant the room was flooded in the unforgiving white light of the bright bathroom fixture. The image of Ted's form, lying in the bed, was burned into her mind and eyes, as if she had been blinded by a sudden camera flash. She walked across the room using the image seared onto her retinas as a bleary, rapidly fading map.

Ted awoke slowly from a dream that he was in his old house in Orange County, in the bathroom, standing over the stool relieving himself. As he dreamed, he was surprised that no matter how long he continued, his need was not abated. Slowly, unconsciously, he realized he was dreaming and he would need to wake up, get out of the strange hotel bed and go to the bathroom. Still mostly asleep, he tried to convince himself that he could wait, but it was no use. As he willed himself to full consciousness he reached for her. She was not there. He felt very alone as he leaned forward and stared into the darkness.

When she neared the bed she knew that she had awakened him. She heard the soft rustling of the bedclothes as he moved in the bed to face her in the blackness.

"Are you all right, Jeri?" she heard him ask in the darkness.

"Yes. I just had to go to the bathroom. I got a drink of water." Using small, unsure steps, she walked to the bed until her knees finally met the mattress. She bent over, searching with her hands, trying to locate him, and discovered his legs where she thought his head should be. She was surprised that she had not arrived at the end of the bed where her mental map had led her.

"Wow. Where are you?" she asked.

"Up here. You should turn on the light."

"No, I'm OK. I'm sorry I woke you." She climbed into the bed, feeling her way up to him. As she put her head on the pillow, he cast the sheet and comforter over her body, kissed her on her cheek and got out of the bed.

"I was awake. I have to go to the bathroom, too. Are you sure you are OK? You're clammy."

"Yes, I'm all right. I was having a bad dream, it woke me up. I guess I was pretty frightened."

"Are you OK now? Do you want to talk about it?" He spoke over his shoulder as he moved to the bathroom.

"No, I'm all right. It was just a bad dream. I can't remember all of it now." He had not closed the door all the way, and he could hear her clearly above his own, somewhat embarrassing, sounds.

"Somehow my records had been misplaced, and the med school at Irvine wouldn't let me register." The light from the bathroom made a bright triangle across the floor. She could hear him standing above the toilet—probably missing it as much as he was hitting it.

"Only, the registration seemed to be here, and not there, and Angie was the clerk. You were with me at first, and then you were gone."

Finished, he moved to the sink for a drink and found Jeri's bottle of aspirin still there. He tossed some in his mouth and bent over to drink directly from the tap.

"I couldn't find you in the lines of people. It was like being lost when you're a little kid. Powerless, you know? I knew it was a dream, but it was somehow very real and frightening. But then I woke up." The light in the bathroom went out, and she waited for him to find his way to her.

"You're right here, Jeri, with me, at Mardi Gras," he said as he got back in the bed. "You can get weird dreams when you go to sleep with cocaine in your system. Your body is asleep but your mind works overtime."

"You know, I haven't done any coke since our first night here. Could it only be three days? It seems like three weeks." She decided impulsively to tell him about doing the X with Donna during their trip uptown. "Ted, I should to tell you about doing something else. When we took the streetcar up Saint Charles, at the Italian restaurant, Donna and I—"

"I love you, Jeri," Ted interrupted. "I just don't want you to be hurt. If you want to tell me something, I'm listening, but it's the future I'm concerned about. Sometimes it's better if the past stays in the past. I have one too, you know." He tried to sound upbeat, trying to lighten the moment.

"No, it's OK." She wanted to make that day the end of it. "Donna had some Ecstasy. I did a hit with her."

"Yeah, I thought it was something like that. You were...that is, you weren't as...*modest* as normal."

"Modest?" Jeri smiled in the darkness, "Hell, I flashed my tits to a hundred thousand people. I'll say I wasn't very modest! I'm so sorry, Ted, if I embarrassed you. Every time I think of it I can feel my face flush." She put her hands up to her cheeks and frowned.

"No, Jeri, it's not that. I just don't want to end up like the Williamsons. I really couldn't believe them last night."

Ted thought about the night before when Williamson and Angie had brewed and drunk their strange elixir of viciousness and love, vindictiveness and kindness, hate and sex. The foul vapors of their psychotoxic alchemy had permeated the atmosphere of the party that roared late into the night on the connecting balconies of the Royal Sonesta, suspended above the heads of thousands of drunken revelers on Bourbon Street below. Ted had been unable to comprehend how Angie had accepted the girl-woman Tara; it had been as if the situation had become less invidious as the night had progressed, as the three had drunk and had smoked pot and had consumed line after line of cocaine.

Ted had watched them as they had stood together at the rail. Sam had stood in the middle, holding a plastic bag of the beads and coins, with Angie and Tara at each side, all three drinking and laughing and throwing the Mardi Gras toys to the crowd. They had stood apart from the others, throwing the valueless trinkets to the rabble that had rioted below them as if they were tossing expensive golden necklaces or authentic Spanish doubloons. They had seemed like old friends—Sam standing with his chest pushed forward over the rail, with Angie on one side and Tara on the other—all of them, even Angie, having a wonderful time.

"They were incredible, weren't they?" Jeri asked. "It's incredible that Angie went along with it. When he first brought her up to the room I thought Angie was going to kill him, but it was like she took a big breath and just went along. She must love him very much to put up with this kind of shit."

"Love? I hope what they have isn't love," Ted said.

"Angie was drinking straight vodka, did you see that? On the rocks, anyway. And she was right there, face down to the coke all night. It was like she wasn't even the same person we started the day with. She seemed trashy. I liked her better the other way."

"Yeah, me too. I wonder how often they go through this sort of thing. He seems in some way unbalanced—but they must have some kind of normal life in New York. I mean, he has a position of responsibility in his company. He must stay normal long enough to get his work finished."

"I wouldn't bet on it. Windy says his job is a farce. He comes into the office a few times a week, but mostly he plays golf and tennis with the clients who are impressed that he used to be a football player. They don't even like him to come into the office because he harasses all the women. I guess they have had to buy off several sexual harassment suits."

"That seems to fit with what I've seen of him over the last couple of days. He's what we used to call a weasel—always sniffing around the women."

"You're telling me, he's been hitting on all of us every chance he gets. Donna says that Windy did it with him in the bathroom the first night they were here—before her long-lost love Sal Benito showed up. Donna and I have been scooting around two steps in front of him to avoid listening to his come-ons."

"Damn, Jeri. Why didn't you say something? We don't have to stay around these people. They may have the need to abuse one another, but we don't have to let them abuse us."

"I don't know. Donna and I just made a joke about it. Dogs like him are everywhere. If a woman can't handle them, she'll never survive in the real world. I think he's a little pathetic, to be honest. Donna thinks he's good-looking, but she wouldn't get involved with him either. She says he is a misogynist at heart."

"I can't believe he has been hitting on you. To tell you the truth, I thought John would be the one doing that," Ted said.

Jeri felt a rush of heat surge through her body as she remembered the night with John. She hoped Ted wouldn't feel it. She had put the episode out of her mind, but now it came back and she felt ashamed again. She answered quickly to prevent him from sensing something was wrong.

"John is another story," she said. "He's not someone I like to be alone with either. But if he finds out that Sam has been trying to bed Donna, he'll turn into the jealous boyfriend. I mean, John already knows that Sam is a womanizer—so is John, for that matter." She felt stupid and naive for ever having permitted him to touch her. "But it's like honor among thieves. They don't screw each other's girlfriends. Dates and pickups, yes, they are fair game. But wives and girlfriends are supposed to be off-limits. It's a contest for them."

"Great. All this party needs is another fistfight."

"No, I don't mean that John would attack him physically. His way of getting back at someone is to play some kind of a practical joke. He would set him up—try to make him look silly or ineffectual. But I don't think he would do anything really terrible. After all, they have been friends a long time." She rolled back to her side of the bed. "What time is it? I'm wide-awake."

"I don't know, but it feels like the middle of the night." He pushed himself toward the nightstand and raised his head to see the time. "Hell, it's eight thirty. What time did we get to bed anyway? Three, three thirty?"

"Something like that. I stopped drinking early, but I still have a hangover. I don't like being hungover every day. I can handle it if I get my rest, but not on four or five hours sleep. In a way I'll be glad when this is over." And as she spoke, she realized that the partying was getting old. She hadn't done any coke for days, and she had only smoked one joint with Donna the night before. She could have fun without being loaded all the time. She had a life—work to do, and she knew she would be incapable of real work if she continued to get high every day. Ted was right. It wasn't worth it.

"Let's sleep in, OK?" Ted hoped that he could treat his own hangover with a few more hours of sleep.

"You go ahead, I'm wide-awake. I'm going to order a big Pepsi from room service." She got out of bed and carefully stood in the darkness.

Ted turned on the small bedside lamp. He watched her naked back as she walked to the bureau and then to the bathroom, and regretfully, he knew that the time for sleep had passed. He swung his legs out of the bed and sat with his head in his hands, thinking about his hangover.

"That sounds good. I could use some breakfast too." He raised his voice slightly as he spoke through the closed bathroom door. In a moment she reopened it, and he could see her peeking around its edge. The sound of the shower came from behind her.

"Yeah," she said, speaking over the shower sound. "Or maybe a club sandwich and fries." Rich waves of steam rolled into the room while she spoke. She pushed the door partially closed, disappearing into the mist.

Ted had deliberately slowed his drinking the night before and still he had drunk too much. What was that quote from Fitzgerald? "You never know how much is enough until you've had too much." He was reminded of the Tooth Fairy Project. Fitzgerald's statement worked for nuclear technology too. The project had collected baby teeth from children living near nuclear facilities and had found increased levels of Strontium 90—and the increased levels correlated with cancer clusters. But it was too late; the isotope was already in the food chain. Enough had already become too much.

Jeri had wisely stopped drinking early, he thought, and he couldn't remember her taking coke or smoking pot all night. She was awake now, but he felt she would need a nap before the day was over, and that would be his chance to get some more sleep. He forced himself to stand and again shuffled to the bathroom, feeling very tired and old. He climbed into the shower as Jeri was coming out. As usual, the water was much too hot and he had to adjust the temperature.

Jeri wondered how the others were doing as she selected her outfit and got dressed. She and Ted had been the first of the group to give up on the party on the balcony and go to their room. When they had said their good-byes, the others had shown no signs of wearing down and had urged them to stay awake. She remembered the strange interplay between the Williamsons and the new girl; she felt terrible about the way Sam had treated Angie. She was an intelligent woman, and Jeri loathed seeing her degraded by the egotistical ex-football player. Jeri wondered how Angie had let her life become so twisted by the man. No love should be so strong as to permit the loved to destroy the lover. Yet, when Jeri thought about her own lost husband, she realized that it was indeed possible that love could be a destructive emotion. It was just that now, in her relationship with Ted, the idea of a hurtful lover seemed improbable and far away.

She wondered what time the others had gone to bed, then walked to the connecting doors to put her ear against their side. She listened carefully, but couldn't hear a sound coming from the adjoining suite. They were either still asleep or were not in the room. She walked to the French doors and peeked out to the balcony; it was empty. The day was overcast but inviting, so she opened the doors to let the cool breeze come in to clean the stale air from the room. She sat on the bed while she called room service, ordering two large Cokes and two club sandwiches.

He had showered slowly, letting the warm water soothe him as he washed. When he was finished, he felt much better. The shower had awakened him and the aspirins had cured his headache. He stepped out of the bathroom refreshed, with a towel wrapped around his waist. The room was open to the street. Jeri had opened the drapes and French doors, and a cold wind blew through the room. The light outside was gray and depressing; it seemed incapable of finishing the job of illuminating the room. The bedside lamp was still on, casting a dim ring of yellow light on the carpet. He saw Jeri out on the balcony; she stood with her back to him, looking over the railing into the street.

"Damn, Jeri." He spoke in a stage whisper as he rushed across the room to the dresser and his clothes. "It's cold outside. Close those doors before I freeze my ass off."

"California boy, this is not cold, it is merely brisk." She came back inside, closing the French doors behind her. "Maybe if you didn't run around naked, you wouldn't be so cold, city boy."

She walked over to him as he began to dress. Stopping him before he could put on his shirt, she hugged him and kissed his bare shoulder. He was very cold, but she felt warm and inviting next to his cold skin.

"You'd better put that shirt on before you catch cold." She took one step back, watching him as he buttoned his shirt. He was shivering before the last button was clasped. He took a pullover sweater out of the dresser and put it on over the shirt. When he had finished, he pulled her close in another hug. She rubbed his back and upper arms to help warm him.

"I don't care what you say, Nanook of the North, it's cold outside." He walked to the glass doors to look outside. The sky was close and heavy, and deeply overcast. "I wonder if it is going to rain."

"When it's cold in the mountains it doesn't rain. The clearest days are the coldest." She spoke as she waved to the silent newscast fluttering brightly on the television. "Besides, the local weather on TV says no rain today. It wouldn't dare, too many big parades."

They ate the sandwiches sitting on the bed watching the television. Jeri didn't care for the flavor of the sandwich; it tasted plain and dry. She watched Ted eat and realized he must be ravenous; he took large bites and concentrated on his plate. She picked at her own meal without relish, managing to finish one-quarter of the sandwich and some of her fries. Their soft drinks were finished almost before they had started to eat. Jeri refilled their glasses with ice and water so they could wash down the dry food. After they had finished eating, they put the plates and rubbish back on the room service tray and Ted slid it out into the hall. Then they lay on top of the bed to rest, with their heads elevated on propped-up pillows.

Jeri felt good in his arms. He was contented as they quietly watched the televised replays of Sunday's parades out on Saint Charles Avenue in the Garden District. He was unaware of falling asleep. They slept there on top of the bed, embracing in all their clothing, until the noises from the suite next door brought them back to consciousness. It was after noon when they woke again.

"Oh-oh. Here we go again," Jeri said, as she raised herself from his chest. "Sounds like the gang is leaving their coffins for the night. I think they need more bloooood." She pronounced the word blood like an actor in an old vampire movie.

"I think I'm getting too old for this, Jeri. Why don't you just shoot me and be done with it," Ted said. He was still chuckling at her parody of a vampire as he sat up on the edge of the bed.

"Come on, old man." She pulled him to his feet. "Just today and tomorrow, and we can go back to our rocking chairs. I'm beginning to think I'm too old for this too."

"I need to wash my face." Ted broke gently free of her tugging and went to the bathroom. He tossed cold water on his face and dried with a clean hand towel. His eyes were puffy and tired-looking. He decided it wasn't only a joke; he was too old for this kind of party. He wondered how his former company was doing back in LA.

Jeri passed through the doors that joined their bedroom with the main part of the suite and looked around the room that had been so alive with the party the night before. Most of the group was there, but they seemed subdued and isolated around the quiet suite. Angie and Tara were seated at the breakfast counter, eating something and drinking coffee. John and Sam sat slumped at opposite ends of the sofa, their heads barely visible over its back. Donna was standing out on the balcony. She was leaning back against the elaborate wrought-iron railing, facing into the living room, holding a coffee cup in one hand and a cigarette in the other. She waved Jeri over as soon as she noticed her, gesturing with the hand that held the cigarette, arcing a circular trail of smoke in the cool mid-day air. Jeri walked across the living room toward her. She deliberately avoided acknowledging John and Sam, who were sitting near the door, but she waved to Angie and Tara. She noticed, as she drew closer, that Donna was smiling with the familiar impatient grin she used when she had a particularly juicy bit of gossip to share. As Jeri passed through the French doors, Donna indicated she should hurry with another series of smoky circles.

"Hurry up, girl, I've been waiting for you to get up. Are you sick or what?" She dropped the cigarette to the wooden floor and ground it into a messy black spot with her shoe.

"No, we just fell back to sleep after we ate. What's going on, anyway? I didn't expect to find Tara still here this late. Especially not with Angie." Jeri looked into the suite to where Angie and Tara sat at the breakfast counter. They were sitting side by side as they ate, and between bites they were speaking to each other in the easy manner of old friends.

"That's just it. Angie and Tara are together now. Angie wooed her away from Sam last night. It was really something. You shouldn't have gone to bed so early."

"What do you mean?" Jeri was confused by Donna's revelation. "What do you mean, she wooed her away from him?"

"You know, she just sort of got closer and closer, and she talked to her, and she made her drinks, and little by little they just sort of paired off." Donna's eyes grew round and large in exaggerated excitement. "I thought Sam was going to kill somebody. He probably would have too, except he got too drunk to walk." Her pleased excitement dropped to a less happy tone as she finished. "John too, the two of them got sloppy drunk and passed out sitting on the couch. First thing they did when they woke up is make Bloody Marys." Donna nodded her head to where the two big men sat. Jeri followed the look to find them sitting almost motionless, at either end of the sofa, drinks on the table in front of them.

"They look terrible. Did they ever go to bed?"

"No, they've been living on that couch. Drinking, smoking, and tooting coke all night. Except for when they were passed out, of course."

When Ted returned to the bedroom Jeri was gone and the double doors to the Williamsons' suite were both open. He walked across the room, turning off the murmuring television as he passed it. "Here we go again, is right," he said out loud as he left the empty room.

He walked through the connecting doors without closing them, surveying the living room as he entered the suite. Jeri and Donna were standing out on the balcony, facing each other, and Donna was speaking excitedly. Donna stood with her legs wide apart, jerking her arms and hands up and down with theatrical emphasis, bending occasionally at the waist from laughter. Jeri seemed to be listening closely to her friend; her active listening was punctuated with head movements that alternated between empathetic nods and disgusted shakes. At times Jeri too burst into silent laughter. Occasionally they would turn wide-eyed looks into the room, turning their heads at the same instant, parting their lips to bare toothy grins, evidently discussing someone or something inside. Angie and Tara were sitting next to each other at the kitchen counter eating room service breakfasts. There was no sign of Windy Lee or Sal Benito. Ted remembered Windy had a complimentary room in another part of the hotel, and Sal lived close by in an old converted slave-quarters apartment. John and Sam were sitting in the living room, facing the glass table, but leaning heavily back into the cushions. Ted walked over to the two men.

"Good morning." He sat down across from them, pulling one of the light chairs close to the table. There were four short rows of cocaine on the glass top of the table; a length of drinking straw and a single-edged razor blade lay near them. A ziplock bag containing more of the white powder sat, top opened, in a cigar box. Two Bloody Marys, one in front of each man, appeared to be untouched; the ice had melted into a pale brown layer on top of the red liquid. Sam raised a joint to his lips, puffed at it sluggishly and passed it to John without looking at him. "Or should I say good afternoon?" Ted continued.

"Hey, Ted," John said slowly. "You two were smart to go to bed early and get some sleep. Last night ran out of hours. Want a Bloody Mary?" His eyes were glassy and blank. He held the joint between his first two fingers like a tobacco cigarette, but did not smoke it.

"No, too early for me. Did you get any sleep?" Ted asked, but he felt he knew the answer. Both of the men looked as if they had been walking the razor's edge between alcohol and cocaine most of the night.

"Yeah. Got four or five hours this morning after the action settled down," John said with a limp smile. "But I'm going to take another little nap before long."

"Pussy," Sam said, "you passed out before I did."

"That's not my fault, Romeo. You just couldn't give it up." John leaned forward and set the joint on the glass next to the lines of cocaine.

"Yeah, I should have got some sleep. Those two cunts ruined my whole night. Matter of fact, I think I'll go get some right now." Sam stood up slowly, then leaned back down to pick up the cocktail. He drained it in a series of large noisy gulps, shook his head with his face wrinkling in distaste, burped loudly, and walked stiffly to the stairs leading up to the loft.

"Hell, I'm gone too. Tell Donna to wake me up when you get ready to go to dinner, OK?" John tried to push his large bulk out of the deep cushions, but fell back with a sigh.

"Sure thing, John. Need any help?"

"Nah, I just got to build some momentum." He turned a little to one side and pushed himself up. He ignored the drink and the drugs and left for the other connecting room, nodding his acknowledgment to Ted as he left. Ted stood up, following him with his eyes, wondering how soon the bartender would recover. Then he noticed that Angie was watching him, her head turned over one shoulder. She continued to stare at him after the other two men had tottered away. She seemed to be waiting to talk to him. Finally, she motioned with one hand the unmistakable message that he should come to her at the kitchen counter. She greeted him happily when he walked over to her.

"Good morning, Ted. How are you feeling? You two left before the party really got started."

"Good, I suppose. Tired, for sure. How are you?" He walked into the kitchen so the two women could face him comfortably. He stopped in front of the refrigerator and leaned against it.

"We feel like shit, don't we, Tara?" she said, as she turned to the girl eating breakfast next to her. Tara's black dress seemed inappropriate in the daytime.

"I'm feeling better now that I've had something to eat. I don't usually drink, you know, Angie." She spoke as she held a forkful of scrambled eggs in front of her face.

"You are such a little angel, Tara. Too bad you had to fall in with us decadent Northerners." Angie reached around the girl's shoulder, leaned in to her and kissed her softly on the lips. Tara responded instantly to her kiss; the forkful of eggs floated, forgotten, a few inches behind Angie's head. The kiss was a closed mouthed series of small, slow lip kisses. Ted was stunned by the intimacy of the act and realized that he and Jeri had indeed left early the night before. He felt that Angie was doing it deliberately to shock him, so he pretended that he hadn't noticed the kiss at all. He waited until the kiss had ended and Angie had started to pull back to her own plate.

"How are the eggs, Tara?" He looked directly into the girl's big dark eyes, willing her to eat the forkful of eggs before answering him. She didn't take the bite first; the eggs remained in their tiny glide pattern as she spoke.

"They are wonderful, Mr. Ted. Would you like some? There is plenty." She put the fork down in the plate and began to stand.

"No thank you, Tara. Jeri and I ate in our room before we came over. You go ahead and finish before your breakfast gets cold." He watched her as she settled back down in the chair, raised the fork and finally put it in her mouth. She was very hard to dislike, but surely she could not have won Angie over in a single evening. Ted felt that there was something else happening around him. Was Angie normally bisexual? Did she do this sort of thing all the time? It wouldn't be that surprising of a stranger, but Ted felt that he had developed an immediate understanding of Angie, and this result just did not fit with his paradigm.

He watched the two women eat their breakfast, wondering how his life had evolved to this point. He had no serious connection to these two women, and yet he was concerned that they were being hurt in some way, damaged by Sam's manipulations and the cold, selfish reality of life. A reality that would not acknowledge the intrinsic value that lay only molecules below the makeup and the skin and the flesh—and, for Angie, below the power and the wealth. His mind felt slow and inefficient as he leaned against the cold metal of the appliance, wondering if it was just a bad hangover or if there was some incomprehensible complexity in the situation. Too much scotch or convoluted melodrama? He could not think his way through to understanding, but must feel his way through, bumping along in the darkness, hoping that his gut feelings could give him some guidance.

Without being aware that he was doing it, Ted cleared the two women's breakfast plates and deposited them in a remote corner of the counter surface. Tara looked up into his eyes with distrustful gratitude, as if she expected him to ask her for some bodily payment for the tiny act. He struggled for a way to displace the discomfort her eyes were causing him, and opened the refrigerator, the first time for him, to look inside. It was not empty—it held mostly beer and wine—but it was without the pretense of a place where the next meal might be found. He took a small bottle of mineral water, wanting Tara to think he had opened the door for a reason. When he tipped the plastic bottle up to his mouth, he discovered the water was icy cold and wonderfully refreshing; he drank until the bottle was empty. As he brought the bottle down, he saw Jeri and Donna coming back inside from the balcony.

Donna smiled and pointed to the glass cocktail table before moving to sit down on the sofa. Her eyes invited Jeri to join her. Jeri shook her head, cast a momentary frown down at the drugs, and continued through the room to the kitchen. Ted felt an overwhelming desire to hug her.

"Today's the big day, Ted. Fat Tuesday. Mardi Gras day. We get to wear our costumes today," Jeri said, rounding the counter to join him in the kitchen.

"Do we have costumes, Jeri?" Ted dreaded the answer as he asked the question.

"We do now. We are going to be Crayolas." Jeri spoke up to his face as she hugged his chest. "At least that is what Donna told me." She turned to face Angie, an open question in her eyes.

"That's right. We've rented a whole…box. Green, yellow, red, blue, and a couple of more, I guess, six colors—costumes—in all." Angie put a friendly arm around Tara's bare shoulders. "And with John going as the court jester, that means we even have a crayon for Tara."

"Oh boy, costumes," Ted said without joy.

"No, Angie, I couldn't bother your nice party. I've got to go home and get ready for work." Tara began to stand, her face pursed with concern.

"Nonsense, Tara," Angie said. "You just call in to work and tell them you are sick." She leaned sideways in her chair, extending her short legs, to push her hand into the pocket of her jeans. She pulled out a crumpled ball of money and began to pull hundred-dollar bills from it. "And I will not let you tell me that you need to go to work because you need the money. Here. Here is five hundred dollars. Is that enough, sweetheart?"

"Oh yes, Miz Angie. You are so good to me." Tara took the money, leaned over to Angie and kissed her on the cheek.

"Now what did I say about calling me miz?" Angie said with mock anger.

"I'm sorry, Angie. I was just so happy." Tara leaned away for a moment and then bent over to give Angie a grateful hug. "Just point me to that old Crayola, Angie."

"You just call up work and tell them that you are all right. The costumes can wait a few minutes." She picked up the receiver of the phone and handed it to Tara.

"OK, Angie. I'll call." She tried to turn her back on the group, pulling the phone to the limit of the cord, but the cord was too short. She dialed her number and bent her head in a submissive bow. She held the phone with both hands, her elbows pressed tightly to her chest. She tried to keep her conversation private, but the location of the phone on the breakfast counter prevented anything but easily overheard whispers.

"Is Charlie there? OK, I'll wait." She stood motionless as she waited for her party to answer. "Hi, it's Tara. Yes. Working. Yes, I have it…I'll tell you later. No, later. OK, five hundred. Tonight? No, they want me to stay. Yes, another five hundred so far. You know I will, Charlie. Good-bye." She raised her head slowly as she replaced the receiver, her teenage face beaming an angelic smile.

Lent

If there is a meaning in life at all, then there must be a meaning in suffering...It goes without saying that suffering would not have a meaning unless it were absolutely necessary...

—Viktor E. Frankl, *Man's Search for Meaning*

Jeri looked at herself in the mirror over the dresser and laughed out loud. She was wrapped in a white cylinder from her shoulders to her knees, a matching white body tight covered her arms and legs, and a conical hat topped her head and encircled her face. Large black ellipses, with the word *Crayola* printed in block letters within, extended down each side if the tube, completing the costume. She turned awkwardly toward the bedside where Ted was sitting. He was frowning as he struggled to pull his own tights onto his legs. She could see the whiteness of his skin through the black stockings where he was pulling them too tight.

"Hey, be careful there. You'll run your stockings, big boy." She laughed at his obvious lack of enthusiasm for the costume.

"I didn't sign on for costumes, you know."

"Oh, don't be a spoilsport. You'll have fun, wait and see." She waddled over to help him, giggling at the awkwardness caused by the bulky, if lightweight, outfit. "Here, roll them up first. You can't pull them on from the top, silly." She tried to pose with her hands on her hips. "Men," she said with mock exasperation. Then she helped him.

Earlier in the day, when she had learned of Angie's sexual humiliation of Sam through her own self-degradation, she had felt deflated and soiled—reluctant to join in the mounting celebration.

She had found herself thinking about the things Ted had been saying since their first days together at the Iron Horse Inn—concepts that implied an intractable senselessness of their roles in civilization. She had wondered if the lives of all successful New Yorkers were as seemingly meaningless as those of the Williamsons. She had been astonished by the brevity and emptiness of the chemically synthesized good times. It was so transient and false, not at all like the true happiness she had experienced while growing up, during the holidays with her family, or when she had excelled at school, or even, if she were honest with herself, on her wedding day. *Ted is right,* she had thought, *we need to get away from this craziness.* But later, once Angie, Donna, and the new addition, Tara, had donned their costumes, Jeri had felt her mood lighten. What did it matter if Angie was having a strange fling with the young prostitute? Donna had certainly enjoyed the way it had affected Sam. The macho ex-football player had moodily gone to the loft bedroom to sleep and had not returned for the rest of the day.

John, on the other hand, had taken a three-hour nap and had emerged from the other room apparently refreshed. His animated return in the role of clown, wearing his brightly colored jester's costume, had catalyzed the universal change into the crayon Carnival raiment. Jeri was happy with the costumes. Once she had seen herself in the clothing of masquerade, she had, as if energized by the illusion, regained her passion for the riotous party roaring outside and below their open French doors. Even Ted had given up his final resistance to the costume under a barrage of teasing and coaxing from the others.

Jeri looked at the reflection of the two of them in the mirror as Ted pulled the cylindrical portion of the outfit over his head and down below his cargo shorts. She liked the contrast of the black and the white; it made them different from each other, but it also differentiated them from the other brightly colored Crayola costumes Angie had provided for their group. She laughed at Ted's discomfort as she helped him pull the pointed hat onto his head.

"Cheer up, Ted, there are worse costumes than this, you know. How about if she had gotten us something sexy? Remember that guy we saw last night wearing the chaps, his bare ass hanging out?"

"Oh yeah, that would be an outfit I would agree to wear." His eyebrows rose in a way made comical by the round framing of the black conical hat and she laughed at him again.

"Don't worry, sweetie, I would only let you wear that in the privacy of our own room." Jeri tried to pull herself close to him, but the bulkiness at the tops and bottoms of the costumes precluded anything more than a hand around his waist, where the cylinders were only draped cloth.

"Not even there, my love, not even there." He pushed down on the fronts of the upper hoops to allow them to lean forward and kiss lightly. "I don't know about these things. If you fall down you might not be able to get back up." Ted laughed for the first time since they had started to put on the costumes. Jeri could see he was beginning to have fun with the outfit. She knew they would have a good time together during the Fat Tuesday climax of Carnival.

"I guess we just can't fall down tonight. Come on, let's go back into Angie's room, everyone is waiting."

They maneuvered their way through the narrow doors between the rooms to find the others at the kitchen counter. Sam had still not joined the group. John and Donna were in the kitchen, he in his jester's outfit and she in the red crayon costume. John was making drinks, and he called to them as soon as they entered the living room.

"Hey, you two, what do you want to drink? I've made up a batch of kick-ass margaritas. You've got to try one."

"Sure, I'll have one," Jeri said, as she shuffled happily across the room to join the other colors of the Crayola box.

"OK, why not. Might as well finish destroying my liver," Ted said, and walked behind her to the little counter where Angie, costumed in yellow, and Tara, in bright pink, were seated. They had the bottom hoops of their costumes lifted up to their waists to accomplish sitting down. He noticed Angie also wore shorts underneath, but Tara still wore the black dress from the night before.

"Come on, Ted," Angie said, "tomorrow's Ash Wednesday. You can give up drinking for Lent. Tonight we paint the town red—or whatever one's respective color may be."

"Smart, Angie. I see you two have figured out how to sit down in these things." Ted spoke as he reached over Tara's shoulder for the plastic cups John offered them. The drink was icy frozen and sweetly tart, contrasting with the dry saltiness on the rim of the cup. Jeri looked to Ted and noted his enjoyment as he drank. "Not bad, John. Not bad at all," he said.

"Not bad? That Maggie has won drink contests from coast to coast. What do you think, Jeri?"

"I think it is perfect, John, a wonder of mixology."

"Why, thank you. It's good to be appreciated by a crayon as white as you."

"Hey," Donna objected with a push into the jester's upper arm and a thrust of her red cylinder, "red is every bit as good as white. No more off-color jokes."

Tara chuckled happily at the banter.

"I can see this is going to be a long night of bad jokes," Ted said with a smile between sips of his drink.

"Enough!" Angie yelled, jumping from her perch on the bar stool. "To the streets. We need to get down into the streets. We have to meet Windy and Sal at Jean Laffite's Bar at seven and it is already six fifteen."

"What about Mr. Sam, Miz Angie?" Tara asked in a tiny voice.

"Don't worry about old Sam. He'll manage to find us. I left him his costume and a note telling him we're going to base out of Jean Laffite's. He'll find us. Let's go, everybody." She reached down to gently pull Tara to her feet, took her by the hand and led the party to the hall door.

Jeri held Ted's hand during the short trip down to the lobby in the old elevator, each of them holding their margaritas in their other hand. As they walked across the crowded lobby, they became mini celebrities, the objects of encouraging waves and happy pointing. They passed through the doors onto Bourbon Street the objects of admiration, but once outside they became just half a dozen more Carnival tourists wearing brightly colored costumes. Angie led the way down the tightly crowded sidewalk to the bar where they would rendezvous with Windy and Sal.

Jean Laffite's Bar was a small wooden structure in the storefront of an ancient brick building. It was open to the street, with wooden doors and shutters that appeared to have fallen into dysfunction through nonuse. The paint was old and moldy and peeling where it could be seen, but mostly the walls and ceiling were covered with layers and layers of paper money, all turned a uniform dirty brown by time and humidity. The paper money came from every imaginable country and from every point in time, leading back into the distant, unfathomable past. Jeri fell in love with the place as soon as she got inside.

It was even more crowded inside than out on the sidewalks. They pushed their way through the shoulder-to-shoulder revelers, taking advantage of the slight parting of the throng created by the universal appreciation of their costumes.

"Six Dixie beers," Angie called across the bar to the bartender, yelling to be heard over the noise of the music and loud conversation. The bartender was a startling woman with short platinum blonde hair and brown eyes; she wore a top hat and tails and a black sequined mask. "You guys have to start off with a Dixie beer. You don't have to drink it if you don't like it, but it does give you the flavor of the town!" Angie yelled above the noise of the bar. She spoke to Jeri after she had paid for the beers. "You know, we need to buy ourselves some little masks. I forgot them, but they're sold everywhere. They'll be easy to find once we link up with Windy." She turned from the bar and started to move across the narrow room toward the windows. They all followed behind her, beers in hand, pushing through the crowd. "We'll be able to spot them from here!" Angie yelled, and they stopped in a small circle near a big wood-framed window. There was no glass in the opening and the people passing by outside were as much a part of the bar's activity as the people inside. "You know, they say that this place has been open continuously, I mean night and day, for a hundred years or something, longer than any bar in North America. Hey, look, they're leaving." Angie pushed her way nearer the window where another group was collecting their things prior to standing. She hovered over the table, ready to pounce for its possession, until the strangers got up.

The table was too small to comfortably fit them all, so Donna sat in John's lap, their costumes becoming a confusion of colorful ornamentation, and Tara stood next to Angie. They sat at the worn wooden table, watching the crowds walk by the window, often exchanging compliments regarding Mardi Gras costumes with strangers. They quickly finished the small draft beers, and when the waitress came around they ordered another round of drinks. Jeri ordered a rum and Coke because she felt a pirate's drink was appropriate in a pirate's bar. The waitress was just leaving the table as Windy Lee and Sal Benito arrived. They were dressed in the clothes of *Gone with the Wind.* Windy wore the wide red dress of Scarlett O'Hara and Sal wore a white Southern gentleman's suit, complete with vest, top hat, and walking stick.

"Well, if it isn't Miss Scarlett and Mr. Rhett Butler," Angie called through the window to the couple as they walked by on the sidewalk outside the bar. They stopped, and when the waitress returned they ordered screwdrivers through the window. They didn't bother with an attempt to force their way into the crowded bar; instead, they simply leaned inside and joined them at the table, although still standing outside on the sidewalk.

"You all look wonderful, Angie," Windy said. "I wish we were crayons too. Too bad we had already rented our costumes. It would have been perfect to all be the same."

"Nonsense, you two look great. I love your costumes." Angie's praise was echoed by the rest of the group at the table, the waitress, those seated at the next table, and all those standing within earshot. Jeri was beginning to feel the effects of the drinks and found the friendly, somewhat nosy, crowd delightful. She leaned her face to Ted's and kissed him messily on the lips, then laughed at the lipstick that remained. She pulled the tight sleeve of her leotard over her hand and held it in her fist as she wiped his mouth with exaggerated, motherly daubs.

"There, Ted, that's better. That lipstick was just not your color." She felt his hand move up under the camouflage of her costume to rest, hidden, on her breast.

"I have found something I like about these suits," he whispered up to her as he removed his hand. She bent over again to kiss him, but this time she took care to be dry and dainty.

"Hey, everybody!" Windy yelled. "We just came back from the gay beauty contest. It was the strangest thing I've ever seen. This guy who won had these huge breast implants, and he wore this cute little tight halter top." She pushed her chest out and shimmied her breasts, her flesh wiggling inside the low bodice of the old-fashioned dress.

"Yeah, so what?" John answered from the other end of the table. He had finished his drink and was looking for the waitress as he spoke.

"Well, the guy also had big body builder muscles, a shaved head, and this big bushy beard. The beard was kind of like yours, come to think of it, John." Windy's explanation brought a general guffaw from the now slightly intoxicated group. "Have you guys had dinner yet? I'm famished."

"Not yet," John answered, "I'm hungry too. Anybody else ready to get something to eat?" They agreed to head out of the bar to find a restaurant where they could get dinner. Angie wanted to go to the Court of the Two Sisters because it was close, but Windy recommended a place less well-known to tourists, a restaurant called Mr. B's. She insisted they made the best crawfish pasta dishes in the city. Angie relinquished her leadership with a shrug, and Windy took over as guide during the walk to the restaurant.

Jeri found herself walking with Angie as they journeyed through the crowds on the side streets off Bourbon. Tara was walking ahead of them, following the rest of the group, and she couldn't resist asking the question that she and Donna had been asking each other all day.

"So what's this thing with Tara all about, Angie, revenge for Sam's bull crap?"

"Well, partly. But it was also a way to keep him from going any farther with her. It was a way to get back at him and to control him at the same time."

"So did you—you know?" Jeri felt embarrassed when Angie laughed at her question.

"We kissed a little, and we slept in the same bed, but no, Jeri, we didn't go all the way." She laughed again and shook her head. "Tara was certainly willing. Thank goodness he passed out. I don't know what I would have done if he had stayed awake last night. I suppose I was ready to do anything at the time."

"Man, you must really be in love with him."

"Yeah, you could say that. How's it going with you and Ted, Jeri? You look like newlyweds." Angie was smiling up at her with what appeared to be genuine interest.

"I think I'm in love, Angie."

"Yeah, and by the looks of the big, sad dog eyes he keeps shining back here to you, I would guess that you are not alone, Jeri."

"Isn't he sweet? He is such a good man and I know he cares for me. It's just that…" Jeri stopped in mid-sentence, realizing that she was beginning to speak about something she really wanted to deal with on her own.

"What, Jeri? You can't just get me all interested and then just stop. It's not fair." Angie spotted something in a window of a small shop and grabbed Jeri by the arm, pulling her into the doorway. "Here they are! Little colored masks." They went into the tiny store and Angie bought six of the masks that cover only the area around the eyes and top of the nose—one mask to match each of the colors of the crayon costumes they wore. They were quickly back on the narrow street. The others were stopped at the end of the short block, faces turning in all directions, searching for their lost pair. They waved to them and hurried to catch up.

"Well, Jeri? Are you going to tell me what isn't perfect about your perfect man?" Angie was still smiling, but Jeri felt that she wouldn't let the subject go. As they drew close to the waiting group, Windy grabbed John with one hand and Ted with the other and pulled them across Royal Street. The others followed loosely behind. Jeri wanted to talk to Angie, but she was afraid she would sound immature. She admired Angie, even after the unexpected events of the last twenty-four hours, maybe even because of them a little, and she wanted her to respect her.

"It's all right, Jeri. You don't have to tell me if you don't want to, but it might do you good to get it off your chest. After all, nothing you could be worried about could compare to the disaster of a marriage I'm living through. I just thought we could share our troubles."

Angie finished speaking, and with the noise of the crowd filling the silence between them, they just walked for a time. Finally, Jeri began to speak, planning only to fill the emptiness with pleasantries.

"Oh, I don't know, Angie. He is a great guy, and I know that he cares for me..."

"But?" Angie finished the sentence and stopped walking to face Jeri as she did so.

"Yes, but. Well, he sometimes gets kind of morbid. Sometimes he has this cloud hovering over him. He had some kind of nuclear accident when he was in California, you know."

"No, I didn't know. Is he all right?"

"Yes, I think so. He doesn't like to talk about it much. I don't think he was hurt seriously, but it caused him to, sort of, give up on life. Anyway, he has this thing about technology. It's bad enough that he has these feelings, but when he talks about them, he tends to be depressing. I just can't stand it when he gets negative like that."

"Yes, I can see where that would be irritating." Angie wound her arm around Jeri's and they started walking again. "So he thinks that technology is out of hand. You know, I've tried to start up a conversation with him, but he wouldn't take the bait. I really am interested in this stuff, but I couldn't get him to open up. Being a woman, you were easier." She smiled up at her, and Jeri felt comfortable with their friendship.

"Well," Jeri said, "he thinks—let me see if I can get this right— that the industrialization of society is a good thing for civilization. But it is a harmful thing for the individuals within the civilization. The culture progresses at the expense of personal freedom and personal happiness."

"Yeah, I can see that, like using economic slaves to build the pyramids, I suppose." They turned up Royal, the rest of their group still half a block ahead of them.

"He is really against partying, against drugs and all, yet here he is with us at the biggest party of them all. Sometimes I just don't know what to think about him."

Angie avoided the wild, intoxicated mob surging around them as they reached the midway point in the street and looked up to Jeri as they crossed. She looked strangely polar, her facial expression serious but comically framed by the circular hole in the yellow, pointed Crayola headdress. "Jeri, that's one of the reasons why I wanted to talk to him. You know, his ideas aren't new or ridiculous.

Certainly nutcases like that Unabomber don't seem to fit within the rational world, but there are very serious and very old philosophical theories that address even the ideas of the crazies."

"What? That we need to abandon all our technology and live in dirt huts?"

"Yeah, right," Angie mocked her lightly. "But there was an Italian philosopher in the early 1700s that had a theory that organized the world in a way that does make some sense in our modern times. His name was Vito or Vico something or other. I studied him in graduate school, and I should remember his name—but it was a long time ago. Anyway, he said that civilization passes through three stages. The first was a 'bestial' period, where all difficult-to-understand phenomenon is explained by the intervention of the gods. The second was an age of 'heroes,' where a civilization's military prowess provides security at the expense of a rigid class society. And the third was an age of 'men,' where class struggles create a society of equality among men. The interesting thing was that Vico said that the third and final stage, of men, is characterized by all kinds of corruption and vice. And that this stage could end with the reversion to the 'bestial' age. He said that this comes about from too much science or from an overdependence on technology." She spoke the last word with the emphasis of a point taken; then, she continued to explain as they walked. "The people of this phase of civilization become weak and cowardly and accept any despotism in exchange for comfort and security. Money becomes their only god. He said they would become servants of science, unmoderated by conscience. Sound familiar?"

"Wow. He said all of that hundreds of years ago?" Jeri tried to count the centuries without using her fingers. "Did he say how we were supposed to avoid this terrible merry-go-round?"

"Yeah, well. He said that God had to step in and help us out. You know, I don't think he could ever have considered the possibility that we would someday have the technological power to send ourselves back into the Stone Age with a push of a button."

"Do you believe in God, Angie?" Jeri asked.

"I've tried, dear, I've really tried. I just can't get over the mystical part, but it would be comforting, wouldn't it?" She lurched toward the door of a small bar. "Look, here's a place we can buy a hurricane." In thirty seconds they were back out on the sidewalk, each of them carrying small plastic cups. "We still have to go to Pat O'Brien's to get a real hurricane, but these will do until we get dinner."

"Angie, I'm beginning to understand what you and Ted are saying, but it is a hopeless, cynical view of life. I don't think I could survive believing that all our work, the sum total of our human understanding, would be the very method of our demise. It is just too hopeless."

"Oh, I don't know. There is always God. He might step in just in the nick of time and save us from our own knowledge. Hey, there's someone who might be able to help us with some religious wisdom." Angie pushed through the crowd to the corner where a small clearing had formed around a clean-cut teenage boy in a cheap black suit, a white button-down shirt, and a narrow black tie. He was standing on the corner holding a Bible, urging the crowd to go home, begging them to accept Christ as their savior, extolling the life of the saved. Angie walked up to the inner edge of the small clearing, pulling Jeri along behind. Jeri stood silently watching Angie, waiting for what would come next. The young man turned to Angie and looked into her face as he continued to quote scripture and decry the Carnival debauchery. Angie chuckled then stepped forward slightly.

"And what wisdom do you have for two lost crayons seeking the perfect hurricane?" Angie raised her drink up to her mouth and the small crowd that was watching and listening broke into drunken laughter. Jeri was also laughing when she saw the young man's gaze stop at her own face, singling her out from the crowd.

"Increased wisdom is increased sorrow, and he who increases wisdom increases sorrow. Ecclesiastes." He spoke clearly above the laughter of the crowd.

Jeri felt embarrassed by his frank stare into her eyes and turned away. "Come on, Angie, I don't want to get separated from the others." She pushed Angie forward to the curb. The two of them left the spontaneous sermon in a cascade of laughter and catcalls from the crowd.

Above the din of Carnival Jeri heard Ted's voice calling to her from just ahead. Their group was standing outside the restaurant, waiting for Jeri and Angie to catch up with them before entering. Ted was walking toward them calling and waving. They met him halfway, and they walked together to the entrance of the restaurant. Miraculously, they were seated quickly; the only table available was a large one that had been reserved for large parties. The host led them through the main dining room, a wide room with a low wood-beamed ceiling, to a small area on one side of an airy but busy kitchen grill.

They were seated at a long table in front of a wall-to-wall wine case with glass doors. As everyone sat down, Angie separated herself from the group to search for a quiet place to make a phone call; she told Jeri she wanted to call Sam, to tell him where they had stopped for dinner. They were ordering drinks when she returned to the table.

"Well, he's not answering his phone, but I left him a message. Let's hope he gets it before we take off." Angie sat down where they had left two empty chairs next to Tara. She took the one that left the empty place between herself and the girl. "Just in case he does get the message, we better leave him a good seat."

Jeri felt she had a better understanding of the woman after the conversation they had shared during the walk. She knew that Angie was hoping Sam would come and join them, and she believed that Angie was sorry she had used Tara to humiliate him. Leaving the empty seat in the middle would allow the man's machismo to again be satisfied; he would have a willing woman on each arm. Jeri moved her hand under the table, resting it on Ted's leg, and she felt his hand come to rest in her own lap. She was glad that she would be able to feel him during the meal. She needed the reassurance of his touch, the security of his closeness. She understood him better, too, now that she had talked with Angie. He was not just an eccentric, he was a man with complex ideas; ideas that other, brilliant minds had shared for hundreds of years. He was right; the parties and the excitement were meaningless diversions compared to the passing of time through history. Maybe he was right about careers too. Did it matter what one did to live from day to day? He had owned his own nuclear engineering company, and he felt no satisfaction from it, no accomplishment. He seemed to drift without direction, without goals. She squeezed his knee and he leaned toward her.

They struggled with their costumes for a moment before managing a small, short kiss.

Jeri ordered a Cajun crawfish and linguine dish that was perfect. The tiny morsels of shellfish were perfectly done in a wonderfully spicy sauce. It was even better since she had not needed to shell the tiny crustaceans herself. All at the table voiced their pleasure in their own selections and food was generously shared, passed around the table on bread and butter plates. Angie had ordered wine, a chardonnay and a merlot, and the waiter was kept busy refilling their glasses and opening more bottles. Everyone had too much to eat and plenty of wine before the table was cleared. Then they sat at the table talking and drinking the last of the wine and considering items on the dessert menu.

They were sated and rejuvenated by the food, and the conversation turned to the animated topic of their next party destination. Their mood was happy and friendly, and even Tara joined in with suggestions regarding the night's parades and open parties. Jeri was laughing and sipping her wine when she noticed the gayety drain from Angie's face. Angie was looking across the table and over Jeri's shoulder, toward the glass entrance doors on the other side of the bar. Jeri didn't have to turn around to know that Sam had arrived. Then, in an instant, Angie's face regained a lighthearted expression, and she raised her arm to wave. "Looks like Sam got my message, after all," she said, as she waved across the room.

Jeri watched Sam walk around the table unsteadily; he wore blue jeans, a red polo shirt, and a brown leather bomber jacket. The crayon costume had apparently been rejected. He glanced around the table at the others with glassy, cynical eyes before settling heavily down in the empty chair.

"Well, I see you all have your costumes on," he said in a dry, disdainful tone of voice. His eyes were red and inflamed around the edges and grossly dilated. Jeri waited for him to explode in anger or degenerate into tears, but neither occurred. "I thought you would all be out on Canal watching the parades by now. Lost your interest in parades?" He said this to Angie, his lips twisted up to reveal a distorted smile.

"As a matter of fact, we were just discussing where we wanted to go next. You are just in time, dear."

"Yeah, I bet you are all just ecstatic to have me."

"Come on, Sam. Let's have a good time," John said from the end of the table. He seemed odd speaking with a serious tone of voice from within the jester's mad headgear.

"Sure, let's have a party. I'm raring to go. Absolutely, let's party. I've got two of the best little whores in town to show me a good time. Don't I, girls?" He put his arms around both Tara and Angie and pulled them roughly into his chest, their tall conical hats meeting in front of his face. He pulled them together a few more times but quickly lost interest. The hats spoiling his view, he released them back to their own chairs.

Conversation at the table had ended. Only the nearby sounds of the restaurant interrupted the silence. Jeri was astonished that Angie had not objected or replied in any way. She had only reached for the dinner check. When she lifted the bottom of her costume to dig for money, everyone else at the table raced her in pulling out money for the check. Ted and John each produced their wallets, and Windy and Sal counted out bills, their heads together in muted conversation.

"Put your money away, people, let the New York Jew banker pay the check. Angie gets all the money she wants from Daddy. She's loaded, you know. Isn't that right, Tara?" He gave the girl another, final yank around the shoulders before standing up. She didn't answer him, and Jeri thought she could see, for the first time since the oyster bar, a break in her happy demeanor, a momentary hint of fear. "Let's go, everyone, the night is young and we have a Mardi Gras to attend," he bellowed, and diners at nearby tables turned to his voice.

Tara looked confused and frightened, uncomfortable with the way the evening had suddenly developed. Jeri knew she was about to go; it was there in her eyes, the need to run, like a terrified animal the instant before a human gets too close.

"You know, Mr. Sam and Miz Angie," Tara said quietly as she stood slowly, stepping away from the big man, "I really need to get back now. I've really enjoyed being here, and I'm very grateful, but I need to get back." She started to pull the pointed hat from her head.

"Bullshit, Tara," Sam objected. He started to take a step toward her and she backed away from him, fear in her enlarged eyes. "Fine, you little bitch. Go ahead, get out of here. We don't need you anyway. Plenty more whores out on Bourbon Street."

Tara continued to back away, still working on removing the hat.

"Don't worry about the costume, baby," Angie said softly. "Just go on home. You can send it over to the hotel in the morning."

"Thank you, Miz Angie, thank you for everything. I sure will. I'll bring it by myself, tomorrow." Tara was already walking around the table and toward the exit as she spoke. She finally pulled the hat free as she reached the end of the table. She held it in both hands as she crossed through the dining room to the exit.

"Well, that is that, folks. Let's go get a drink, OK?" Sam reached behind Angie and politely helped her up by pulling out her chair. Angie stood up from the table, then seemed to remember the check, again lifting her costume to get to the pockets of her shorts.

"It is all taken care of, Angie. We've got it. Do you hear?" John said, as he pushed his wallet back into the leather pouch hanging from the cord belt of his costume. She nodded as she let the yellow hoop fall back into place. They all stood to go. Sam took Angie by the hand, and the two of them led the way out of the restaurant. Jeri looked up to Ted; he cocked his head to one side and shrugged, as if to communicate his total lack of understanding of the situation. As they followed the Williamsons out of the restaurant, Donna and John walked up next to them.

"Oh boy, Sam is back," Donna said with heavy sarcasm.

"He really isn't a bad guy, you know. He's just too full of pride sometimes," John said in Sam's defense. "And I think he has been hitting his little box a little hard the last couple of days."

"No kidding, Mr. Holmes. Did you see the guy's eyes? What is he on, anyway? That isn't just coke." Donna's voice contained unrestrained anger. "Did you catch that crack about Jews? And look at Angie. She's up there walking with him like nothing's happened."

"Yeah, ain't love grand?" John said, as he jingled the bells on his hat.

When they got back outside, the streets were even more crowded than when they had entered the restaurant. Everyone walking the streets had multiple strands of colorful plastic beads around their necks and plastic cups in their hands. As they passed under the parties roaring on the balconies above them, they stopped to call up for the beads, and their necks were soon clicking with plastic necklaces too. They followed the Williamsons down Royal and back toward Bourbon on Saint Louis Street, where they stopped outside Pat O'Brien's bar.

Jeri saw Sam give the doorman a folded bill surreptitiously. He unfolded the bill to check its size before leading them through the crowd to the front of the line. A middle-aged black waiter in a green jacket greeted them there. Inside the door, a long entranceway led to a large interior courtyard. There were bars on both sides of the entranceway; on the left was a small room with people crowding up to a long bar, on the right was a larger room with two copper-clad grand pianos on a central stage. Two women wearing long formal dresses were preparing to sit down at the pianos. The waiter led them into the narrow bar on the left side of the hall as the pianos began to play behind them. Sam gave the waiter a tip, and he left them to push through the crowd on their own.

The room was long and narrow, with the bar running the length of the far wall. It was crowded with drinkers, pressing up to the bar and sitting at bar stools. Loud music blared from speakers mounted high on the old brick walls. Jeri was standing next to Ted, enjoying the loud, festive atmosphere of the bar, when Windy handed her a curved glass with the green Pat O'Brien's logo printed on the side. She realized it was another hurricane, the bright red color brilliant in the clear glass.

When they finally made it up to the bar, Donna and Angie were sitting on stools, with John and Sam standing next to them. Windy and Sal were welcomed by the bartenders and waiters as old friends; they seemed to know everyone who worked there. Soon a waiter brought seats for the two singers, pushing through the crowd with the stools held high over his head. She pulled Ted in close to the group, and they were all together again, pressed next to the bar by the throng.

"Wow, this place is crowded," she screamed to Ted over the noise of the sound system, the pianos, and the laughing, talking drunks nearby.

"Yeah, and these bulky things don't help!" he yelled, as he lifted the upper ring of the black cylinder he wore by pushing it from below with the rim of his glass. It looked like scotch. She looked up at the walls and ceiling of the room, again astounded by the age of buildings still in fashionable use in the French Quarter. Pulling down on the wide hoop of Ted's costume, she leaned in close to speak him. The plastic beads around his neck became entangled in her hair and they both laughed as they tried to get them free. They stayed close so they could talk without screaming at each other.

"The only buildings in Colorado as old as this were built by the Indians," she said over the barroom noise.

"I know what you mean. A fifty-year-old house in LA is a historic structure. This place is incredible. Imagine the roaches they must have."

"No thanks. I'm still eating and drinking in this town, you know."

"Only one more night. Tomorrow we head home."

"I'm ready. This has been a great time, but I'm ready to get back to reality. I have a thousand things to do to get ready for my move to Irvine."

"California. I sure have some bad memories from California. I hope you have better luck than I had."

"Don't worry. I'm going to take you along as guide." Jeri made the statement lightly, as a joke, but she desperately wanted him to want to go with her. She wanted to be with him, and he needed to stop drifting. He had to get a grip and settle down—and maybe she was the woman to help him do it. She looked up into his face, still ringed by the ridiculous black hat, and smiled. He looked like a medieval magician; all he needed were a few stars and a half-moon on the pointy hat to complete the image. Only the expression on his face had become serious. His eyes were narrow and his lips were thin as he stared down at her.

"Do you want me to go to Irvine with you, Jeri?"

"Yes, Ted. More than anything else in the world. At this moment, I want to be with you more than going to Irvine at all." She felt herself start to tear up, and she sopped up the moisture with the sleeve of her leotard.

"Wow, Jeri. I was hoping you would let me come along with you, but I never expected you to say that. I'm stunned. Of course you'll go to Irvine and go to med school. It's what you have worked for your entire life. And I'll go along and do my thing again. It won't be hard to pick up where I left off."

Jeri pulled herself closer and upward to kiss him hard on the lips, their drinks spilling without care onto the backs of their costumes. "Ted, you have made my future perfect. I love you so much."

"I love you, too, more than anything, more than life itself. Only I have something else on my mind, Jeri, but I'm a little afraid to broach the subject."

"Anything, Ted, there is nothing you can say that will damage my mood now."

"OK, here goes. Will you marry me?"

The suddenness of the question stunned her for an instant; then the meaning became wonderfully clear. She could not control herself and she began to scream at the top of her lungs and jump up and down, pulling roughly at Ted's neck. She screamed without being able to speak, and then the meaningless sounds became the single critical word.

"Yes, yesss, yessss." She reached up and pulled down so she could kiss him again, and he was smiling so broadly that their teeth crashed together painfully. She didn't care. She only cared that she was getting everything she wanted, and she was overwhelmed with happiness. She turned to see the others in their group. They were staring at her, their lips parted in sympathetic, if unknowing, smiles. Then she saw Donna scrambling to her feet, her eyes and lips smiling the wide, knowing smile of a best friend. In a moment she was next to her and they were both jumping up and down screaming at the top of their lungs. Then Angie and Windy were there too, hugging her as tightly as the bulky Mardi Gras costumes allowed. Then they were rotating, arms around each other's shoulders, bumping into annoyed strangers, a colorful mass of screaming friendship. Then she saw the guys were next to Ted, shaking his hand and pounding him on the back.

Gradually, the wild excitement ran itself down and someone ordered champagne. By the time the bartender had opened and poured it all eight of them were standing shoulder to shoulder, costume hoop to jester hat to costume hoop, at the bar. The air of the party was upbeat and happy, the earlier darkness at dinner forgotten in the celebration. They toasted with the champagne repeatedly, and the first two bottles were gone almost as fast as the bartenders could pour them. Then the manager of the club, who was a friend of Sal Benito, joined them with two more bottles of champagne, with which he wished them a happy life. Jeri was getting drunk, but the happy endorphins were still energizing her mood. They finished the new champagne quickly and someone, Jeri wasn't sure who, suggested they go back outside to play in the streets. As they grouped to leave Pat O'Brien's, the bartenders, waiters, and customers applauded the newly engaged couple. They hugged and waved to them as they departed.

They walked up Saint Louis Street toward Bourbon, the party raging around them and above them on the balconies of the second-floor apartments. Doubloons and beads showered down on them as they walked, drinks in hand, through the masses. They wandered through the narrow streets for several hours, visiting bars they passed to renew their cocktails, stopping to call to the balconies for Mardi Gras throws. All of them, even Sam, had numerous plastic necklaces draped colorfully around their necks, and Jeri had dozens more hanging from her bent elbow below her drink.

They were all playfully intoxicated when they stepped through a doorway into a small, dimly lit, and poorly decorated bar some blocks off Bourbon Street. They entered the bar a clumsy, noisy, happy group of drunken Carnival revelers. Jeri was surprised to see that the place was completely empty. She thought it was probably the only bar in the French Quarter that wasn't standing room only. But this bar seemed abandoned. Aside from the bartender, there was only one another man inside, and he was apparently a waiter judging from his white shirt and black bow tie. The two men were sitting on the customers' side of the bar, near its end, facing a small television on the back bar, playing a computer game. Neither of them stood or welcomed the group as they approached the bar.

"Where's the bathroom? I'm about to pee my pants," Windy Lee called to them as she looked around the room.

The man Jeri had first judged to be a waiter stood up, and she realized by his size and demeanor that he was probably the bouncer. He was broad and thick across his chest and arms. His shirt collar looked too tight and there were dirty gray splotches on one arm and shoulder. His shirt was torn at the elbow on the dirty side, and some dried blood was mixed in with the dirt there.

"You have to buy something to use it," the bouncer said as he stood. He was not smiling. Jeri noticed for the first time the strange atmosphere that permeated the dingy bar. It was as if the men didn't want them to be there.

"No problem," Windy said, "I want a screwdriver." She continued to walk to the back of the bar. "Are the bathrooms back here?" Disappearing through a doorway to the bathrooms, she didn't wait for the answer that never came. The bartender got slowly off his seat and stepped behind the bar.

"What will you have?" he said to them without interest. They ordered their drinks cheerfully, but the bartender prepared them slowly, banging the ice and the glasses together noisily. All the while the bouncer stood at the end of the bar with an angry expression on his face. John passed the bartender the money to pay for the drinks as Windy returned from the blackness at the rear of the bar.

"Wow, that bathroom is a damn mess," Windy said, pulling her wide skirt up as she climbed on the bar stool in front of her screwdriver. "Don't you have a mop or something?"

"Listen, lady. Nobody asked you to use it," the bartender said, the dislike in his voice palpable.

"Hey," John said in a quiet and calm voice, "no need to talk like that. She was just asking a question."

"Well, we don't want to listen to any damn questions from her, or any bullshit from you either." The bouncer spoke as he moved away from the bar to stand ready, legs wide.

"Hey, calm down, we just want to have a good time, OK?" John said, using his friendly bartender voice.

"Don't tell me to calm down. Who the hell are you, anyway? You know, I think you better leave, you and all the rest of you too."

Jeri watched in wonder as everyone in their group froze in shocked disbelief. Ted took her hand discreetly and pulled her closer to him, inching her slowly away from the angry man. She was wondering how Angie would react when Sam, his forearms still leaning heavily on the bar, turned his head slowly from his drink to face the bouncer. Jeri could see the hatred in his eyes when he spoke to the man.

"Not me, I still have a drink to finish. And if you're not as dumb as you look, you'll shut up and sit back down while I do it." Sam's voice was very low, but she could hear the rage in it. He continued to stare at the bouncer, with both of his hands holding his drink.

"Come on, Sam," Angie said. "Let's get out of this dump. It's not worth the trouble."

"That's right, Sam," the bouncer mocked, "get the hell out of here. Now!"

The loud challenge seemed to impact against Sam Williamson with physical force. Jeri backed into Ted's chest as the former professional football player sprang from his seat, his drink spilling and the bar stool tumbling backward.

"You think you're a tough guy, eh, punk? OK, enough fucking talk."

Sam squared himself to face the bouncer, and Jeri knew that a fight was inevitable. They moved closer, two bull animals ready to battle. Then, in a flash of arms and hands and metal, the bartender rose from behind the bar pointing a shiny chrome-plated handgun at Sam.

"Get the fuck out of here before I blow you away, asshole." The bartender was slight of build, but with the pistol pointed at Sam, his voice exuded confidence.

Angie raced to her husband's side, where she pulled at him hard, both of her small hands tugging at his still flexed biceps.

"Come on, Sam. Let's get the fuck out of here. These guys are crazy," Angie begged, as she pulled on his arm.

He seemed to relax slightly and turned his face down to her, removing her grasp from his arm with his opposite hand. "Yeah, OK, Angie. Let's get out of here."

He seemed for a moment to turn from the bar, and Jeri watched as the bartender lowered the gun slightly. Jeri felt a wave of relief wash over her, and her arms exploded in goose bumps. Then, before she knew what was happening, Sam leaped across the bar at the surprised bartender, grabbing him by the wrist. She watched in stunned amazement, frozen by the sudden violence. The bouncer jumped onto Sam, hitting him in the head with his fists, but Sam was oblivious to the assault. John grabbed at the bouncer as Sam pounded the bartender's hand, and the pistol it held, violently on the bar.

Then Jeri saw the blinding white flash and heard the loud discharge of the weapon as she was pounded backward into Ted. She couldn't understand what had happened. She tried to turn her face up to him, but she felt faint.

Then she realized she was on the floor, her head in his lap, looking up at him. He seemed oddly terrified, and she realized that it was because she had been shot. Then she was also terrified and confused, and she only wanted to be home, away from the terror.

"Steven?" she said.

He shivered. Icy air had penetrated the room; a cold draft droned sadly through the gap where the French doors failed to meet. He wandered, still shivering, into the bathroom and took a very hot shower, washing mechanically under the heat of the flow.

Wearing a thick sweater and his down jacket, he looked down onto Bourbon Street from the balcony. A few people were again in the street, evidently unaffected by the frigid weather, drinking happily from plastic cups as they crossed in front of slowly moving cars and trucks. One man pushed a steaming hot-dog-shaped handcart down the opposite sidewalk until he was stopped by a customer.

My God, he had thought, *she seems so light in my arms.*

He turned from the surprisingly normal activities in the street and walked the few steps to the French doors of the Williamsons' suite. They were locked from the inside, and the drapes were pulled closed. He continued on to the other connecting room, the Colorado bar couple's room; the French doors were shut but the curtains open. They were inside, hurrying about, packing their suitcases that lay open on the bed. He knocked gently on the glass and Donna looked out to him. Her face looked drawn and worried as she opened the door for him to step inside. She stared into his face for a moment, her waxy expression unchanging, then turned away and went back to her packing.

"You're leaving?" he heard himself asking.

"Yes, we're checking out and starting back to Durango today." Donna spoke rapidly as she crossed the room from the dresser to the open suitcase, her arms full of clothing.

"But what about Jeri?"

"I gave the cops her parents' address and phone number. The detective called them last night. They're flying in today. Here..." She went back to the dresser, dug into her purse and pulled out a slip of blue paper. Walking back to him, she extended it in her outstretched hand. "This is the flight they're coming in on. The detective's name and cell number are here too." She handed him the slip of paper with both hands, holding his wrist with one as she pushed it into his palm with the other.

He had held her in his lap, rocking slightly, supporting her strangely heavy head from behind her neck, occasionally wiping one of his fallen tears from her cheek, calling to her softly, begging her to wait, to please try to wait for the medically astute saviors who were surely racing to their aid.

"You're just leaving?"

"You're damn right we're leaving," John said as he entered from the bathroom, zipping his shaving kit in front of him. "I had my fill of cops last night. They say we can leave, and we are going to leave. Hell, Sam and Angie packed up and left this morning, as soon as they said we could go. They have some lawyer talking to the cops for them. They're probably sleeping in their own bed right now."

"They're gone? Already?" His mind felt dull and slow; he was hungover and tired.

"We're lucky the cops didn't come and search the rooms last night. We would all be in some Louisiana jail right now," Donna said. She released his hand and turned back to her packing.

He had carefully removed the tangled rope of multicolored plastic beads from around her neck, pulling them gently over the crushed conical hat.

"Ted, you look wasted. You should get something to eat and get some sleep." John spoke to him as he bent over his bag, pushing the shaving kit inside.

Ted looked down at the forgotten scrap of blue paper, put it into his jacket pocket, and turned back to the French doors and the balcony.

He returned to his own room and carefully packed her things. She didn't have much, really: underwear, a few pairs of jeans, some tops, a few sweaters. He could smell her scent as he placed the clothing in the nylon shoulder bags. When he had difficulty making everything fit, he remembered that she had packed in a very organized, thoughtful way, first rolling her things into tight, compact cylinders. He followed the bellmen downstairs and checked the nylon bags under her name, explaining that they might be there a few days, that her family might come for them later.

There had been policemen and questions, but his memory of this time was incomplete. He couldn't remember his answers or even their questions; only the faces were clear, impatient with his inability to remember the details they sought. His mind reduced his memory of the events to disconnected images: the policemen and the emergency vehicles; the blinking colored lights—blue and red and yellow; the strange faces during his confused interview; the others being questioned—her friends from Durango, the couple from New York; the ambulance pulling slowly away from the curb, unhurried and without the urgency of lights or siren; and the police leading the stringy-haired bartender away with his hands cuffed behind his back.

He wandered outside without direction, walking on the sidewalk along Bourbon Street. The bitter cold had caused people to bundle up with heavy coats, but it had not kept the many small storefront businesses from opening as usual. He walked past the T-shirt stores and the souvenir shops without fully noticing them, continuing on to the corner of Bourbon and Orleans Streets, where he found himself turning toward the river and Jackson Square. He walked under the big flags that fluttered over the entrance of the Bourbon Orleans Hotel, past Saint Louis Cathedral and through Jackson Square, his eyes averted, staring at his feet and the old stone of the sidewalks and gutters.

The policeman in the front seat had announced, "Police Parade," as he pointed out through the windshield of the patrol car. Inevitable and irresistible it had plunged slowly up Bourbon

Street toward them. Spanning from doorway to doorway, arranged hubcap to hubcap, a huge piston of city vehicles had pushed the reluctant stragglers of Carnival toward Canal Street. With a leading edge of slowly moving parking scooters and police motorcycles, a massive ram of street sweepers had ground slowly up Bourbon while mounted police pressed up the sidewalks.

Above the engine roar from the machines and the intermittent blare of sirens, an amplified electronic voice had intoned the monotonous dirge to disperse: "Mardi Gras is over. Please leave the area. Mardi Gras is over for another year. Come back tomorrow. Please leave the area."

He watched his feet as they stepped mechanically on the recently hosed sidewalks. The dirty gray concrete of the night before had been transmuted into the fresh white sidewalks of bright winter mornings. The cold morning light was brilliant and clean, casting sharp-edged shadows under his feet as he walked. Occasionally a fragment of broken plastic doubloon from some unidentifiable krewe passed beneath his stride, or a dirty length of cotton string, encrusted with the crushed synthetic residue of Carnival beads, crunched under his weight. At the height of the Carnival the beads had been of great value, though they were the least expensive colored plastic, but when the festival was finished, and the street sweepers had pushed the revelers out onto Canal Street, the strands had regressed to their true worth, and were tossed aside and stepped upon, broken and smashed. Street artists were staking out their territorial claims to space, on the sidewalks, outside the wrought-iron fence surrounding the square, on the walk outside the Cafe Du Monde in the old French Market.

An old black waiter led him to a round table with a stained gray top. The waiter seemed tired or in pain as he walked. His uniform—a white dress shirt, a black bow tie, and a white paper hat—seemed too light for the morning's chill. His white hat had a sooty black smudge in front, where it had slipped down on his forehead and into a crudely drawn cross of ashes, evidently placed there during an early morning Ash Wednesday Mass.

The color had drained from her face unbelievably fast; lying in his lap, her failing attention directed helplessly up and into his eyes, her skin had blanched as shockingly white as the ridiculous costume that framed her ashen face. All white. Vacant of tone from head to foot, save for the red splotch, obscenely bright, expanding remorselessly from a central font in her chest, she had closed her eyes.

The air was still very cold, and the space heaters inside the cafe were burning loudly, warming the large volumes of air that had chilled during the night. Around the perimeter of the cafe, waiters were rolling up heavy canvas tarpaulins, barriers that had been lowered against the dark inactivity of the night. As each green curtain was rolled up, his view of the outside world gradually increased.

Pushing him back from her, working over her briefly, pulling off the absurd hat and cutting the bloody costume from her, they had taken her from him. They had worked without emotion; methodically correct, mechanically competent. Someone had pulled him away from her, strong hands on his shoulders, pulling him back from behind. Quickly they had taken her away from him forever, her body shrouded under a sheet of purest white.

The coffee was startlingly bitter. He added cream and sugar to soften the chicory flavor before taking another sip. The old waiter, with the expression of pain on his face and the symbolic ashes on his forehead, returned to offer him another cup of coffee and another order of beignets. The beige plate in front of him was empty save for a light dusting of powdered sugar.